praise for you're the reason

"Wow, Tari Faris is a master storyteller - so many twists and turns in this roller-coaster ride. But spoiler alert: love wins! Against all odds, just when you think all is lost, she untangles the plot - bit by satisfying bit - and love comes out on top! It's uplifting, encouraging, and heart-stopping."

—SARA, GOODREADS

"I've been ugly crying for the last hour over Seth and Grace. Their story is so beautiful and flawed and genuine and just—all the feels! Faris has a way of drawing you in within the first pages and holding you emotionally hostage until the final page. Hope, grace, letting go, pressing through adversity, and embracing who you are in Christ are found in these pages. I already want to read it again!"

—DEENA, GOODREADS

"A beautiful story of learning how to forgive yourself before you can accept the forgiveness of others. This was my first Tari Faris book, and I enjoyed it so much. Grace and Seth's journey is heart wrenching, filled with joyful ups and tragic downs as they learn to overcome their past mistakes and trust in God for their futures."

—NATALIE, GOODREADS

You're the Reason was a refreshing return to Tari Faris' world of Heritage. It was wonderful to see old faces while meeting new ones. Seth and Grace's story was a sweet story of redemption and coming home. It's a beautiful reminder that we can't live in the past. Grab a cup of coffee and cuddle up in your favorite spot because you won't want to put this story down.

—KATE, GOODREADS

you're
the
reason

HOME TO HERITAGE

you're the reason

TARI FARIS

sunrise
PUBLISHING

A Note from Susan May Warren

Dear Readers,

From the moment I met Tari Faris, it was evident she was not only a natural storyteller but also a woman of profound faith. Her original Heritage series captured my heart, and the opportunity to partner with her on this beautiful continuation—and eagerly anticipate Mandy Boerma's forthcoming contribution—has been an absolute joy.

As I turn the pages of Tari Faris's latest book, *You're the Reason*, I'm reminded of the warm, enveloping charm of a story that feels like home. Tari possesses a writing style that is both sweet and fresh, inviting readers to settle into the quaint town of Heritage, Michigan—a setting that echoes the cherished community of my own Deep Haven series.

When Tari and I first brainstormed this project, I knew her exceptional talent would give life to a series that would resonate with readers far and wide. I had the joy of helping Tari shape her story, but truly, it is her unique voice that infuses this tale with its sweet and poignant spirit—a voice that brought me to tears and will no doubt capture the hearts of all who visit Heritage.

Tari is a fantastic writer, a craftsman of characters, and a weaver of worlds that beckon you to stay a while longer. As you delve into *You're the Reason*, you too will feel the embrace of a place that feels like coming home. It's an honor to play a part in the continuation of her mesmerizing Heritage series, and I am thrilled to invite you to experience the journey that is as endearing as it is unforgettable.

Enjoy!
Susan May Warren

He gives strength to the weary and
increases the power of the weak.

ISAIAH 40:29

To my boys Zachary and Joshua,
Your passion for weightlifting helped inspire
Seth and his journey. Thanks for sharing your
successes and struggles with me.
I love being your mom.

one

H E MIGHT NOT BE ABLE TO OUTRUN HIS PAST, but Seth Warner could outrun Grant's wife before she roped him into another ridiculous baby shower game. He owed Grant his life—literally, but whatever Caroline had planned next involving those diapers, he was out. He sipped at his pink punch, eyeing the swinging door that led to the kitchen, then glanced at the front door. The entire Kensington house had been transformed into a cacophony of pink as if they feared someone might forget that Jon and Leah Kensington would be welcoming a baby girl any day now.

He'd never cared for pink, but today he found it extra annoying. Balloons? Pink. Tablecloths? Pink. Even the banner of baby clothes that wound up the grand staircase in the foyer—all pink.

The plan for Memorial Day had been simple. Come to the baby shower, drop off the gift, ask his cousin Jon for a job. The three-part plan should have been foolproof. But he hadn't realized that half the town of Heritage would be invited. And although he'd received a few smiles, it was clear not all were glad to see him back in town.

Maybe he should cut his losses and put the zip code of Heritage,

Michigan, in his rearview mirror once more. But he really couldn't. He'd run out of options and he'd run out of time.

"Don't go anywhere." Caroline Quinn spoke in a loud voice to the entire room, but it seemed to Seth that her green eyes paused on him a moment. "We have one more game before we serve the cake."

He'd never had a sister, but if he did, he imagined she would be bossy like Caroline. And as soon as she looked the other way, Seth ducked through the swinging door that led to the kitchen. He walked straight to the three trays of sandwiches that had been discarded on the island after lunch. They'd been well picked over, but food was food, and this was still better than anything he'd eaten this week. Seth lifted another sandwich from the tray and took a hearty bite.

Jon Kensington's six-four frame filled the door for a moment as his gaze found Seth. "Trying to escape."

He and his cousin hadn't looked much alike as kids. But as adults, the similarities were unmistakable. Same brown eyes. Same brown, unruly hair. Same square jaw. It was weird and a little confusing to others. That was unless they were standing. There was no mistaking the seven-inch height difference. Jon stepped into the kitchen followed by Grant and Nate, each with a piece of pink cake.

"Nice try." Grant Quinn slapped Seth's shoulder and then brushed some of his slightly too-long blond hair from his face before forking another bite of cake. "Caroline saw you make a run for it."

"But I applaud the effort." Nate Williams downed the last bite of his cake and set the plate aside. Seth didn't know the local pastor well. Nate had arrived in town about the time Seth made his grand exit, but with the tattoos poking out of his collar, he didn't look much like the stuffy preacher that he'd replaced. And from the few things he'd picked up from Grant and Jon, Nate had quite a story. "When did inviting guys to a baby shower become a thing?"

Jon shook his head. "Who knows, but you know when Leah and Caroline get something in their head, there's no talking them out of it. If Abby was here, she would have sided with me."

"Where is your sister these days?" Seth hadn't seen his younger cousin in a few years.

"Nannying in England. She plans to visit after the baby is born."

Seth lifted another sandwich from the tray and took a bite.

"Dude, is that your fifth?" Nate laughed as he dropped his plate in the trash.

"This guy can eat like no one else I know." Grant nodded toward him. "But what do you expect from The Storm?"

Seth winced at the nickname. Of course they knew. Looking back, the fact that he'd thought he could keep it a secret had been naive. "I'm not The Storm. That was just a gimmick for the show. Which is over. It was a onetime thing."

"Onetime?" Jon pulled some Cokes from the fridge and passed them around. "The onetimers are the people you crushed at the Detroit city qualifier. You're officially a Ninja Warrior, my friend. You've got a date at the semifinals in Chicago in July."

"I needed the money to pay off my school bill. It's paid. I'm done. Time for me to get a real job." A real job, like one at Kensington Fruits. He should just say it. It was why he came to this shower, after all. It should be easy. But now that he stood here next to Jon, the timing felt off. Jon might be his cousin, but he was also the owner of a major corporation and probably didn't want to talk business at his own baby shower.

"Why wouldn't you go for it?" Grant cracked open his pop and took a drink. "You're good and the crowd loved you. You'll kill it at the semis."

"I'm done." His voice came out harsher than he planned, but not one of these guys knew what it was like to be him. He set his sandwich down and leaned on the kitchen island. "You've seen the show. The more popular you become the more they dig into your life—your past."

Jon looked ready to say something, but Grant shook his head. They all took the cue and went back to their pop.

Right. Uncomfortable silence. Because he'd bet the last five hundred dollars he had in his bank account that every one of them had the same word running through their head. *Felony.* The same word that had shown up in every background check in every job interview he'd been to. Which was why, awkward or not, he needed to talk to Jon. It was now or never.

"Jon?" Leah stood a few feet away. Her red curly hair framed her face and emphasized the shock in her green eyes. That, combined with a large wet spot on her colorful dress, seemed to jolt Jon into action.

"Now?" Jon rushed toward her and placed his hands on her stomach. "I'll get the car. You get the bag. No, I'll get the bag. You get the car. No—"

"Jon. Relax. It will still take hours." Leah gripped his arms. "Caroline is already upstairs getting my bag. She'll meet us at the front door."

Seth blinked back and forth between the two as his brain finally connected the dots. "Is she having the baby now?"

"Hopefully not right now." Leah patted her husband's hand. No doubt because he'd gone pale.

Seth followed them and the now-gathering crowd through the living room, then to the driveway. He nearly collided with Jon when the guy came to an abrupt halt.

"We're blocked in." Jon scanned the driveway of more than fifty cars all packed in bumper to bumper. Then he pointed to Seth's at the end. "Seth, is that your white Lumina?"

Seth eyed his beater, with its rusted doors and the half-dislodged bumper. It was painfully out of place next to all the respectable sedans, EVs, and fifty-thousand-dollar pickups. It had served him well over the past four years, but it wouldn't win any prizes for style.

"Should I move it?"

"No, I need to borrow it." Jon pulled his keys from his pocket, then held them out in his right hand with his left hand waiting for Seth's keys. "I am not waiting for all these people to move. Take my Mustang, and you bring it to the hospital later to trade me back."

Jon was ready to hand over the keys to his Mustang in exchange for the '94 Chevy? The guy had really lost his mind. "We can get everyone—"

"Seth, please." Jon thrust his keys toward him again as Leah leaned forward on one of the cars and released a moan. "We don't have time."

"Jon, relax." Leah's voice came out strained. "That was the first big contraction."

"First *big* contraction?" Jon's attention snapped to his wife. "How long have you been having contractions?"

"Since I woke up. But they weren't too bad, and they were far apart." She offered a little shrug as she bit her lip. "I was going to tell you after the party."

When she bent over with another moan, Seth took the keys to the Mustang, then jogged toward his car. "The door is tricky."

By tricky, he meant the passenger's side didn't open from the outside. He hurried ahead and leaned over the driver's seat to pop it open so Jon could help Leah in. It had become second nature, but usually he didn't have an audience. He climbed out and held the keys to Jon. But his cousin was staring into his back seat.

Right. That.

This just wasn't his day.

Jon finally turned and looked at him. "Are you living in your car?"

"You need to go." Seth pointed to Leah and took a step back as he pocketed the keys to the Mustang.

Jon nodded once before he climbed into the car. "We *will* talk about this."

No doubt they would.

By the time Seth made his way back to the room of never-ending pink, half the guests had left with the other half making their way to their cars. He found a trash bag in the kitchen and began gathering discarded plates and cups that seemed to litter most surfaces. An hour later, the pink decorations remained but the main areas were clean once more. He switched off the lights, then carried the two large bags of garbage out to the can on his way to the three-car garage.

He hit the garage door and stood next to the black 2008 Shelby Cobra GT500. Was he really going to do this? Jon had gotten it as a graduation present from his parents, and he'd been tempted more than once to take this baby joyriding in his teen years. He'd even gone so far as to take the keys and sit in the driver's seat one time. But he'd had too much respect for his cousin even back then.

He clicked the fob and slid into the driver's seat. The leather welcomed him like a glove as he adjusted the seat and mirrors. Jon always downplayed it by simply calling it a Mustang, which it technically was, but it was so much more. With the way this hugged him, he could see why Derek—Jon's cousin from the other side—had added all those extra miles on it when Jon had been in Europe. This could get addictive. His Lumina would never be the same, not that it had been that great to begin with.

He ran his thumb across the silver cobra logo in the center of the steering wheel. When he'd started college, he thought if he studied hard enough, worked hard enough, he could own a car like this. Seth rested his head back as he released a humorless laugh. Four years had knocked that notion out of his head. No matter how hard he tried, no matter what he gave, he was always one step

18

behind. But not tonight, he lifted his head, started the car up, and revved the engine. Tonight, the road was his.

Seth shifted it into drive and eased out of the circular driveway, finding he had to consciously hold the car back like an unruly horse that just wanted to take off at full speed. He could take the long way to US 31 or the most direct route through the heart of Heritage. He had no desire to rouse old memories, but if he was going to work for Jon, he'd have to face them sooner or later.

At just under three thousand people, Heritage was more of a smudge on the map than a real town, but there was something different about Heritage. Something that he found harder to let go of than he'd once imagined. As he got closer to town, the fields and farmhouses gave way to vintage Victorians and old businesses. Some open, some boarded up.

The entire town centered around one square that was home to a gazebo, playground, and library that once had been a one-room schoolhouse. Years ago, it had held a stately Victorian mansion next to a row of run-down houses. They'd all been condemned, and probably rightly so, but he'd had a love-hate relationship with them, and their absence still sent a shock through him.

Otis sat at the corner of Richard and Henderson, as if guarding over the square. The old hippo statue had been an icon of the town for generations. But the shine on his brass back and nose meant that kids still loved to climb all over him on a regular basis.

The statue's soft smile was still in place as if he held a secret no one else knew. He did. Lots of them. Everyone assumed the statue's only secret was how he mysteriously moved about town. But the hippo also knew better than anyone how often Seth had snuck into those abandoned houses for a place to sleep as a child.

He turned left on Henderson and parked along the curb in front of the two-story, cottage-style house that had been his childhood home. Same peeling white paint. Same bricked-in porch. Had it looked this bad when he'd lived there? Probably close.

With the dark windows and overgrown grass that half covered the sidewalk, he guessed it wasn't occupied.

He climbed out of the Shelby and walked up on the porch, taking care with each step. The weathered wood had seen better days. A quick peek in the window revealed not a single piece of furniture in sight. Maybe no one had lived there since he and his mom. He squatted down to a familiar brick on the porch and wiggled it free. His mom hadn't known about this hidden spot.

After retrieving the key, Seth let himself in, bracing himself for the impact of memories, but they didn't come. Someone else *had* lived here recently. The peeling wallpaper was flowered instead of the plaid pattern they'd had. The brown stained carpet had been replaced with a cheap wood floor. Even the odor of cigarettes that had always hit him when he entered had faded to a distant smell covered by something he'd expect to find in an old attic. Nothing about this place felt familiar.

He hurried up the steps toward his bedroom in the front corner. The worn yellow walls he'd always hated were now pink with a few peeling duck decals. Couldn't say he liked it any better.

His phone rang in his pocket, and he pulled it out. "Hey, Grant. What's up?"

"Sorry to abandon you. We went to get the girls settled at Caroline's brother's house. Now we're on the way to the hospital." His friend's voice sounded a bit distant, which meant he was probably speaking though the car phone. "Where are you at?"

"Still in Heritage." Seth would leave the exact location out of it. "Did you need me to get something?"

"No, I just wanted to say we expect this to be a long night. I probably won't be around for lifting at the ranch tomorrow. Maybe next weekend."

A week without lifting? He ignored the unease that spread through him. "That's fine."

And one more reminder that he needed to find another option

for lifting soon. He loved lifting with Grant, but the ranch was two hours away. But since his car had become his place of residence, it was his only option. At least for now, Grant let him keep his weights there.

"You sure you're good to wait?" There was no mistaking the tension in Grant's voice.

He didn't blame his friend. When Seth had landed at Quinn Ranch for rehab, Grant had tried to get him interested in every sport under the sun. He'd had just enough bitterness about his past back then that he'd refused all of it. That was until Grant had introduced him to weightlifting. Since that day, it had become his anti-drug—literally. But he'd been clean for over five years, and a few missed gym sessions weren't going to change that. "Positive."

"You know, Seth, it was good to have you there today. Caroline said that Leah was so happy you decided to come. She really adores you."

Adored him?

The idea wrapped around him and made it difficult to breathe. Leah had treated him like family from the time she'd gotten engaged to Jon. He couldn't imagine that someone would want him around—someone who wasn't even obligated by blood—and there went that tightening of his chest again.

He pushed away the emotions, cleared his throat. "I'll be at the hospital to change cars soon."

He ended the call and circled the room, finally stopping at his closet. He knelt down and felt along the wall but came up empty. He pulled out his phone and tapped the flashlight. It lit up the small space. His fingers found the bent nail and twisted it, releasing a small section of paneling.

One thing hadn't changed. He pulled out the old wooden plaque not much bigger than two inches by four inches. There were toothpicks glued roughly to it and if possible, it looked worse than he'd remembered. He dropped it in his shirt pocket then resecured the wall and stood.

He circled the room once more and paused at the window. His gaze snagged on the window straight across the street from him. He'd spent half his childhood wishing that was his home instead of this one. Not just because it was bigger and fancier. But it always looked clean and homey.

The curtain in her room moved.

Grace?

He hadn't seen her in years. Last he'd heard she was starring in a ballet in Chicago, so what would she be doing here? This trip down memory lane was playing tricks on him. His gaze skipped over to the next window, where Gabe had shared a room with Gregory. His hands broke out into a sweat, and he ran them down the lengths of his pants. Maybe he hadn't completely moved on.

He stepped back from the window, then made his way back down the stairs and out the door. He took a second to lock the door and rehide the key. Maybe it was silly, but it just seemed right.

He hurried over to Jon's car and got in. Then followed Henderson to Heritage Road, where he turned toward 31. In half an hour, he'd get his car back and still have no job. Because no matter how desperate he was, he wasn't going to bother Jon with that tonight.

He'd just gotten the Mustang up to speed when lights flashed in his rearview mirror.

Just great. He pulled the car that he had no business driving to the side of the road, rolled down the window, and waited with both hands on the wheel.

The officer approached and leaned down. "License and registration."

He didn't have to look to recognize the voice. Officer Hammond.

Of course. But that was what happened when you had one officer in the area. Everyone knew who was in charge. Wasn't he supposed to retire soon?

His hair and mustache were a touch grayer, but he pretty much hadn't changed. "Evening, Officer."

The man's eyes widened slightly as recognition seemed to sink in. "Seth Warner. I hadn't heard you were back."

There was no affection in the words, and Seth didn't blame the guy. Hammond had been the one who'd busted Seth more than a dozen times in his teen years. Alcohol, curfew violation, the infamous drug possession, and the doozy of them all . . . suspicion for Gregory's death. If Seth were a betting man, he would guess that it was the last one that was circling Officer Hammond's mind as his jaw seemed to tighten and his hand went to rest on the gun at his hip.

"Care to explain yourself, son?"

"Was I speeding?"

Officer Hammond motioned to a forty-five-miles-per-hour speed limit sign about twenty yards ahead.

Guess the gazebo wasn't the only thing new around here.

"Is there a reason you're driving Jon's car out of town?"

Well, this didn't look good. "He borrowed mine because Leah went into labor. I was driving down to Muskegon to trade it back at the hospital there."

Hammond stared at him for a long moment as if weighing the truth of his statement. But it wasn't like Jon would take his call right now to confirm it. Hammond, like everyone else in town, probably had already heard through the gossip mill that Jon's wife was in labor.

Hammond gave a curt nod, then walked back to his cruiser. He'd only been gone a minute when he returned. "We just received a complaint about a break-in in an empty house on Henderson. The person was driving a black Mustang. Know anything about that?"

His face must have said it all because Hammond took a step back and rested his hand on his gun again. "I am going to need you to step out of the car slowly and put your hands on the car."

Of course, because no matter what anyone said, Seth would always be a criminal in the town of Heritage.

*

Ballet had always been the one thing Grace Howell could count on, but now even that was failing her. She got out of her car and looked up at the two-story Victorian that had been her childhood home. With the new white siding and the white flower boxes on the porch bursting with daffodils in full bloom, it was picturesque—the quintessential Midwest family home. And from the outside it was.

Grace squared her shoulders and hurried up the steps as fast as her aching knee would let her. She knocked twice, then stepped into her parents' house. "Hello?"

The word seemed to echo off the bare white walls and hardwood floors. An outsider might guess that her parents were just moving in . . . or out. But her mother wasn't one for clutter or sentiment, and every time she came home, there were fewer knickknacks, fewer family photos, fewer memories. As if every day they were a little more detached from the family they had once been.

She stepped into the entryway and shed her shoes by the door as a spicy aroma surrounded her. "Dance to the Music" interrupted the stillness from the small speaker in her phone. Her best friend Mallory's designated ringtone. "Hey, Mal. You should be stretching not calling me. The show's in an hour."

"Thank you, *Madame* Grace." The sarcasm was thick in her friend's tone. "Now, what did your magic doctor say?"

"He isn't magic." She dropped her purse on the kitchen table with her keys and lifted the lid of the Crock-Pot. Homemade soup.

One piece she missed of home. "And he didn't say anything because they had to move my appointment to tomorrow."

"Did you get a hotel?" Mallory's voice grew muffled. No doubt her friend had wedged the phone between her shoulder and her cheek as she slipped on her pointe shoes.

"I'm staying with my parents." She walked over toward the garage, pushed open the heavy door, and flicked on the light—no cars. "It's after five so they should be home any minute."

The barre her father had secured to the wall when she'd been just eight remained, but other than that the place was swept clean of both dirt and anything else that would point to her childhood.

"Are you going to tell them?" Mallory's voice cleared, but the increased background noise meant she was at least in the green room stretching now.

"I don't see a way around it." She flicked off the light and pulled the door shut.

"Maybe it will be fine." Mallory was ever the optimist.

"Maybe." But unlikely. They would see it as her failure. Maybe it was.

She walked into the living room and over to the mantel, running her finger over a photo of herself and her two brothers. They were eating ice cream. Gabe had it everywhere, but Gregory's was licked clean.

She stepped back and took in the entire mantel. Had her mother added another photo of Gregory? Maybe they weren't detaching from everything.

"You've gotten quiet. You only get *this* quiet when you're thinking about your brother. Are you going to try and find out more details about his death while you're there?"

"What would be the point? They seem to have swept it all under the rug about as fast as they swept me back to Paris after the funeral. They see it as protecting me. I see it as they're treating me like a child."

"It's a small town; someone should know something."

"Because that's a fun question. 'Grace, good to see you home.' 'Good to be home. Do you know how my brother, who didn't do drugs, died of an overdose'?"

"Are you going to be okay?" Mallory would probably jump in her car and drive up from Chicago if Grace were really honest with her, but she couldn't ask that. Mallory had a show tonight. A show that Grace was supposed to be in.

"I'm fine." The familiar words left her mouth as she blinked away the tears. "Besides, surely I can make it through one dinner with my parents peacefully, and I will be back dancing with you tomorrow." Probably.

Her gaze landed on the one solo photo of herself. She was about five and decked out in all her pink ballet glory. Pink leotard, pink tights, and pink ribbons in her hair. When was the last time she'd been that happy? "Do you ever think about quitting?"

"Every day." Mallory laughed but her tone grew serious. "But then I think about how much my parents sacrificed to get me here and of all the people who would kill to be in my spot, and I decide I have it pretty good. And I love what I do . . . most of the time. And so do you."

But did she? She honestly didn't know anymore.

"And let's face it." Mallory's voice grew soft. "It's all we know. It's who we are. We've been on the high-speed train our whole lives, there's no easy exit."

"Well, look who's home."

Grace jumped and spun toward her brother's voice. Gabe was leaning against the side of the archway that led toward the dining room, sporting torn jeans and a black Metallica T-shirt, both in need of a wash. His long, stringy hair drew attention to the dark circles under his eyes and unnaturally dilated pupils. He was a little high, and a lot lost. "It's become quite an impressive display of Gregory the Great, hasn't it? I think Mom will commission a gold statue by the end of the year."

"I'll call you later." Grace ended the call with Mallory, pocketed her phone, and narrowed her gaze on Gabe. "Don't you miss him at all?"

A look she couldn't quite interpret flashed across his face before he nodded toward the dining room. "Don't worry. Dad still keeps all your accolades in his den. Good thing I'm a two-bit loser so mom can have her Zen-producing bare walls."

"What are you doing here?" Grace wasn't going to take his bait. Gabe was always up for a fight, and today she had no desire to give it to him. "Mom and Dad said you haven't been around in a while."

"I've been around, just not when they're here. It's easier that way. Even you know that. I just show up and grab a little food. Help myself to a little of this." Gabe lifted a ten-dollar bill from the end table. "A little of that."

He picked up a Bluetooth speaker and weighed it in his hands as if trying to estimate its value.

"Put it back." Grace crossed her arms over her chest and tried to look tough, but he had a good four inches on her five-seven.

"A guy's gotta do what a guy's gotta do."

"You mean a drug addict has to do what a drug addict has to do."

Gabe shrugged as he set the speaker back down. "Judge all you want, but you have your own addictions."

His same old pattern. Deflect and attack.

"I don't have any addictions."

"Are you saying you would be okay not being the best one out there? That you would settle for something other than the starring role?" He offered a sad attempt at jazz hands. "Prima ballerina."

He waited for her comeback, but she'd already given him more of a fight than she'd planned. Besides, he had no idea how much his words hit the target right now.

Gabe shrugged and shoved the ten in his pocket. "Mom and

Dad are certainly happy to live in denial when it comes to me. Because as much as Mom says I haven't been around, there's a ten-dollar bill here every day. As much as they want that son back"—he motioned to the photos of Gregory—"they're pretty happy to keep this son invisible. After all, I was the one who should've died. No one would even miss me."

"That isn't true." Her voice came out a raw whisper.

"Isn't it?"

Her parents thrived on perfection, and Gregory had been perfect. Until he wasn't.

Gabe smirked, but there was a pain in his expression she hadn't expected, something even his well-rehearsed act couldn't hide. His gaze flicked out the window. "Mom and Dad messed us all up pretty good. Then again, we make our own choices . . . and live with the consequences. See you around."

Gabe walked out the front door, letting it slam behind him.

Maybe she should follow him, but to say what? Maybe that he could be more than a druggie living off his parents? That Gregory's death wasn't his fault? That she wished things could be different between them.

She walked out onto the porch, but he was gone. That was Gabe, quick to come, quick to disappear, and quick to leave damage in his wake.

Grace leaned against the porch railing and eyed the house across the street. With the chipped paint, overgrown grass, and dilapidated shutters, it had seen better days. She often wondered what had happened to Seth Warner and his dark, mysterious eyes.

The first time he talked to her, she'd been just almost eight years old, and he'd been nine. She'd fallen on her bike, and he'd rushed down his porch steps to help her. She'd cut her ankle pretty bad, and he'd helped her to her porch, then ran home to get a rag for the bleeding. By the time he got back, her mom was there. Her mom yelled at him and told him to get the dirty cloth away from

Grace. He hadn't said much, just nodded and left. They didn't really talk after that, as he was mostly Gabe's friend but had this way of watching her with those dark eyes. Not in a creepy way. Just in a way that said he'd be there if she ever needed him again.

Her phone rang in her pocket, and she answered the call. "Hey, Mal."

"You hung up so quick I just wanted to make sure everything was okay." There was music in the background now, they must be moving into warmups.

"Just a run-in with my brother. I'm fine. He's gone." Grace sank onto the top step of the porch, her eyes still fixed across the street. "Have you ever been on a date?"

"We eat, sleep, and breathe ballet. Who has the time to date? Is this why you asked me about quitting? Who's the guy?"

"No one, I swear." Grace leaned her head against the pillar.

"Then what's this about?" The background music had quieted, which meant Mallory had stepped out of warmups again. "Are you really thinking about quitting?"

Yes. No. Definitely, no. Her parents would flip. "Like you said, there's no easy exit at this point."

"Then what is this about a date? Did someone ask you out?"

"Yup, six years ago. The guy who lived next door asked me out." The memory of Seth as he asked her to go to the movies was still fresh in her mind. He'd shoved his hands in his pockets as he shuffled his weight from one foot to the next, then back as his face grew red.

"What did you say?"

"No, of course. It was right before I left for Paris, and I knew my parents would never agree. They wanted me to stay focused." She closed her eyes, remembering the sadness in his eyes as she'd turned him down. "But then I told him we'd go out as soon as I got back. And I was determined to, no matter what my parents said."

"But you didn't?"

"When I came back, it was for Gregory's funeral and he'd already moved away. Never saw him again. I've often wondered what would have happened if I'd just gone. Just enjoyed one night."

"Maybe you should've."

She should have? *No.* Mallory was supposed to tell her that all they had given up had been worth it. That ballet was all that mattered. She was the one who said there was no getting off this train. But before she could argue all that, her mom's car turned onto the road.

"My mom's pulling in the driveway. I have to go. And so do you. Break a leg." Grace slipped the phone in her pocket as she stood.

The silver Lexus came to a stop in front of the house, and her mom stepped out and blinked at her. Her mom was tall and slender with straight shoulder-length hair that was grayer than it had been at Christmas, but other than that, she hadn't changed. Her mother had appeared the same as long as Grace could remember. "What are you doing here, Grace?"

"I wanted to know if I could stay the night." When her mom just lifted one brow in question, she added, "I'd rather talk to you and Dad about it at the same time."

Her mom nodded and pointed at her car. "You're blocking the garage."

Hello, Mother. Good to see you, Mother. I love you too, Mother.

But that wasn't the Howell way.

She eyed her car and the two feet of clearance her mom had to get past her. But what was the point arguing? "I can move it."

She took a step toward the car, but her mother just handed her a small bag of groceries, then reached into her car to pull out a second. "It will be fine for one day."

Grace's gaze traveled across the street again. "Mom, do you know what happened to the Warners?"

Her mom seemed to jolt at the question, then her eyes hardened. "Last I knew, that boy was in jail. Let's pray he still is."

Jail? A heaviness washed over Grace that seemed to press in from every side. She couldn't name it or even explain it, but there had just been something in Seth that had always made her feel protected and that he wanted her to be herself. The real her. The her she didn't even know she could be. "Who lives there now?"

"Another family lived there awhile, but it's been empty a few years. Now help me get dinner on the table." Her mom walked past her up the steps and pulled open the front door. "Your dad will be home soon."

Twenty minutes later, they sat at the kitchen table sipping their soup as Grace took in the changes her parents had made to the house. "I like the white cupboards and new marble countertops."

Her father didn't look up from the paper he was reading. The top of his salt-and-pepper hair was the view she'd had at dinner most often growing up. Although he too seemed to have more salt and less pepper lately. But his focus hadn't changed. Always business all the time.

Her mom just nodded and continued to eat in silence. Right. Because talking during a meal was frowned upon. Guess she wouldn't mention that she liked the new wooden floors as well. Every dinner had been quiet, but not just quiet—complete mind-numbing-bang-your-head-against-the-wall silent. Better for digestion, her mom always said. However, Grace's digestion had been just fine for the past six years while she ate with friends who talked nonstop through every meal.

Grace spooned the last of her vegetable soup into her mouth letting the perfect blend of flavors linger on her tongue before she swallowed. Then again, maybe home cooking was worth the long quiet meal. She reached for the ladle.

"Seconds, Grace?" Her father looked up from the paper for the first time. "You didn't dance today and therefore don't require the same amount of calories as usual. Maybe sit with that and see how you feel in twenty minutes."

Grace let go of the ladle and sat back. "And of course, I need to save room for dessert."

Both parents' spoons dropped to their bowls as they stared at her. Only in the Howell family did refined sugar bring the same reaction as if she'd just announced she was getting a face tattoo.

"I'm kidding." She lifted the napkin from her lap and wiped her mouth. "Stop looking at me that way. I haven't had sugar since I was thirteen."

It had been cake at a friend's birthday party. Chocolate with chocolate frosting. She still dreamed about that cake. The reality couldn't be as good as what she had built up the memory to be, but she kept it tucked away for cold nights. Or for when she was denied a second bowl of soup.

Her father wiped his mouth with his napkin and then set it beside his plate. "Are we going to talk about why you're here and not taking the stage in Chicago as Giselle in ten minutes?"

"The scar tissue has built up in my knee again. The orthopedist the company uses wants to do surgery to clean it out."

"But that would take you out for the season—or longer." Her mom crossed her arms over her chest. "You're already twenty-three, can you afford that in your career?"

"Madame Laurent agreed and decided I should move to the role of Myrtha."

"Myrtha?" her father spoke up. "But you're Giselle."

"Madame Laurent hopes that if we reduce the strain on my leg, it could extend my career by a couple of years."

"We'll get a second opinion. That's not an acceptable spot for you." Of course her father wouldn't think so. After all, he hadn't bothered to attend any of her performances unless she was the star. He pulled out his phone and started tapping at it as fast as he could.

And this was why she hadn't called her parents when this first came up a week ago. "I agree, and I told them I needed to get a second opinion before I would make a decision. And if you re-member, Dr. Medler helped me with the scar tissue problem I had in early high school. I already made an appointment with him."

"What did he have to say?" Her dad paused his typing and looked up. Was that a tinge of respect she saw in his eyes?

"The appointment got moved to tomorrow morning."

Any light in his eyes dimmed as his mouth pressed into a line. "Maybe we should try to get you into Dr. Simmons. He did your mother's knee replacement and—"

"No." She tried to make the word kind but firm. "I have an appointment tomorrow morning. I will let you know what—"

"You will let us know, like you let us know about the appoint-ment you had today with him?" Her mother tapped her finger on the table to punctuate her words. "Tell me, would you have even called us had he not had to move the appointment until tomorrow?"

No. But it wasn't because she didn't want to talk about it with them. She wanted their opinion. She wanted to talk through this *with* them, walk through this *with* them, but they didn't give opin-ions, they gave demands.

"I am sorry I didn't call before. But—"

"But nothing." Her mother stood and carried her bowl to the sink a few feet away. "You didn't call. See how that turned out? Now you can let your father call Dr. Simmons—"

"No, I won't." Because not only did she believe Dr. Medler would have a solution, but letting her dad step in wouldn't just be one appointment. "I plan to head back to Chicago right after the appointment tomorrow. I will call you and let you know how it goes. I promise."

"Head back to Chicago?" Her dad's eyes narrowed. "Didn't you turn down the part of Myrtha?"

"I told them I would give them an answer after talking to Dr. Medler."

"Taking time off for recovery isn't a good idea." Her mother folded her arms across her chest again. "You have invested too much, done too much, to consider it."

"But taking a lesser role isn't okay either." Her father carried his bowl to the sink, letting it drop a little too hard with a loud clatter, but nothing seemed to have cracked. "You have built a reputation in the industry. Don't tarnish it. Another company would pick you up."

And they wondered why she hadn't called them a week ago. Grace added her bowl to the sink, then began clearing the rest of the dishes. "I'm not deciding until I talk to Dr. Medler."

Her mom lifted her hand in the air in frustration. "I won't let you throw away everything—"

She spun to face her mother, some of the water splashing on the floor. "This isn't your decision."

Grace shut off the water, then leaned her back against the counter. "It's my leg. My career. My life. My decision."

When neither responded, she pushed away from the counter and walked toward the stairs. "I'm going to bed. See you in the morning."

So much for thinking she could make it through one dinner peacefully. She climbed the stairs to the second floor and pushed her way into her bedroom, instantly transported back six years. She hadn't lived here since she'd studied a year in Paris at sixteen, but nothing seemed to have changed. Same white-cotton curtains defusing the summer evening light, same pink floral bedspread, same cream carpet. Her packing list from the day she left for Paris was still sitting on her white desk.

She set her bag on her bed, then walked to the window. She pulled back the sheer curtain, her gaze going automatically to the roof of the porch across the street where Seth always sat. But it was empty.

She was about to look away when a small light flickered in one of the windows. Then again. Someone was in the house. Surely Heritage hadn't turned into the hub of crime since she left. But there was someone in that house. Suddenly, the faint silhouette of a man appeared in the window. Grace dropped the curtain and backed up. She couldn't make out his face, but his wide shoulders filled the window. This guy was definitely not to be messed with. She reached a shaky hand toward her phone.

"Grace?"

Grace let out a small scream as she spun to face her mom.

Her mom's eyes narrowed in concern. "Everything okay?"

Grace turned back toward the window, but didn't see anything. Maybe she'd imagined the whole thing. She angled back to her mom. "What's up?"

"I'm sorry I lost my cool downstairs, but you must not take time off or even step back. Trust me, you'll regret it." Her mom stepped closer and laid her hands gently on Grace's arms. "You're the principal—the prima ballerina—but as soon as you step out of the limelight, they'll forget about you. I know."

She didn't have to ask. Growing up, they'd heard often of her mother's budding television reporter career that had just started to take off when she opted to take a season off to have Gregory. When she was ready to return, her spot had been filled.

Her mom's eyes filled with a bit of sadness. "And when that happens, there's no going back. Your dad is right. Other companies would be happy to have you. You are *the* Grace Howell."

She appreciated her mother's support even if she doubted that her name carried that much weight. "But if my knee continues on this path—"

Her mom shook her head. "We have worked too hard to fail now."

We?

And suddenly it all came into focus. The little girl in the photo who had just wanted to dance had disappeared the moment she'd been put on a high-speed train to success. A train that didn't leave room for anything else in her life. She couldn't quit. She couldn't slow down. Because if she took it all away, she was nobody, and she had nothing.

She nodded at her mom, and that seemed to be enough. As soon as her mom was out the door, she went back to the window. She pulled the sheer curtain back again and froze. The figure she'd seen in the window was back. But now he was exiting the house with something in his hand. She couldn't see much besides the top of his head, but the way his gaze darted around, he looked guilty. "What are you stealing, mister?"

The man climbed into a black Mustang and revved the engine before pulling away from the curb. She might have no life, but it didn't mean she didn't still love this town.

She lifted her phone and dialed 911.

"911. What's your emergency?"

"I need to report a break-in."

two

IF THERE WAS ANYTHING MORE HUMILIATING than being picked up at the jail by his cousin, Seth didn't know what it would be. He waited for Officer Hammond to unlock the holding cell, then stepped out. He followed the man through the all too familiar hall conveniently lined with wanted posters, as if to announce a cautionary tale to those being released.

Would he ever be seen as anything but a criminal? Probably not. Why had he even thought coming back and asking Jon for a job was a good idea? Maybe between the years at Quinn Ranch and years away at college he'd started to believe that he really was a new man and that others might see him that way too. Guess not.

Seth stopped by the window and waited as Officer Hammond opened a large manila envelope and dumped the contents out. "One cell phone. One wallet. And one . . . wood thing."

He added the contents back to the envelope and passed it to Seth. "Sorry about the confusion."

"No problem."

Not that he didn't appreciate his cousin rescuing him. He just had hoped that by twenty-four, he wouldn't need anyone helping him with the schoolyard bullies.

Okay, that wasn't fair. Officer Hammond wasn't a bad guy. He'd always been decent to him even when Seth had been in the wrong. But that didn't erase the sense of embarrassment he'd felt from the moment he'd been loaded once again into the back of the man's squad car.

The man motioned to the chairs. "Jon will be right here. He had some papers to fill out and sign. Not to mention he has to show off photos of his new daughter to anyone who will look."

So, the pink had been right.

Seth settled in a plastic chair that wouldn't win any award for comfort and leaned forward with his elbows resting on his knees. The door to the station opened, and a woman walked in, wearing gray leggings and a long pink button-up shirt. Her blonde hair was pulled tight in a bun, minus a wisp of hair that had escaped and curved under her right cheek. His eyes landed on her face, and—

"Grace Howell?" The name was out of his mouth before he considered the wisdom of it. He was probably the last person she wanted to see right now. Or ever again for that matter.

She blinked at him a moment, and her eyes narrowed before recognition seemed to sink in. "Seth?"

He didn't really blame her. The last time they'd seen each other, he'd been a couple inches shorter and barely a hundred pounds soaking wet. Weightlifting had changed all that.

He stood but didn't take a step toward her. "I didn't know you were back."

Her pale blue eyes traveled over him a moment, her cheeks slightly flushed. "What are you doing here? How've you been?"

He focused on the second question. "Good."

Not really but he wasn't about to tell her about his night in jail by answering the first question. He'd missed his one chance with

Grace, so no need to feed the bad image she probably already had of him.

"It's been a long time." She brushed the wisp of hair back, but it refused to stay.

"Are you still dancing in Chicago?"

"How did you know I was . . ."

Her words faded as her eyes seemed to register the words on the envelope in his hand. Her eyes widened slightly as she took a step back, then another toward the counter. "I'm just here to give my statement on a break-in."

Seth turned the envelope around. *Inmate Property* was stamped in large block letters with *Seth Warner* handwritten below that.

He opened his mouth to say something, but what could he say? The envelope said it all. Seth sat back down in the chair. Could this day get any worse?

She gave him one last look, then stepped over to the window where a guy who couldn't have been out of high school for too many years sat typing away at a computer. "Yesterday I called in a break-in that I witnessed, and they asked me if I'd stop and give my statement."

The guy behind the counter paused his typing and looked up. He blinked and then stood. His cheeks went instantly red, and he nodded and fingered though a pile of files in front of him. "Y-yes, of course."

Poor kid. Seth knew what it was like to be the recipient of one of Grace's smiles. He'd almost failed biology for the second time just because she'd been assigned his lab partner for the first few weeks of the semester.

"Here it is." The guy leafed through the file, then looked back at Grace. "Looks like we don't need your statement anymore, the owner of the property isn't pressing charges."

"How could that be? I saw—"

"The property owner turned out to be related to the individual who . . ." His gaze jumped to Seth for the briefest glance. ". . . was trespassing."

Seth blinked and stood again. "You called the cops on me?"

She spun back toward Seth. "You were sneaking around in an abandoned house."

"I wasn't sneaking, I was looking. And what was there to steal?" Nothing besides that stupid wood craft he'd taken. The envelope wrinkled in his hand, and he relaxed his grip. "But I guess that's what I should expect from a Howell."

Her eyes narrowed. "What do you mean by that?"

Was she kidding? To put it in Shakespearean terms, if the Howells were the Montagues, then Seth had become a Capulet.

Jon emerged from a door off to the side as he pulled his keys from his pocket. He must have picked up the Mustang from impound before he came here. "Ready?"

Seth nodded a quick farewell to Grace. She still looked ready to argue, and he wasn't getting into it. Not here. Not now. "See you around, Grace."

She didn't respond. Not a big surprise. If their history wasn't bad enough, that whole interaction would feed everything she probably thought she already knew about him.

He pushed out the precinct door, then slowed his steps to wait for Jon. "Congratulations on . . ."

"Isabella." Jon yanked out his phone, pulled up a photo, and turned it toward him.

"She's beautiful." That was what people always said about babies, right? Truth was, she looked pretty red and wrinkly, but he wasn't about to say that. And by the huge grin on Jon's face, he guessed that was how newborns were supposed to look.

Jon tucked his phone back in his pocket as he unlocked the Shelby with the fob. "Breaking and entering? Really?"

Seth shrugged and climbed in. "The house was abandoned. I

didn't think anyone would notice. I just had some things to put to rest."

"And did you?" He started the car and turned toward Heritage.

"Not really." Seth eyed the passing signs. "Where are we headed? Michigan Ave. is faster to your place . . . which you just passed."

"Your car is at the MIM."

"Mim?"

"The store on the square Leah and I opened three years ago. Stands for Made in Michigan, but we just call it the MIM."

Awesome. Back to Heritage. Twenty-four hours ago, he was trying to build up the courage to ask Jon for a job, now he just wanted to get away from this town, even if it meant living out of his car for another six months.

"Did you know I caught Leah breaking into the MIM once? Of course, it wasn't the MIM then, and cops weren't involved that time."

"Well, I guess people look the other way when spunky redheads who they know break in. Not so much for former druggies with a felony on their record."

"It's kind of funny actually." Jon flipped on his blinker and turned onto Richard Street.

"Probably will be. But not today."

"It could've happened to anybody." Jon turned right on Henderson, then a moment later pulled into the parking lot behind a row of businesses. Jon parked next to Seth's Chevy, which looked sadder than ever after his time in the GT.

"Could've . . . but it didn't." Seth popped the door open and stepped out of the car and walked to his Lumina. "You don't have to wait. I'm sure Leah is waiting for you."

Jon hopped out and glanced at him over the roof of the Mustang. "Leah told me . . . to take my time."

Seth pulled the door, but it was locked. Seriously, as if any self-respecting thief would bother. "You locked it?"

"You seem to have your whole life in there."

Caught.

When Seth didn't respond, Jon nodded toward one of the alley doors. "Let me show you something."

Jon worked the key in the old lock, then eyed Seth over his shoulder. "Who's Grace?"

"What?"

"When we were leaving the station. You said bye to a woman named Grace. Who's Grace?"

"Someone I hadn't seen for a long time. And someone who probably wished it had been longer."

Jon finally clicked the lock and pushed the door open and stepped into the main floor. It had once been a dance studio. There were floor-to-ceiling mirrors, and two wooden bars circled the room about waist high. "It's been a while since anyone's been in here."

"You could say that." Seth crossed the large open space and laid his hand on one of the bars but quickly removed it before dusting his hands off. "I forgot about this place. You own this?"

"Yup. This and many more properties that my uncle Dale acquired under the Kensington Fruits name while I was in Europe."

"You could do so much with this place. Why do you leave it empty?"

"Because lately I have just too much on my plate. Which is where you come in. I offered you a job three years ago, and the offer still stands."

He had nothing. He just stared at Jon. "What?"

"A job. I need someone to find someone to rent this place. This place and all the other properties that sit vacant that Kensington Fruits owns. Properties including the one you broke into yesterday. I don't know what you've got going on right now, but if you've got a few months to give to me, then I would really appreciate it."

"Why me?" He just blinked at Jon. "I don't have a real estate license."

"I have lawyers for the legal stuff. I just need someone to find the right tenants or buyers. You have a business degree. Help me find the right business for the right space."

Seth made a face. "A business degree. That's why you desperately need me? Business grads are a dime a dozen."

"You have the ability to see the possibilities in a situation and place. You'll have a good idea of which properties to sell and which to develop."

"I think last night was a red flag telling me that my returning to Heritage is not a good idea."

"I disagree." Jon motioned to a door in the side wall then walked over and gave it a tug. The door stuck, but it gave on the second pull. He hurried up a set of steps that led up to the right.

Seth eyed the back door. Maybe he should just leave anyway. But shoot, Jon still hadn't given his keys back.

Fine. Seth arrived at the landing just as Jon flipped a switch. Light flooded the room.

It had once been an apartment. One corner still had several cabinets with gaps where appliances once stood. The only walled-off section was a bathroom. The rest of it was one open room. Which meant that the bedroom, living room, and dining room were all in a shared space.

Jon walked the edge of the room but there wasn't much to it. "And it isn't a handful of properties. Dale bought over thirty. Some commercial, some residential, one is some empty warehouse in Lansing. Trust me, it would be a full-time position."

Seth ran his hand along the wall. The dark paneling dated back twenty or thirty years. "Who lived here?"

"Leah and her family, minus her dad when they first moved to town. Not much for a mom and three teenagers, is it? I think it was short lived. Then they moved into the farmhouse with the grandparents within the year." Jon tapped the wall opposite the upstairs of the MIM. "I think this wall is new. The wood looks like the same stuff they paneled the upper floor of the MIM with. But what's left is still big enough for a bachelor."

Seth shook his head and stepped over to the row of windows that looked out toward the square, but the dust was too thick to see through.

"Okay, Leah didn't say to take my time. She told me to not come back until you said yes. Please say yes."

"This town doesn't want me here. That will never change. Maybe yesterday I thought it would work but . . . I was wrong. Thank you for the offer, but I just can't."

"That's not true. Ask Madison Westmore. She came to town believing that same thing, but she realized that we could change the way we saw her if she took the risk of letting people in."

"But she didn't kill anybody in town."

"And neither did you. Drugs killed Gregory Howell. End of story."

"Drugs I gave him." Seth wiped a thick layer of dirt from the window. Most of the dirt was on the outside, but at least he could see the square.

Jon stared at him for a moment as if ready to say more but seemed to change his mind. "So, back to Grace."

"Nope." He was all for changing subjects, but they weren't going there.

Jon stepped up next to him. "Is Grace an ex?"

"No." Seth released a humorless laugh as he walked over and opened one of the kitchen cabinets, then another. "But I did ask her out once."

"She turned you down?"

"Me and my perfect timing asked her just before she left to study ballet in Paris for a year." The third cabinet revealed a stock of canned goods. He pulled one out and searched for the date. 2005. "We made a plan to go out when she was back from Paris."

"And?" Jon leaned against the wall and crossed one foot over the other.

"The next time she was home was for her brother Gregory's funeral." Seth turned to inspect more of the apartment, but the fifteen-second tour had pretty much covered it all.

"As in Gregory Howell?" Jon's brows rose to his hairline. "Wait, that was little Gracie Howell?"

"The very one." Seth leaned his shoulder against one wall.

"Man, last time I saw her she was in pigtails and braces." Jon shook his head again as if trying to reconcile the little Gracie with the grown-up Grace. "I *was* gone a long time. She . . . grew up."

"No kidding." Seth rubbed at his temple. And Seth had thought she'd been pretty back then.

"I thought I heard she moved to Chicago."

"She's evidently back. I don't know for how long. We didn't get that far in the conversation." Seth pushed off the wall and walked toward the stairs but paused at the top and turned back. "We were too busy discussing the fact that she was the one that called in the break-in last night, so that should tell you something. The Howells don't want me here. Maybe I need to respect that."

"Then where are you going to go? You need *something*."

Seth shrugged. "I'm a survivor. Always have been. I still have five hundred in my bank account and three jobs I'm waiting to hear back on. I appreciate the offer, but it's a no."

Shoot, and he'd really wanted to work with his cousin too. Not just because he needed a job, but because Jon was a wise business-man, and he wanted to learn from the best. But that had been before.

Seth hurried down the stairs before Jon could call him a liar. Jon might not see it, but he'd never be welcome again.

Dr. Medler had told her exactly what she had been hoping to hear. Then why didn't she feel better? Grace flipped on her blinker and took the exit toward Heritage as her phone rang. She tapped the steering wheel and answered through the car stereo. "Hello."

"You're driving north." Mallory's no-nonsense tone carried over the line. "You do know warm-ups are in just over four hours, right? You should be headed south if you want to make it in time."

"Good morning to you too, stalker." Grace slowed her speed as she got closer to town. Her appointment had been early—very early—so she was arriving home just as Heritage rush hour was headed out. Rush hour of fifty cars that was.

"Hey, you're the one who convinced me to get 360. My stalking you is your fault." Mallory's voice muffled a moment, then there was a loud clatter followed by her voice far away. "One second."

No doubt her friend was trying to juggle the phone as she readied her hair or something. Then Mallory was back, voice clear. "Are you going to tell me why you're headed the wrong way?"

"I forgot my bag."

"Your bag? How do you forget your bag? That's all you had with you."

"I blame Seth." Shoot, she hadn't meant to say that out loud.

"The guy who asked you out?"

And the guy who'd been practically best friends with her brother Gabe when she'd left. She'd thought she'd see him at the funeral, but he had all but vanished, until today.

"He was at the police station because evidently he thinks breaking and entering is no big deal." He'd seemed almost glad to see her until he'd found out that she'd called the police. She flipped on her blinker and turned down Henderson.

"I guess that's what I should expect from a Howell."

What had he meant by that?

"Hello, are you going to explain?"

"Shoot." Grace ducked down as she passed her house. "I was hoping my mom had already left."

"Grace, you're talking like a crazy person. A crazy person who shouldn't be driving."

She turned on Richard Street and pulled along the curb, as her gaze landed on Otis just across the street on the sidewalk by the new playground. The brass hippo must have moved in the night. That was Otis, always keeping the town on its toes. She cut the engine and popped the door open. "Fine, I stopped. I'm even getting out."

"Thank you. Now what is going on?"

Grace slid out of her Sonata gave a quick glance up and down the street then crossed the street and sat on her old brass friend. "I am still headed to Chicago. I just had to come back for a second because I forgot something. But I want to wait until my mom leaves to grab it."

"I got that part but what did the doctor say? Why were you at a police station? And why are you talking about Seth?"

"He said that with exercises, stretches, and some ultrasound therapy he thinks we can possibly get my leg back in shape—Dr. Medler, not Seth."

"Then why don't you sound happy?"

"Because he said possibly." Grace leaned forward putting her elbows on her knees letting her head fall forward. "And it will take at least a month. Who knows what that type of time off looks like to my career. Not to mention, what if I take the time off and it gets worse, and I can't even get secondary roles."

"When do you have to decide?"

"Today." Grace sat up and ran her hand over the shiny brass ear of the hippo. "Any answers for me, Otis?"

"Otis?"

"My town hippo."

There was long pause on the phone and Grace checked to see if they were still connected. "Should I be concerned?"

"Grace?" A feminine voice came from behind her. Grace jumped up and spun around. Margret Bunting, her old ballet instructor, stood about twenty feet away on the sidewalk. Her gray hair was a little thinner and her skin almost paper thin. But the twinkle in her eyes remained. "Are you going to give your old teacher a hug?"

"I need to go." She waved at Ms. Margret and stepped around Otis as she started making her way toward her. "I'll call you later."

"Wait. What about Seth and the jail?"

"Later."

"I am holding you to it."

Grace ended the call and embraced the woman in a quick hug. "How are you?"

The older woman gripped her hand with the strength of a much younger woman. "How am I? What are you doing parked in front of my house? Aren't you supposed to be in Chicago?"

"I . . . well . . . it's a long story. I'm only here for the morning."

The woman slipped her hand in Grace's arm and half led, half dragged her toward Margret's porch. "Well, turns out long stories go great with tea, and I was just going in to have my morning tea. Will you join me?"

Tea wasn't her favorite. But even dirt-flavored water sounded better than sitting here waiting for her mom to leave. Not to mention, with Ms. Margret's grip on her arm, the invitation wasn't really a question.

Grace opened the door and held it for Ms. Margret. The woman stepped in and pulled her hat pin from the blue old fashioned straw hat that rested at the back of her head. She hung it on a hook just inside the door before motioning Grace inside. The entryway was covered in dark paneling and wood flooring. It looked original. Maybe it was. After shedding her coat and shoes by the door, Grace followed the woman to the kitchen. After the dark elegance of the entryway, the kitchen was unexpectedly light and bright. Big windows, gauzy curtains, and a white crocheted tablecloth.

The dining nook off the kitchen had the same large windows and enough shelves for a room twice that size. Every space filled with a knickknack, photo, or souvenir. Every one so unique, it was as if they each told a story more fantastic than the next. Yet all shouting one common theme—*this woman has lived*. It was a stark contrast to her parents' plain house.

Ms. Margret filled a brass teakettle at the sink and then set it on the stove. "So, what brings you back to Heritage? I am guessing it wasn't just to have tea with an old lady?"

"You aren't old."

"If I'm not old, something has gone terribly wrong with this body." Ms. Margret pointed to the cupboard. "My shoulder is aching today. Can you reach the cups for us?"

Grace hurried over and pulled two china teacups from her cupboard as Ms. Margret pulled a canister of tea from the pantry. "How does peach tea sound?"

Extra gross. But Grace just smiled and set out the cups on the table.

"Thank you, dear." Ms. Margret dropped a tea bag in each cup, then hurried over to get the teakettle as the whistle began to blow. She poured in the hot water, then carried the kettle back to the stove. "My great nephew keeps trying to talk me into moving into an assisted living place. He's afraid I will fall with no one to help. I have lived here for sixty years. I'm not moving anywhere just because I struggle with getting dishes to and from the high shelves."

"Have you considered a roommate?"

"Why? Are you looking?" The woman carried a delicate sugar bowl to the table, then sat in the seat next to Grace.

"I live in Chicago."

"I'm just teasing, sweetheart. Now tell me about dancing. What's the summer production this year?"

"My company is doing *Giselle*."

"And what part are you?" Ms. Margret added a scoop of sugar and offered some to Grace.

"No, thank you." She covered her cup with her hand. "I was Giselle until last week. But Madame Laurent wants to move me to Myrtha."

Ms. Margret stirred her tea in a slow, graceful circle with a miniature spoon, then set it aside. "But you've been the principal the last three years."

"I have scar tissue built up in my knee. The doctors said I needed to take time off to treat that or take a less strenuous role."

"What are you going to do?"

"I just came from an appointment with Dr. Medler." Grace took a sip of her tea and tried not to wince at the tart liquid. "He was optimistic that with stretching, strength training, and a new ultrasound therapy, I could get back to where I was."

"But?"

"Optimistic, not a guarantee. I could go through all that and not be any better. And it could continue to get worse. And you know how it is, it doesn't take much time out of the limelight to be forgotten. If I don't come back better, she might not even give me roles like Myrtha."

"A secondary role isn't as bad as your father always made it out to be." Before Grace could stop her, Ms. Margret added a spoonful of sugar to Grace's tea and stirred it. "And neither is sugar."

Grace took a polite sip of the tea. Oh, that was good. She took a bigger sip. Then another.

"It isn't just this production. We always reprise *Swan Lake* for a fortnight at the end of the summer, and she already has me down as the Queen. I've always been Odette."

"Have you considered that dancing as Myrtha and even the Queen would allow you to still enjoy dancing without everything resting on your shoulders?"

A small snicker escaped before Grace could stop it. How long had it been since joy and dance belonged together in her mind? But maybe Ms. Margret and her mother were right—a secondary role was better than being forgotten altogether.

Ms. Margret laid her soft, wrinkled hand on Grace's. "Why do you dance?"

The words seemed to snap Grace out of the mini-sugar coma she was headed toward. She set the cup down. "I'm a dancer. It's what I do."

The woman eyed her a moment then stood. "Let's take a walk."

"To where?" Grace stood and carried the cups to the sink.

"So many questions." Ms. Margret's voice faded as she walked back out of the kitchen.

So many questions? It was just one question and a pretty important one if she was going to get back to Chicago in time. Grace checked the time on her phone, then followed her former teacher. But ten minutes later as they stood on the sidewalk staring down the old ballet studio on the far side of the square, she wished she'd asked a few more questions. Ms. Margret pulled an old key on a single pink ribbon from her pocket and inserted it into the lock.

When the lock stuck, Grace stepped forward and wiggled it until it gave way. "You still own this place?"

"Oh no. The Kensingtons own it now. But I kept a key for days like today."

"Ms. Margret, this is breaking and entering."

Her mind flashed to Seth and their conversation this morning. Maybe it wasn't as big of a deal in Heritage as it was in Chicago.

"Jon and Leah don't care. I helped them get together, you know." Ms. Margret stepped inside the room and settled into a rusted folding chair in the corner. Because the room was long and narrow, it was set up so the front door was stage left and the mirrors—they were always considered the front of the room—really ran down the left wall.

The place was just like Grace remembered, except then the floor-to-ceiling mirrors had been streak free rather than clouded with a heavy layer of dust. The barre and black Marley dance floor too for that matter.

She walked a large circle in the room, stopping at a door that was smack in the middle of the wall opposite of the mirrors. "I always thought this was a strange place for a door."

"It leads to an apartment above this place. But it was only used for a little while in all the years I rented the space. I don't think it is a very nice place. And it did make it tricky for them to come and go during class."

Grace tried the knob, but it was locked. She turned and stepped over to the mirror, her first day of ballet vivid in her mind. New slippers. New tights. New ribbons. And dancing had just been . . . fun.

"Dance for me."

"Now?" Grace pointed at her pink Converse. "I don't have my shoes."

"Floor is too dirty for your pointe shoes anyway. Just do a favorite sequence not on pointe."

Grace slipped off her coat and studied her muted reflection as she struck a pose. Giselle's opening sequence was familiar enough. She was only on her third eight-count when Ms. Margret stood.

"What was that?" She took a step closer.

"I told you my knee—"

"That wasn't just a knee problem. That was a heart problem. Where is the joy? The passion? What are you afraid of?"

What was she afraid of? Maybe that her career was at its end. Maybe that her best years were behind her. Maybe that if she didn't dance, she didn't even know who she was anymore. "I don't know. I—"

A little tap on the door echoed though the room.

They'd been caught. Maybe someone would call the police on them.

Margret opened the door, and a young girl about seven stood with a grin from ear to ear. She wore a red jacket that looked at least two sizes too big and tennis shoes with a hole in the toe. Her crooked pigtails that were so blonde they were almost white swung back and forth as she hopped from one foot to the other then back.

"I saw you go in. And I thought you might be dancing." Her blue eyes jumped between Ms. Margret and Grace. "Who are you? Are you a dancer? Can I dance with you?"

"Susie, this is Grace." Ms. Margret hugged the little girl to her side. "Grace was one of my students when I taught ballet. Susie is my new neighbor. She just moved next door to me with her brother Zane and her father."

"Ms. Margret teaches me ballet in her kitchen." The little girl lifted her arms and did a fairly impressive pirouette. "But I thought the studio sounded better than the kitchen. Sometimes I kick things there."

The little girl rushed in and took a ready position next to Grace.

Grace sent a questioning look to Ms. Margret, but the older woman just smiled and returned to her seat.

"Do you know grand plié?" Grace demonstrated with a deep bend in her knees then up.

"That's easy." The little girl squatted then stood. "I want to try something hard."

"Ballet is different than many things in that from a beginner to a master you do many of the very same moves. What makes a person great is how graceful and effortless they make it look." Grace stepped over next to Susie and placed her finger under her chin. "Chin up, back straight, tuck your bottom under . . . and again."

This time the little girl wobbled as she bent down. "That's harder."

"But prettier and more graceful."

Susie nodded and stood. "Now what?"

Grace's gaze darted to Ms. Margret, but the woman just nodded.

Grace stepped back to provide more space, lifted her right leg to ninety degrees in front of her, then lowered it to the ground. "How about a battement."

"That's called a Batman?" Susie kicked into the air with abandon and zero control.

Grace bit back a chuckle. "Not Batman. Baht-mah. And just like before, it isn't how high. It's about control and grace. Back straight, shoulders down, and lift your leg, don't bend to it."

Susie did it again this time with more control.

"Very good."

The little girl spun around on one foot. "I could do this all day."

There was another knock at the door, and Susie made a face. "That's probably my brother. He went to the library and said he'd pick me up when he was done."

She ran over and wrapped Grace around her middle. "Thanks, Miss Grace. See you later Ms. Margret."

With that, Susie hurried out the door. Ms. Margret peeked through a tear in the paper covering the windows but seemed satisfied that Susie was taken care of and turned back to Grace. "You're a natural."

"That was what you told me when I was young." Grace lifted her own leg in battement.

"Not dancing—although you are. I was talking about teaching. You could come home and open this studio back up." Ms. Margret tapped at her chin, as if making mental plans. "Susie and many girls like her would be over the moon."

Grace dropped her arm and leg and turned away from the mirror. "I'm not really a kid person."

Ms. Margret pulled a handkerchief from her pocket and laid it on the dusty barre before resting her hand on it. "I think Susie would say differently."

Grace shook her head as she pulled her coat back on and then stepped toward the door. "Besides, I'm not a teacher. I'm a dancer."

"One does not exclude the other. You're a dancer. But the last few minutes proves you're a teacher as well." The older woman studied her for a moment, then followed her out the way they came in. "When you were helping her, I saw a bit of your joy return. That has to mean something."

Grace secured the door, then dropped the key back in Ms. Margret's hand. "It means that ballet at age seven was easier."

"Or that a season of teaching might help you remember why you love it." The woman held out the key as if it were hers to give.

Grace shook her head, and the woman tucked the key back in her pocket. The two started walking across the square toward where she'd left her car, Grace making sure to match Ms. Margret's pace. "I have to decide if I am going to dance or heal. Teaching isn't on the list."

Ms. Margret slipped her hand in Grace's arm again. "Sometimes life makes you choose, but sometimes you can do both."

"Both." The word hit her in the chest as a new idea formed. "That's it. I need to both dance Myrtha and do therapy at the same time. It would be a full schedule, but I can do it."

Ms. Margret's face twisted into a frown. "Myrtha is a full-time role. I meant both teach and do therapy. Take the summer to heal and find your joy. I could find several girls to make a class for you. Just say the word."

Grace just shook her head and walked on.

"And where would I live? You know my parents." She motioned in the direction of her house. "You think that would work?"

They had just reached Grace's car when the woman's soft hand landed on hers, eyes calculating. "You could be my roommate for the summer. I have two rooms that I don't even use."

"Why would you offer all that?"

"Because you think your problem is here"—she touched Grace's knee—"but I think your problem is here." She moved her hand over Grace's heart.

Grace took a step back as she shook her head. "Thank you for the tea and visit, but I think it's time for me to go back to Chicago."

Ms. Margret sighed and nodded. "I'll pray that God leads you through this."

What was there to say to that? She and God hadn't been on speaking terms for years. She'd heard people say that God was love. But all love came with high expectations and conditions, and she didn't need more of that in her life.

She walked Ms. Margret to her porch, then Grace jumped into her car and checked the time. If she hit traffic, she'd be late to practice, and she still didn't have any solid answers. Her only hope was that Madame Laurent would approve her doing both therapy and Myrtha at the same time.

As she pulled from the curb, movement on the porch of the house next door snagged her attention. Susie, with her back to the road, bent in a grand plié then rose. Much better. Grace had taught her that. The little girl must have been pleased with her own efforts because she did a little jump and clapped her hands. Grace couldn't hold back her own laugh. Maybe next time she visited home she would stop by and see how Susie was doing. Because Grace had once loved ballet that much, and no doubt more time with Susie would help her remember why.

three

THIS HAD TO WORK . . . REHAB AND DOWNGRADing her role. Now to convince her director.

Grace slipped her toe into her pointe shoe and tied off the elastic ribbons at her ankle in record time. She rose on relevé and down. She hurried out onto the stage and did her best to blend into the warm-ups without missing a beat.

To her left, Mallory did a double take and nearly stumbled out of her arabesque. "You're back. I didn't think you were going to make it in time."

"I did." Grace lifted into an arabesque. With a smile in place, she spoke softly through her teeth. "Sort of."

"So, which did you choose? Therapy or Myrtha?" Mallory wasn't nearly as cautious with hiding their conversation.

"Both." Grace moved to the side of the stage with the other dancers and lined up.

"How will you do both?"

"Shh." Grace took her place next in line and did a series of chaînés across the floor.

As soon as they both reached the other side, Mallory pulled her behind the edge of the curtain.

"How will you have time to see your magic doctor if you're Myrtha?"

"Stop calling him that."

"Answer the question."

"He said he could set me up to do therapy here in Chicago with a friend."

"Madame Laurent agreed to let you take that much time off for therapy?"

"I—"

"Grace." Alec appeared at her side, clipboard in hand, causing Grace to jump. He wasn't scary—after all, he couldn't be much older than she was—but the sharp angles of his face, the haughty way he talked to them, and the overuse of product in his black hair made him feel more like a villain than Madame Laurent's assistant. Like he secretly wanted them all to fail. He tapped his clipboard with his pencil. "Madame Laurent is waiting for you in her office."

She looked at her friend. "Here goes nothing." Grace hurried off, pausing only to swap out her pointe shoes for slides.

Grace hurried down the long white corridor of black doors to the one at the end. She knocked twice and waited until she could hear the faint voice on the other side. "Enter."

Grace opened the door but was greeted by several racks over-flowing with costumes. "Hello?"

"Over here." The thick French accent came from the other side of the clothes. Must be choosing time for the next show, but this office was barely big enough for the woman's desk and chair. Why she chose to do this here instead of one of the other spaces always baffled Grace.

She wedged herself between them and found the hard-back chair she was looking for. She dropped into the seat, but across from her was just her instructor's empty desk.

"Madame Laurent?" Grace leaned forward but that didn't really help. There were just too many tulle skirts.

The woman stepped between two of the racks with an ornate white costume in hand. The iridescent sparkles on the skirt were a stark contrast to Madame Laurent's ever-present black long-sleeved fitted top and black pants. She'd never seen the woman wear anything else. Her black clothes were a staple just like her severe bun and scowl. Madame Laurent passed the costume to someone Grace couldn't see on the other side of the rack. "Dis one. Now leave us."

As soon as the door clicked shut, Madame Laurent settled into her chair and steepled her fingers under her chin. "What did your doctor say?"

"He's optimistic that with therapy, I could get back to where I was." Cautiously optimistic but still optimistic.

Madame Laurent's eyes gave nothing away. "So you want to do this therapy?"

"I do."

Madame Laurent nodded and lifted her pen.

"But I want to do therapy and dance at the same time. This way, if all goes well, I may be able to dance Odette—"

"No." It came out more like *nu*. She dropped her pen. "Myrtha is a full-time part. You must be here or there. Not both."

"But I can—"

"No, you must choose."

When Grace didn't answer, Madame Laurent removed her glasses and set them on the desk. "Do you know the difference between a good dancer and a great dancer?"

She thought back to her lessons with Susie earlier. "Technique?"

Madame Laurent gave a slight shake of her head. "A great dancer is a good dancer who faced a difficult road and overcame, emerging stronger on the other side. Like a beautiful butterfly."

"So you think I should do therapy and get stronger." When

Madame Laurent just stared at her, she tried again. "I should take the part of Myrtha and be stronger for it? I am not actually sure what you're saying."

"I am saying that part of your difficult road is that very decision. You must decide what you really want. Taking Myrtha is less risky, and you get to dance every night on that stage. Therapy is a risk. But a risk that could lead to great reward. Or not. But you cannot have both. So choose."

Grace closed her eyes a moment, then let out a deep sigh. If she did therapy here in Chicago, there was still a chance Madame Laurent would see her progress and change her mind. "I want to do therapy and reaudition for Odette for the end-of-summer show."

"Excellent." Madame Laurent slid her glasses back on and made a note on the paper in front of her. "Tell Alec on your way out, and you will need to turn in your key to him by the end of the day."

Grace started to stand but then nearly tripped over her own feet. "My key?"

"Rooms are only for dancers of the current show. We will need your room for another dancer." She moved her hand as if to shoo Grace away.

Grace wasn't going anywhere. She leaned on the desk. "But I am coming back."

Madame Laurent's lips pressed into a thin line. "Then we will reissue you another room at that time."

"Where will I go?" She dropped back into the chair with a thud.

"I am sure you will figure it out."

"If I—"

"Take the roll of Myrtha? No. Follow your courageous road. You will come out stronger. You'll see. You may go." She motioned with her hand once again for Grace to leave.

Grace stood and walked toward the door. Slow, steady breaths, in and out. It wouldn't support Madame Laurent's theory that her road was courageous if she passed out during the first few steps.

TARI FARIS

But what was she going to do? She couldn't afford to rent a place in Chicago on her own. She couldn't sleep on a friend's couch. All of her friends lived here with the company. And where would she dance to even be ready to try out for Odette?

Ms. Margret's face flashed in her mind. Like it or not, Heritage just might be her only option.

Grace lifted her phone and found Margret's number. The woman answered on the third ring. "Grace?"

"Were you serious about me coming to Heritage for the summer?"

"Absolutely. What changed your mind?"

"I told them I am not taking Myrtha, and I lost my housing."

"I've been praying, and God does work in mysterious ways."

Well, Grace had never liked His mysterious ways. "You really think I could use the studio to practice?"

"And to teach."

She let out a deep sigh. She didn't want to teach, but if she had to, she would. "And to teach."

"I already texted Leah, and she's all for it."

"You already asked?"

"I had faith God would bring you back. You need this, and we need you."

"Leah was really okay with it?"

"At least that's what I think the little cartoon picture of the thumb means."

"Thumb?"

"Let me send you a screenshot. My grandnephew Kade showed me how to do that because he has to talk me through phone problems all the time." There was a tapping then a chime on Grace's phone.

Leah's response was just a thumbs-up emoji. "I guess that's a yes."

"She did just have a baby yesterday so we may want to clarify

61

later with a contract, but for now, I say it's a go. When will you be back in town?"

"I think I will stay in Mallory's room tonight and drive back in the morning. I will have to come for the rest of my stuff this weekend."

"I look forward to seeing you. And Grace, don't forget to buy—"

"Signs to advertise the class?"

"I was going to say a mop and bucket. It's going to take a lot of cleaning to get that studio ready."

Ugh. She hadn't mopped a floor since she was sixteen, and she'd never taught a class in her life, but what she did know was that with hard work and enough determination, she could accomplish almost anything. Now she had to figure out how she was going to tell her parents that not only was she staying in Heritage for the summer to heal, she was not staying with them.

Two more interviews and two more nos. The temp agency had been optimistic that they could get Seth set up with a job on an assembly line, or there was always McDonald's. The job and apartment that Jon had offered him five days ago flashed in his mind. But whether Jon could see it or not, it just wouldn't work. Because the truth was, nobody wanted a former felon on their payroll or in their town even if he'd cleaned up his life, got a degree, and was a success on reality TV. At least according to *Ninja Warrior*. Thankfully, that was all they knew about him, because if the network dug very deep, they would find not just his criminal record but also his mother.

Seth signaled his blinker and took the exit toward his mom's apartment. He passed a playground, but it was empty. Seemed wrong for a Saturday morning. The area didn't look too bad. In fact, if he didn't know the crime rate in Muskegon Heights, he'd say it didn't look that much different than Heritage. But he knew better than anyone that crime often hid in plain sight.

Not that he wanted his mom back in Heritage. It might be safer *for* her, but he didn't want to have to protect the town *from* her. If she still lived in Heritage, she might have tried to come to the baby shower. Not that family meant much to her, but all the unattended purses would have been a gold mine. Nope. The thirty-minute buffer was just about perfect.

A couple of young teens stood by an old building passing around a joint. Everything in him wanted to stop the car, but it wasn't his place. And by the look of an older man not too far away, his efforts wouldn't be welcomed. He was an outsider.

Little did they know he'd probably be right there with them had the felony not landed him at Quinn Ranch, where Grant had helped him see that a different version of himself was possible. A version where he went to college. A version where he could be strong. A version that recognized his need for God. He'd love to be able to help other kids the way Grant had helped him. He just didn't know how. His mind flicked back to the property in Lansing that Jon had mentioned. The empty warehouse sounded like the perfect place to start his own ninja gym. But gyms needed startup money. And money and Seth had never been good friends.

His mom's apartment building came into view. The pale blue, one-story building was in desperate need of new paint. All doors faced the parking lot, and if he had to guess, it was once an old motel. But other than the brass door numbers, nothing really confirmed that.

He pulled into a spot near his mom's door, shoved his car into park, and grabbed his legal pad from the passenger seat. He uncapped the red marker and drew a thick red line across the two job leads. He eyed the last uncrossed name on the list without any real hope. JBL had been a long shot, and they were based out of California—talk about starting fresh.

He tossed the pad back on the seat, then lifted his phone and checked his bank balance. He needed a job. Soon.

If he didn't find something, he was going to have to sell off his weights. And in his life, they were the only things he really had left.

He popped the door open and waited for a rat to scamper back to the dumpster before climbing out. There wasn't anyone hanging around, but then it was a Saturday morning. Most of the tenants here were probably still sleeping off the night before.

He grabbed the two bags of groceries from his back seat and walked toward her door. Seth had just pulled out his keys when his mom's landlord stepped into his path. Jack was a decent guy but wouldn't win any prizes for friendliness. Or hygiene.

It wasn't so much the need for a shave or shower as the stain of grease from a recent meal that covered his stomach. A worn-down cigarette hung from his mouth. He sucked in one more long breath from it, then dropped it at Seth's feet. "I need rent today."

The guy was no nonsense when it came to rent. He'd ignore anything he didn't want to see as long as the rent was paid.

Seth shifted the groceries to the other arm.

"I left it with her last week."

Jack seemed like a straight up guy. He had never tried to cheat Seth or his mom before. "I ain't seen it, and that's two months unpaid now."

One check, his mom could have misplaced. Two? Maybe Jack wasn't as honest as Seth had thought.

The suspicion must have shown on his face, because Jack ground the smoldering butt on the ground with the toe of his steel-toed boot and narrowed his eyes. "I'm telling you how it is. She never paid her rent last month, and I ain't seen a dime this month."

"I'm on my way there, I'll make sure you have it before I leave." With any luck, she'd just forgotten to give Jack the checks, and he'd find them buried under the mess she called a life.

Jack nodded and stepped back as he pulled out a fresh cigarette and lit it. "Most people I wouldn't let walk out of my sight until things were square. But you seem like a stand-up kid. Not sure how you survived, let alone turned out all right with a mom like that, but I trust you. Don't make me regret it. My buddies aren't as nice as me."

How had he survived? Because he's been the one raising his mom, not the other way around. That, and because of Gabe. Ironic how the tables turned.

Seth made his way past the landlord to her door. He started to unlock it, but it just pushed open. A musty dank stench of garbage and stale alcohol hit him in the doorway. A lesser person might have gagged, but the smell was too familiar. Home sweet home.

He stepped into the dim room and immediately switched to breathing through his mouth. When he kicked the door shut, a moan lifted from the couch.

His mom lay face down on the old seventies couch, hair splayed across the orange-flowered cushion. She wore an old T-shirt that had once been Seth's dad's. A blanket covered her bottom half. The arm that hung off the side of the couch was skin and bone.

An empty bottle of vodka lay next to her on the floor, while a used syringe had been abandoned on the coffee table next to a lighter, a spoon, and an empty baggie. Awesome.

Seth carried the groceries to the kitchen and started putting the refrigerator stuff away. He'd stopped giving her money for groceries long ago, knowing that half of it would go to alcohol and the other half to meth, but she'd always been good about paying rent since it wasn't cash but a check made out to the landlord himself.

He searched the counter where he'd left the check, but it wasn't there. Guess she figured out a way around that as well.

He gathered the bags of trash scattered around and added all the garbage that hadn't quite made it to the can, including the remnants of last night's binge—there were at least three empty vodka bottles sitting next to the sink. He carried it all to the dumpster and stopped at the mailbox. It was crammed full. Good thing he hadn't waited another day.

He pulled the mail out and sorted it on the way back. Half was his since he'd been using this place as a forwarding address until he found a place to land.

By the time he came back, his mother had risen from the couch, found different clothes, and was digging through the grocery sacks.

"Did you buy me any cigarettes?" Her bloodshot eyes were desperate. She now wore threadbare sweatpants and a tank top that hung on her frame, emphasizing the sharp lines of her collarbone and the top of her rib cage just below her neck.

"No cigarettes, no alcohol—just some fruit, vegetables, peanut butter, bread, and milk."

"What about cold medicine? You know I have allergies." Her raspy voice lowered as her eyes flicked around the room. Finally, she pulled a banana from the bag.

He couldn't force her to take care of herself, and he couldn't force her to get help. "Mom, why does your landlord say he hasn't gotten rent in two months? What did you do with the checks I gave you?"

His mom suddenly look anywhere but at him as she peeled the banana, her movements more childlike than that of a forty-five-year-old woman. "Lost them."

"They were cashed." He'd checked that on the way back from the dumpster.

"Something came up."

He wanted to question her further but what was the point? He knew what came up. No doubt whatever had been in that baggie. She'd once been all about heroine, but she seemed to favor meth these days.

Her eyes darted back to his. "Just leave another check on the table. I'll drop it off today. Promise."

Few things pushed his buttons like the word *promise* coming out of his mom's mouth. *"I promise it will be different this time." "I promise I'll be there." "I promise it will never happen again."*

He opened the fridge and started pulling out some of the rotten food and shoving it into another trash bag. "I'll pay your landlord from now on."

"Oh, come on, Sethy, you remember how it was. It wasn't so long ago you were begging me for money."

The only thing he'd ever begged for from her was food, but she was correct about one thing at least. He did know what addiction had done to him.

"I changed." Seth shut the fridge, tucked his mail under his arm, and carried another bag of trash to the door. "You could too."

When she just stared at him, he opened the door. "See you next week. And keep this door locked."

He let it slam behind him and tossed the final bag in the dumpster then headed to the landlord's door. He pulled out his checkbook and calculated what his new balance would be. Two months' rent would clean him out. But what was the alternative, let his mom be homeless with him? That wouldn't make things any better.

He scribbled out the check and knocked on the door.

Jack answered, the odor wafting out the door from his place not much better than his mom's had been. He eyed Seth a moment, then took the check. "Better not be late again."

"I'll pay you directly from now on." Jack nodded, then slammed the door in his face.

Seth knew Jack preferred cash since most of his tenants bounced checks left and right, but Seth had always been good for it. Then again, after that check, his next one wouldn't be good unless he could get a solid job.

He climbed into his car just as his phone rang. An unknown number flashed across the screen. He tossed the mail on the seat next to him and took the call. "This is Seth Warner."

"Seth, this is Brad from JBL Corporation. We have decided to go in another direction. Thank you for applying."

That didn't take long. Although it was better than the companies that took the time to explain something had come up in his background check. Otherwise, he was perfect. Like that made it better.

"Thanks for the call. If anything opens—" The line went dead. Right.

Seth snatched the legal pad from the seat and scratched out the last option. He tossed it back in the seat and let his head fall back as he pressed his eyes shut. Now what?

He only had one option and that option was probably a very bad idea.

He stared at his phone for a moment, then pulled up Jon's number. His cousin answered on the third ring. "Are you ready to say yes?"

"I have a proposition for you."

"I'm listening."

"I will help you figure out what to do with your properties, but I want to turn the Lansing warehouse you mentioned into a ninja gym."

"The Storm is back."

"No. I don't want to attach my name to it. The Storm is gone. I just want to run it."

"I think it's a great idea, but you may want to look at a few of the other properties. There's one right in Heritage—"

"I want the one in Lansing." It might only be two hours away from Heritage but that should be enough. "It's better for us both that way."

"Okay. Deal." Jon seemed to hesitate a moment, then pushed on. "What about the apartment? I know you don't want to live in Heritage, but you need some place."

"How much?"

"Free."

"I don't need your charity."

"It's just sitting there empty." When Seth didn't respond, Jon's sigh came though the line. "Fifty a month for added utilities."

"Hundred."

"The more you save, the sooner you can leave town."

"Fine. Fifty but I'll buy my own furniture. Don't think I don't know how your mind works."

"Deal but only if you use the studio below for your weights until you get your ninja gym set up."

He took in the pathetic amount left in his account. "Deal."

"So what happened?"

"Happened?" He tossed back the question as if he had no idea what Jon was talking about. "Can't I have just changed my mind?"

"You don't have to do life alone, Seth."

But didn't he? If Jon knew the condition his mom was in, he probably would rescind the offer.

Jon finally sighed again, his voice tight. "You can pick up the keys at my place."

"See you in an hour." Now if he could keep his head down and away from all Howells for the next few months, this might turn out just fine.

four

ONLY LESS THAN FORTY-EIGHT HOURS AFTER accepting the job and Seth had already landed in the back of the squad car. Again. Talk about a Monday morning. And it wasn't just any squad car, the very squad car that hauled him off to the precinct more than once in his life. The first time he'd been picked up, the vehicle had been fresh off the line with a new car smell. Now, there was a fair amount of scratches and dents in the hard plastic seat which, by the smell, had been hosed off with disinfectant not too long ago.

He stared at the open MIM window twenty feet away. Why had he listened to Leah?

"You really want me to break and enter?" Seth had questioned Leah on the phone one more time as he examined the back window of the MIM.

"Preferably just the entering and not the breaking." The teasing in Leah's tone hadn't put him at ease. "It's easy. If you slide your hand down the left side of the window pane, there should be a nail slightly sticking out. If you pull that out, the window will push open. My grandpa came up with that years ago to keep from getting locked out."

Seth ran his hand down the pane like she said and found the nail on the first try.

"Did you pull it?"

"I still think this is a bad idea."

"Then don't lock yourself out of your apartment the day after you move in." Leah sighed. "Sorry. I am not upset. Just so tired from being up with Isabella. I would come, but I just got her back to sleep, and—"

"Don't sweat it." He tugged the nail, and it came right out. "Nail is out. But didn't you guys remodel this part of the building a few years ago?"

"We did, but I made Jon leave that. Partly for nostalgia, partly to keep me from getting locked out. Just push the window open, and you're good. The keys are in the cabinet to your left. But before—"

Seth pushed the window open, and it swung inward.

"—you do, you'll only have two minutes until the alarm goes off. The alarm code is #2477#."

"That would have been helpful information about thirty seconds ago."

"Sorry. Better hurry. I'm getting back to my nap before Isabella wakes up. And I'm putting my cell on Do Not Disturb so you sure you're good?"

"I'm good."

"Oh, and Seth?"

"Yeah?"

"We're glad you're here." With that, she ended the call and Seth slid his phone in his pocket. She was glad he was here. The pressure he felt at Grant's words was back. What was with this place?

He eyed the dirty windowsill and then his new dress pants and shirt. Maybe they weren't *new* new but they were new to him and the best he could afford at the thrift store in Mason. He didn't want to wreck them the first day, but what choice did he have?

And with the way the alarm code blinked on the opposite wall, he'd better hurry.

Seth placed his hand on the window ledge at the top and tested his weight. He lifted his feet and threaded himself through the window. It wasn't huge, probably easier for a girl Leah's size than his. But if he angled his shoulders, he should get through all right.

He had just begun to twist his body when a police cruiser pulled into the parking lot, lights flashing. He didn't even try to move. He knew the drill. Both hands where they could see them, even if that meant the top half of his body still hung out the window.

The officer stepped out of the car. "Hold it right there."

He winced as the voice registered. Hammond. He lifted his head and looked at the man. "Morning, Officer Hammond."

The man's eyes widened slightly as recognition seemed to sink in. "Again, Seth? Care to explain yourself?"

"I work for Jon. And I'm living in the apartment above the ballet studio—or what used to be a ballet studio. I locked myself out, and Leah told me how to get in this window."

"Break into the MIM? But I thought you said your apartment was above the old studio." He gestured to the next door over.

"The apartment is upstairs, and after they remodeled the MIM you can only access it though the old studio. She said there was a spare key in here."

"Along with the safe."

Yup, this wasn't going well, and his side was beginning to pinch as he hung half in and half out of the window. "Any chance I can climb out?"

"Sure. Just keep your hands where I can see them."

Seth lifted himself out of the window, taking care that none of his movements would be taken as threatening just as Hammond's radio crackled to life: "Dispatch to Unit Two. Silent alarm notification at the location of the 10-62. Proceed with caution. Copy?"

"Copy." Hammond spoke into his radio as he met Seth's eyes.

"Why would Leah tell you how to get in this way if she knew there was an alarm?"

"She gave me the code, only you showed up before I could get all the way in to turn it off." Seth brushed at the dirt on his clothes, but they wouldn't come clean without a wash, maybe not even then.

As if Heritage itself was determined to point out that returning was a bad idea, large rain drops began to descend from the sky.

Hammond had his notebook out and jotted something down. "If you work for Jon, why did he say you were just visiting when he picked you up from the station?"

No doubt he was trying to catch him in a lie. They'd done this dance before, and Hammond had usually won. Only before, Seth had actually been lying, and this time there was nothing to catch. "He just hired me on Saturday and offered me this place to stay."

"Do you have any work ID that would collaborate with your story?"

"I don't officially start for—" Seth checked the time on his watch and winced. "Thirty minutes ago. If the alarm hadn't gone off yet, how did you know I was here—"

"Someone reported seeing a break-in."

Seth scanned the area. Who? They were pretty hidden back in this parking lot. No direct line of sight to any window or building. And the big oak trees by the road made a drive-by unlikely.

The black nose of a Sonata was parked along Henderson. He could just make out someone sitting in the driver's seat but no details.

"Is this your car?" Officer Hammond pointed to Seth's car parked a few feet away.

"Yes, sir."

"Where are the keys to it?"

"With the apartment keys."

"Which would be up in the apartment."

"Actually, no."

Hammond paused his writing and eyed him as if he'd found a hole in his story.

"I set my keys down to do some quick chin-ups to release a little . . . energy before work. First day jitters and all that."

"A chin-up bar in your apartment."

"No, in the studio below. Jon said I could set up my workout equipment in there. I was distracted when I left and hurried to my car after fifteen reps and locked myself out."

"I want to believe you, Seth." Officer Hammond pulled his phone from his vest. "If I call Leah, will she back up your story?"

Seth winced. "She was going to put her phone on Do Not Disturb."

When the officer just lifted an eyebrow at him, Seth shrugged. "She's tired because of the baby. I woke her up."

"And if I call Jon?"

"He's at the factory. He may or may not pick up. He didn't answer for me."

"Sorry, Seth. It looks like you get to sit in my car until I can get a hold of one of them."

Seth hadn't bothered arguing, he just walked over and placed his hands on the car for a pat down before he'd climbed in. At least this time, Hammond hadn't cuffed him.

Now he sat in the cruiser as the rain fell in the still open window of the MIM and hoped no important papers would get wet. Jon was just going to love him after today.

The rain picked up, and suddenly Seth was glad he was in the dry car. He peered out the window to watch Hammond, who stood with a woman under the small overhang. He tried to make out who it was, but the water cascading down the window made it impossible.

Whoever it was unlocked the door to his place and strode in. What did she think she was doing? It might not be a great apartment, but it was his.

A moment later Hammond pulled the door open and motioned for him to follow. They hurried through the now open door to the studio and climbed up the half dozen steps to the main area where he'd set up his workout equipment. It wasn't much but it was scattered all over the place. A few dumbbells here and there, a bench, and a full set of free weights next to a weight rack, which also served as his chin-up bar. He hoped to install the pegboard by the end of the day, but right now, that wasn't looking good.

And sure enough, his keys sat on the floor next to the chin-up bar just as he'd said.

"Good news is that with your stuff here and your keys right where you said they'd be, I'm keen to believe your story."

"Bad news?"

"She says she rented this place from the Kensingtons on Tuesday." Hammond motioned to the wall behind Seth.

He turned and locked eyes with one very angry Grace Howell. That answered the question of who called the cops. Seemed to be her specialty. That also answered any questions as to what she'd thought about him since their run-in at the police station.

He knew her parents hated him, but trying to get him arrested for a second time in a week while making up stories was crossing the line.

She hadn't spent her entire day last Wednesday cleaning this room and carrying out fifteen buckets of dirty water for some ape of a man to turn it into his personal sweat-producing factory. Grace couldn't believe all the workout equipment that littered her dance space. With the weight of that bench, she'd be lucky if he hadn't permanently damaged the Marley floor.

Officer Hammond stood by the door talking to Seth. Of course it would be him. Breaking and entering again. She pulled out her phone and sent off a text to Ms. Margret.

GRACE

Seth Warner is in my studio.

Ms. Margret's reply was almost immediate.

MARGRET

He's a fine boy. Invite him to dinner.

Is he still handsome?

What? Handsome? Very. Invite him to dinner? No way.

GRACE

Why would I invite him to dinner?

MARGRET

My house is your house. Invite anyone you want.

Especially fine-looking young men.

She ignored that last bit.

GRACE

He's saying the studio is his.

MARGRET

Oh dear, that is a pickle.
Maybe you two can talk about it over
dinner while he is here. You can make something
that will impress him. They say the way to
a man's heart is through his stomach.

GRACE

I'm not inviting him to dinner.

I can't even cook.

And I don't want a way into his heart.

I just want him out of my studio.

MARGRET

Show them the message from Leah.

Then invite him to dinner.

I'll cook.

She started to type back but stopped as officer Hammond walked toward her.

She did her best not to cringe as his shoes left wet spots with every step. Sure, the place had been covered in a thick layer of dust less than a week ago, but street shoes on the dance floor? But it wasn't like she could ask him to take them off. He was helping her after all.

"He says Jon gave him the space for a gym on Saturday." Hammond shrugged and ran his hand roughly through his hair. "Do you have a contract of your lease?"

"I have a text." She pulled it up on her phone and passed it to the officer.

"This is a photo."

"It's a screenshot of the text Ms. Margret sent Leah and her response." She pointed to the line. This had to work.

"Margret Bunting. Of course she'd be involved. That woman is the source of half these gray hairs." He studied the photo a little more. "I'm not sure a thumbs-up emoji is enough to build a case. It's definitely not enough for me to ask him to leave."

"But I cleaned this place. He didn't." She pointed to Seth, who moved a few steps closer as he listened in.

"What type of argument is that?" Seth took another step closer.

"So, can every cleaning service claim the right to any house they clean? Besides, who asked you to clean it?"

"Seth, stay over there." The officer pointed to the other side of the room, then turned back to her. "Do you have any type of written agreement with the Kensingtons for use of the room when they asked you to clean it."

"They didn't ask."

Hammond's brow wrinkled as he seemed to be processing the new information. "So you're saying that Leah gave you a key and you just volunteered to clean it, then expec—"

"She didn't give me the key. Margret did."

"Because Leah gave Margret the key to give to you?"

"Margret still had it from when she taught—"

"Okay, let me get this straight." The officer closed his eyes for a moment as he drew a calming breath. "Margret gave you a key she shouldn't have had. You used said key to break in and clean the place. Seth, on the other hand, has a key given to him by the owner and you want me to kick him out? And if you've been here since Wednesday, how did you not notice he moved all this equipment in?"

"I drove to Chicago to pick up the rest of my stuff yesterday." And see the opening show of *Giselle*. The first opening show she hadn't starred in for the past three years.

Hammond shook his head. "I swear, retirement can't come soon enough."

As if on cue, Jon walked in the back door. And after they all had given their side once again, Jon's only response as he glanced at the thumbs-up emoji was to offer a sympathetic shrug. "Sounds like Leah. She's been pretty tired with Isabella."

"But I can use it, right?" Grace stepped forward. Maybe she did sound like she was begging, but the flyers had already gone up. And it was the only place to practice in town. "I need a dance space."

"And I need a gym." Seth took a step forward.

Jon's gaze bounced between them. "Is there any way you two could share this place?"

Seth stared at her a moment, then looked away as he shrugged. "You won't bother me, and I won't bother you. Feel free to use that corner over there to dance, and I'll keep my stuff over here."

She walked over to the space barely big enough to do a full fouetté. "You want me to dance in this corner?"

He looked at the ten-by-ten space and then back at her. "Is that bad?"

"Why would you think that this little space is enough for me to dance in? Not to mention I am doing a summer ballet camp for the month of June with at least six girls in it." She hoped six.

"Fine. I'll take this half and you take that half. Better?"

He couldn't be serious. Her face must have said as much because he sighed and drew an invisible line with his arm.

"You can't fit six little girls in half this room?"

Grace pinched the bridge of her nose and drew a calming breath. "How do you expect me to practice Giselle or Odette?"

The leap sequence alone would land her right in the middle of his bench.

"Are those the names of two of the girls?"

"You're such a . . . an . . . ape. I need this room. The entire room. You can sweat anywhere." Okay, now she sounded like a toddler, but everything hinged on the use of this room. To practice. To teach. "I need the whole room."

"This is where I live. It's technically a part of my apartment."

"Okay, time out." Jon held up his hands. Hammond must have decided he didn't need to be a part of this and had disappeared during their little discussion. Jon focused on Grace. "What exactly do you need?"

"I need to be able to not just do moves but practice entire sections of stage choreography that will take most of the room. And

I will be teaching the camp during the late mornings as soon as school gets out."

Jon nodded at Seth. "You work days. So, what if she uses this space during the day? You use it in the evenings. And you keep your weights lined along the end wall."

Seth stared at Grace for a moment. His dark eyes seemed to study her, saying words that she couldn't decipher at this point. Then he focused back on Jon. "I can do that."

Grace took his cue and directed her words to Jon. "I'll be done by five o'clock every day, and he can use it in the evenings."

Jon flipped the keys over in his hand as his gaze bounced between them. "Anything else?"

"What about Saturdays?" She finally looked back toward Seth. "Can I share the space with you on Saturday mornings?"

Seth hesitated a moment then took a step closer. "Sure."

"Your shoes." Grace winced at the wet footprint he'd just made.

Seth's hand lifted in confusion. "What about them?"

"You aren't supposed to have street shoes on a Marley floor."

"You want me to remove my shoes every time I walk in and out?"

"Yes."

"No."

"How about"—Jon stepped between them—"Seth will use the back door that's closer to the door to the apartment, and you can use the front. Closer to your parents' place. He'll only wear his shoes along that wall."

Jon pinned Seth with a stare.

Seth nodded and looked back at Grace. "I'll stay off the rest except for when I am working out, then I'll be barefoot. How does that sound?"

Not ideal but that was probably the best offer she'd get. "I'm not living with my parents. I'm living with Ms. Bunting, but that works."

"Seth, why don't you walk me out, then you can come move your weights out of her way." Seth nodded, and the two disappeared out the back door.

As soon as it clicked shut, Grace hurried over to where she'd dropped her bag and pulled out a roll of white athletic tape. She measured off the space he'd need to walk along the wall and stretched the tape from the steps that led to the back door all the way to the door that led to the apartment. The white line ran parallel to the wall about two and a half feet out.

Then she hurried over to the end wall and began boxing out a space for his weights. She had just secured the final side when the back door rattled as it opened, then shut. She stood and spun to face him.

Seth's gaze followed the white line from the back door to the door leading to his apartment, then looked back at her. "Is this for me?"

"Just didn't want there to be any misunderstanding."

"Despite what you may think, Grace, life doesn't always fit in a box." With that he walked through the door of his apartment, letting it slam behind him as he went.

There he went again, acting like he knew her. But he didn't. Maybe they had been neighbors when she was a kid, but a lot had happened since then.

She stepped over to a bar of weights and tried to lift it. The thing didn't move. She bent her knees and tried again. Nothing. Maybe she could roll it into the square.

"Don't hurt yourself. Seth is just changing clothes, then he'll move his stuff out of your way." Jon stood by the steps. "I came back to make sure you're okay. Do you think this arrangement will work?"

She forced a smile and took a step toward him. "Is he safe? I mean . . . do you trust him?"

Seth had broken into not one but two of Jon's buildings in a week. Did the guy really think Seth was trustworthy?

Jon winced. "I wouldn't have suggested it if I didn't trust him a hundred percent. I would trust him to babysit Isabella if that gives you any indication. But if you don't feel safe, then—"

"It's only for a little while anyway." Because there wasn't any other option that ended with her having a space to dance. "I hope to be back in Chicago before the end of the summer."

Some of the tension eased from his shoulders. "You could always stay. Heritage seems to have that effect on people, and we could use a ballet studio again."

"I have a career and a life in Chicago that I need to get back to. This is just for the summer."

"Well, it's good having you here in the meantime. I'm sure your class will be popular." Jon offered a wave and headed to the back door.

The door had just shut when Seth's apartment door opened. He stepped back into the room in athletic shorts and a loose tank top. Wow, he definitely hadn't had those shoulders when they were in high school. He locked eyes with her for a moment, and all the warmth in his gaze from when she'd seen him at the police station was gone. But the dark, smoldering look that had replaced it did not detract from his appeal. In fact, quite the opposite. His dark eyes seemed to look right into her, melting any barrier she'd constructed.

He looked away as he stepped over to the bar that she'd tried in vain to move and picked it up with little effort then carried it to the box she'd marked out. The muscle on his freshly shaved jaw twitched slightly. When he set the bar gently down, he cast a look back at her. "Is that okay, Your Highness?"

Right. That snapped her out of it. Hot or not, this was still Seth. The guy who seemed to make a hobby out of breaking and entering, not to mention hating her for some unknown reason.

"I'll leave you to it." She spun on her feet toward the front door and hurried outside.

She'd only just crossed Teft when her mom's silver Lexus stopped along the square. The window rolled down, and her mother leaned across the passenger side. "Grace?"

Great. She should have stopped by her parents' before now to tell them the new plan. She'd texted that she was doing the treatment but had left it at that. Maybe she should have added a few more details. But she was just waiting. Waiting to not feel like this.

Grace leaned down, propping her elbows on the window. "Hi, Mom."

"Why aren't you in Chicago?"

"I'm rehabbing my knee. Remember?"

"Here? Where are you staying?"

"With Ms. Margret?" Why did that sound like a question?

Her mother's red lips pressed into a thin line. "What were you doing in the studio?"

Grace glanced back at the lit front window, but the butcher paper still hid the inside. "I will be teaching classes for the summer."

"Teaching?" The word dripped with disdain.

"Yup."

Her mom's nose flared a moment. "Get in. Your father and I need to talk to you."

"I am actually on my way somewhere." Like anywhere but home at the moment. They might need to have this conversation, but she needed to be prepared and on her terms. "How about dinner tomorrow?"

"Nonsense. Your father and I have plans tomorrow night. We'll expect you tonight at five thirty." Her mom started to lean back.

"No." Grace leaned down in the window and met her mother's eye. "If tomorrow won't work, then Thursday, and I'll make dinner at Ms. Margret's."

Her mom's eyes narrowed a moment. "You cook?"

No. But surely Ms. Margret's offer to help extended to meddling parents and not just attractive young men. She just needed to be on the high ground for this battle. "Six o'clock Thursday, at Ms. Margret's. I'll be ready."

With that she straightened away from the car and continued down the street. Would she be ready? Never. But if she could fake being brave in the face of Seth Warner, surely, she could fake it in front of her parents for one dinner.

five

S ETH HAD HOPED SHARING THE SPACE WITH
Grace wouldn't be that bad—after all, they'd probably barely
see each other. But maybe he should've asked Grace what she
meant by *morning*, because the six a.m. wake-up call in the form of
Bach was not what he had in mind. Seth smashed his pillow over his
head, but that didn't help—there just wasn't enough soundproofing
between the studio below and his new apartment. Maybe if he was
on a real bed, but the few blankets that separated him from the wood
floor did nothing to lessen the sound. He might as well have his ear
pressed to the floor.

He'd hoped he'd at least find some peace and solitude in this
apartment, but that seemed like a big no. He'd have to get extra
coffee to keep from falling asleep at work. He couldn't let Jon
down. He'd only worked a half day after yesterday's rough start.
But at least he'd managed to make a central list of properties, which
was no small feat.

He closed his eyes, but returning to sleep wasn't an option.
Not with the way the hard floor dug into his shoulder blades.
Then again, he couldn't blame the floor for his poor night's sleep.

He'd spent many nights in worse conditions than this. Crashing anywhere had become his superpower.

But those anywheres weren't usually plagued with pale blue eyes blazing as she yelled at him. He still couldn't believe Grace had called the cops on him again. The whole Howell family was out to get him, and had he known he'd have to live this close to one, he'd never have agreed to Jon's deal. No gym was worth this.

Not that they'd see each other much. But with him living here, there would be no avoiding her. And right now, knowing she was twenty feet below made returning to sleep impossible, even if Bach hadn't still been vibrating through the floor.

Seth sat up and stretched his neck to the right and then to the left. The first item on the agenda was to buy a mattress. Maybe an air mattress would do.

His gaze landed on the wooden plaque he'd pulled from the wall at his mom's old house. Why had he bothered to save it? Probably the same reason he'd pulled it from the trash back when he was ten.

Making that with his mom had been the last time he'd heard her laugh, really laugh. He hadn't known in that moment how much that memory or this stupid thing would come to mean to him. They had nearly glued their fingers together as they laid each of the sticks on the little wooden board, only to discover after it dried that they had done it wrong.

"Would you look at that, Sethy. We spelled Jesus's name wrong. It says Jeus. I guess it's a good thing He loves us even when we mess up."

It had been the next day that a sergeant and a captain had shown up in uniform with hats in hands to tell them that his dad had been killed in action.

The two men hadn't even pulled out of the driveway before his mom had dug out a bottle from the cupboard and tossed the wooden plaque in the trash. She just stared at him with cold eyes as she uncorked the bottle.

"I was wrong, Sethy. Jesus doesn't love us. Sooner you realize that the better you'll be."

Seth rolled to his back and let out a deep breath. His mom's problems hadn't started with his dad's death, but it was definitely when she'd stopped trying to overcome them.

It had still been in his pocket when Officer Hammond had patted him down. He had asked Seth about it in processing, but Seth had dismissed it with a shrug and told him he'd had it for a long time. It wasn't a complete lie. He just hadn't had it in his possession the whole time. But it wasn't like whoever ended up owning that house wanted a child's craft that was misspelled and poorly done. And admitting he did want it and explaining he had gone in to find it meant opening up, and that was not Seth's way.

"You don't have to do life alone, Seth." Jon's words still circled his mind three days later. But he did. And being in Heritage for a couple months wasn't going to change that.

It was more than just that memory though. He'd kept it because he knew in his mom's broken way, she'd been trying to help Seth find the faith that his father had.

He stood, letting the blanket fall away just as a cool morning draft from the window whipped down his spine. He released an involuntary shiver as he reached for the old worn Bible that had been his dad's. Jon had found it at his parents' place a couple years ago. Evidently Seth's dad had left it with them before his last deployment. It was well marked up, and every day when Seth read it the past couple years, he felt that not only did he get a glimpse of who his heavenly Father was but who his earthly father had been also.

He flipped open the marked page as another concerto vibrated the floor. Maybe he would run first. He strode across the rough wood floor toward his duffel bag until he found some athletic clothes.

He'd normally burn his restless energy with a hard workout, but if Grace was already started, then he'd have to settle for a run.

He changed and hurried down the steps. He hated the fact that the only way out was through the studio. He knocked, although that didn't seem right. But the last thing he needed was to slam into Grace with the door.

A moment later she opened the door in a black leotard, pink tights, and a sheer pink skirt wrapped around her middle. The color pink was suddenly growing on him. "Are you knocking to leave your apartment?"

"I just didn't want to surprise you."

"If I am dancing this close to the door, something is way off." She wore her hair up and back into a tight bun, which only accentuated her face and especially those big blue eyes as she laughed with the words.

"Still." He shrugged and secured the door. "I wouldn't want you to call the cops on me."

"Since you're using the door and not a window for once, I think I'll let it go. Besides, that's what the tape that you made fun of is for." She pointed to a white line. "The door space and along the wall to the steps down to the door are all yours to use at any time with your shoes on. Even if I'm dancing, you're free to come and go."

"Gracious of you." He nodded and followed the marked-out path toward the back door. Who was he kidding? Sharing a space wasn't difficult because she was a Howell. It was because she was beautiful and light and petite and toned. And seeing her every day wearing that, as she held herself as if she were made of air, might just drive him insane.

Okay, he really needed that run.

He forced his gaze around the room—anywhere but lingering on her and that sheer skirt. "Did I miss a weight?" He took a step toward the dumbbell sitting in the middle of the room—

"Shoes." Her elevated voice stopped him midstep.

"I was just going to grab the weight."

"I borrowed it. My doctor wants me to do some strengthening." The haughtiness finally dropped away. "Is that all right?"

"Sure." Because he couldn't put his shoe in her space, but she could go use his equipment without asking.

"If you don't want me to—"

"It's fine." He took a step toward the back door, taking care to stay in his lane.

"Obviously it's not." Her lips pressed into a line.

"I said it's fine."

"Can you just be honest with me?"

"Probably not." Sounded harsh but it was true. Would he tell her that she intrigued him and angered him at the same time? Not a chance. Would he tell her how many times he had wondered what might have happened if he hadn't waited until she was leaving for Paris to talk to her—to ask her out? Another solid no.

A sadness crept into her eyes, and for just a second, the polished, poised Grace melted away. The hard shell was gone, and she was just Grace, the girl next door.

His tone softened. "Just be careful. If you lift wrong, you'll mess up your knee worse."

"Oh." Grace eyed the weight a moment, then looked back at him.

"Can you help me?"

"No."

"I don't mean now. But my doctor told me to consider a trainer. I would hire you."

"Still no."

"Why? I thought we could start over. Be friends."

Friends? Training? No, way. All that would lead to more time with her which would lead to him wanting what he couldn't have. He'd already spent enough years of his youth wasted on that.

When he didn't answer, her hand clenched at her side. "Why are you so difficult?"

He shrugged. It wasn't like he would tell her all that. He shifted his weight to the other foot. "And I would appreciate it if you could wait on the Bach wake-up call until a little later."

Her eyes rounded as her hands came to her face. "I didn't realize the sound would carry. Or that you would know Bach."

Cause why would Seth Warner know anything civilized, right? "It's fine. I'm going for a run. But in the future, if you could wait until after eight o'clock to start, I would appreciate it."

He was up before seven but if she waited until eight, then just maybe he wouldn't have to have the image of her dancing branded on his mind every day before he started work.

With that, he hurried out the back door and broke into a steady jog, slightly faster than his normal pace. He'd been wrong—sharing this space with her, even for just a couple months, might just kill him.

Grace punched the mound of bread dough in the antique bowl and then again. When she admitted to Ms. Margret that she'd invited her parents over, the woman decided it was a great time for Grace to learn to make bread. When Ms. Margret had suggested she take her frustrations out as she kneaded the dough, one face had come to mind.

Seth had shot down the idea of training her faster than she could have done a petit allegro. No explanation, nothing. Just no. She'd even offered to hire him, and by the look of his car she'd seen in the parking lot, he could use the money. But he wanted nothing to do with her. *Punch.* Which was fine. *Punch.* She didn't need him or his help. *Punch.*

"That's some frustration." Ms. Margret wandered back into the kitchen and peered in the bowl.

"Sorry." Grace pulled her hands from the dough. "I hope I'm not ruining it."

"Not at all." Ms. Margret patted her shoulder. Her former instructor was certain if they made this one together today, then Grace could make the one for her parents' dinner in two days all by herself. Gace wasn't convinced, but she appreciated Ms. Margret's confidence in her. "What has you so worked up?"

"I need to weight train, but Seth won't help me. And I will never get back to the stage without it."

"Is that the worst thing that could happen?"

"Not getting back to the stage? Yes. My ballet career is all I have."

Ms. Margret covered the dough with a cloth. "While we wait for this to rise again, would you take me for a drive?"

Grace did a quick wash of her hands, then walked over to the entryway to slide her shoes on. "Oh, sure. To JJ's?"

Grace checked her watch. Hopefully, the local grocery store would still be open. It definitely didn't provide the variety or long hours that Meijer did, but it was great in a pinch, and Margret preferred to shop local.

"I said a drive, not grocery shopping. I have something much more special in mind." The woman lifted an old-fashioned tan hat with a spray of pink flowers from the hook and ran a pin through it, securing it to her low bun. Then she stepped past Grace and out the door.

Once in the car, it didn't take Grace long to deduce where they were going. Even though she couldn't see beyond the thick foliage on either side of the road, there wasn't much west of Heritage besides Lake Michigan. And with the road they'd chosen, they would come out on the beach just about on the point of Little Sable Lighthouse. But since Ms. Margret kept her mouth shut as they drove, so did Grace.

And unlike when she was with her parents, this silence she didn't mind. Driving in the country up here was one thing she missed while living in the city, with the trees stretching over the roads creating living tunnels. The quiet, shaded miles had always felt calming, peaceful, and welcoming. "Beautiful."

Ms. Margret nodded from next to her. "Once upon a time, this area was all covered in mostly white pine. The deciduous trees didn't really make an appearance until they deforested the area for the lumber."

"That's sort of sad."

"True, but sometimes you have to cut away beautiful things to make room for even more beautiful things." Ms. Margret sent her a look to make sure she got the analogy. Yeah, she got it. But how did one know what to cut down and what to keep?

"Where did all the lumber go?"

"Chicago-bound just like you. Built most of the city." The woman seemed to be playing the game of how many lessons could she squeeze into one talk. And Ms. Margret was definitely a worthy player. "Although it *was* the part of Chicago that burned in the fire of 1871."

Grace darted her gaze to her then back to the road. "Just like me?"

"What?" The woman's brow pinched as if she wasn't following.

"I went to Chicago, and now I'm on the verge of burning down?"

Ms. Margret chuckled, then reached across the car, patted Grace's arm, and pointed to a parking spot. "I might not take that analogy too far."

Grace put the car in park, then climbed out and hurried around to help Ms. Margret with the door. They weren't far from the lake, but because of the series of large sand dunes that stood between them and the water's edge, they couldn't see it. The parking lot bordered a wide gap in two of the dunes and if they followed that sandy path, they'd come out directly in front of Little Sable Lighthouse.

Ms. Margret accepted Grace's hand, then waited as Grace locked the car. "I know I was being over the top earlier, but I might just need your arm in this sand. Balance isn't what it used to be."

"Of course." Grace secured her arm in hers before leading them on.

Ms. Margret's steps were slow but steady as they moved forward. "I assume you have been here, growing up so close."

"I have. I showed a friend a photo once in Chicago, and she thought it was photoshopped. She said that you couldn't build a lighthouse in the sand."

As if her statement had conjured it up, the tall structure jettisoning out of the sand came into view. The deep red bricks, backdropped by the blue sky and accented by the pale sand at the base, always took her breath away no matter how many times she saw it.

The lake was fairly calm today and still very cold, if the fact that none of the beachgoers were actually in the water was any indication. They continued to the base of the lighthouse, then Ms. Margret pointed to a small rise in the sand nearby. "This is far enough."

Grace held the woman's arm as she settled her into the sand, then took a seat next to her.

"I might never be able to get up again, but it's a beautiful place to die." Ms. Margret dusted off her hands with a chuckle. "You know, I have sat here hundreds of times over the years, but I've never sat in the same sand."

"I never thought about it like that." Grace dug her hands in the sand on both sides of her. The top had been warmed by the sun but the underneath was cool.

Ms. Margret picked up a handful and let it fall through her fingers. "Ever shifting, ever changing, but I enjoy it every time."

Ah, they were back to lesson-speak. Hopefully, this comparison wouldn't end with her burning down. "Are you suggesting that where I find my joy in life will change but that's okay?"

Grace leaned back on her elbows. A little girl screamed and laughed as she ran from her brother closer to the shore. Right now, life without ballet seemed too empty to consider. "I love ballet—you taught me to love ballet. Why are you now trying to talk me out of it?"

"I'm not."

Could have fooled her.

Ms. Margret pointed at the lighthouse. "Do you remember the old Sunday school song about building your house on the rock rather than on the sand?"

Another lesson? She hadn't even really understood the last one. It was like hanging with Mr. Miyagi or Yoda. Why couldn't older people just speak directly. "I remember the song."

Ms. Margret crossed her ankles and dusted her hands off again. "That always confused me when I would come here as a child."

"Because this is built on the sand and doesn't fall down?" That was a big testimony against it. "Isn't it celebrating its hundred and fiftieth anniversary this fall?"

Ms. Margret nodded. "Along with the town."

"So did you decide the old song was wrong?"

"Well, the song came from the Bible, so I believed it had to be true, so I asked my dad." She pointed to the base where the red bricks disappeared into the light sand. "He told me that the lighthouse isn't built *on* the sand but *in* the sand."

On. In. What was the difference? But Grace sent a smile like she did, in fact, understand the significance. It must not have been convincing because Ms. Margret continued.

"If it were *on* the sand it would shift with the winds and storms. That would be very unstable. But the builders dug deep to a firm foundation—a solid rock you could say. So as the sands shift around it, that solid rock keeps it strong." She picked up grains of sand like she had done earlier. "Many of the things of our lives will come and go. If we try to find our source of joy there, we will be an unstable lighthouse. But if we dig deep and anchor ourselves to something unchanging—even when life shifts around us—we can stay strong."

"You mean faith." And there it was. The big lesson. She'd have to be dense to miss that one. But what sounded simple out of Ms. Margret's mouth wasn't that simple when it came to her life.

"Faith is definitely my bedrock. And I think it's the best place to ground yourself. That is why I chose it." She sent Grace a wink. "But you must make that choice for yourself. Because as much as I loved ballet in my own life, it was shifting sand. You need to dig deeper to find out who you really are."

"I'm not sure faith is my thing. I don't know what my thing is. Everything just seems cloudy."

Grace's phone pinged with an incoming text, and she pulled it out.

ALEC
We are running some auditions in the Auditorium Theatre
6/22 12:30 p.m.
Madame Laurent wants to see you dance Giselle.
Don't be late.

Dance Giselle? Did that mean they wanted her back? The idea of it spread an energy through her body all the way to her fingers. That was what Ms. Margret didn't get. Ballet wasn't *shifting sand* in her life. It had always been her bedrock. Her identity. Which meant if that crumbled now, everything in her life would tumble down.

But the twenty-second was in just over two weeks. Could she be ready by then? Dr. Medler had been thrilled with her progress on her first visit, but if she was ever going to be ready, she needed to get stronger.

For as high of a level as Grace had trained for ballet, Madame Laurent had believed in pushing through pain, not rehabbing. She had already felt uncertain about how to follow the instructions Dr. Medler had given her for PT exercises. Last thing she needed was for them to make her knee worse.

But it wasn't like she had a plethora of training options in Heritage. Which meant she had to convince Seth to help her. Besides, she suspected Seth would be an expert. But with the quick way he dismissed the idea, that wouldn't be easy. Then again, Grace hadn't gotten to where she was by giving up when things got hard. She glanced from the lighthouse back to her phone.

GRACE
I'll be there.

Besides, all she needed was one or two sessions. How could Seth say no to that?

six

H E NEEDED MONEY AND SOON. SETH PUSHED his run a little harder as he turned north on Henderson back toward his place. Maybe he'd cut across the square. Paychecks were issued every other Friday, but his hours this week would be on the next paycheck, which meant it would be another two weeks and two days before he saw any money. That timing worked for his mom's rent and his place, but he needed money for gas, not to mention he'd been reduced to eating ramen. And for a guy who normally ate three sandwiches for lunch, the lack of calories was killing him. Maybe he should have saved his energy this morning, but lately he'd needed to run more than ever.

Seth gave a quick glance up and down Henderson and Richard, then angled toward the square, determined to beat his time from yesterday. Checked the time on his watch then started to pick up the pace. He lifted his head just in time to narrowly avoid Otis, who sat in the middle of the sidewalk. He had definitely not been there yesterday.

Grace had started her workout again at six, leaving Seth with the need for a run by six-fifteen. She no longer started with Bach, but somehow, he'd become highly attuned to her every sound. The opening of the front door, the creak of the floor when she jumped, even the pounding of her slippers with her leaps and turns seemed to come through the floor. Maybe he could invest in some better insulation.

He'd only been at this faith thing a few years, but wasn't God supposed to help provide? There was that verse about the birds and flowers. All he needed was a tank of gas. He'd make it to work and back today but tomorrow?

A little help, God.

He slowed to a walk and checked his pulse. He was about to turn into the parking lot toward his apartment when a bang followed by a groan came from a nearby porch. He glanced over as Pastor Nate massaged his hand and seemed to be biting back a few choice words. A green recliner sat half-in and half-out of his front door. The chair wasn't huge, but big enough to be awkward for one person.

Seth stopped next to the fence. "You okay?"

Nate looked up. "Hey, Seth. Jon said you were moving back. Glad to hear it. I was hoping to talk longer at the baby shower, but well . . . no one expected the baby to take the party as a green light to make an appearance. But welcome to town."

Seth hurried up the steps. "Let me help you. Are we going out or in?"

"Out." Nate ran an affectionate hand over the back of the chair. "Olivia said it had to go. Not sure if it's the ugly green or that the material has finally worn through on one arm, but the replacement is set to arrive later today."

"What are you going to do with it?"

"Take it to the dump." He motioned to the truck sitting in his driveway. "Borrowed Luke's truck."

"Can I have it? The chair—not the truck." Asking for things

wasn't his style, but if Nate was trashing it anyway, then it wasn't charity.

"Absolutely. There's a lot of good life left in this baby."

Olivia stepped to the door. "Don't let him talk you into it if you don't want it, Seth. He can't see how ugly it is."

"It's better than what I have." Which was nothing, but he wouldn't mention that. In his experience, when people found out he didn't have stuff, they started with the pity gifts. He didn't need that—he just needed to get his first paycheck. This chair would make a nice bed until then.

Thirty minutes later, they had managed to get it through the studio door and up the stairs, although they had to step over the tape. Grace had said it was fine, but he could have sworn she cringed while she watched.

They set the old recliner in the center of the room and stepped back.

Nate sank down into the chair and sighed. He obviously was going to miss the thing. "When does the rest of your furniture show up?"

"I don't need much."

"Not much, but some." Nate stood and wandered around the room, pausing at the pile of mail. The invitation to the Ninja Warrior Regionals was sitting on top. He didn't blame Nate for looking, the thing was colorful enough to be an invitation to a kid's birthday party. It had even come with blue and red confetti that was now all over his table. He should have just thrown it away. Nate picked it up. "Are you going?"

"Nope." He didn't leave room for discussion, and Nate seemed to recognize it.

"If you need some more furniture, I can ask arou—"

"I can take care of myself."

Nate stared at him a moment, then marched over to the fridge and opened it. The shelves were empty except for a box of baking soda that Jon had left there. "Obviously. Looks like you don't need a thing."

"Once I get my first paycheck—"

"You can't wait two weeks to eat."

"I'll make do." Seth walked toward the door. Maybe Nate would get the hint. He still needed to shower for work.

He glanced back, but Nate hadn't moved. Nate's eyes were more kind than intense, but it felt like he could see into Seth's soul. After a moment, he pulled his wallet from his pocket.

"I'm not taking your charity."

"Not charity. I'm hiring you."

"To do what?"

"Be my personal trainer." He patted his middle. "Marriage has been treating me too well. I want to get back in shape. We start today. Here's your first payment."

"I'll train you for free. I'm not taking your money."

"Seth may train me for free. I'm paying for The Storm." He pointed to the invitation.

When Seth didn't move to take the money, Nate shifted his weight, tilting his head to the side. "I've been where you are, Seth. Letting people in, letting them help you, letting them care about you isn't the worst thing in the world."

"Then what is?"

"Going it alone."

Seth opened his mouth, but before he could speak, Nate held up his hand. "And don't tell me it has worked so far, because if you were honest with yourself—Grant, Jon, and others have been there for you, and it made a difference. Maybe a friend in town who knows what a life after addiction is like wouldn't be such a bad thing."

Right. He'd forgotten that Pastor Nate's past was almost as dark as his own. Almost.

When he still didn't respond, Nate leaned against the wall with one shoulder. "God has given you people who are on your side. Don't slap His hand away in the name of being self-sufficient."

Was that what he was doing? *A little help, God.* His own prayer came back to him. What had he expected, the answer to come in the form of cash falling from the sky? If God was providing, maybe he needed to be willing to accept.

He finally looked at Nate and nodded. "All right, I'll train you, but not for money."

"I told you—"

"I want home-cooked meals. If I have to eat another bowl of ramen, I might go crazy."

"Deal." Nate slapped him on the shoulder, then moved toward the stairs. "But I'm not sure that's saving me money. I've seen the way you eat. But I can't have my trainer passing out from lack of food."

His mouth almost started salivating at the idea of a real meal. "First session is tonight at eight."

"Perfect." Nate walked to the door. "I'll tell Olivia to know to expect you for dinner, but be warned, it's my night to cook."

Even if Nate wasn't a great cook, it would be a huge step up. Now he just needed money for gas. As if on cue, Bach began vibrating the floor below. This might be a very bad idea, but if it was how God was going to provide, he couldn't ignore it.

He hurried down the steps and flung the door open to the studio and waited until Grace looked his way. "If you want to hire me, I'll train you. Three nights a week."

Her arms crossed over her chest as her head tilted to one side. "I was thinking like once or twice, then I can do it on my own."

"I can't just show you something and not help you with technique. And that technique needs to happen over and over again to make sure you're working with your joints and not against them. That will take more than once or twice, it will take regular training.

So, if you want to do this right and you want to get better and back to the stage, you need to do it my way."

She seemed to weigh what he said in her mind. Then she nodded and took a half step closer. "Thank you. That would be helpful."

That was all. He'd admit his tone had been a bit rough, but he'd assumed she would come back with both barrels loaded.

"But I don't have much money." When he opened his mouth to respond, she held up her hand, cutting him off. "I can pay some, but I know it isn't what a trainer costs. But the sooner I'm better, the sooner I will leave Heritage, and the sooner I can get out of your hair. Deal?"

The studio to himself. That was exactly what he wanted, right? Then why didn't this feel like a bargain? He shook off the uncomfortable feeling. As long as it was enough for gas to and from work, it was enough. "Deal. When do we start?"

She shrugged and offered a half smile. "The sooner the better."

"Tonight, at seven. Don't be late—I have another client at eight." With that he headed back up to his apartment to get ready for work. *Another client.* Seemed funny to say. An hour ago, he'd woken up with no food and no money for gas. Looked like God *had* provided. Now he just needed God to provide a way for him to set up that ninja gym in Lansing. Because right now, that would take more clients and more hours of working than he had to offer.

Grace refused to let her parents bully her into moving home, but the past twenty-three years had taught her this would not be easy. As much as she loved them, she had to be the one calling the shots in her own life. Grace sipped her sugarless tea as she perched on the edge of one of Ms. Margret's armchairs and waited for her parents to speak. Her parents sat side by side on Ms. Margret's blue and mahogany Victorian settee with both of their gazes fixed on her.

She wasn't completely sure if they were trying to stare her into submission, which they'd perfected over the years, or waiting for the right moment for a unified pounce. She had honestly believed that the worst part of this dinner would be the silent dinner itself, but she'd underestimated how painful a silent after-dinner conversation could be. She drew a calming breath and tried not to think about all of the things she could be doing instead on a Thursday night.

She could be dancing right now, or training with Seth. *That* she would definitely prefer. She still couldn't believe that he'd agreed to train her. After the way he'd so rudely dismissed the idea of helping her the first time, she'd come up with a long list of reasons to convince him to change his mind. But before she could do that, he'd shown up and laid out the reasons she needed his help. All the reasons she'd already thought of the day before.

All except for the fact it would take regular training rather than just once or twice. It did make sense though. If she was going to get back to 100 percent as quickly as possible, she needed someone who knew what they were doing every time she lifted. So she'd agreed and hoped that they could limit their hostile encounters as much as possible.

But for as grumpy as he'd been in their first few encounters, he seemed to let his guard down when they were discussing training. Although he had also been so in-the-zone that he seemed to see her only as a client and not as a person of the opposite sex. She couldn't say the same. So much so that the memory from yesterday still sat rent free in her mind.

"Good, now put your hands a little farther apart on the bar." Seth had stood on the opposite side of the bar, supporting most of the weight. Their heads just inches apart. *"You got it?"*

She had no idea. All she could think about was how close he was. She'd just nodded. He slowly let go and stepped back. Okay that was heavier than she thought.

It must have shown on her face because he rushed forward and took the weight again. "Maybe we aren't quite ready for this yet."

No kidding. "Can't we go back to squats?"

"I know you're concerned about strengthening your legs, but your legs are amazing." He stared at her legs for a moment, then seemed to realize what he was doing and what he'd just said. His gaze darted out the window as his cheeks reddened. "I just mean, they're very strong for your size."

"Good to know." Grace bit her lip to keep from laughing. "But I need to be able to dance for hours without tiring, not to mention jumps and leaps."

"All right. Legs it is." He walked over to where they had done the squats and started adjusting the weights. "I have a new one for you to try."

Grace grabbed her water bottle and downed a few swallows. "Where did you learn all this?"

He seemed to hesitate on his first words before he finally stood and looked at her. "I got into weightlifting at Quinn Ranch."

He seemed to be waiting for some sort of reaction, but since she'd never heard of the place, she just smiled and waited for him to go on.

Finally, he released a slight sigh and reached for his own water as if he'd passed some sort of test. "I loved working out so much I studied it in college."

She capped her water bottle and blinked at him. "You studied weightlifting?"

"No, Exercise and Sports Science. Just a minor though. I majored in business." He tossed his own water bottle to the side and motioned her toward the weights he'd just set up.

"So, you want to open a gym?"

"That's the hope. But that takes money. So I'm just taking it one day at a time." He then had lifted one of the weights and handed it to her.

One day at a time. Boy did she ever get that. Even now, staring at her parents who had their own plans for her recovery. She didn't know what to say to them. Maybe she should follow Seth's approach and take it one day at a time—one conversation at a time.

"I saw Dr. Medler this morning." Grace winced at how weak her voice came out. She set the teacup on the side table and cleared her throat. "He's happy with the progress in how well the ultrasound therapy is working. He believes I could be back dancing on stage as soon as a month."

Slight exaggeration, but that was her hope. She wouldn't mention that he wasn't happy with the strength of her leg. But now that she had Seth, that would change too. *She had Seth.* The words echoed in her mind. No, just friends—not even that. He was her trainer.

"But why must you live here?" Her mother's words pulled her back to the moment. "If you lived with us, then we could—"

"I am helping Ms. Margret." The words came out forced and a little desperate, but if she let her mother finish that sentence, they'd no doubt twist her answers into such knots that anything but moving home would seem illogical.

"She sure is a sweetie." Ms. Margret came shuffling into the room with a cane in hand. A touch of a waver in her voice. "Not sure what I'd do without her."

Grace covered a laugh with a cough. The woman had miraculously aged ten years as soon as her parents had shown up. She sent a look that hopefully said *Laying it on a bit thick, are we?*

Ms. Margret just smiled at her and settled into the wingback chair. Her parents didn't really seem to notice anyway. Their only focus was on her.

"What is this your mom tells me about you teaching." The disdain in her father's voice wasn't any better than her mother's had been. "If you're going to heal, then you shouldn't be wasting your time—"

"I like it. I only had my first class today, and I only had two students, but it was fun." The memory of the girls giggling and laughing as they learned seemed to lift a weight she hadn't even known she was carrying. "And the girls like it. Maybe it will help me find my joy in dancing again."

"This is ridiculous. You need to come home." Her father stood.

"No." She stood and met his eyes and prayed he didn't notice how her lip quivered. "I am an adult, and this is what I've chosen."

After a moment, he motioned to her mom. "Well, you seem to have made up your mind."

She had done it. She'd put on a brave face and won. Maybe he even respected her decision a bit.

"But this is the wrong choice. You will see that eventually. Don't come to us for help when it doesn't get you back to center stage." He opened the door and waited for her mom to walk through. Then turned back for one final barb. "You need us. You'll see."

Then he followed her mom out without even a glance back or a farewell as the door rattled in their wake. Grace sank back into the chair and closed her eyes. "No going back now."

This had to work, or her parents would never let her live it down.

seven

THERE WERE FEW REASONS TO INTERACT WITH the people of Heritage, but Donny's bacon cheddar melt was probably top of that short list. Seth shoved the last bit in his mouth and reached for another napkin, doing his best to ignore the Friday night dinner rush around him. He'd been craving the burger for days, but with cash in his pocket from his first couple training sessions with Grace and Nate and Olivia out for the evening, he hadn't been able to resist any longer.

And he'd definitely earned every cent and more if he counted the taxes taken out. Jon had gotten him an office with a name-plate and everything. It all felt a little over-the-top for just a few months, but he suspected Jon was angling for it to be longer. He'd divided the properties between commercial real estate, residential real estate, and possible places for development. That was definitely the smallest. He'd toured more than half, with plans to tour the other half next week. Some would move quickly, others he couldn't imagine what Dale Kensington had been thinking. But he'd figure out something. It was like a giant puzzle, and he really did enjoy moving the pieces around.

So after he clocked out at Kensington Fruits for the day, he'd wandered in to Donny's, chosen a seat at the counter, and kept his head down. So far, so good. He popped another fry in his mouth. So very good.

"Want a second burger?" Janie, one of the owners, stopped in front of him and refilled his Dr Pepper.

"I'll pass." He needed to save every penny if he had any hopes of opening a gym anytime soon.

The bell over the door chimed as a few kids walked in. All about junior high age, and all a little too loud for the space.

A kid with dark hair and dark eyes raised his hand as he passed. "Hey, Seth."

Jimmy, maybe? Or it could be Zane. They'd both come with Nate last time he'd worked out with Seth, and he hadn't been clear on who was who.

"Hey." Seth greeted him but left it at that. They seemed like good kids, but Nate seemed worried about them, and Seth didn't blame him. There was a lostness in their eyes that was probably not too different than what others must have seen in his own face at that age. They were searching, and no doubt, Nate wanted to offer answers before they chose a destructive path.

The bell rang again as Grace walked in. Her blonde hair was in its normal bun but looser, softer. She must have just come from working out because she wore her black leotard, but she had covered it with a pink half sweater and gray sweatpants. Her footsteps paused as she met his gaze. She offered a quick smile, then hurried to the counter and chose a seat at the opposite end, leaving about five seats between them.

Their training sessions had gone better than expected. She hadn't brought up the past and neither had he. He'd even tossed a comment out there about his time at Quinn Ranch, expecting she'd jump all over it. But she'd just smiled like there was an unspoken truce regarding the past, and he was good with that.

She might never forgive him for everything that happened with Gregory, and he didn't blame her. He wasn't so sure he deserved or needed to be forgiven. What he did need was more money to get his gym up and running. And even if it wasn't a lot, if she was willing to pay him, he'd take it.

Although as he feared, spending more time with her had only increased his awareness of her. Even now as she sat at the other end of the bar, every cell in his body seemed painfully aware of where she was and how she tucked that wisp of hair behind her ear every few minutes.

It wasn't just physical attraction, which was a given. There was something about her determination to beat the odds that he identified with and respected. The girl didn't quit. And the more he learned about her, the more he wanted to learn about her.

"I hear you're going to build a ninja gym out in Lansing." Janie was back. She passed over his check. Her dark hair was tied up in a messy bun, and the stains on her apron testified that it had been a long day, but her ever-present smile didn't waver.

"That's the plan." He pulled the cash from his wallet.

"I still think you should look at some of the other properties." Jon dropped onto the stool next to him, his elbows resting on the counter.

"I like the Lansing property. Bigger city, more customers." Seth grabbed another fry and then eyed the pies in the display behind the counter.

"You haven't even seen it. You just like that it's two hours away."

Seth didn't comment. Jon wasn't wrong about that. Two hours meant it was close enough to keep a bit of the family connection here but far enough to start over and to not have people in his business all the time.

"Just saying, the property in Heritage off Teft would be perfect." Jon spun so his back was leaning against the countertop.

"Not going to happen."

"We need to put something in there, Seth. Why not your ninja gym?"

"Why not a basketball court. You could probably fit two."

"One court is plenty. You of all people know that not every kid wants to play sports. What were you interested in, in high school?"

"I am pretty sure my only extracurricular activity in high school was my next hit." Seth kept his voice low so Grace wouldn't overhear. Not that it would matter, but he still didn't feel like reminding her of that part of his life.

"What if we'd had a weight room back then? Would that have been a place to go and burn your energy more effectively? There are lots of Heritage kids who could benefit from that right now." Jon had cast a glance toward Grace and matched his volume. He never missed much.

Seth's gaze flicked to Zane and Jimmy with their friends in the corner booth. Maybe Jon was right, but that didn't mean he was the guy to make it happen. "They don't have kids in Lansing?"

"The property isn't even near residential living. It's located in the industrial section. How many kids do you think you're going to get?"

"Heritage doesn't want me here."

Jon pressed his lips together a moment, then seemed to let the issue drop. "How's the rest of the apartment? You get it furnished yet?"

The last thing he wanted was to explain again to his rich cousin all that he didn't have.

His flight instinct must have shown on his face. "You know if you walk away, I am just going to follow you, and at six-four, my stride is longer. So again, how's the place?"

"I have a recliner. It's enough."

The satisfied smirk dropped from Jon's face. "Why are you so opposed to help? Your pride will be your undoing one day."

"It isn't pride." Maybe it was, but he wasn't going to admit that to Jon. Seth reached for his pop and polished it off. "We agreed that I'd take care of it. And I will after my first paycheck. And no, I won't let you give me an advance."

Jon shook his head, then twisted his stool, so he was facing Seth. "What if you could spend less than a hundred?"

Seth thought about what he already had planned for his first paycheck. "I could afford a hundred."

Jon looked like he was about to argue but let it go.

"Mayor Jameson," Jon yelled across the diner. "What did you do with that couch that you just replaced?"

"It's in my garage." The mayor ran his hand across his balding head as a frown wrinkled his large forehead. "The stupid thing is keeping me from parking my truck in there."

"Decent condition?"

"Great. But the missus wanted a gray one and this one was brown. I swear she gets the craziest ideas." Mrs. Jameson shook her head as she swatted his shoulder.

Jon motioned to Seth with his thumb. "Seth here needs a couch. How much will you sell it for?"

Seth cringed. No doubt with his name mentioned the price would go up.

"He can have it as far as I'm concerned. I just want to park in my garage again. Can you pick it up, son?"

Before he could answer, Luke Taylor spoke from another booth. "I have a truck."

Seth blinked at the men. Why were they helping him?

"Oh, but I can't move it until tomorrow." Luke spoke up again. "Does that work?"

"Yeah. Sure."

"You wouldn't need a set of table and chairs would you?" Gary Hoover spoke from a few booths away. "We just got a new set, and I don't want to mess with selling it. You can have it if you pick it up."

"That would be great." Seth cleared his throat. Why did his voice sound so rough?

"Look at that," Jon said. "Furniture and you still have your hundred bucks to buy another burger."

"I know what you're trying to prove, but it won't work." If anything, all Jon had done was put him in debt to the whole town. Nothing came free. "I'm not setting up my gym here."

"Fine." Jon held up his hands as if to surrender. But Seth wasn't under any impression he was really giving up for good.

Seth headed toward the door, but Hannah Taylor stood in his path, clipboard in hand. She was built a lot like Grace but with dark hair and dark eyes. If he remembered right from what Jon told him, she was married to Luke and largely responsible for the transformation of the town. "Hey, Seth. How do you feel about signing up for the bachelor auction?"

"I'm sorry. What?" Surely, he hadn't heard her correctly.

"Our annual bachelor auction. It's during the Fourth of July festival, and this year we're raising money for new books for the library."

He was in favor of new books, but really? "Can't I just donate?"

Jon slapped him on the back as he passed. "We've all been there. It isn't so bad. Luke snagged his wife at his auction. But my date was with an eighty-nine-year-old woman. Honestly, that's more likely."

Seth looked back at Hannah with a solid *no way* on his lips, but one look at all the grinning, nodding heads around the room confirmed that resistance was futile. Yep, everything came with strings. He took the clipboard, scratched in his information, and handed it back.

"Wooo-wee." Margret Bunting spoke up from a booth a few feet away where she sat with a group of older ladies who all had their eyes fixed on him. "That horse will sell. I know I'm saving my pennies."

His eyes darted back to Jon, who seemed to be holding back a smile while he offered a half shrug that telegraphed *Told ya*.

Hannah bit her lip, no doubt to keep from laughing herself, then slid back into the booth with her husband and kids. "I'll email you."

Seth offered a curt nod and hurried out the door. He needed out of there before he got trapped into anything else.

The night was a little cool but not uncomfortable. He shoved his hands in his pockets and hurried across the street to cut across the square. The setting sun cast a golden tone over the town, giving it an almost storybook quality.

"I thought that was you." Nate walked toward him across the square as he tucked a book under his arm.

"You told me earlier you were going out tonight. Are you just tired of feeding me?" Seth nudged his shoulder in humor, but there was a fair amount of truth to it. The last thing he needed was to become a burden to his friend.

"Never." Nate shook his head and stopped next to Otis, who lay on the sidewalk a few feet away. Same place as when he'd nearly tripped Seth while running the other morning. "Olivia wasn't feeling the best, so I'm picking up a book for her and takeout from Donny's for me."

"It's nice having a library again." Seth surveyed the square. The one-room schoolhouse really changed the whole look. It went from a set from *A Nightmare on Elm Street* to *Little House on the Prairie*. "But I'm not sure I will ever get used to the old houses being gone. This is about the spot where I'd break into one of the back windows to escape the cold."

When he'd found out they'd burned, he had wanted to both celebrate and weep at the same time.

As if reading his mind, Nate turned toward him. "Sometimes we have to burn down what is holding us to our past to make room for something new and beautiful. Sometimes those things are buildings. Sometimes those things are lies."

"Lies?"

Nate pointed at Otis, then took a seat and waited for Seth to do the same.

When Seth finally sat on the brass back, Nate turned toward him. "Lies that you don't belong here. Lies that no one wants you here. Lies that you'll never be more than what you've done."

Seth shook his head. "You and Jon talk too much."

"He's worried about you. And he cares. We all do." Nate's phone chimed and he stood and pulled it from his pocket. "My food is ready. See you tomorrow? I think Zane and Jimmy are going to join us again."

Seth nodded as Nate hurried over to the diner.

Lies.

Seth leaned back on the hippo, letting his gaze travel to the night sky. But were they lies? Just because Nate and Jon refused to see it didn't make it not true.

"What are you doing here?"

Seth's head jerked up and he practically jumped to a stand. Mr. and Mrs. Howell walked toward him from the other side of the square, daggers shooting from their eyes.

"I'm working—"

"You should be in jail." If possible, her look was steelier than her tone.

Evidently, they weren't looking for actual answers. He straightened his shoulders and waited for more barbs to come.

"Does Officer Hammond know you're in town?"

"I've seen him. Twice actually." He wouldn't mention the circumstances. But why did they seem so shocked? Surely Grace would have mentioned him being at the studio.

"You need to leave." Mrs. Howell was almost hissing at him now.

"I'll be gone by the end of the summer."

"End of the summer?" Her eyes narrowed on him as she took a step closer. "Oh no. You will be gone long before that. I will see to it."

They hurried off into the darkness, her heels clicking on the sidewalk as she went.

They were definitely not lies. A job and a few pieces of furniture were nice, but that didn't change the fact this place wasn't for him.

Maybe the burger hadn't been worth it after all.

It was already Monday, which meant her audition that was in just twelve days would be a complete waste of time if she couldn't get this move. Grace placed a hand on the barre and lifted her foot. But as soon as she removed her hand from the barre, she swayed to the left.

Grace dropped her foot and peered at Mallory through the screen of her phone propped up a few feet away. "See, it's not working."

"It's called a *supported* adagio for a reason. You need support." Mallory's voice held a touch of annoyance as if she were tired of repeating herself. She probably was.

Grace lifted the phone from where she'd balanced it. "I know that, but what am I supposed to do about that here? It isn't like there are a plethora of male dancers in Heritage."

"No, but there's a strong physical trainer you've hired." Mallory sat in front of her laptop on the floor of her room. Her knee was pulled up as she bent a new pair of shoes she was sewing the ribbons on. "Pay him extra to help you with the adagio."

Grace sat on the floor and leaned her back against the mirror. "I don't think dancing is what he'd consider a part of his agreement. Besides, I don't think it would be a good idea. I need to keep things professional."

"And your relationship with Tony when you danced with him in *Giselle* wasn't professional?"

"It's different."

"How?"

"The more time I spend with Seth, the more time I want to spend with him. And it isn't just because he's good-looking. He's kind and so patient with me. And so giving. I swear that if I walked into our session and asked him for his shirt, he'd just take it off and hand it to me, no questions asked. Who does that?"

"So you're saying he's good-looking and now you want him to take off his shirt."

"Mallory. Focus. I don't know what to do. What is wrong with me?"

"Nothing is wrong with you. You have a crush on a boy. It's that simple. Up until now, you have made ballet your whole life. You have lived, slept, and breathed ballet. But there's more to life than that. There's a whole world out there. Welcome."

Ms. Margret's words from the drive to the lighthouse came to mind, but she shoved them away. "First, I don't have a crush on anyone. Second, I don't have time for that world. If I am going to get back, I need a hundred percent focus a hundred percent of the time."

"Is that you talking or your father?"

The barb found its mark. That had always been her motto, but she didn't have to dig very deep to know that had been drilled into her from the moment Ms. Margret told her parents she was a natural with a lot of potential.

"What does Magic Doctor think of your audition?"

She didn't even bother correcting the name. "He says that my knee is progressing faster than expected. But he fears I could set myself back if I push too hard."

"There's something you should know." Mallory's teeth tugged at her lip as if debating if she would, in fact, tell it. "I know I told you last week that Jami wasn't cutting it, but she has found her stride, and . . ."

"And?"

"She's really good. The *Chicago Arts Online* even featured her—"

"The *Chicago Arts*? Do you know how long I tried to get them to do a feature on me? She dances a few weeks and she's there?" Grace tapped at her phone until the article appeared. "They call her a breath of fresh air. Opposed to what? My musty scent?"

"You know that's not true." Mallory leaned into the camera.

She knew this would happen. "My mom was right, step out of the limelight, and they forget you immediately. Love is earned."

At least she hadn't gotten a text canceling the audition yet. Grace put the phone on the floor leaving Mallory staring at the ceiling as she pulled her legs into the butterfly stretch.

Mallory's eyes narrowed on her through the screen. "Real love isn't earned. Maybe you have to earn the love of the public, but that's because it isn't really love—it's fandom."

Grace stretched her legs to the side and leaned forward pressing her shoulders into the floor. "Maybe you're right."

"I know I am right. And you're going to blow Madame Laurent away on the twenty-second and the fandom will come back. But if that's going to be the case, you need to nail the supported adagio. So you have to ask for his help."

"Seth's?"

"What?" Seth's voice echoed in the room.

Grace pushed up into a seated position faster than she ever had before as she snatched up her phone from the floor. "What?"

"Sorry. I thought I heard you say my name."

He was in dress clothes, but his tie was in his hand and the top button of his shirt undone. Why was she actually hearing her pulse right now? Okay, maybe she had a little crush.

"Is that him? You only said he was cute. You didn't mention that he had one of those deep husky voices. Turn the camera toward him." Why did the speaker seem twice as loud as it had a minute ago?

She tapped the button to take it off speaker, but it was Face-Time, so it refused. She grabbed her earbud and shoved it in her ear. "I was just talking to my friend."

Seth's head tilted to one side. But then he seemed to think better about whatever he was going to say and took a step toward his door.

"Ask him," Mallory nearly shouted in her ear. "This isn't about him or you. This is about you getting your own article in *Chicago Arts*."

Mallory was right. All personal feelings aside, this was about her career. She hurried to her feet. "Seth?"

Seth paused with his hand on the apartment door, his brow wrinkled when she didn't go on. "Yes?"

She opened her mouth, but nothing came out.

Mallory spoke into her ear again. "This is seriously painful. Just ask him."

"I need your help," she finally blurted.

"I thought I *was* helping you."

"No. Not just with weight training. I need help dancing."

Seth let out a loud laugh as he opened the door. "You don't want me to help you dance. Trust me."

"Wait."

He stopped with his foot on the first step.

"Not dance with me. I mean you would be with me but not dancing. *Helping* me dance. It's easy."

"For the love, land the plane, Grace," Mallory nearly screamed in her ear.

"It's called a supported adagio. And I dance and you just keep me balanced. No actual dancing required from you."

"When?" Seth's stance relaxed, but he remained in the doorway.

"Whenever. I mean if now works or—"

"I have an hour now. Is that enough time?" He folded his tie in his hand.

"That would be great."

"Let me go change, and I'll be down in five." With that, he disappeared up the steps.

"Grace. Grace. Grace." Mallory's words were laced with compassion. "Maybe having a guy that's a friend is good for you. Show you there's more to life than dancing."

"Goodbye." Grace ended the call as Mallory's laugh traveled though the line, then set the phone aside. There wasn't more to life for Grace right now than dancing. There couldn't be.

Seth appeared in the door moments later. How did he make basketball shorts and a T-shirt that had seen better days look so good? "Where do you want me?"

Want? She'd never thought about what she really wanted. She just did the next thing that would help her succeed.

"Grace?" His brows rose, waiting.

Perfect, now she looked like an idiot. Wants were dangerous, but she needed his help. There was no denying that. "I *need* you to support my waist."

He stared at her a moment, then at her waist, then back at her face. He didn't say anything, just stretched his neck to one side and then the other, then stepped up behind her. "Where do I put my hands?"

Had his voice just gotten lower?

She met his gaze in the mirror, then pointed to her sides. Suddenly, want and need seemed to be blurring together in her mind. No, this was just like working with Tony—professional. "Place your hands here."

His hands hesitated about a foot away, then settled onto her middle, the warmth of his fingers soaking through her leotard. Each point of contact filling her with the desire to sink into him. Maybe a little different than when she danced with Tony.

"Now, as I lift on pointe"—she drew a slow breath, willing her pulse to even out—"you just have to keep me balanced upright."

Grace lifted her leg, poured all her focus into her balance and not the hands supporting her or the way his breath eased across her neck. The supporter normally left a little more space between them, but right now she had no desire to correct him.

She did it two or three times before making eye contact with him again in the mirror. She'd been ready to offer a correction, but the intensity of his dark eyes stole every thought from her head. This was definitely different than dancing with Tony.

"Perfect." She cleared her throat and lowered her gaze. "This time when I lift, you will walk in a circle, and I will turn on my toe."

"That sounds simple enough. How big of a circle?"

"Whatever seems right." She'd never paid attention to the male role before.

She lifted her leg and he started walking in a circle, but she tipped to the side. He caught her just as her toe slipped on the black Marley floor. "Sorry."

She got her feet under her and righted herself. She refused to think more on how easily he'd caught her. "Maybe we should try that again. Don't watch the floor. Stand to the side slightly and lock on my eyes, and that will help you adjust as needed."

His gaze lingered on her for a moment before he looked away, his expression tortured. "Maybe this isn't—"

"One more try. Please." Maybe she should have let it end there, but she needed this move.

He nodded and assumed the position, holding her slightly to his right side. Her arms lifted, and her gaze moved from the mirror to him over her shoulder. Their faces just inches apart. He took a few steps, and when she didn't tip or sway, his tortured expression gave way to the molten eyes from a few moments ago. She couldn't quite interpret what it meant, but it made her want to stay like this for a long time.

When they made the full circle, she dropped her leg, but her head remained turned. "Perfect."

His eyes traveled over her face, stopping on her mouth for a half second before he took a hasty step back and dropped his hands. "You good then?"

No. She was definitely not good. She might never be good again after that. Were they done? Maybe they should be, but she had one more move she needed to practice. "The final one is a little more complicated."

"I'm not sure I can do more complicated than that." His voice was so low it was almost a rumble.

"Hands, same place. But this time hold me loosely because I will spin in your hands."

His hands rested on her waist for a moment. "Here?"

"Yes." But truth was, she hadn't looked. Which was obvious the moment she lifted into a basic pirouette. He stood way too close, and she spun right into his chest.

She'd collided with a fair number of partners over the years—which was always awkward and painful—but both dancers moved on without missing a beat.

But here she stood with her face pressed against Seth's chest, and she couldn't seem to make herself step back. Leaning against him felt so natural, right. His hands that hung loosely around her waist slowly moved toward her back. Each finger seemed to leave a trail of fire behind.

She began to contemplate if spontaneous combustion was really a thing when a ringtone she didn't recognize filled the space. Seth jerked back and retreated about three feet as he pulled the phone from his pocket, scanned it over, then returned it.

"So, you're good?" His eyes darted around the room as he inched toward the door.

He finally looked at her and when she offered the slightest nod, he practically flew out the door.

What was that?

"You have a crush."

Mallory's words came back. Crush suddenly didn't seem an adequate description for the unfamiliar desire, or passion, or, okay ... inferno he ignited in her. Oh no. What was she going to do now? Nothing. Absolutely nothing. Because her focus had to be Chicago and no man—not even a handsome, sweet, gentle, kind, crush from her past—was going to sway that.

eight

SETH HAD A LIMITED TIME IF HE WAS GOING to get his full workout in before he met Jon. But the two kids Nate had dragged here with him were determined to slow the process down. Seth did another ten reps on the bench press, trying to ignore the way the bar dug into his palms as well as the junior high laughter that echoed in the room. He didn't want to know.

Jimmy and Zane hadn't done much besides goof around and try to play catch with some of the smaller weights. He'd put a stop to that. But by the way they snickered, they were probably getting into something else they shouldn't.

He finished his set then settled the bar into the stand, Nate spotting him as he went.

"Why did you want to bring them again?" He'd kept his voice low so only Nate could hear him.

"Not a lot of good options around here for them on a Friday night." He sent a pointed look that no doubt hinted at how Seth had spent a fair share of Friday nights. "Besides, they need it."

"They need a little discipline, but I'm not sure that's my area."

Seth sat up and reached for his towel and dried off the back of his neck. "Let's add five to each side."

"You're awful grumpy today." Nate removed the lock at the end of the bar. "What's eating you?"

"Nothing." Nothing but being tormented by a set of blue eyes and a tiny waist he'd had his hands wrapped around again yesterday. He held out a five-pound disc to Nate. When Nate just lifted one brow, Seth added, "I've been training with Grace, and it's getting to be a challenge."

Nate took the weight and added it to his side. "Because you like her?"

It wasn't just that he thought she was pretty. He'd met his fair share of pretty girls in his life, and not one had ever had this effect on him. "She's different."

"The best ones are." Nate locked the weight in place. "You should ask her out."

Seth locked his side and settled onto the bench. "She's Gregory's sister. It would never work."

"Start with friends. You never know where it will lead."

Friends? Maybe he could do friends. Seth managed four reps on the new weight when his phone pinged. He set the bar back on the stand and walked over to his phone.

JON
_____
I stopped by the Lansing property.
We need to talk.
Where are you?

SETH
_____
In the studio.

JON
_____
About five minutes out.

He set his phone aside as Nate's voice carried across the room. "Zane, Jimmy, can you come over here a moment."

Nate walked over to his bag and pulled out a rough three-foot-wood sign with burned-in letters on it and held it up.

HE GIVES STRENGTH TO THE WEARY AND IN-CREASES THE POWER OF THE WEAK.
~ Isaiah 40:29

"Awesome." Jimmy laughed and nudged Zane's arm. "We don't have to work out to look like him." He pointed at Seth. "We just need to pray."

"Not what I was saying." Nate laughed it off as he carried the sign to a wall without a mirror and nailed it up there. "But as we work on our muscles, let's not forget where real strength comes from. That's it. Lesson over."

The boys ran off, and Seth raised one eyebrow at Nate. "That was brief."

"They're twelve-year-old boys, they have the attention span of squirrels."

Seth nodded at the sign. "Good verse."

"I thought so." Nate nudged one of the bottom corners to straighten it.

"I'm just glad I'm not weak anymore." Seth adjusted his lifting gloves.

"We're all weak at some time. Even with muscles like yours." Nate sent him a meaningful look.

"Right." God had helped with the money situation. But it was nice not to be so dependent on others like he had been as a kid.

Nate clapped to get the boys' attention. "Jimmy, help me change the weights on this, then you can give it a try."

The kid ran over as if Nate had promised him ice cream and a new video game all at once. Maybe one of the kids was more open to being here than the other.

Seth walked over to where Zane stood staring at the pegboard screwed into the wall about six feet off the ground.

Seth slung the towel around his neck, holding it on each side. "Give it a try?"

The kid sent him an eye roll worthy of the sassiest junior higher. "I can't reach that."

"Then the first challenge is getting up there . . . Figure it out." He turned away to give the kid a moment. Zane was all attitude, and if he tried to walk him though the process, there was no way the kid would even try. At least with a room full of mirrors he could keep an eye on him without being obvious, so he wouldn't hurt himself.

Zane jumped several times but couldn't seem to get more than a couple fingers on it. Not enough to pull himself up. Then the boy pushed a stool over and grabbed the pegs on the first try. "Now what?"

Seth turned back to Zane, crossing his arms over his chest. "Now pull them out and move them around the board."

"No way. That's impossible." He wiggled as he adjusted his grip, straining with the effort of holding himself up.

"Difficult. Not impossible."

The kid dropped and wiped his hand. "Then let me see you do it."

The kid obviously didn't think he could, but this was part of Seth's standard workout. Seth jumped up and navigated a few before glancing at Jimmy over his shoulder. "The key is to support your weight on one before moving the other. When you get good enough you can try following different number patterns. Sometimes I go in order. Other times I do odd numbers."

He demonstrated a few more, then jumped down. "Try again."

The kid jumped up and strained against his weight. He didn't have an extra ounce of fat on him, but he didn't have an extra ounce of muscle either. Poor kid. But they all had to start somewhere.

He managed to move one peg, and he dropped, a smile on his face. "I did it."

The look on his face struck a chord in Seth. Like he was looking back at a younger him. How would life have turned out differently if he'd had something like this back then? If he hadn't been so determined to figure it all out on his own. He offered Zane an approving nod and a fist bump. The kid strutted over to tell Jimmy about his triumph, standing noticeably taller than before.

Seth glanced over to get Nate's attention, but he hadn't missed it. He nodded at Seth. "Now you get it."

This was exactly why he wanted to set up that ninja gym. It wasn't just about the weights. It was about creating an environment where kids could challenge themselves in a fun and entertaining way. That was what had made the *Ninja Warrior* training so fun.

He hadn't really thought beyond the money the first time he went to compete, but the course had tapped into something that made him come alive. Part parkour, part gymnastics, part weight training. All he could think after it was over was why had it taken him so long to try it? He would have loved it as a kid, and just maybe it would have given him the confidence to steer in a different direction.

Both Nate and Seth had taken the hard path, but at least they had come out okay on this side. There were others in his life still lost on that path. And others who needed to be saved from ever entering it. If he could provide options for those kids, not only would it make them stronger and fitter, it might just be the one thing that kept them from self-destruction.

He'd make the Lansing property work no matter what Jon said. How bad could it be?

As if on cue, Jon walked in the front door. One look at his face and he knew Jon was going to try to talk him out of it. Not going to happen.

Jon held out his phone. "It's the last ones in the album."

Seth took the phone and studied the first photo. It didn't show much beyond a dilapidated pole barn in the middle of an over-grown field. That was probably just a bad angle.

"It gets worse." Jon motioned for him to scroll.

He scrolled to the next. Jon had zoomed in on a row of windows running the length of one side. Most of those were cracked or missing large sections. He scrolled again. The next focused on a large, damaged section of the roof. Just getting better and better.

The last photo was taken from the inside. It was dim, but he could make out a fair amount of debris and puddles of moisture that covered the cement floor.

"And let me just say"—he pointed to the puddles—"that'd better be rainwater. But by the smell, I'm guessing it was not."

Seth shrugged and held out the phone. "It's not the best location, but I've seen worse."

"I'm not sure I believe that." Jon took back his phone and crossed his arms over his chest. "After seeing it, you can't say this is where you want to set up your gym."

When Seth didn't respond, Jon tapped at his phone, then turned it around again. "You need a place like this."

It was the building down the road. And the worst part was, Jon was right. It would be perfect. Unlike that dump of a property in Lansing. His thought must have telegraphed more than he hoped because Jon just slid the phone in his pocket. "Put together a proposal for the board. You can present it at the next meeting."

"Ninja gyms are expensive."

Jon shrugged and took a step toward the door. "So are fruit packing plants. That turned out okay. Lay it all out in the budget."

His job had gone well because the only person he'd really had to deal with in town had been Jon. Just the idea of staring down the board made his neck feel hot. "Maybe you should present it. I doubt they'll go for it if I'm involved."

"Nope." He shook his head then pointed at him. "Your idea, your presentation, and it will be *your* gym."

Seth walked out the front door toward Jon's car. Last thing he needed was Jimmy and Zane to hear this part of the conversation. "I still don't think this is a good idea."

Jon's long legs caught up with him in a couple strides. "Just because the Howells want you gone doesn't mean that everyone does."

Seth eyed Otis who had moved in front of the studio a few days ago. "This guy has been moving a lot lately."

Jon rolled his eyes and leaned his back against his car. "Too much some might say."

"What?"

"Nothing." He seemed to shake off whatever he'd been thinking. "The Howells don't speak for everyone. Don't let them bully you."

Seth leaned against the side of the brick building and looked up at his cousin. "So you heard about our run-in in the square."

"You had a run-in?" His face shifted to one of concern.

"Nothing happened really. They just told me to leave. I'm not sure they knew I was back." He dismissed it with a shrug, then narrowed his eyes on Jon. "If you aren't talking about that, then what—"

"They've been talking to people." He dropped his head, then looked back at him. "Trying to convince people that you don't belong. They encouraged me to let you go."

"Are you serious?" Seth pushed off the wall and paced a few steps away. "You tell me this and you still think I should open a gym here?"

"I don't agree with them and said as much." Jon took on a more relaxed pose. "I am serious about this. Let me know when you're ready, and I'll put it on the agenda."

He didn't answer, because what could he say? Jon wouldn't take no for an answer, but with the Howells campaigning to get him run out of town, Heritage wouldn't work either.

Jon offered him one last look, then took a step toward his car. "What do you have to lose?"

His dignity. The last shred of respect he clung to. He couldn't spend his whole life fighting against the Howells.

Nothing would work. Which meant the gym would be like so many things in his life. A dream that would never happen.

If she'd had any lick of sense, Grace would have cancelled this morning so she could just focus on the audition and nothing else. But her ballet class had grown to four girls, and when they had begged her to have it, she agreed only if the class met from seven to seven forty-five that morning. She assumed it would be a deal-breaker. She'd been wrong and it wasn't like she could say no after that. Just like she couldn't say no to Susie who'd asked her to wait with her for her brother after class. But now seven forty-five had become eight o'clock, and she still wasn't on her way to Chicago.

The little girl sat next to her on the front steps of the studio, swinging her pigtails in her face as if she didn't have a care in the world. Of course she didn't. She wasn't the one who had to make an audition in—Grace checked the time on her phone again and added the hour she'd gain crossing into central time—four and a half hours. Should be still enough time, but the drive alone was three and a half hours with no traffic, and when it came to Chicago, there was always traffic.

The little girl paused her hair swinging and looked up at her. "Where are you going again? I forgot."

"I have an audition in Chicago." She stretched her feet forward and winced at the way her tights scratched on the steps. *Please don't tear.* She had an extra pair in her bag but at this rate she wouldn't have the time to change.

"To dance on stage? Is it big?" Her eyes widened.

"The stage? Yup."

The audition? Huge. She still couldn't believe Madame Laurent had invited her to reaudition. After her talk with Mallory almost two weeks ago, she'd assumed any hope of returning as Giselle was gone. But when she had talked to her friend yesterday, Mallory had said that the new lead's moment in the sun was fading as she struggled more each night with the difficult dances.

Grace knew better than most that the challenge of dancing as prima ballerina was more than physical. The mental endurance to handle the expectations that came with the lead night after night could chew a person up. But handling the big roles was her sweet spot, and Alec had made it clear that Madame Laurent needed to see her dance the part today. And he hadn't reached out to her to cancel, that had to be a good sign.

Even Dr. Medler had cleared her yesterday at her appointment. He wanted her to continue her exercises and therapy but was confident it was safe for her to return to the demands of the role.

But if she got the part, would she be able to finish the summer dance class? Probably not, which meant today's class could very well be their last class. A weight settled on her with that thought. But if she were offered Giselle, she couldn't turn it down.

"I want to dance on stage." Susie's words pulled her back to the moment.

"Maybe we can figure out a way for you all to do a show for your parents." She bopped the little girl on the nose with her index finger. And she would. Even if she had to cancel the rest of the summer's lessons, she'd find a way for them to do a show.

"Not my mom, she left. But I know my dad would come if he isn't working. He calls me his dancing princess." Her face twisted up. "But he does have two jobs so we don't see him too much."

Suddenly, she had a lot more appreciation for all Zane did and compassion for him running late.

"And you. You can be in it too." Susie bopped Grace right back. "And you can show us how you are lifted in the air sometimes."

"That would take another dancer to lift me."

"Have Seth do it."

"How do you know Seth?"

"My brother's been exercising with him and Pastor Nate and Jimmy. I wanted to go, but Zane said I was too small. My brother says Seth is super strong, so I'm sure he could lift you."

No doubt he could lift her, but the idea did very strange things to Grace's insides. But Grace was saved from answering as a kid who was all legs and arms came running across the square, his brown hair flopping in his face. "Sorry, Susie."

"You must be Zane." Grace stood and lifted her purse to her shoulder. "Susie has been waiting for you."

The boy cringed. "Sorry."

"I'm okay." Susie jumped to her feet and then proceeded to hop down each step. Zane scooped up his sister's hand.

It was so reminiscent of the way Gregory used to pick her up that Grace stood frozen, unable to move. Life had been so simple before—

"You're going to be late." Susie pointed at Grace's car parked along the curb. "Get going, teacher."

Grace blinked away the memory and hurried to the driver's side. Teaching was definitely different than she'd expected. She had expected it to drain her, but instead it made her come alive, if not a little distracted.

She climbed behind the wheel of her Sonata, tossed her purse into her open duffel bag on the passenger's seat, and started the engine. The dash lights dimmed a moment, then flickered, but seemed to find their footing. That was weird. She'd have to have that checked when she returned.

She pulled out onto Heritage Road and was almost to 31 South when the lights dimmed again. She turned on her blinker, but that wasn't working either. Luckily, she hadn't gotten on the highway yet. She pulled into a gas station and had just made it to the closest parking spot when the whole car went dead. Dead-dead. No turning over. No dashboard. No nothing.

This couldn't be happening. Over two weeks of strength training, working and reworking Giselle's solo, and now it was a complete waste. Grace turned her key once more in the ignition. Still nothing. She clicked it back and tried again. Nope. She rested her head against her steering wheel. Now what? Nothing. There was nothing she could do.

She'd have to call a tow and then message Alec. Madame Laurent would be angry, but what choice did she have? Her parents were gone this weekend, and there was no way Mallory could get here in time to get her back to Chicago for the audition.

Grace eyed the Marathon station. At least she was mostly out of the way. She gave the starter one more try, but nothing. She pulled out her key then reached for her cell phone.

"Dan's Garage." A feminine but no-nonsense voice filled the line.

"Hi, Danielle. My car is dead at the Marathon just off 31, the one by Heritage exit. I need a tow."

"We can, but it will be a couple of hours before we can get there. Both the trucks are out right now. There was a wreck on 31 just north of the Heritage exit."

She sighed and let her head fall back on the headrest. "I'll be here."

"If you can get a ride, just leave your keys with Charlie. He's the owner of the Marathon. He's a good guy."

"Okay. Thanks." She ended the call and stared at her phone. Get a ride?

The biggest problem with making ballet her life was she had no one to call on when things went wrong. Especially at eight fifteen on a Saturday morning.

The only friends she'd even made since returning to Heritage had been Ms. Margret and Seth. Ms. Margret didn't drive anymore. Which left Seth. Were they friends? And he was often up early for a workout. She couldn't overthink this, it was this or count the number of broken bulbs in the gas station lights for a few hours while she waited. She tapped his number on her phone, and he picked up on the third ring.

"Grace?" His voice was thick with sleep.

She cringed. "I woke you, didn't I?"

"It's all right." His voice became clearer with every word. "I was just trying to catch some extra sleep after the early ballet class."

"Ack. We woke you then too."

"What's up?" She could almost hear him sitting up.

"I broke down, and I need a ride. I'm not far. Just over at the Marathon where you get on 31. But if you're sleeping—"

"On my way." He hung up.

This shouldn't be weird. After all, they worked together daily on her strength training, and he was still spotting her on her turns. Although now he always kept a wide space between them as he spotted her.

By the time Seth's old white Lumina pulled into the parking lot, Grace had already delivered the keys to Charlie, locked the car, and waited with her duffel bag on her shoulder.

He popped open his door and stepped out but left the engine running. It wasn't fair that he could look that good fifteen minutes after waking up. He had on a flannel over a T-shirt, jeans, and a black stocking cap that let just the edges of his dark hair peek out from beneath. "Need anything from your car?"

"Just my bag." Grace motioned to the gray bag on her arm.

He eyed her large duffel a moment before reaching for it and carrying it to his trunk. He climbed into his side, and she reached for the passenger's side handle, but it was locked.

He leaned across the car and pushed it open from the inside. A grimace accompanied the move. "Sorry, it only opens from the inside."

He hurried to straighten a towel that covered the passenger seat. "There are some bare spots on the upholstery, so you'll want to sit on that."

Grace climbed in. The mid-'90s' sedan had seen better days, but it was clean with a hint of oranges in the air.

When she didn't say anything, he started fidgeting with the radio that didn't seem to work either. "It's not pretty. But it's clean and reliable."

She laid her hand on his arm. "It's fine, Seth."

"I'm just saying that it isn't as nice as your Sonata." He didn't move, just stared at her hand.

She dropped her hand and reached for her seat belt. "Well, my *Sonata* isn't working, so it's a lot nicer at the moment."

Finally, he sat back, put the car in drive, then pulled out on the road toward Heritage.

"Did you buy citrus recently?"

"Air fresheners under the seats."

"I'm really sorry I woke you."

"I was awake. My mom had called several times. I just didn't answer her."

"How did you know I wasn't her?"

"Special ringtone."

"I have a special ringtone?"

"N-no." He shot her a look across the car. "She does."

"Oh right." A giggle escaped. Well, that was embarrassing. Things had been extra tense between them since he'd helped her dance the first time. It was like they didn't know how to be around each other.

She glanced at him out of the corner of her eye. Maybe if she wanted them to be friends, she should talk to him like she talked to Mallory. "Maybe I should have a special ringtone."

He gave a slight chuckle, but his shoulders seemed to relax a little. "What would it be?"

She lifted his phone. "May I?"

He nodded and looked at it to unlock the screen.

She set to typing and soon had it set. She locked the screen then picked up her phone and called him again. "Dancing Queen" filled the air.

"You cannot make that your ringtone. You have to change it." But the laughter in his eyes undermined the instruction. "So where are you coming home from with such a large bag?"

"Going to. I was on my way to Chicago for that audition."

"Wait, the one you've been training so hard for?" He gave her a quick glance, then focused back on the road.

"The very one." She lifted her cell. "That reminds me, I need to message Alec that I won't be there."

"But I thought this audition was important."

"It is. But the audition is in four hours. Unless I can learn to fly, I'll have to reschedule." *If* they let her reschedule. She should probably message Mallory too.

Seth pulled the car to the shoulder.

She lifted her gaze from her phone. "What are you doing?"

"I'm getting you to Chicago for your audition." He checked his mirrors and then made a U-turn back toward 31.

Grace gripped the armrest on the door. "I'm pretty sure that was illegal."

"No one was coming."

"Why are you doing this?"

"I know what it's like to want something. I was—"

Red and blue lights flashed in the car as a small blip of a siren said the rest. Seth pulled the car to the side of the road, his lips

136

pressed into a flat smile as he withdrew his license and registration. He rolled down his window, then placed his hands on the steering wheel. "Sorry."

"You're sorry? You turned around for me. I'm—"

Her words were cut off by the appearance of Officer Hammond at Seth's window. The man eyed Seth for a moment. "I assume you know why I pulled you over, Seth."

"Yes, sir. My bad." Seth lowered his eyes.

"It's a new day, Seth. I'd like to believe it." The man took the documents and tapped them on the window. "But I keep seeing you. Just two months until I retire, Seth. Two months. You're killing me."

"It won't happen again." His voice was flat, his eyes unmoving.

Officer Hammond leaned down and peeked at Grace. "Grace Howell?"

"Hi." She offered a little finger wave and smile.

"Everything...okay?" His gaze darted back and forth between her and Seth. Seth's gaze just stared straight ahead, his face growing red.

"We're really sorry, officer. You see, I'm late for an audition in Chicago and Seth was trying to help me get there."

"You two are headed to Chicago?" His gaze flicked to Seth, but he directed the question to Grace. "For how long?"

"Just the day."

Officer Hammond nodded and stood, then walked back to the squad car. It wasn't long before he returned with Seth's documents and a white piece of paper. "I cited you for the illegal U-turn. I didn't cite you for the ten over. Keep the speed down, alright?"

Seth nodded, rolled up his window, and shoved all the papers in his glove box. His movements were jerky.

When he just sat there, Grace angled her shoulders toward him in her seat. "You still want to go to Chicago?"

"More than ever." Seth started the car and pulled onto the road, then merged onto 31 South.

nine

GRACE HATED THAT SETH WAS GIVING UP HIS day for her, but if it meant getting back to center stage, at least he might see it as worth it. Grace pulled open the side door of the Auditorium Theatre, then held it for Seth. This area wasn't open to the public unless there was an emergency evacuation, so it didn't have the charm of the rest of the nineteenth century building. But the deep red carpet that matched the rest of the building hushed their steps as they walked.

"I don't know how to thank you for giving up an entire day for me." Grace glanced at her phone and released a sigh. Seth had made good time. "I will pay you for this."

"You aren't paying me anything."

"I will at least pay for the gas." When he didn't argue that point, she pushed further. "And the ticket."

"You aren't paying for the ticket. I pulled the illegal U-turn, not you."

"I didn't call the cops this time." She held up her hands and hoped he would laugh. "I swear."

He eyed her for a moment but finally cracked a smile.

"I love when we get to do auditions here." Grace did a little turn as she walked.

"You don't always?"

"Oh no. We perform here but so do a lot of other productions. We have a practice studio a few blocks from here. But on occasion we get to use the space for auditions." Grace walked to a set of doors on the left side of the hall. She eased it open and peeked in, then leaned back. "It isn't quite the Paris Opera House, but I love it."

"What do you love about it?"

Instead of answering, she opened the door and led him in. She knew the moment he got it when his mouth dropped slightly open. "Wow."

Thirty-five hundred lightbulbs arched across the high curved ceiling, making the room seem to glow. Each arch above them was bigger than the one before as they moved away from the stage. It was like they were standing in a giant trumpet, a giant shiny brass trumpet. *Wow* pretty much summed it up.

"This was the tallest building in Chicago when it was constructed. Of course, it isn't close now, but it was an engineering marvel at the time."

"I bet it was." He continued to turn as if attempting to take it all in. She'd been trying for years and still found new things all the time.

Grace checked the time but they were ahead of schedule. Traffic had been good, and Seth had made good time. She made her way to row D then through the row of chairs until she found what she was looking for. "Want to sit?"

She settled into the chair then waited for him to join her. "These are my parents' seats."

He settled down in the seat next to her. "They own seats?"

"No, but I have a friend in the box office, and I know this is where my father likes to sit, so I always have the two seats at will-call, under the name Scooby-Doo."

"Scooby-Doo?"

"I did that to drive my mother crazy once, and what can I say, it stuck."

"They come to every performance?" His brows pinched.

"No. They rarely use them, but sometimes they let friends use them. If they aren't picked up thirty minutes before the show, the box office sells them. But if I don't get the lead back, I can probably tell Stephanie not to bother."

"They'd come to one show at least, wouldn't they?"

She shook her head as she fiddled with the drawstring on her shoe bag. "When I was ten, I moved from Ms. Margret's School of Dance to Belle Pointe in Grand Rapids. My dad didn't think Ms. Margret could take me further. Being the new student, I went from being the star to the bottom of the class. But I knew it would be worth it, and I was just happy to dance. At the first performance, I stepped on stage determined to be the best poppy that had ever taken the stage."

"I'm sure you were adorable." His eyes crinkled at the sides as his face split into a grin.

The impact of it hit her in the chest, making it slightly hard to breathe. It was more than the fact that his smile seemed to transform him back into the shy kid who'd lived across the street, and definitely more than the way it highlighted a soft set of dimples she'd never seen before. There was something in his gaze that was personal. Intimate. And being the sole focus of that smile made her want to forget the audition, forget the future, forget everything around her and just sit right here for the rest of the day.

"So, what did your parents say?"

Right. She blinked, and then again, as she tried to ignore the effect that smile had on her. "After finishing my number and holding my pose, I scanned the audience for my parents. Fourth row left."

"Just like these."

"And there was my mom, smiling, clapping, but my father wasn't there."

"Did he step out for a second?"

"No, there wasn't even an empty seat. Later he told me he'd only come to shows where I was the star. The rest weren't worth his time. After that it wasn't about the fun of dance. It was pushing myself to be the best. It became my job. A job I am very good at."

His face pinched as his grip tightened on the armrest.

"Easy." She patted his forearm. "They would like the chairs to last another century. Besides, don't look at me like that. It was fine. He taught me that hard work was rewarded. And failure had consequences."

His grip relaxed as his gaze lingered on her hand still resting on his arm. "No, he taught you that love was based on performance."

"Isn't it?"

"No. Real love doesn't come with conditions." He finally lifted his gaze to meet hers. "It isn't based on your performance, it's based on who you are. We all have wins and losses. People who love you are with you for both."

She must not have looked convinced, because he leaned a little closer. "You already believe that. If you didn't you wouldn't have waited with Susie this morning."

"How did you—"

"You were sitting on the step right outside my window." He rotated her arm so her hand now lingered on his forearm.

"Right." Her breath slowed, and as if by their own will, her fingers began toying with the material at his wrist.

"And you wouldn't be here with me." His hand slowly shifted until his fingers caught hers. "The criminal."

Her pulse pounded in her ears. "Breaking and entering isn't too bad."

His brows pinched together, and his mouth opened. But a door slammed open, and Seth pulled his hand away.

Grace lifted her bag as the room filled with the voices of her friends. "I guess everyone is arriving. Do you have anything you can do in Chicago while I audition?"

"I'm not allowed to stay?"

"You can, but the whole process can take hours."

"Would you like someone here?"

The question caught her off guard. She had never considered it because it had never been an option. "I would."

"Then I'll stay." His eyes softened.

When she stepped away, his fingers snagged hers once more. She sucked in a quick breath and turned back to face him.

"You've got this. You deserve this part. I know it, and so do you. Now sell it to them."

She nodded and let her fingers drop. She immediately missed their touch, and it took every ounce of willpower to walk away from him. She needed to clear her head if she was ever going to pull off Giselle.

Grace hurried back along the corridor until she found Alec. "I'm here."

He didn't even look up from his clipboard. "Get stretched, you'll be up first."

Grace pulled off her sweats, then tugged her convertible tights over her toes and reached for her pointe shoes.

"The Storm?" Mallory plopped down next to her, stretching her long legs out. "Tell me how you know him and how do I get one for myself?"

"What are you talking about?" She sat up straighter, then stretched over her leg.

"The guy you were sitting with when we came in."

"Seth?" She sat up and switched legs. Mallory was still on the same leg, not that she seemed to be doing much stretching.

"Seth is The Storm? No wonder you couldn't talk to him." Mallory faked a swoon backwards. "Can you get me his autograph?"

"What are you talking about?"

"Hello?" She sat up, really studying Grace's face like she'd gone mad. "*Ninja Warrior*?"

"That show you're all obsessed with?"

"Yup." Mallory pointed out toward the auditorium. "And you just walked in with one of the hottest guys of this season. Do you call him The Storm to his face?"

"Stop calling him that. It's Seth. Just Seth. And we're just friends." The way his fingers had snagged hers a few minutes ago flashed in her mind. "By the way, he did help me with my turns."

Mallory wiggled her eyebrows and leaned in as if waiting for juicy gossip. "And by helping you with your turns, you mean—"

"No!" She shoved her away.

"Don't destroy my fantasy."

"It's true." There had been some looks and some flirting, but nothing had really happened, and by the way he was quick to pull back every time they got close, she didn't expect anything to happen.

"Well, maybe you should stake your claim because he has caught the attention of all the other dancers." Mallory nodded toward the edge of the stage where several girls stood whispering and staring in the direction of Seth still sitting in the audience.

An unfamiliar swirl of anger filled her stomach. Why was she angry? No, this felt different than anger. She just wanted to yank them all back by their tight little buns and say *back off*.

"Grace." Mallory snapped her fingers in her face.

She blinked at her friend. What had just happened?

"And that, my friend, is a green monster called jealousy." She helped her to her feet.

Grace shook her head. She had to clear her head. She had no reason to be jealous, he wasn't hers. He wasn't hers, and she needed to nail this audition. She didn't need to think about how easy and fun the conversation had been the whole way here. Or that he made her laugh like she hadn't in a long time.

"Grace Howell."

Grace's head jerked up at her name.

Focus.

A skinny guy with horn-rimmed glasses and floppy brown hair tapped his pencil against his clipboard.

"You've got this. You deserve this part. I know it, and so do you. Now sell it to them."

Grace stepped out onto the stage with all the poise she could muster. She struck a pose and waited for the music to start. When the first note hit, everything faded into the distance. The weight of the audition, Seth watching, and even the chatter off to the side disappeared. It was just her and the music.

She had just made it through the first third of her piece when the music cut off. Grace's heart dropped and she looked to Madame Laurent, but the woman was staring at a paper before her. She shot a look at Alec just as he waved her over.

She rushed toward him. "Was I off? I can start—"

"You did great. Madame Laurent is happy with your progress and wants to see you back in two weeks."

"Progress? I thought this was to audition to come back as Giselle."

"Come back? She is not recasting Giselle." His brow pinched as if the idea repulsed him. "This was just an update for Madame Laurent. You may go."

An update? "I drove three and a half hours for a two-minute update?"

"Three and a half hours? You should have told us. We could have done it over video. Plan on that for the next update."

With that, he rushed away, looking for another dancer.

How was she going to tell Seth that he'd wasted a day for nothing? That he'd gotten a three-hundred-dollar ticket for nothing.

But worse yet, what was she going to do with this new emotion inside her? Because everything in her wanted to run toward him and away from him at the same time. She needed to face the fact that the worst thing that could happen to her this summer wasn't losing out on the next big role. It just might be falling in love with Seth Warner.

Grace hadn't said a word all the way back to the car, and Seth had no idea what to make of it. Her dancing had looked beautiful to him. Sure, he didn't know much about dancing, but everything had been so fluid and graceful. And when she leaped like that, he honestly didn't know a human could go that high without the assistance of a spring somewhere.

Maybe he was biased—okay, he was definitely biased—he was falling for her all over again, and he couldn't stop himself. He should've never rotated his hand or grabbed her fingers. It was too intimate. Too much. But it had been minor compared to how he wanted to scoop her up in his arms and hold her after the story about her parents. He'd never cared for Mr. and Mrs. Howell. Long before the Gregory incident, Gabe had offered many reasons for Seth to dislike them. But now?

Some people shouldn't have kids. Then again if they hadn't, there would be no Grace. And any scenario he imagined without her in the world was dark indeed.

He cast her a glance. Why had the director cut her off? He didn't know anything about auditions either, but that didn't seem like a good sign.

He started to unlock Grace's door but froze. The door didn't open from the outside. She had him so rattled he was forgetting his own car. So instead, he leaned his back against the car and laid his hands gently on her arms. "Do you want to talk about it?"

"I'm so sorry." She covered her face with her hands as her head fell onto his chest.

When she didn't move, he leaned her back, loosely captured her wrists, and pulled her hands from her face, but she didn't lift her gaze. "What are you sorry for? So you didn't get the role. It's not the last audition you'll have. It wasn't a waste."

He looked at his large fingers still circling her tiny wrists and slowly let go. If he didn't, he might just be tempted to do something stupid like pulling her back to him.

"That's just it." She finally met his eyes. "It wasn't an audition."

"What are you talking about? I saw you up there."

"Oh, I danced. But evidently, I wasn't auditioning. They just wanted to see the progress on my knee. I could've done that via video." She stepped back, finally lifting her head.

"Okay, so no audition, but were they happy with your progress?"

"Yes, but don't you understand? I could've done that from Heritage. You wasted your whole day. I don't blame you if—"

"Hold on. Are you crying because you're disappointed about the part or because you think I'll be upset?"

When she didn't answer, he walked to his side of the car, climbed in, and popped her door open from the inside and waited for her to get in. "Are you afraid of me, Grace?"

Her head whipped toward him. "Why would I be afraid of you?"

"Why else would you be so upset with the idea you wasted my day? I don't know who you think I am, but I'm not going to hurt you or yell at you. The only person I am mad at right now is whoever put it in your head that you aren't worth people's time unless you produce results."

"I am not afraid of you. I just know you had plans and—" Her voice cracked again.

"And I'd gladly cancel them again to drive you down here. You're worth people's time. Even when it's just an update."

She stared at him. The tears gone. Replaced with an intense look he couldn't quite decode. He didn't know what she wanted from him, or what he wanted from her, all he knew was that he wasn't ready to go back. And all he wanted to do was make her smile again like she had on the way down. "What's your favorite thing to do in Chicago?"

"What do you mean?" She blinked away whatever she'd been thinking.

"I mean you lived here for what, five years? What was your favorite thing to do when you weren't dancing?"

She offered a half shrug "I was always dancing."

"But on your time off."

"I slept. We had a tense, full schedule. I mean some of the girls would go out, but I didn't."

"Why not?"

She tilted her head back on the head rest and closed her eyes. "Why didn't I have sugar? Why did I never go on a date? Why did I never stay up a minute past ten? Why? Why? Why? It's always the same answer and not a very interesting one. I am a dancer with a singular focus."

They both sat quiet in the car a moment. "Well, I think that should change today."

Her eyes opened, wide. "What should change?"

"All of it. Seeing Chicago. Eating sugar." *The date.* Yeah, maybe he wouldn't mention that. "Maybe even staying up past ten at night."

He reached over and tucked a strand of hair behind her ear. "What do you say?"

"Why are you being so nice to me?"

Because you deserve it even if you don't think so. Because you're beautiful and can't even see it. Because he was falling in love with the girl and he couldn't stop, no matter how hard he tried. "What can I say? You're easy to be nice to. Have you ever been to Navy Pier?"

"I've heard of that. Isn't that where the Ferris wheel is?"

"The Centennial Wheel and that's perfect. We're going to get you a ride. But first we need to get you some sugar."

Thirty minutes later they stood in a line that stretched twenty yards down a busy sidewalk, inching their way forward. "Stop number one, the famous Sprinkles cupcake ATM machine."

Grace tried to lean around the person in front of her to get a better view. Her hair was still in her performance bun, but she had slipped into the back seat of his car and traded the leotard and tights for leggings and a button-up white blouse. He'd stood watch while she did her quick change and it had taken every ounce of willpower to keep his gaze outward and away from the car. Really, he deserved an award.

She inched forward again. "How have I never even heard of these?"

"The world of sugar is a strange place." He pointed at the pink rotating door that had just delivered a brown box to a little girl.

They were up. He stepped up to the ATM and tapped the screen. "What kind do you want?"

"I don't know." It wasn't the I-don't-know of someone debating over the menu at their favorite restaurant. It was pure and utter panicked confusion.

"It's okay. What type of cake do you like?"

She breathed deep and nodded. "Chocolate cake and chocolate frosting."

Seth navigated the screen until he found one like that, then added their classic red velvet to the order for himself. As soon as the machine spit their cupcakes out, Grace grabbed her brown box. After turning it over in her hands, she opened it and pulled out the chocolate-on-chocolate creation with chocolate shavings over the icing. "This is amazing."

"And they taste better than they look." Seth peeled open his box and pulled his out. It was domed with white frosting and topped with the signature red-and-blue dot. It was something straight out of a cooking show. "Ready?"

He tapped his cupcake to hers before taking the biggest bite he could. Seemed fitting.

She mimicked his action, leaving a glob of chocolate frosting across her upper lip and nose. But she didn't seem to notice. She just closed her eyes and moaned at the goodness.

"Good, right? When was the last time you had cake this good?" He offered her a napkin.

"When I was thirteen." She accepted it and took a moment to clean her face. "So, ten years."

"That was rather specific." He took another more modest bite.

"It was the last time I had cake."

"You really don't eat sugar."

"I didn't eat sugar." She lifted the cupcake in salute.

"Well then, I can't wait to introduce you to a funnel cake at the Heritage Festival on the Fourth." He froze. Why had he said that? Chicago streets where hundreds of people passed around them, where they didn't know anyone, were one thing, but there was no way she wanted to hang around downtown Heritage with him. "I mean—"

"I'd like that." She took another bite, this one quite a bit smaller.

He sighed as a little of the pressure lifted. "Besides, I got roped into that bachelor auction. I need you to at least offer a pity bid."

"I'll think about it." She lifted her chin and sent him a cheeky smile.

"You'll think about it?"

She downed the last of her cupcake and wiped off her hands on the napkin, then tossed her trash into a nearby can. "Well, I need to see who else is in the running before I decide."

Seth tossed his trash as he shoved the rest of his cupcake in his mouth and pointed at a bus slowing down at a stop twenty yards away. They ran to catch it, and that was just the beginning.

For the next several hours, they bought popcorn, navigated water fountains, and rode the sky swings. Which might not have been the best plan after their little sugar binge. At least the Centennial Wheel moved at a slow pace and offered a great view of the city. But the slow pace meant it also never completely stopped, so boarding the moving blue pods could be tricky. Although he doubted Grace would struggle, he still held her hand as they stepped into their private pod and waited for the door to seal them in.

It wasn't a big space, just two benches that faced each other. Each bench could fit three adults comfortably, but with it being just the two of them, they chose opposite sides.

Grace stared out the side window as the ground below them slowly dropped away. Despite the busyness of Chicago, it felt like they were cocooned in their own little private moment.

She met his gaze across the small space. "You never took me on that date you promised."

He motioned to the carriage around them. "Does this count?"

She seemed to consider it a moment, then shook her head. "Nope, I guess you'll have to ask again."

That was something he very well could do.

She sat back and looked out again at the city. "Why did you wait until I was leaving to ask me out?"

Why? Because he'd been in love with her for as long as he could remember. Because he'd been terrified that she'd say no. Which she had. But it wasn't like he'd admit all that here. He offered a half shrug as he stared toward the city where people crowded the sidewalks, waiting for their turns on this ride. He wasn't good with crowds or raw honesty. "I'm not sure. I saw you on your porch and just asked. Bugged your brother to no end, so that was a bonus."

It wasn't a complete lie. It had made Gabe mad, and Seth knew it would, but that had definitely not been a motivating factor.

"You and Gabe were so close before I left. It's still a little shocking to me that you two aren't friends anymore."

Friends? Of course they weren't friends. They were borderline enemies, but she had to know that. Could she not know— How on earth could that be possible? He must have misunderstood.

"I always hoped he would change." She focused on her feet a moment, her face pinched as if she were in physical pain.

"At one point when I was younger, I used to think Gabe was my hero."

She looked up. There was a smile on her face, but there wasn't really any joy in it. "I even defended him to my parents, only to find out later I was just helping him lie."

It wasn't a stretch to imagine that. Seth knew a half dozen ways to get good people to help him lie.

He debated his next move with more than a little dread. Finally, he leaned forward, dropping his elbows on his knees. He snagged her fingers with his. "Don't give up on him. I wouldn't be alive today without him."

The words pained him but were true. He had to believe that guy who was there for him when no one else had been still existed.

Instead of pulling back her fingers, she toyed with the calluses on his palm. "He saved your life?"

"After my dad was killed in active duty. My mom did not handle it well. And she turned to drugs, alcohol, and not-such-reputable company. But she was concerned about me—sort of." He swallowed and let his gaze travel out the side of the carriage toward Lake Michigan stretching out in the distance. They were about halfway to the highest point, just high enough to see quite a distance. This type of openness wasn't so bad. It was just the facts. He could do facts. "Her way of protecting me from the people she was associating with was to not let me come home on nights she had . . . visitors."

"How old were you?"

"The first time? Eleven." He dropped her fingers and leaned back, stretching his arms across the bench seat. "Gabe found me shivering on your guys' back porch and snuck me into your basement and then found me some dinner."

"He should've told our parents."

"Probably." Seth drew a slow calming breath, the night still so clear in his mind. "I begged him not to. I knew my mom was upset about my dad's death, and I didn't want to make things worse. Looking back, they would've just moved me to my aunt and uncle's. So, I missed out there."

"How did your other family not know? Why didn't anyone step in?" Between the indignancy in her voice and the way she gripped the bench seat, she seemed more upset about this than her audition.

"I think they tried." He leaned forward again, lowering his voice to a calming tone. "They would ask me so many questions, trying to get me to open up, but I think you underestimate how far kids will go to protect their parents. Secrets were the comfortable place I lived in, and I refused to let anyone see what I didn't want them to see. Gabe was the only one who knew."

"I don't get it. The Mrs. Warner you're describing and the one I remember don't line up in my mind." Grace closed her eyes a moment. "I didn't know her well, but I just have this memory of her standing on the porch in a pink flowery dress with her thick brown hair pulled back on the sides calling you home for dinner. She was always smiling and so beautiful."

"She was beautiful, that's true, but the smile was a show. Where do you think I learned to keep secrets?"

"Was? Did she—"

"No. She's alive. But years of drug and alcohol abuse stole her

153

beauty. She held it somewhat together in public for years. But when my aunt and uncle died my junior year of high school, she really hit rock bottom. But by then, I was so caught up in my own life choices, I barely noticed. We lost touch for a little while. But she reconnected with me when I was in college. As soon as she thought I had money, she was back."

"Did you live in our basement long?" She reached for his fingers again. She probably meant it as a comforting gesture, but every movement, every touch traveled the length of his fingers to his arms. He could barely focus on her words.

He looked up and found her waiting. Right, she'd asked a question. He leaned back, letting her hand fall away. "Um, no, we knew if we kept it up, your parents were going to find me. So we found a way to break into those old houses that used to be on the square. I pretty much lived there on and off and saved your basement for the very cold nights. But Gabe got me food, most nights. Sometimes I even found bags of groceries on the steps to my house. He literally kept me from starving."

"I am so sorry." Tears clung to her eyes. And something hit him square in the chest. Those tears were for him. He couldn't remember a time when someone had cared enough to cry for him.

"It's all right, I'm not that thrown-away kid anymore." Their eyes locked and held. There was something so raw and open in her expression. And for the first time in a long time, he didn't want to offer easy-out answers or avoid the hard questions.

He wanted her to see him. Really see him. The good parts and the really painful parts.

His gaze traveled across the water that disappeared into the horizon. They had just passed the highest point of the wheel. They were beginning their descent. If he didn't do this now, open up now, he might never do it.

He bent down and pulled her foot onto his lap and traced the faint white scar that circled around her ankle with his thumb. "I lied a minute ago. Asking you out wasn't on a whim, it wasn't no-big-deal, and it had absolutely nothing to do with your brother. I pretty much had a crush on you from the day you fell off your bike and got this scar. But we were young, and my life was a mess."

He shrugged, letting his thumb trail once more over her ankle, then lowered her foot back to the floor. "I only gathered the courage that day because I figured it was then or never. Turned out to be never. I know—" His phone vibrated from his pocket, breaking his line of thought. "One second."

He pulled it out and scanned the text from his mother.

MOM

Where were you today?

Need food.

Maybe I'll come find you.

Since moving to Heritage, he shifted from going on Saturdays to Sundays. But his mom had a hard time keeping track of the days of the week—or the past month. But if she was reaching out to him already under the pretense of food, she was desperate for money. The last thing he needed was for her to wander into Heritage looking for him, and she knew that. So was she really threatening, or just saying that to get him to act? It didn't matter, he wasn't willing to take the chance. He sent off a quick text in return.

SETH

I'll drop off some food, but it'll be a while.

In Chicago.

He slid the phone back into his pocket. "Sorry, but I'm going to have to call it a day. I have to get you home, then take my mom some groceries."

"Where does she live now?"

"Muskegon Heights."

"That's on our way back. Why don't we stop on the way?"

Was she kidding? "You know it has a higher crime rate than Detroit, right?"

"It's not like we're moving in there. And you'll be driving back there tonight anyway. Which would put you there over an hour later. Wouldn't it be better for you to be there earlier?"

Like crime only happened at night. "No."

Her brow creased into a frown. "You gave up your entire Saturday for me. Let me do this."

"No." The carriage was almost to the bottom of the wheel. He moved across the bench closer to the door.

She sent him one last frown as the door opened. Then stood and exited, not stopping to wait for him. So much for their fun day. His mom had a way of ruining everything in his life. Grace could frown all she wanted, but he wasn't taking her anywhere near Muskegon Heights or his mother.

ten

THAT UNFINISHED SENTENCE HAD THE POWER
to mess with her mind like nothing else Grace had ever known.
I know ... what? I know I still care about you or *I know it would
have never worked*? Both possibilities. Both very different statements.
Grace crossed her arms, watching the road go by out the passenger
window of Seth's Lumina as they headed north on 31.

They had talked about a lot on the drive home—her class, his
new plan for a ninja gym, even about the upcoming fall festival—
but they hadn't circled back to finishing that sentence, and he
refused to discuss stopping at his mom's. And here she'd thought
for a moment there on the Centennial Wheel that she was finally
getting to see behind the armored wall he kept around himself.

At least she had talked him into stopping to buy the groceries
when they were passing through Holland but now that they were
approaching the Muskegon exit, he was back behind his thick
armor, refusing to budge on the idea of dropping her off in Heritage before taking the food to his mom.

"Do you honestly think I'm such a snob that I couldn't handle being at your mom's place?" From the stories, she could guess his mom lived in a not-so-nice place, but was that really the reason?

"It's just not a good idea. That place is not for you."

"What's the big deal? I go to Muskegon three times a week for my doctor appointments. How different can Muskegon Heights be? According to Apple Maps, they're only ten minutes apart."

"They just are, okay?"

The whole thing just didn't make sense. Unless for some reason he was embarrassed of her. Her gaze unfocused reducing the passing foliage to a blur of dark green out her window.

His phone buzzed, and his gaze flicked to it, but he didn't pick it up. His hands gripped tighter on the wheel.

That wasn't good. "Do you want me to read it to you?"

There was a long pause, and Grace had given up on him answering when he finally let out a slow breath. "You'd better."

Grace lifted the phone. "It's from your mom."

He didn't react so she supposed he already knew that. "Hey, Sethy, Jim said I could borrow his car so I can drive up to you in Heritage. Leaving soon."

"Ugh," Seth practically growled into the car. He looked at Grace, then flipped on his blinker, his jaw tight. "Text back that we'll be there in ten and we already have food."

She did as he said, then waited until the three little dots produced a heart emoji. When she looked up, he was pulling into a gas station but chose a spot alone rather than going to a pump.

"I know you don't think it's a big deal, but you have to trust me and do exactly what I say," he said suddenly.

"What?"

He looked at her across the car, his gaze intense. Gone were the warm brown eyes that she'd seen in Chicago. What had she gotten herself into?

"At my mom's. You have to stay with me at all times and if I say no to something, it's no. Meet me by the trunk, we need to fix all that." He motioned to, well, all of her, then he cut the engine and climbed out.

Ouch.

She climbed out and walked to where he'd just opened the trunk. He turned and let his gaze rake over her. Not in the same way as earlier. His eyes were distant, hard, and calculating. "First your bag needs to go in the trunk. Along with anything on you that has any value whatsoever."

He circled back and pulled her duffel from the back seat and tossed it in the trunk. "Not only do we not want it stolen out of the car, but my mother is a master at pickpocketing. I'm not having her take that fancy watch off your wrist when you're not looking."

"I think you're being a bit dramatic." She slipped off her watch and added it to her bag, then her necklace.

"I'm not. Trust me. Take down your bun." He pulled his stocking cap off and handed it to her. "Put this on and tuck as much of your hair in there as possible."

"I will look ridiculous—what will your mom think of me?"

"Hopefully, she won't think of you."

"Ouch." Her ego was taking a hit tonight.

He closed his eyes a moment then opened them and looked at her. "It isn't you. It's her. I swear."

She nodded and tugged her hair down then added the hat.

"Take off that pink coat." He pulled off his flannel shirt, leaving him in just a white T-shirt. He handed it to her and scanned her over again. "I can't do anything about the leggings but at least they're black and nondescript."

"Really?" She turned the flannel shirt over in her hands.

"Remember when I suggested that you didn't need more than a corner to dance and you told me I didn't understand the world of dance? Well, this is my world and you, in all this, are a walking target. It says rich, it says—"

"I am not rich."

"Your jacket alone would pay for at least one fix if not two. Flannel on. Jacket in the trunk."

Maybe she didn't understand his world at all. But she'd be safe with him, wouldn't she? Some of her hesitation must have shown on her face because Seth's movements halted. "You sure you want to do this?"

"Is it safe?"

He took a step forward and put his hands firmly on her shoulders. "I will never let anything happen to you."

Oh. Oh my. She felt his gaze all the way through her body. And one look at his arms and she had no doubt he could probably keep that promise.

And to add to the weird sense of protection, when she pulled on the flannel, his incredibly male, heady, musky scent surrounded her.

This guy was not Mr. Nice from the studio.

Except maybe he was, too, because he stared at her a moment, then reached up and tucked a little of her blonde wispy hair back under the hat. "Honestly, I'm not that worried about her neighbors. They might break into the car if there's something obvious they can see, but if they can't see it, it isn't worth the risk to break in and hope they find something. My car doesn't really say posh. And as long as they know you're with me, they'll leave you alone."

With him. The idea did strange things to her.

"I just . . . I haven't introduced anyone to my mom since I was ten." The rawness in his voice nearly broke her heart.

Grace laid a hand on his arm. "It'll be okay. I promise."

He flinched, then drew in a breath.

What? Did she say something wrong?

Then he swallowed. "Don't promise. Just being there will be enough."

Seth shut the trunk and waited for her to climb back in the car before he got into the driver's seat.

He reached into his wallet and pulled out a five-dollar bill. "Put this in the front pocket of the flannel shirt."

She took the money and did as he said. "What for?"

"Call it an experiment for why I had you put everything in the trunk. We'll see if it's there by the time we leave."

He pulled back out on the road but away from the highway.

"When were you going to tell me about The Storm?"

His movements froze. "I thought I was recognized at your audition."

Nonaudition.

When he didn't elaborate, she lifted her brows and waited.

"It's not a big deal. I needed money to pay off my college debt. So I entered as a dark horse and ended up winning the city qualifier."

"Does that mean you go on to the next round?"

"No!"

Grace jumped at the strength behind the word, and he winced.

"Sorry. I mean, yes, that's what it means, but I just can't." He didn't say anything the rest of the way, but it didn't keep Grace from replaying the conversation in her mind. She didn't understand his world, and she had a feeling she was the first person he'd ever tried to explain it to.

By the time she stood with a bag of groceries in hand at his mom's front door, Grace was convinced he had, in fact, overreacted. Sure, the building needed to be painted. But it wasn't that bad.

Seth knocked but didn't seem that surprised when his mother didn't answer. He sent Grace a this-is-your-last-chance-out look. When she only nodded, he opened the door and stepped in.

The room was dim, but she followed Seth, staying just a few inches behind him. She bit back a gag when a musty, dank odor hit her about three steps in. Seth secured the door and then flipped the light switch, but that just illuminated a single light bulb from the ceiling. The furniture and carpet seemed to be from the era of her grandparents, but it was the large dark stains on the cushions and carpet that she couldn't look away from.

"Mom, I have your food." Seth's voice rose but not in an angry way. He didn't seem fazed by any of it. As if this was normal. This was okay. This was home. The image of an eleven-year-old Seth came to mind, and she bit back the tears. How had he come out of this and not self-destructed himself?

"Bring cigarettes?" The voice was rough without even a touch of appreciation.

"Just food." By Seth's tone, this was a regular question with the same answer. He also didn't seem surprised she'd lied about driving to Heritage.

"It wouldn't hurt you once in a while—" His mom emerged from the hall and froze when her eyes locked on Grace.

It took all Grace's mental energy to not physically recoil. Different was an understatement. The once dark, thick hair was a thin, dull, ratty mess. Her once round face was skin and bones, along with the rest of her. She wore a large T-shirt, no doubt to try and hide it, but with the way one bony shoulder poked out the neck hole, she clearly needed every calorie Seth could bring her.

She'd always remembered Mrs. Warner as younger than her parents, but right now with the dark circles under her sunken eyes, she appeared to have at least two decades on them.

His mom reached up and made an effort to smooth her thin brown hair as she smiled a gray smile missing several teeth. And for the first time Grace saw the slightest hint of who she once had been. "You didn't tell me you have a guest. Who might you be?"

Seth seemed to be debating whether to point out that his mom had met her before but must have decided against it. "This is my friend Grace."

Seth opened the fridge and began exchanging fresh food for some that was rotten. "Grace, this is my mom, Angel."

"Aren't you pretty." Angel's bony fingers caught a piece of

Grace's blonde hair between her fingers. "Seth has never brought home a girl before. You must be special."

Seth winced and hurried forward. He stepped between them and lowered his mom's hand.

His mom didn't seem deterred though. "He's a good boy, no matter what anyone says."

Other than her mom, Grace had never heard anyone say a bad thing about him.

"Mom." Seth pointed to the pile of food in the garbage. "Why do you want me to buy you more food when you didn't eat what I bought you before."

She waved his hand away. "Stop buying me broccoli."

"Fine. But you have to find something healthy to eat." Seth walked back to the fridge and took the broccoli out.

"Is he this bossy with you?" His mom stood right by her again.

Grace couldn't keep the smile from her face as the conversation from fifteen minutes ago ran through her mind. "Sometimes."

Seth sent her a look, but there wasn't anger in it. Maybe a touch of amusement. "I'm only bossy with her when she's wrong."

"Typical man." His mom shook her head. "His father was the same way. Looks just like him too."

"Really?" Grace looked over at Seth and tried to imagine him in an Army uniform. Yup, he could pull that off. "Do you have a photo?"

"No." The word was sharp as her eyes dimmed and she spun away, disappearing down the hall.

Grace looked toward Seth, but he wasn't much help. His jaw was locked again. "We got to go, Mom. I'll be back next week."

The only response was the song "Look Away" blasting from down the hall, and Seth motioned toward the door.

"Don't we need to check on her?"

"Nope." He handed her the bag of broccoli. "My guess is she went to find a hidden bottle and *Chicago's Greatest Hits*. Memories of my dad will do that to her. And every time my dad comes up, *Chicago* comes out."

"I'm sorry. I never meant to . . . I mean, she brought it up."

He cupped her face in his hands, making sure she met his eyes. "You did nothing wrong. She's an alcoholic and a drug addict with many regrets. One is burning all of my dad's stuff in a drunken rage shortly after he died."

"What was he like?"

"Kind, loving, giving. He was a good guy."

Grace couldn't wrap her mind around a dad like that. A dad that wasn't demanding and harsh.

He dropped her face and she immediately missed the warmth. "You don't have any photos of him?"

"I had one for a long time." He gathered the bag of garbage and stepped toward the door. "I kept it and a few other personal things in the vet houses to keep them safe from my mom."

"The houses that burned?"

"Very ones." He held the door and waited for her to walk out into the cool evening air. "The town wanted to erase an eyesore. And in turn, I lost every last bit of my childhood."

"I'm sorry."

"Life happens." Seth just shrugged and followed her toward the car, stopping to drop the garbage in the bin. "But this is just one of the reasons The Storm has to disappear. The further you go, the deeper they dig."

He was so casual about it, but it broke her heart. All of it. His childhood, his mom, and even the way he used it as a reason to push everyone away now.

Grace reached in her pocket for the five, but it was gone. She opened her mouth to say something but stopped. She didn't have to tell him. He already knew.

He shook his head. "I still don't understand how she does that when she can barely walk straight most of the time."

Seth was right. This was his world, and she didn't understand it at all.

Suddenly, it all came together. His friendship with Gabe. Officer Hammond asking her if she was all right. His mom.

Seth had a whole life she knew nothing about.

"So what do you think, Jon?" Seth had spent most of yesterday putting together his slide presentation on his day off. But after spending the entire day before that with Grace, he had to keep busy, otherwise he would no doubt show up and beg her to go on that date he still owed her.

Jon turned his office chair toward Seth as the presentation ended, his elbows propped on the sides. "What changed your mind?"

"I thought about what you said." Not to mention the conversation with Grace on Saturday. Seth adjusted his tie. "I think this town—the kids—could benefit from a place to go. But it can't be a one-size-fits-all. This would be half rec center, half ninja gym."

"So The Storm is back."

"No." Seth shook his head and leaned forward. "I'll head it up, but as Seth. Not The Storm."

"But the money—"

"It isn't about the money, it's about the kids."

"Says the guy not paying the bill." Jon turned a pen over in his fingers, then again. "I know I told you to present this to the board. But after my meeting with them a few days ago, the board was clear about looking at trimming, not expanding. So this kind of budget is—"

"I get it, I do. But this is really important to me."

Jon hesitated then nodded. "Me too. I should have been here for you instead of off in Europe."

Something tightened around Seth's heart. "It wasn't—"

"I know. But I should have been here. And I am determined to be here for other kids. So"—Jon sat forward and locked eyes with Seth—"I want to personally invest in this. I'll use my money, not company money. And I want you to run it. And if that's as Seth and not The Storm, I'll take it."

Was he serious? He couldn't be serious.

This was what he wanted. Everything he wanted. "Are you—"

"Sure? Absolutely. I'll fund it, you run it." Jon stood and stuck out his hand. "What do you say, partner?"

Seth stood and shook Jon's hand and resisted every urge to whoop and yell. "Partner."

"I am proud of you. It's a good plan." Jon dropped his hand and lifted his coat from the back of the chair. "And just so you know, once it's up and running, I want you to be working there, full time. At the rate you're moving the properties, you'll have worked yourself out of a job before the year is up. That will be about the time it'll take to get this build-out done."

"But I . . ." Why was his throat so tight?

"Wanted to be out of town by the end of the summer? Do you really?" Jon walked out of the conference room and paused in the door to look back. "And take the rest of the day off. You look like you were up all night working on this."

He had been, but he'd hoped he'd hidden it better than that.

His phone buzzed with an incoming text.

GRACE
I know I said only two weeks, but what
do you think about continuing to help me?

He couldn't keep the smile from his face as he tapped back a reply.

SETH
Training or dancing?

It honestly didn't matter. He'd do both.

GRACE
Yes. Yes. And something else.

SETH
?

GRACE
You have to wait and see.

He set the phone aside as an uneasiness settled in his chest and seemed to build with every text. As much as he wanted to see her, they also had to talk.

Because the more he'd let his conversations from Saturday with Grace roll around in his mind, the more the pieces just didn't add up. The fact she seemed surprised he wasn't friends anymore with Gabe. Her confusion about the way Officer Hammond had questioned him, and then there was the fact she didn't know what she was walking into with his mother.

Before this weekend, she had never given any indication that she didn't know how he was connected to her family. It didn't make sense, everyone in town knew. But she *had* been in Europe at the time. Maybe her parents hadn't told her. But surely it would have come up. Then again, beyond their initial greeting, most of their conversations revolved around her knee or her dance. And he'd been happy to keep it that way.

He shook his head. It had been these yo-yo thoughts that had kept him up into the wee hours of the morning working on that presentation instead of sleeping.

But with the way things were continuing to develop with their . . . friendship, there was no denying all cards had to be on the table.

And that meant risking everything. There was no telling how Grace would react when she found out he was implicated in her brother's death. But he couldn't afford to wait and risk having her find out from her mom. Who knew what kind of poisonous spin she would put on it. The truth was bad enough as it was. It needed to be now. He lifted his phone again.

SETH

Done early. Are you at the studio?

GRACE

Yup.

He stood and shoved the phone in his coat pocket. As good a time as ever to clear the air. It could ruin everything. His mind drifted to their conversation on the Centennial Wheel. Then again, maybe not. He'd been honest there, and tragedy hadn't struck. She hadn't judged him, she'd simply cried. For him.

Fifteen minutes later, he stepped in the back door of the studio. A classical piece he wasn't familiar with filled the air, and he took the few steps up to the main floor and leaned against a wall. Grace wore her familiar black leotard with her hair in a tight blonde bun. A wisp of a pink skirt hung around her toned waist.

The color pink was definitely growing on him.

Grace lifted her arms in the air and floated more than danced across the floor. He loosened the buttons at his wrists. He really could watch her dance all day and never tire of it.

She focused on her reflection, a small V between her brows as if silently judging and correcting every move. They looked perfect to him.

When her gaze met his in the mirror, she dropped down from her toe and turned toward him, a smile stretching from ear to ear. "And?"

"And Jon loved it." He pushed off the wall and took a few steps toward her. "He and I are going to open it together. I start working on it tomorrow. By working, I mean spending the day on the phone with contractors and filing permits."

She hurried toward him and wrapped her arms around his neck, squeezing him. "I knew he would love it."

He hugged her back, letting her words and embrace wash over him. She had believed in him. When was the last time someone had believed in him? When was the last time someone had really hugged him?

There was that pressure in his chest again. He loosened his hold and took a step back. "There's something we need to talk about."

"And guess what?" she said at the same time, then added, "What is it?"

He shook his head. "You go first."

He wanted to hear what was behind that smile before he dumped all this on her.

"Alec called. Madame Laurent was so impressed with my progress and said if I can manage the lift, she would consider me for Odette at the end of the summer show."

"The lift?"

"Yes, and I think I am coming close because look at this." She turned back toward the mirror and stepped over to where she had been dancing. She lifted her arms and then raised her leg, never dropping off pointe.

"You did it without help."

"I know and my leg is getting strong. I think I'm now ready for you to help me with a lift. Can we try?"

"Whoa." He held up both hands and took a step back. "Holding you steady is one thing. I don't think I'm ready for a lift."

"You pretty much just have to deadlift me above your head. If you think you can hold my weight—"

"That isn't a problem." He slid his bag off his shoulder and dropped it in the corner. "But I'm guessing it's more complicated than you think."

"Here. Maybe if you see it." She walked over to grab her phone. She navigated the screen a moment before pointing it toward him.

That did help, at least he could see what his role was. And she was right, his part was just a dead lift as long as he didn't have to stand in that fancy way.

He kicked off his shoes and pushed them toward the mirror.

"Stand behind me and place your hands on the small of my back from behind."

He loosened his shirt at his waist, rolled up his sleeves, and then did as she said. His thumbs crossed over each other in the back as his fingers wrapped around her middle.

"Okay." Why was his voice coming out so ragged?

"Oh, did you want to talk first?" She met his gaze in the mirror.

Should they? Probably. But he knew the reality that the talk could change everything. He just wanted five minutes of this. Five more minutes before—

"Lift first then talk."

"Okay, on three. One . . . two . . . th—"

He lifted but it was awkward, and she pulled up. He set her back down.

"You lifted too soon. Wait until three. Then I can jump into it."

Grace took her position again and waited for him to grab her waist once more. "One . . . two . . . three."

This time they were more in sync, but he only got her about three feet off the ground. Seth shook his head. "You have to lean back more."

Grace eyed him over her shoulder. "*You* are coaching *me* now after one video?"

"I may not know about dancing, but I know I can't deadlift you unless I can get under you. And I can't get under you if you stay vertical."

She didn't comment but nodded. On the next attempt, she did better but she still seemed to be holding back. "Do you think I'll drop you?"

She walked a few feet to the mirror. "Last time I did this lift I didn't have enough strength in my leg to jump, so I wasn't high enough, and my partner did drop me. So yeah, maybe I'm not as ready as I thought I was."

"Hey." He walked up behind her, his hand finding her waist again as he leaned toward her ear. "You can trust me. I won't drop you no matter what."

She only hesitated a second before she nodded and went back into position. On three she threw herself into the lift, and he was there to support her. With her arms stretched out, her back curving over his hands. Wow. He looked a little like an oafish wrestler holding up the championship belt, but she looked good enough for the both of them.

His arms began to tense. Maybe they should have watched the end of the video too, because he wasn't exactly sure how to get her down from this position.

After a moment, she placed her hands on his, and he began lowering her down. The unpracticed move landed her half on his shoulder, then sliding down his chest, only to launch forward when she touched down.

She landed with an *oof* on her hands and knees. "We'll have to practice that part."

Seth rushed forward and helped her up. "I'm so sorry."

He pulled her hands up and examined them. The skin was a touch pink but none of it was missing. His thumb trailed over her palm. Then again. He met her gaze. Her blue eyes were wide, lips slightly parted.

"We should probably talk." But he didn't step back. He couldn't. It was as if he were trapped in her orbit and now that he was this close to her, he couldn't willingly pull away.

Her free hand slid over his heart. "I know you don't like to let people in here. But just like you asked me a few minutes ago to trust you, trust me."

She had no idea how very much he wanted to. But . . . but what? His mind had gone cloudy with need. Not just the physical need for her to be close. But the need for someone to see him, know him, and still love him.

He didn't remember moving, but now her lips were just a breath away. He needed to stop this. To back up. To get everything on the table. But it was as if an invisible thread tugged him forward.

"We really do need to talk." He finally managed the words rough and low.

"Okay." The breath from the word brushed across his lips as her hands settled on the sides of his waist. "We will."

And when her fingers began to lightly toy with the skin where his shirt had come untucked, his last bit of self-control crumbled. Seth brushed his lips across hers. Then again. Her lips were so soft and intoxicating that he was nearly going out of his mind.

He waited for her to pull back, to push him away, anything that would ground him. But when her lips pressed into his, hunger like he'd never known traveled through him, and he stopped fighting the pull to deepen the kiss. And in that moment, every cell in his body lit up, and his skin began to hum.

This was better than any high he'd ever had before, because it wasn't just the touch of their lips, it was Grace. Grace, who knew him. Grace, who he'd found himself wanting to open up to. Grace, who had met his mother. Grace, who had a glimpse into his world and had not run screaming.

His hand slid up to her neck, her pulse hammering against his thumb. He needed to slow the kiss, but when she released the tiniest moan, Seth couldn't remember why he wanted to end it or what they'd even needed to talk about. His fingers dug into her hair, pulling her closer.

Without warning, the music cut off, leaving the room eerily quiet for just a half second before a humorless laugh filled the air. "Well, if this isn't the joke of the century."

Seth jerked back as Gabe's voice echoed around the room. The heat traveling through him was replaced with an icy chill.

No.

His former friend stood in the doorway, arms crossed, eyes wide and a touch wild. He had his hair slicked back, and the fact he was wearing clean pants probably meant he was on the way to a party. He'd probably only stopped to try to beg money off Grace. The idea sickened him.

His gaze shot back to Grace, who was still in his arms, but her eyes also fixed on her brother. "What are you doing here, Gabe?"

"What am I doing here?" His arms flew out in an uncontrolled gesture. "What are you doing here with *him*?"

"Why wouldn't I be here with Seth?" She stepped away from Seth and to glare at her brother. "He was our neighbor. You guys were friends. Or have the drugs erased that part of your memory?"

Gabe jerked back as his gaze flicked to Seth. "She doesn't know?"

Oh no.

"Gabe." He hadn't meant for it to sound quite so threatening, but this was not how he wanted Grace to find out.

"Know what?" Grace's eyes bounced between them.

"Grace, let's go somewhere and talk." Seth held out his hand.

"Like that's going to happen." Gabe took a step toward them. "I'm not letting you hurt her."

Grace propped her hands on her hips. "Don't be ridiculous, Gabe. Why would he hurt me?"

"I don't know. Why would he kill Gregory?"

And there it was. The words traveled through him like ice.

Grace frowned, shook her head. "You're confused, Gabe. Gregory died of an overdose."

"A drug overdose that was his fault." He poked Seth's chest, and Seth clenched his fist to keep from laying the guy flat. "You're kissing a convicted felon, Grace. And here everyone thought you were the good kid."

Her face twisted in confusion as she looked to Seth for answers. But what could Seth say? Everything Gabe was saying was true. And suddenly, the hope that someone who knew him could also love him vanished.

eleven

EVERYTHING SEEMED TO BE HAPPENING ALL at once, and none of it made sense. Grace let her gaze bounce between Seth and Gabe, each standing a few feet apart in the studio, but still nothing they said found a place to land in her brain.

Gabe hadn't closed the door, and the humid afternoon air filled the room. He still laughed, but it had shifted from a shocked laugh to something more angry and bitter. Gabe shut the door, sealing the sticky air away, but his gaze never left Seth's. His hair was neater than normal, his eyes excessively dilated.

Her brother was wiry and didn't have an extra ounce of muscle or fat on him, but she couldn't deny the desire to protect Seth from him. When he moved toward Seth again, she took a step between them. "Go home. You're high."

Gabe's beady eyes finally turned on her. "Wait, I'm the bad guy here? Did you even hear me say—"

"Leave Grace out of this." Seth grabbed her arm and tugged her behind him, his wide shoulder shielding her from her brother's anger.

"You're the one who brought her into this when you plastered

175

your lips on hers. I'm protecting her from *you*." Gabe went to move around him, but Seth blocked his way.

Gabe had never been violent with her, ever. But she couldn't deny that the wall of Seth added a level of assurance that she hadn't realized she desperately needed.

"Let's go, Grace." Gabe's voice faded as if he'd stepped toward the door expecting her to follow. "I said let's go."

"You don't even know what you're talking about." She peeked around Seth's arm. "Go home and sleep it off."

"I don't know what I'm talking about?" He marched back toward them, his dilated eyes fixed on Seth. "What do you say, Seth? Do I know what I'm talking about?"

Seth didn't say a word, just shoved his hands deep in his pockets like a wall blocking her.

"Are you going to deny that you killed—"

"Gabe." The word came out harsh and laced with a warning as Seth took a step toward him.

Gabe had always tried to pull her into his lies, but he was going too far this time. She waited for Seth to defend himself. But he didn't say a word. She stepped out from behind him. His face had gone pale, and he eyed the front door as if it were calling to him.

"Seth?" She took a step toward him, but he backed up as his gaze shifted to her, empty and vacant.

"It can't be true."

He opened his mouth, but nothing came out. He seemed to draw a breath to try again. "I was there the night Gregory died."

"You were there? You were more than just there. It was your fault," Gabe finally filled in.

Her eyes darted back to Seth, but he wouldn't meet her eyes. If possible, his face had gone even paler. Like the life had been drained out of him.

"I don't believe it." Grace took another step toward him, but he retreated again.

"It's true." The words were ragged, as if they shredded his throat on the way out. "I thought you knew. And then I sort of figured that you might not know—probably didn't know. And I didn't know how to tell you. But I was going to tell you . . ."

She closed her eyes a moment as the last several weeks fell into place. How nervous he was the first time they met. The way Hammond had questioned her at the stop. "When did you realize I had no idea?"

"In Chicago I began to wonder. I mean, certain things you said didn't seem to add up." He stepped toward her and lifted her hand. "Before that, I thought . . . you'd forgiven me. Giving me a new start. I didn't—"

She pulled away and stepped back. "Why didn't you bring it up in Chicago? Or on the three-hour ride home?"

"At first, I didn't see how it could be. I couldn't imagine your parents not telling you. But as I replayed some of our conversations, things didn't add up. I didn't really figure it out until last night. Then it was late, and I couldn't call you. I needed to look you in the eye. I came here today to do that very thing."

"Convenient." Gabe's snicker jolted her. How had she forgotten he was here?

Seth took a step toward her. "That was what I wanted to talk to you about. Then you wanted me to lift you and then the kiss—"

"So this is my fault?"

"No."

She shook her head and held up her hand. "I need to be alone."

"I'm not leaving you with him." Gabe's face twisted as he leaned against the wall.

Seth sent him an icy stare as he squared his shoulders and tilted his head that pretty much telegraphed *Back at you*.

"I need to go think, and I need you both to leave so I can lock up."

Which didn't make sense at all because Seth had a key. But Gabe seemed too high to notice. He waited for Seth to turn toward the front door then he followed him out. The glass rattled as he slammed it.

She stood there in the empty studio and wrapped her arms around herself. What had just happened? None of it made sense. She'd seen Seth's disdain for his mother's lifestyle. The stories of what that life had stolen from his childhood. She couldn't imagine him like Gabe.

How had he become like that?

"The first time my mom kicked me out for the night, I was eleven." That might do it. But Gabe had been the one to help him. What happened? Part of her wanted to go to him. Hold him and try to right every wrong his mother had done to him. But one word stopped her as it echoed around her mind.

Gregory.

Was he really responsible for Gregory's death? The idea sickened her. How could she ever be with someone who had done that to her family? To her brother?

Grace pressed her hands against her temples as a headache began to form. She had to get out of here. She had to think. Grace slipped on her shoes and hurried to the door. She flipped off the lights, then went outside and pulled out her key, her hands shaking as she shoved it into the lock.

"You're welcome."

Grace made a little scream at Gabe's voice. Her head jerked around until she spotted him against the building a couple yards away.

She turned back to the door and secured the lock. "Leave."

"You're mad at me? What did I do?" He pushed off the wall and took a step toward her, propping his foot on the back of Otis, who still rested under the front window. "I'm saving you from him. He was lying to you. He's the criminal."

"Don't step on Otis." Great, now she was defending a statue. But

178

maybe Gabe was right. Everything from the last few weeks with Seth suddenly seemed muddled in her mind. "You're a criminal too. Or doesn't it count because you're never caught?"

His eyes hardened for a moment but then he looked away and dropped his foot. "You better not be going to him."

That didn't even make sense, because his apartment was on the other side of this door. But if Gabe didn't know that, she wasn't going to fill him in. "Why do you care all of a sudden?"

"I care." He shoved his hands into his pockets and met her gaze again. "Take my advice and stay away from that guy."

His advice? He hadn't been around for the past several years of her life and suddenly, he wanted to offer advice?

"If not for yourself, then at least do it for Gregory." He offered one last hard look and was gone.

The air whooshed out of her lungs with his final words. For Gregory. Defend Seth, betray Gregory.

Grace darted across the square toward Ms. Margret's house. She hurried up the steps, rushed in the door, and collapsed on the couch. As everything over the past fifteen minutes caught up with her at once, Grace pulled her knees to her chest and began to sob.

"Oh, dear." Ms. Margret's voice was soft, and the cushions dipped slightly as the woman joined her on the sofa and pulled her to her shoulder. "I think it's going to take more than a cup of tea to fix this."

After a moment, Grace lifted her head, and Ms. Margret wiped away her tears. "What has gotten you so worked up?"

"Did Seth kill Gregory?"

She sighed and brushed back a bit of Grace's hair. "That's not quite right."

"Not quite right but kind of right?" She stood and pulled the tie from her bun, letting her hair cascade down. Somehow, she'd held out a trace of hope it was all a sick joke. But Ms. Margret wouldn't lie.

"He *was* convicted of a felony." Ms. Margret patted the seat next to her. "But I don't believe it was murder. I do believe it was connected to what happened that night."

Grace sat back down but stayed perched on the edge. "What happened that night?"

Ms. Margret reached up and wiped away another tear. "Don't you think that's something you should ask Seth?"

"Seth, the convicted felon?"

The woman gripped her hand, her aged fingers still displaying a fair amount of strength. "Seth, your friend."

"How can I even trust what he says?"

The words slammed into Grace with enough force to steal her breath. *You can trust me. I won't drop you.* But he had. Maybe not in the lift, but he'd dropped her heart, and after experiencing both, she'd much rather be dropped on her head.

"Has he ever lied to you?" Ms. Margret's blue-green eyes seemed to look into her soul. But the woman knew he hadn't. He'd left some key pieces out, but he'd never lied.

"I don't even know where he is. Gabe interrupted us kissing, I told them both to leave. He just took off."

"Did you say *kissing*?" Ms. Margret wiggled her eyebrows at Grace.

Had she? She needed to work on that think-before-speaking ability. "Yes?"

"Well, that answers the question of if you trust him. Unless you go around letting people you don't trust kiss you?"

"No. I mean not usually—not ever. That was my first kiss. But that was before."

"Before what? Seth hasn't changed. Have you?"

Everything from Saturday replayed in her mind. Seth giving up his day to drive her four hours to Chicago. Seth helping her relax and have fun with a special day at Navy Pier and cupcakes. Seth being kind but firm with his mother—the drug addict.

She'd guessed there was more to his story after all of that, she just hadn't guessed it was this.

When she didn't answer, Ms. Margret pushed on. "That boy has been through a lot. And I believe he's changed, and I think Jon agrees or he wouldn't have offered him a job."

"I know, but—"

Ms. Margret lifted Grace's chin with her finger and waited for Grace to meet her eyes. "We trust him, but that doesn't matter. What matters is, do *you* trust him?"

"Trust him not to harm me? Absolutely." She pulled a throw pillow to her stomach and tightened her grip. "Trust him to tell me the truth? I don't know."

Ms. Margret dropped her finger and patted her hand. "Then at least hear him out."

"What if he won't talk about it?"

"I think he will. But with a guy like Seth, you have to make room for him to talk."

"What does that mean?"

"Know when to talk and when to be silent. You can't make him talk." She reached out and squeezed her hand once more. "Trust is a two-way street—he also has to trust you to listen. Can you do that?"

There were only a few times since he'd become sober that a hit grew from a want to a desperate need. The moment he realized he'd lost the last photo of his father with the town fire. The time he'd found his mother beaten after she hadn't been able to pay her dealer. And the moment Grace had looked at him waiting for him to deny what Gabe said—her face morphing from irritation at her brother to revulsion at the sight of him.

Seth gripped the steering wheel tighter as the next green exit sign grew in the distance. If he gave in and turned the car around, there was no way he'd stay sober for the rest of the night. There was only one place he could go. It was where he'd always gone when life imploded. Quinn Ranch. He hoped and prayed he had enough gas to get there because he didn't even trust himself to stop at a gas station.

Two hours later as he took the long driveway to Quinn Ranch, he let his shoulders relax for the first time in an hour. He'd made it. The first time he'd been dropped off here, he'd wanted a hit too. Only that time he'd been angry he couldn't get it. He'd been brought by court order and was sure no one here understood him. He was certain he'd never survive. But he had, and he had come out a stronger man because of it.

He turned into Grant's driveway instead of toward the bunk house that had been his home, although maybe he should have gone that way. Maybe this was proof he needed to move back.

His desire for a hit had faded to a dull need by the time he stepped on Grant's wraparound porch. But it must have still shown on his face, because as soon as Grant opened the door, his smile dropped. With a nod and a quick shout to Caroline, he grabbed his coat and stepped out on the porch. "Let's walk."

"Daddy." His three-year-old daughter, Vangie, ran out the door. "Hug."

Grant scooped her up and planted a kiss on her cheek. Her strawberry blonde curls were the perfect combination of her mother's red and her dad's dark blond. He set her back down. "I'll be back."

He hadn't seen Grant since the baby shower. That had only been a month ago, but it felt like forever from where he stood. Grant had been more than just his sponsor. With his military background, he'd reminded Seth so much of his dad. At least what he could remember of him. Even now, as Grant walked beside him, he didn't know if he was his friend, mentor, sponsor, or all the above.

They were five minutes into the walk before Seth spoke. "I don't think Heritage is working out. I need another job and soon. Maybe I could work here."

"That's interesting, because Leah just told Caroline that Jon was excited about your presentation today and that he offered to go into a partnership with you on the rec center. She also mentioned you went to Chicago this weekend with Grace."

"That's over." Seth shoved his hands in his pockets.

"I didn't even realize it had started." Grant sent him a side glance, but Seth refused to meet his gaze. "What happened?"

"I should have told her." His voice was tight as he fisted his hands in his pockets. "Initially, I thought she knew. It never occurred to me that she didn't. This weekend I finally put it together, and I was going to talk to her today, honest. But we . . . got sidetracked. And then Gabe showed up and started carrying on—"

"Hold on." Grant stopped. "Are you saying she didn't know it was your drugs that her brother overdosed on?"

"She didn't even know I was there that night." Seth kicked a small rock down the path before continuing on. "She didn't know how I was connected to Gabe beyond our childhood years. And she definitely didn't know my own history with drugs."

Grant caught up in a few strides. "How is that possible? Heritage isn't that big of a town."

"That's why I assumed she had to know. But when she met my mom on Saturday, she clearly had no idea that had once been my life."

"You took her to your mom's?" Grant eyed him a moment. "So, you really like this girl."

"Maybe, but it doesn't matter." He backed a few steps away. "Gabe told her I killed Gregory, so it's over. Now I just need to get out of town for a while. Will you help me?"

Grant released a sigh. "I've said it before, and I am going to keep on saying it. You didn't kill Gregory. Drugs did."

"Don't you see? To her—to the town—I'm responsible."

"But why do you need to get out of Heritage? Your job is going well."

"I'm not sure I can continue to share a space with her."

"If that's the case then I think your feelings go way beyond 'maybe.' Which begs the question of why you hadn't talked about Gregory yet. Whether she knew or not—you had to have known it was a conversation you needed to have."

"I told you I was going to talk to her today. I went to the studio for that very reason. But she needed help with a lift. And then we got . . . distracted." He started down the path again.

"Distracted?"

"We sort of kissed."

"You *sort of* kissed?"

"Fine, we kissed. That's when Gabe found us."

"Ah. Let me get this straight. So you make a big presentation to Jon that went well. A presentation for the project of your dreams and he offers you a partnership. Then you kissed Grace." Grant lifted one eyebrow. "I think you need to admit that you really care for her."

"It doesn't matter." Seth stopped walking and rested his elbows on the paddock fence. "She'll be returning to Chicago soon."

"Not everyone walks away, Seth."

But they did. His mom had, Gabe had, it was only a matter of time before Grace did too. He was always left to face the hard moments alone.

"If you never let people close, you may keep them from hurting you, but trust me when I say that doesn't mean a pain-free life. And don't forget there are people who haven't walked away. Jon hasn't. I won't. There are many that are behind you and want to see you succeed."

"And if I don't?" The words seemed to scrape across his throat. What if he did fail again? He'd almost failed tonight.

"Then we will be there to help pick you up, every time. I won't give up on you."

Seth closed his eyes against the burning in his throat. He refused to get emotional. But the only two people who'd never given up on him were his dad and Uncle George. And both had been taken from him. Even if it hadn't been their choice, he'd still been left with nothing.

Grant's hand landed on Seth's shoulder as he cleared his throat. "I'm on your team. Forever, no matter what. We're family."

He shook his head as he leaned back from the fence and looked back at Grant. "We're not—"

"We are. Maybe not by blood but not all family is blood. Adopted families are families by choice. You're my brother. Don't forget that."

A wave of emotions threatened to overwhelm him. A brother. A family. Jon and Leah were family, and Abby was family even if she were half way around the world. But his mom? She hadn't felt like family for as long as he could remember. She used him. Over and over.

And although she might love him in a twisted way, that wasn't what real love was. Love was kind, love was not self-seeking, and love did not rejoice in evil.

"I believe God has a bigger plan for you than hiding from your past." Grant squeezed his shoulder and then dropped his arm. "Go talk to Grace."

"You honestly think she would listen?"

"When I got out of the Army, I was a mess. Not just in my own head, but I came home to my brother announcing his engagement to my ex."

"Ouch."

"Yup. I wasn't into her anymore, but it was still a little bruising to my ego. Okay, a lot." Grant turned toward the house, nodding for Seth to follow. "Anyway, I went to visit Nate—he'd just moved to Heritage. And Caroline ended up trying to be my life coach."

"Your life coach?" Somehow it wasn't that difficult to imagine the no-nonsense Caroline telling people how to live their lives.

"It didn't go well at first. I was afraid if she knew me—really knew who I was on the inside—she wouldn't like me. But you know what?"

"You opened up and she did?"

"Well, after a rollercoaster of a relationship. And had I been willing to open up sooner, I could have saved us both a lot of pain."

"So just open up to her? It's that easy?"

"Are you kidding? It was the hardest thing I had ever done up to that point. But it was worth it."

"And if it doesn't go so well?"

"Then you'll know. And it'll be practice for the next time you have this conversation. Because any relationship worth fighting for will require full honesty and transparency."

"I'm just not good at it."

"Join the club. But being open and honest is like anything else. The more you do it, the better you get at it."

"If she walks away . . ."

"It will hurt like a pain you've never known before."

"Awesome."

"But not talking to her isn't saving you any pain. Is it?"

Grant was right. Possible pain was better than guaranteed pain. This could end in disaster, but having the conversation would be his only chance.

twelve

G RACE HADN'T KNOWN WHAT TO EXPECT WHEN
Seth showed up at her door an hour ago asking her to go for
a drive, but it hadn't been this.

Silence.

She cut Seth a side glance again from the passenger seat, then
back to Lake Michigan. He hadn't said a word on the long drive
up to Ludington. And he hadn't said a word since he parked five
minutes ago in a parking spot overlooking the Ludington beach.
Seth's gaze stayed locked on the lighthouse at the end of the break-
wall, as if the moonlight itself was writing the answers on its side.

"Know when to talk and when to be silent." If this much silence
hadn't been enough, she doubted more would help. Maybe if she
opened up a bit, it would give him space to open up.

"Ms. Margret keeps asking me why I dance." Why had she
started there? Because maybe if she wanted him to be vulnerable,
she needed to be vulnerable herself. "All I can come up with is
that it's who I am. But I can tell that isn't what she's looking for."

He blinked and turned to face her. The streetlight highlighted
the outline of his face. "You're an amazing dancer—"

"Thank you, but—"

"I wasn't done." He blinked at her a beat, but the shadows hid the details of his face. "You're an amazing dancer, but it's what you do, not who you are."

His words slid under her armor, and she turned back to the lighthouse. Maybe staring across the water had its benefits.

"Then who am I?" Her words came out strained, and she cleared her throat. Why were they even talking about this? There were more important things to talk about.

"No one else can answer that for you."

She let her head fall back against the headrest. "You're as bad as Ms. Margret."

"It doesn't have to be that hard. If someone asked you about me, who would you say I am?" He turned back to stare over the lake. "Or what would you have said prior to Gabe's little truth bomb?"

"You're Seth, my former neighbor." Worst answer ever, but saying more felt too raw, and she wasn't sure she could go there.

"That's where I lived. But who am I?"

She met his gaze. She'd planned on telling him she got the point, but he had shifted just enough for the light to catch his left eye and there was a raw vulnerability there. A questioning. No, not a questioning. A pleading.

He wasn't just trying to make a point. He needed to know he was seen. That he wasn't alone. That he could trust her with the darkest parts of who he was and she wouldn't throw him away like his mom had.

Grace angled her shoulder into the seat so she was fully facing him. "You're a protector. You're a survivor. A helper. A problem solver. Someone who loves deeply but has a hard time letting himself be loved."

He blinked a few times, then closed his eyes. His Adam's apple bobbed, then he drew a loud, long breath. He cleared his throat and half shrugged. "I didn't hear anything about my job at Kensington Fruits. Sure, those things help me do my job. But if I change jobs, I'll still be me. Right?"

"Right."

"You are more than a ballerina." He reached out and squeezed her hand, then quickly pulled back. "And if you changed jobs, you'd still be you. Kind. Graceful. Determined. Caring. Gentle."

"I just can't imagine a life without dance." Or without the memory of his kiss that still lingered on her lips.

"Why do you love ballet?"

What kind of question was that? "Because I'm good at it."

"But why do you dance?"

"I dance because I'm a dancer." This was the same merry-go-round that she found herself on with Ms. Margret. Confusing and unhelpful.

Her frustration must have shown because he held up a calming hand. "Think about the last time you danced and it filled you with joy. Or the last time you were so excited to take the stage that it was like a current running through you."

"I honestly can't remember."

"Do you want to quit?"

"I don't think that's an option."

"Do you still love it?"

"I don't know. Everything at my level is super competitive. Intense. Fighting for the best part." She lifted her hands, then let them drop in her lap. "I've made a few friends in the process but a lot more frenemies. When it got hard before, I would remember that little girl on her first day of class at Ms. Margret's, just proud of her pink tights and dancing with all heart and no skill. But the longer I'm in this, the harder it is to pull up that memory in my mind."

"Do you think that's why you love to teach?"

"I'm not sure I'd say I love it. Like it, definitely."

"Are you kidding? You come alive when you teach. You're

practically glowing every time you finish a class. When that little girl with dark curly hair showed up the other day when we were training—"

"Lucy."

"Well, when Lucy showed up, you stopped everything to help her. You gave her an extra hour of private lessons, and I'm guessing you didn't charge her."

"She almost had her chaînés. She got it in the end." Grace bit her lip, unable to keep from smiling again.

"See, you love it."

"Their joy is contagious. You know, I was disappointed with what happened with the nonaudition, but I was also a little relieved. I wasn't ready to end the class yet."

"You should see if you could perform at the Fourth of July festival."

"In less than two weeks?"

"It can't hurt to ask."

They dropped into silence again, Seth shifting in his seat. "I guess it's my turn. Care to walk?"

"Sure." It had been a warm day, but the air blowing off the lake had a bite to it. Grace pulled her jacket a little tighter as she stepped out into the brisk night.

Seth climbed out and nodded toward the sidewalk. Grace dropped into step beside him. Even at nine thirty, there were a fair number of people on the beach.

"I am a recovering alcoholic and a recovering drug addict." His voice sounded almost robotic.

So they were diving right in. She nodded for him to continue, not really wanting to stop his flow now that he was finally sharing.

"You might assume after meeting my mom that I got into that scene at a young age. But after seeing what it did to my mother, initially I stayed away from the stuff." He stared up at the night sky a moment, then back at her. His voice relaxed into their usual familiarity. "My junior year was particularly rough, and I just wanted to . . . escape. Gabe had already been using on the side, and it didn't seem that bad. But whether it was genetics, life choices, or just randomness, that first hit quickly turned into a life of addiction."

"Like Gabe."

"More than Gabe. He seemed to be able to pull back when he needed to, but for me, it became an obsession like I had never known before. It had a hold on me. The same hold I see in my mother."

"How did you finally give it up?" She released a strong shiver.

"I'm sorry. Let's head back to the car. I thought walking would help, but I don't want you to get hypothermia. They turned back toward the car, walking in tense silence while they retraced their steps and got back in the car.

"The night Gregory died is a bit of a blur. I remember buying drugs." Seth tapped his fingers on the steering wheel and then gripped it tight as if it cost him to go back there in his mind. "Gabe and I went to an abandoned shed in the woods off Dearing. Our usual spot. About an hour in, Gregory showed up."

A lump formed in Grace's throat at the mention of his name. Her heart squeezed so painfully that she became sick to her stomach, just like when she heard of her brother's death for the first time. She stared across the water again as the moon dipped closer to the horizon, the lighthouse fading in the dim skyline. "I didn't even know he used."

"I don't think he did. At least he never had around us." Seth returned to tapping. "But he kept going on about his Econ test and how angry your parents were going to be."

She could almost picture her brother's face. He'd get so worked up about grades. The lump in her throat had grown into a large boulder. She swallowed past it as she closed her eyes. "And then?"

"I honestly don't know. One minute he was complaining, the

next he wasn't breathing. We were deep enough in the woods and so high, that by the time we got him help, it was too late."

Her breath left her as she leaned forward on her hands. Too late. Because he was dead. And she never saw him again. Never spoke to him again. Never heard his laugh. His voice.

"Turns out the drugs he took were laced with fentanyl."

Her head jerked toward him. She could have lost more than Gregory that night. She could have lost everyone. "Then why didn't it affect you or Gabe?"

"The labs came back that only Gregory's bag was tainted." He gripped the steering wheel so hard she feared it might snap. "I don't know. I'd never had problems before. I honestly only remember buying two bags. Maybe the guy slipped it in because there were definitely three, and one was bad." His voice broke at the end.

She had lost a brother, and he had lost a friend. Not just a friend in Gregory, but a friend in Gabe that day. "How were you blamed and not Gabe?"

He blinked at her, his eyes red with emotion. "You really don't know any of this?"

No, and it was long overdue that she did. "My parents protected me, or at least what they called protecting me. I came home for the funeral but was pushed back into my program less than a week later. They wouldn't tell me anything. Told me I needed to focus."

Seth rested his head back and closed his eyes. "Gabe was seventeen. I had just turned eighteen. Gregory was twenty, but he had no drug history and was dead. Your parents were angry—still are angry—and I don't blame them. So the DA went after me. Drug possession with the intent to distribute. Felony."

"But Gabe—"

"Left me standing alone." He lifted his head and returned to staring out the front window. "The guy who I thought would have my back no matter what . . ."

"Did you go to jail?" Hadn't her mom said something about that?

"I was given the option of jail or a rehab program. I chose rehab. And Grant went to bat for me to get me assigned to his ranch—Quinn Ranch. It was the best thing that ever happened to me."

"Getting convicted was the best thing that ever happened to you?"

"If that hadn't happened, I'd be just like Gabe." He shook his head and leaned forward again. "I'd be worse off than Gabe. I'd be like my mother."

"Grant saved you?"

"No. God saved me. Grant just pointed me in the right direction and told me to stop being an idiot."

God saved him? Grace turned her face toward her side window. "Then why didn't God save Gregory?"

"I don't know. I wish He had. It should have been me instead."

"I blamed myself for a long time."

"For Gregory's death? How do you figure that? You were in Paris at the time."

"The day before he died, a bunch of us in the program snuck out of the dorms. We didn't do anything horrible, but definitely enough to get sent home. I remember thinking as I climbed into bed that night that my parents were wrong, bad choices didn't always come with consequences. I woke up to the call that I had a ticket on the next flight home. At first, I thought it was because we were found out. But it was Gregory. I thought it was God's punishment."

"God doesn't work that way, Grace. He isn't up there waiting for a chance to punish us."

"Are you sure?"

"I may not have everything figured out about God, but I do know He's ready to forgive us every time we fail."

"God never really played a big role in our family outside of Sundays."

"Maybe that's why you don't know who you are."

She whipped her head to face him. "What do you mean by that?"

"I'm not trying to offend you." He held up his hands. "I just know that before I could really understand who I was, I had to understand how God saw me."

God saw him? Did He see her? "How does He see you?"

"As His child. Not an easy concept since my mom wasn't the greatest example of a parent. But I have a few vague memories of my dad. My dad always believed in me, always loved me, never missed a phone call when he was deployed. He was faithful. Always built me up, never tore me down. He was a good dad."

"Sounds like it." She reached across the car and grabbed his hand. "I bet he'd be proud of who you've become."

"I think he finally would be." He captured her fingers with his thumb and then let it trail across her hand a moment. "He used to say 'Tomorrow's a new day with no mistakes.'"

"Smart man we could both learn from." Why did his touch affect her so much?

"Yeah." He pulled his hand back and tucked it under his leg.

She rested her head back on the headrest. "What are we doing?"

"I wish I could say this will work. But let's be real, your parents will never support this." He met her gaze. "And, you're going back to Chicago."

He seemed to be waiting. But waiting for what, her to disagree? Everything he said was spot-on. And she didn't see that changing. So instead, she just nodded and shrugged. "We've never had the best timing, have we?"

"You could say that." He turned to stare out the front window again. Wall back in place.

Everything in her wanted to scream, but what options did she have? "So where does that leave us?"

"Friends?" He started the car and started backing out of the spot.

Could they be just friends? In Chicago, she would have said absolutely, when he'd shown up in the studio to tell her about his presentation with that big grin on his face, she would have said probably, but now after knowing what it felt like to be held by him, kissed by him, just friends seemed straight up impossible.

She started to say as much, but the hope in his expression stopped her. He needed a friend right now and how could she refuse that?

"Friends. We'll just pretend the kiss never happened."

The muffler rumbled louder than normal as he hit the throttle, but she could have sworn he mumbled the words, "Not likely."

Two days later, the plan for his Wednesday had been simple: come to Jon's house, talk to him, then return to the studio for a few hours of lifting. How did Seth find himself in a playroom having a tea party with two bears, a doll whose hair had seen much better days, and little Becca, who was holding a teacup up to her eye as if she might be able to see through the solid plastic.

Seth caught the straw hat that was way too small, as it slipped off his head. He put it back on and prayed the chair under him wouldn't break. He hadn't even known they made chairs this small.

"Becca, no. It's a teacup." Vangie pulled the cup out of her sister's hand and set it back on the saucer, her strawberry blonde curls swinging. She wore a very colorful apron and pointed to the tiny cup in front of him. "Uncle Seth, you have to drink the tea. And don't forget to stick a pinky out."

That wouldn't be a problem. Seth picked up the tiny cup with his thumb and first two fingers. There was no way he was getting his ring finger on the tiny handle, let alone his pinky. He lifted the cup to his mouth and offered his best pretend sip. "Mmm. Yum."

Vangie stuck her little fists on her waist. "I haven't poured it yet."

Then why did she tell him to drink it? Seriously, the logic of a three-year-old was way beyond him. He looked over at little Becca for help, but she was now trying to balance the cup on her head.

"Vangie, Becca." Leah appeared in the room. "Your mom is on the way. Why don't you get your bags ready to go."

The girls ran from the room squealing.

Leah bit back a laugh. "That cape is definitely your color."

He'd forgotten about the purple cape that Vangie had draped around his shoulders before handing him that hat. He pulled off both as he stood.

"You're a life saver." Leah took the hat and cape, then dropped them in a box of clothes, then started gathering the tiny dishes and adding them to another box. "I was able to finally get Isabella sleeping for a moment. Jon texted. He'll be a bit longer. Now tell me what is going on with you and Grace."

What? Where had that come from?

"I've heard you two were spending a lot of time together." She sent him a smile that had a lot of hidden meaning in it. He just wasn't a hundred percent sure what the hidden meaning was.

"We're just friends."

"Of course you are."

He wasn't going to stand here and try to convince Leah he didn't feel anything for Grace. Because that was a lie. But they were just friends. Wishing that could be different wouldn't change anything.

Before Leah could answer, Isabella's tiny cry sounded from the speaker at her hip. Leah closed her eyes a moment, drawing a deep breath. "I swear she must be going through a growth spurt because this week that kid has not stopped eating. I can't keep up with her.

I blame Jon and all six-four of him. Luckily, I have some milk in the freezer. Can you grab her while I get that ready?"

Leah walked out of the room. He wasn't exactly sure what all that meant, but he was pretty certain she wanted him to pick up Isabella. He made his way down the hall to the wailing infant.

He walked over to the crib and peeked in. Leah kept talking about how big Isabella was getting, but this baby still seemed tiny to him. He reached out and lifted the infant under her armpits. The crying continued.

"That's not how you do it." Vangie appeared next to him. "You make your arms like you're holding a watermelon, then the baby sits in the hole. It's easier sitting down."

For a three-year-old that might work, but for him, she'd fall right through his arms, but he got the gist. He turned Isabella's back to him, and she settled into the crook of his arm. Her fussing halted as her wide eyes watched him.

He'd never held a baby before. And the complete trust in her eyes as she stared at him hit him solid in the chest.

One idea he'd given up long ago was that of a family. Of love. It wasn't for him. But this . . . He'd never experienced anything like it.

"I believe God has a bigger plan for you than hiding from your past." He'd never quite believed that, but looking into Isabella's face right now, he wanted to believe it like never before.

"Don't you have the magic touch," Leah spoke from next to him. "Seriously, I tell Jon you can do this, and he might shift your hours to nursery duty for the next couple of months."

"I teached him how to hold her." Vangie patted his leg with her hand. "He was holding her like a stinky cat."

"You did a good job." Leah lifted Vangie up and dropped her on her hip. "Your mom's here."

Vangie held up her hand to her mouth like she was telling a secret but put it on the wrong side. "Did she have the baby?"

Leah's gaze darted to Seth then back. "That won't be for a long time, sweetie. Not until almost the end of February. Remember, it's a secret."

She shrugged and looked at Seth. "Dats why I whispered."

Leah lowered Vangie to the floor and the little girl ran from the room with a squeal. Seth started to hand the baby to Leah, but she backed up.

"No way. She's happy. You don't wake a sleeping baby, and you don't mess with a happy baby who has been fussy all week. Oh, and Jon's here. He's in his office." Leah disappeared out the door.

He eyed the bundle in his arms who still looked up at him with wide eyes. "I guess it's you and me, kid."

He made his way down the grand staircase, across the foyer and through the living room to the door of the study. This place needed a map. He knocked once before walking in, keeping Isabella rocking as he went. She seemed to like the movement. Jon was digging through a pile of papers. He glanced up when Seth walked in but didn't pause his work. "I have about ten minutes before I have to leave for another meeting. Shoot."

He shifted Isabella and started to bounce her. "I was thinking we could set up a mini ninja gym experience for the festival."

"Dude, we only came up with the initial plan like two days ago and the festival is in a week. What do you think we can accomplish in that amount of time?"

"I'm not talking about the built-in kind that we have planned, but I've found a few companies that rent temporary setups for a reasonable price. It's a series of six to twelve obstacles, depending on which package you get, like rings, climbing walls, and one had tilting paddles. It's all low stuff, but it could be a good sample of what we're planning."

"Okay, I'm following. Is this just to promote the new rec center/ ninja gym? We're a long way from promotion. We don't even have solid plans."

"I figured we could sell tickets, and the money could go toward the books at the library. Isn't that the main fundraiser this year? Connect with the community and all that."

Jon nodded as he tapped his pen on his chin. "I'd have to run it by Mayor Jameson and Hannah. She's in charge of the whole thing, but I don't see why it would be a problem."

"It's also supposed to be pretty humid next week, and the AC guy came yesterday. The building should be cool by then."

"Sounds like you have it all figured out." Jon laced his fingers across his stomach. "What do you need from me?"

"If you could talk to the mayor and Hannah like you said, I can secure the rental for tomorrow. We just need a deposit."

"I like it. And I know what you said, but just imagine"—Jon moved his hands as if displaying a sign—"The Storm's gym. Thunder Arena. Bring the—"

"No, I've told you I don't want my name attached."

Isabella started to fuss, and Jon stepped around the desk and claimed his daughter. "I'm not sure that's a good marketing decision on your part. But I will accommodate. Oh, and since you're signed up for the Fourth of July festival bachelor auction, we can just close it for that hour. Can't have our *prize horse* miss out. Margret is saving her pennies after all."

When Seth's only response was to groan, he added with a chuckle, "Consider it a rite of passage."

A rite of passage. The right to belong in town.

"It has happened to the best of us." Jon slapped him on the back. "I'm just glad that I'm married now."

"Glad to hear that." Leah walked in, lifted Isabella from his arms, and planted a kiss on his cheek. "Although if the biggest pro of our marriage is that you get out of the bachelor auction, we may need to reevaluate things."

Jon pulled out a card from his wallet and handed it to him. "Use this for the rental. This is a great plan. I'm proud of you Seth."

Proud.

That was the second time Jon had used the word. And the word hit him this time as much as it had the first time. Maybe he could see a future with possibilities. A future he'd never considered before.

Jon took a step toward his office door but turned back. "Oh, and you're welcome to move your weights over to the rec center now. Give you and Grace both more space."

Jon walked out the door and was gone before Seth could agree or disagree.

But why wouldn't he agree? After all, a space where he didn't have to move his weights every day would be great. At least it should be. No doubt Grace would love more space. Then why did it leave him feeling so empty?

Ten minutes later as he pulled into the parking lot to the studio, he still couldn't answer that question. He put the car in park and froze. Gabe leaned against the building next to the door to the studio. He took a long drag of something in his hand, his gaze never leaving Seth. One glance at the parking lot told him Grace wasn't there yet, which meant Gabe was there for one reason—to talk to him. Lucky him.

He didn't know what Gabe's game was but whatever it was, Seth didn't like it. He climbed out of his car and walked toward the studio door.

He fit the key into his lock but didn't open the door. "Go away, Gabe. We have nothing to talk about."

"I think we do." He flicked the ash from the joint in his hand. "I'm pretty sure you still owe me a favor or two."

"I owe you nothing." So like Gabe, his first tactic was always manipulation and guilt. But Seth was done playing his game.

"You see, I haven't told my parents what I saw yesterday." Gabe stepped forward as if he were ready to follow Seth inside to settle in for a long talk. "So if you want me to keep my mouth shut—"

Seth blocked his path to the door then put his hand in the middle of Gabe's chest, pressing him against the building. Gabe had a couple of inches on him, but Seth was stronger. A lot stronger. And the fear that flashed in Gabe's eyes testified that he remembered that Seth had once had a very bad temper.

Seth pushed a little harder, bringing a grunt from Gabe. "I owe you nothing. Grace owes you nothing. Stay away from me and stay away from Grace."

Seth backed up and dropped his arm. Gabe straightened his shoulders and took a step toward his car. "And here I was gonna invite you to a party."

"Let me think about it. No." Seth just shook his head and walked in the door, securing the lock behind him.

His phone buzzed in his pocket, and he pulled it out. Hannah Taylor?

He gave a quick look out the window to see if Gabe was up to anything, but he was gone. Seth accepted the call. "Hello."

"Hey, Seth, I hope this isn't a bad time." Was it him or did she sound nervous?

"No, just got home from a meeting." He searched his mind for what this could be about but came up empty. "I sent the photo for the brochure for the bachelor auction, didn't I?"

"Yes, but . . ."

Maybe it was the wrong size. Maybe he'd get out of doing this town event after all. Jon's words about it being a rite of passage rang in his ears. Even if it was embarrassing, at least maybe it would make him feel like a true Heritagite . . . Heritagonian . . . Heritager? Whatever it was called. "I can send a new one if you need—"

"No, it's not . . . I want you to know I don't agree with this decision. But there have been some complaints when your name was released on the auction list . . ."

Oh.

"Got it." Of course. Had he expected anything different? "That works out perfectly anyway. Jon was going to clear it with you, but

I am going to be running a small ninja course in the warehouse on Teft."

Out of sight.

"Oh, that's great. It's supposed to be quite warm, and you'll no doubt draw quite a crowd." Her voice lifted as if she was relieved he wasn't upset.

"Talk to you later." Seth ended the call. He wasn't upset because this was what he'd expected.

thirteen

O N JUNE THIRD SHE'D PRACTICALLY THROWN
a fit about sharing the studio with Seth and all his equipment.
So how was it, that today, July third, Grace hated his absence.
Even with a full class of girls right now, the place felt empty.

Grace tapped her meter stick against the ground as the girls
leaped over it, each one giggling as they landed. Somehow her
class had grown from Susie and a couple friends to almost a dozen
girls ranging in age from four to fourteen. Their skills were quite
varied, but they were her girls. *"You come alive when you teach."*
Seth's words came back to her. Maybe she did.

Grace walked over to her phone and selected "Dancing Queen"
from her playlist. "You can use the last few minutes to free dance."

The girls squealed and began skipping and dancing around the
room, using every inch of space now that they had it. No more
weights. No more pegboard and chin-up bar. No more white box
where they couldn't dance.

A week ago, Seth had moved all his stuff out of her dance hall.
She should be thrilled, but the truth was, she didn't like it. Not
one little bit. Maybe it wasn't the weights themselves.

It was Seth. Because when all *that* left, so did he. He had a way of filling up the room, and she missed that. She missed him. She'd barely seen him since that day because now he spent all his time at the ninja-warehouse-rec-center-building place. Whatever they called it, he was there and not here.

Maybe he was giving her space. After all, his revelation about Gregory had shaken her. How could it not?

But as angry as she was, she couldn't find it in herself to blame him for Gregory's death. Seth had been a lost kid, nothing more sinister than that. He'd had no one to protect him. He had been alone and basically homeless. He was no more at fault than Gabe. Definitely no more at fault than her parents and their impossible expectations, the same expectations that had been suffocating her own life for as long as she could remember.

Ultimately, Gregory had made his own choice, and they'd all paid for it. Gregory, Gabe, and Seth. Those awful drugs had taken all three of them from her in different ways. The part she couldn't let go of was everyone who had known and hadn't told her. She had a right to know. It was her brother after all, and at least Seth had been going to tell her.

So, after all of the soul-searching, she was right back where she had started. She missed Seth. The question was, was he avoiding her or was he just busy doing his job?

Grace stepped over to the music and selected the cooldown mix she'd made on Spotify. "Okay, ladies. Find your spots."

Grace waited for them to find their number on the floor and assume first position. "Good. And lift through your core."

Grace walked them though the five positions, then again, and one more time. "That was a great class today, girls. Remember, even though tomorrow is Thursday, there's no class tomorrow because tomorrow is the—"

"Fourth of July festival," they all yelled in unison.

"That's right. And this year they're extending the events to go through Saturday. And I've arranged—and approved with your parents—for us to perform Saturday at ten o'clock for the whole town in the gazebo."

They all lit up in smiles, and Susie raised her hand.

"Yes, Susie."

"Are you going to do one of your fancy dances too on Saturday?"

"No, Saturday is about you guys."

"Ms. Margret said we should ask you real nice. Then you might do it."

All the girls broke into a round of *please*s as each one clutched their hands to their chest.

"I'll think about it." She lifted the notes she'd printed off for the parents. "Make sure to give these to your parents. It has all the details for Saturday about where you need to be and when."

All the girls lined up to take a flyer, then ran to their bags. They replaced their ballet shoes with street shoes and rushed to the mothers waiting on the sidewalk just outside the front door.

Grace walked over and picked up her water bottle and checked the time on her phone. There was a missed message.

ALEC
_____

We have run into a problem with Giselle.

We will be readjusting the cast for Sunday's performance.

When can you get here?

GRACE
_____

You are reauditioning the part?

ALEC
_____

No, it is yours.

If you can do it to Madam Laurent standards.

205

She read the message once. Then again. What could have happened?

GRACE

I have a commitment, but I can be there Sunday.

ALEC

Saturday

But Saturday was the day of the performance in the square with the girls. But could she really give up this opportunity? Pushing back could cost her everything, but she refused to let her girls down.

GRACE

Sunday.

There was a long pause before the three dots finally appeared.

ALEC

Sunday, 8AM. Don't be late.

She typed-out "Sunday, 8AM. I'll be there." Her finger hovering over the send button as the knot in her stomach tightened. Her father's voice echoed in her head, telling her that she was a fool to put it off a day. Ms. Margret's voice in her head questioning if she wanted to go back at all. And then there was Seth. Amazing Seth, whose voice wasn't in her head because he was just silent.

She drew a calming breath and read over the words again. She was committing to a weekend, not her whole future, and she owed it to herself and everyone else to hear them out. It was one day. She hit send and turned toward the front of the studio.

She screamed as she came face-to-face with Susie. Her hand

flew to her chest as she released a small laugh. "What are you still doing here?"

The little girl giggled as if surprising Grace was half the fun. "My dad is working tonight, so my brother was supposed to walk me home. But he's not here."

"Do you want me to walk you home?"

The little girl shook her head, her blonde pigtails flapping back and forth. "I can't stay home alone."

"Of course." Grace eyed the front door. "Do you know where your brother might be?"

She nodded. "The new gym place with Seth, Pastor Nate, and Jimmy. Can you walk me there?"

Her heart sped up at the idea. But she wasn't chasing him— Susie needed her to go. "Of course. Just let me change my shoes."

Grace quickly replaced her pointe shoes with street shoes and led them out before securing the lock.

"That sure is a lot of people." Susie pointed across the street at the town square where a good share of the townspeople were busy setting up booths, decorations, and a few carnival games.

"Sure is." Grace held out her hand to Susie. "Are you planning on going tomorrow?"

"My dad has to work," she said with an extra dramatic sigh. "And my brother said he has to help Seth at the ninja thing. So, I have to stay there with him all day."

"Maybe you and I could go together for part of it."

The little girl's eyes lit up. "Really?"

Yeah, really? A month ago, she'd told Ms. Margret she wasn't a kid person, and here she was volunteering to spend the day with Susie. "See what your dad says."

"Are you going to do the solo?"

"I told you I'd think about it."

"What's there to think about? Doesn't dancing make you happy?"

"Sometimes." That was the most honest she'd been about that question.

"I looove it." The little girl spun under Grace's arm. "My daddy told me that when I dance it makes God happy."

"Why do you think that is?" What she really wanted to ask was what made her dad think some crazy thing like that, but she didn't want to be rude.

"He says that God put that seed of dancing in my heart, and now He has given me the opportunity so He loves when I do it. Or something like that."

Susie threw her hands up but didn't let go of Grace's hand. "You should do the dance and you should do a lift at the end. It would make God happy."

Grace offered a quick glance up and down Richard Street and Second Street before they crossed. "A lift?"

Halfway across Susie dropped her hand and ran ahead to where Otis sat at the corner as if watching all the setup happening on the square. The girl jumped on his back and walked up and down, with her arms out for balance. Funny, it didn't bother her when Susie stood on Otis. But Otis was always meant to be climbed on and loved by kids, not used as a foot prop for her brother. She held out her hand to Susie again. "How would I do a lift by myself?"

The little girl took it and jumped down. "Not by yourself. With Seth. I told you he's strong."

Yes, he was. She wasn't sure if a lift would make God happy, but it sure would make her happy.

The location for the future rec center sat only twenty yards away, up on the left, and the lights were on inside.

When she got to the unremarkable brown building, she banged on the door, but with the music blasting no one would ever hear them.

She opened the door and led Susie inside. The place had been an old warehouse and still retained most of that look. No doubt they'd change a lot more, given more time, but for now, it was primarily a large empty room with obstacle-course-like structures in the center.

The course, which appeared temporary, started with a variety of rings, ropes, and what looked like monkey bars mounted on rotating barrels that were to swing across. After that was a rock wall designed for climbing sideways rather than climbing up, then a series of angled platforms and balance beams. Another climbing obstacle followed, then a curved ramp that led up to a high wall. There was also an inflatable obstacle course for younger kids. None of the challenges looked high enough to get injured if someone fell, especially since there were thick, padded mats lining the whole floor under them.

"You have to trust yourself and reach for it." Seth's voice echoed in the room, but she couldn't see him. "You only gave a half reach and now you lost your momentum. You won't make it."

Grace followed his voice around to the other side of the structure where a whole different set of obstacles ran the length of it. Zane held on to one ring and reached for another. Seth was right, they were too far apart to reach from one to the next without a swing, but the kid just dangled, refusing to give up.

"Drop and try again." Nate's voice was firm but not unfriendly. And when the kid didn't drop, he added, "There's no shame in it. That's why it's called practice. We're all learning."

"Just like I'm learning ballet." Susie spoke from next to her.

Everyone turned, and Grace's face warmed. She lifted her hand and waved. Maybe she should have announced their presence when they'd arrived.

Zane dropped when he saw them and hurried over to grab his stuff. "Sorry, Susie. I didn't realize how late it was."

"I'm good. I was having a good talk with Miss Grace." Then she pointed at Seth. "She needs your help with a lift Saturday."

Seth's brows rose but he remained quiet. Before anyone could comment, Zane ran over and grabbed Susie's hand, then waved goodbye. "See you tomorrow."

"Tomorrow." Seth nodded.

Nate's gaze bounced between Grace and Seth for a second before he dramatically checked his watch. "My, look at the time. I'll walk you home, Jimmy."

The kid looked at him, his brow wrinkled. "But, I don't—"

"See you tomorrow, Seth." Nate pointed Jimmy toward the door, and the two disappeared, with Jimmy still sending him questioning looks.

"Sorry. Nate isn't known for his subtlety." Seth loosened the Velcro on his lifting gloves and tugged them off.

"So will you be in here most of the day tomorrow during the festival?" Grace stepped over to the rings where Zane had been.

"We'll run the whole day except during the bachelor auction. They're trying to get as many people over there to bid as possible."

She stepped up on the mini platform and eyed the obstacle. It didn't look that hard. "Well, we have to have Heritage's finest out there bringing in money. The library needs those books."

His movement stalled a moment, one glove half off before he nodded and tossed it aside. "Yup."

He pointed to the rings. "It's harder than it looks. But you're welcome to try. It's safe."

Grace let her ballet bag slip from her shoulder to the floor then stretched up on her toes and grabbed the first ring. She swung out and grabbed the second.

"Looking good so far." Seth stood a few feet away, arms crossed, head cocked to one side. "Now focus on the next ring or you'll miss it and lose your momentum."

She swung and let the momentum carry her to the next. "I did it!"

A smile creased his face, and that was all it took for her to lose her focus. On the next swing, she missed the ring on the first try, and by the second swing, she wasn't close enough to reach. She hung from the one ring, dangling in the air. "I made the same mistake Jimmy did."

"Yup. Biggest thing with ninja warrior obstacles. You have to be all in. Any hesitation and you'll miss."

Maybe that was her problem in life. She was a ball of hesitations. Returning to the stage. Teaching. Even things with Seth. She wanted to get to know him better, she liked him, she trusted him, and yet she held back.

"Come over to this obstacle." Seth's words pulled her from her thoughts. "It's much more up your alley." He then swung across the rings as if it took little to no effort and landed on the opposite platform that faced a row of discs that stretched from one side to the other.

"Show off." She joined him on the platform and eyed the obstacle. "Let me guess, they tilt."

"Like six little teeter-totters. But with your balance and quick foot movement, you should be able to make it. Just don't stop. Trust yourself, and don't hesitate."

She lined up and made a mad dash, but just over halfway she paused and that was all it took to tip her off the side. She landed on the mat and rolled. Oof. Talk about a learning curve.

"You done?"

"Do you even know me?" She walked back to the start and gave it another run. This time she made it most of the way. But at the last second, it shifted and tossed her into the foam barrier. She glanced back at Seth still watching her with little or no expression. She climbed out the far side and set up to run it the opposite way toward him.

Don't hesitate. All in. She could do it. She could do it with Seth. She could do it as a teacher. And she could do it with these ridiculous twisting discs.

This time she made quick, light steps and didn't hesitate until her feet reached the landing. She put her arms in the air. "I'm a ninja warrior!"

Seth took a step toward her, then seemed to think better of it and hopped off the platform. "You are."

He walked over to another obstacle, adjusting one of the ropes. "Is your class dancing tomorrow?"

"Saturday. The girls want me to do a solo at the end."

"You should."

"I think I'm going to." Don't hesitate. All in. Make the move forward. "They also want me to do the lift." She spoke slowly hoping it would hide how much she was shaking on the inside. "Which means I need you."

He shoved his hands in his pockets and shrugged. "I don't dance."

"You don't have to dance, just lift. You've done it before." Before when he held her. Before when he kissed her.

His gaze shifted from suspicious to something hungry in a split second, and she had no doubt he was thinking about after the lift as well. But just as quickly as it had appeared, it vanished. Right. Just friends.

"I promise it's easier than you think." She grabbed his hand as he passed and tugged him over to a firm mat that was lying there. She pointed to a spot for him to stand and then walked a few feet away. "We'll be in the gazebo and you'll just wait to one of the sides when I'm dancing like this."

She did a quick pirouette, stopping with her back to him a foot away. "Now you step in and wrap your arms around me like you're capturing me."

"Dancing."

"Hugging. You've hugged people before. I'm a fairy and you were watching me, and now you've captured me. Try it."

He hesitated a moment then wrapped his arms around her loosely.

"More dramatic and sort of lean over me like you're trying to prevent me from flying away."

He stared at her for a long moment, and Grace thought he might walk away. So much for going all in. But just when she'd about given up, he stepped up and did it again, his face landing right by her neck.

"Now what?" The deep timbre of his voice traveled from his chest up her spine, sending awareness through every inch of her body.

"You slide your hands around to my back as you step back and we do the lift like last time. Then you turn a full circle, then lower me, and I dance away." Why was her voice so breathy?

"I'll try." His voice was deep and gravelly. "I'll warn you. I'm no dancer."

"Let me put on some music." She lifted her phone from her bag and sifted through her favorite songs until she found "Perfect" by Ed Sheeran. She tapped play then turned up the volume. She locked eyes with him as the first few words about finding love floated in the air.

His back stiffened. Maybe this was a mistake, but it was like he'd said, she had to go all in. Hold nothing back. She was falling in love with him, and she was tired of trying to hide it. If he thought he could simply walk away from this, from her, there was no way she was going to make it easy on him. She lifted her arms and did a series of turns that landed her close to where he stood.

She gave a slight nod, and he stepped forward and wrapped his arms around her, then his hands moved to her back. They bent in unison as if they'd been dancing together for years and he lifted her in the air. He did the turn and then lowered her. But instead of setting her on the ground, he lowered her to his chest and then eased her to the ground, her head resting in the crook of his neck. The words from the chorus seemed to parallel the moment and wrap a spell around them.

She never realized how much this song fit them, fit their story. They were fighting against the odds. But she wanted their happy ending. Just like the song. Maybe he was feeling it too because he still stood right behind her, his nose brushing against her ear.

"I thought you were supposed to dance away." The breath of his words brushed against the side of her face.

"Yup." Yet she still wasn't moving. They fit. Not just in each other's arms but in each other's hearts, as if they had ready-made spots carved out special just for them.

She lifted her hand up and over his head. She ran her fingers softly through his hair then slid them down past his ear and jaw until she reached her own shoulder. "But this could work too."

Seth finally stepped back, and she immediately missed him. "If that's all it is, I think I can do that. What time Saturday?"

"Ten in the morning."

"I'll be there." He turned back to work.

But no matter how much she wanted this, it would never work unless both of them were all in.

Maybe just friends were all they'd ever be, could ever be.

No. She refused to believe that. Seth was just used to people walking away from him when life got too hard. He couldn't see his own worth. And maybe the only future he could see for them was one where she walked away, but she could see something different. Somehow, she was going to find a way to show him that.

It had been a long day of never-ending festival customers, so shutting the door and placing the sign Closed for Bachelor Auction should come with more satisfaction than it did. Not that he wanted to be out there. The last thing Seth wanted was to be bid on—or not bid on—by the town. What he did need was an hour to work out to get his head straight and that was exactly what he had.

Seth secured the sign to the door, shut off the main lights, and set the timer on his phone. One hour.

Seth walked back to the obstacles, his phone ringing as he went. He scooped it up. Unknown number. Could be about the festival. He accepted the call.

"This is Seth."

"Seth, this is Allen Mets of *Ninja Warrior*. We still haven't received your acceptance to the regional in Chicago—"

"I'm not going."

"I'm sorry to hear that. You were quite the crowd favorite. Is there anything I can do to change your mind?"

"Can I run it without being on camera, doing interviews, or spotlight features?"

"That's sort of how we pay for things around here, Seth."

"I get that. I . . . just can't."

There was a deep sigh on the other end. "I am sorry to hear that. If you change your mind, you have my number."

"Thank you, sir." He ended the call, tossed his phone aside, and peeled off his shirt. Some people wanted to make a poster child of him, others wanted to shut him away in here like the town's dirty little secret.

And him? What did he want?

That was easy . . . Grace. Wow, he'd never wanted anything so much in his life than to hold her in his arms, to see her smile, to go back to that easy day they had in Chicago when he felt like they belonged together.

Stupid just friends. He could barely be in the same room with her without wanting to revisit that kiss. But it was best in the long run. As much as he cared for her, wanted her, even . . . dare he say loved her, the cards were stacked against them.

He jumped up to his pegboard and started moving the pegs through the numbered holes, ready to burn a little of this irritation away. It wasn't that he wanted to go to the auction, or even be in the auction—he was thankful that hadn't worked out. The whole thing just made him mad.

On his third rotation of working the pegs from one to twenty-five, a small feminine "Oh" made him pause.

He looked over his shoulder to find a wide-eyed Grace standing about twenty feet away.

Oh boy.

He dropped to the ground and snagged his shirt from where he'd thrown it. "Everything okay?"

She blinked at him and then again. Now she was really concerning him.

He slipped the shirt over his head and took a step toward her. "Grace?"

She seemed to shake herself back to the present, then turned accusing eyes on him. "Why aren't you in the bachelor auction?"

"What?" He grabbed a towel from his bag and wiped his face.

"The bachelor auction. You told me Hannah asked you and you agreed. But you aren't on the list." She waved a pamphlet in the air. "And you aren't even there. Why?"

He stepped over to his water and took a large gulp. "Let it go."

"I will not let it go." She withdrew a wad of cash from her purse. "I brought my money and—"

"Then bid on someone else. I heard there was quite the lineup this year." He walked over to the table where they'd been collecting money all day.

"I don't want to bid on anyone else." She marched over and stopped in front of the table opposite him.

"Trust me. It's better this way."

"Better?" Grace pressed her lips into a thin line and practically stomped her foot. "Stop suggesting that you have no value or that nobody wants you. People want you here. I want you . . . here."

He crossed his arms and met her gaze. "Not everyone feels the same." His voice came out thick and rough.

"You keep saying that, but from what I've seen—"

"Your parents." The words came out like a loud smack.

"What?"

He lowered his tone and ducked his head. "I found out they called Hannah and said that I wasn't a suitable person to represent the town. They give quite a bit toward the festival and said they'd withdraw their support if I wasn't removed. They said they'd talk to others."

"I'm sorry. They shouldn't have done that."

Her hand landed on his arm, but he pulled back. "Maybe. Maybe not. But aren't you glad now that you didn't bid on me in front of the whole town?"

Her brow wrinkled. "No. I still want to bid on you."

Sure she did. That was easy to say when it wasn't a possibility. He opened his mouth to say as much when she pulled a bill from the stack of cash in her hand and slammed it on the table. "One hundred dollars."

"I'm not doing this."

She pulled out another bill and added it to the first. "Two hundred."

"Grace, it's a nice gesture but nothing changes." He raised his hands and walked a few feet away. "What's first? We secretly bid then have a secret date, for our secret life? I can't be your dirty little secret."

She pulled out a third bill and dropped it on the table. "Three hundred and the date starts now." She jerked her thumb roughly toward the center of town. "Out there in the square. I want a funnel cake and it isn't over until the fireworks by the lighthouse."

"Out there? With the entire town. Where your parents could be? Think this through, Grace." He shook his head. Why couldn't she see this was killing him.

She dropped a few more bills on the pile. "Six hundred. I know what I'm suggesting. You think you aren't worth my time, my money, my inevitable conflict with my parents. But I am trying to show you that you are. You *are* worth all that and so much more."

She stepped around the table, coming to a stop right in front of Seth, her toes just inches from him. "You say you don't see yourself as that thrown-away kid anymore, but I think you do. You don't think that you deserve the friendships this town wants to offer, that you aren't worth someone bidding on you, that someone like me couldn't ever . . . care for a person like you. But you're wrong."

Seth reached up his finger, brushing the edge of her silky cheek. "Why? After what I—"

Her fingers landed on his lips. "Aren't you the one who told me that real love isn't earned?"

Her fingers trailed down his chin then landed on his chest. As if the gravity had shifted, he found himself leaning toward her. She released a small gasp, and her lips parted slightly as her eyes fluttered shut.

The door slammed open as voices filled the room. Seth jerked back just as Grace's eyes popped open. They both took a step back as Nate approached the table, his daughter Charis on his hip.

Nate shifted the toddler to the other side as she kicked and screamed. "Ice cream!"

Grace started at the sound, her gaze darting from Seth to Nate then back to Seth. No doubt she was worried for little Charis, but Seth had seen Nate parent enough to know he did it well. He set a calming hand on Grace's arm and nodded back to the father-daughter pair.

"Stop." Nate's words to his daughter were firm, but he didn't yell.

Her kicking stopped as her lips puckered. "But ice cream."

"You didn't listen to Mommy. So no ice cream."

The little girl nodded as big tears welled in her eyes. "I sorry."

"I forgive you." He dropped a kiss on her forehead. "But still no ice cream today."

Grace offered Seth a small smile, and he dropped his hand.

If what he'd heard from Gabe as a kid was true, Grace's parents' approach was pretty harsh. A far cry from what she just witnessed.

The little girl buried her head in Nate's chest as he claimed one of the chairs at the table, his gaze finally finding them. "Another auction in the books, new record high of bidding. Even set the record for highest bid."

Seth took a step back from Grace. "Then why don't you sound happy?"

"I'm thrilled." His tone remained flat.

"He's just grumpy because the one who set the record was Jackson Mackers." Olivia appeared next to him. Her long white-blonde hair that had been pinned up seemed to be escaping in every direction.

"Olivia's ex, and might I add, a billionaire." He extended his legs out.

Seth's gaze bounced between the couple. "We have a billionaire who lives in town?"

"He grew up here. Doesn't live here. And I never dated him. And here is a solid piece of evidence of who I chose." Olivia leaned over and tapped her daughter on the nose. "I don't get why you're jealous."

"She's got you there." Grace leaned her hip on the table and pointed to the medium-sized bump at Olivia's midline. "And there."

"I'm not jealous. I'm just giving you a hard time." He pulled her close and dropped a kiss on her lips then one on her stomach. "But admit it. I would be more attractive as a billionaire."

"Nope. You're worth more than a billion dollars."

"You are worth all that and so much more." Grace's words came back. His gaze flicked to her, and with the way she was looking at him, maybe she was thinking the same thing.

Without breaking eye contact, Seth rapped his knuckles on the table. "Hey Nate, any chance you can cover for me here? I owe this girl a funnel cake."

"Yes!" Nate and Olivia practically shouted at the same time. Then Olivia added, "I'll help. Take the rest of the night off."

He shook his head but couldn't keep the smile from his face. "Subtle."

But maybe Grace was right—he was of value to his friends, to a good share of the town, and to Grace.

Seth scooped up Grace's six hundred dollars and handed it to her.

"No."

"You made your point." He pulled off one of the bills and added it to the cash box. "You made your donation, but since you can't bid against yourself, the last five hundred didn't count anyway."

She reached in her purse and pulled out a handful more. "I was prepared to bid quite high for you. You might have earned more than the billionaire."

"Well, that deserves a funnel cake and an elephant ear." Then he pointed to his office in the corner. "But let's lock that money away, shall we? I don't like carrying that much cash."

"I'm pretty sure if I'm with you, I'm safe."

His movement stilled and met her eyes. "You really mean that, don't you."

When she only nodded, he pulled her into a giant hug. He dropped a quick kiss on her forehead then motioned toward the office. "Let's lock that money away and get you the funnel cake."

fourteen

HE'D MEANT WHAT SHE'D SAID ABOUT STAND-
ing by Seth, but when her parents started making a beeline
toward her in the funnel cake line, Grace said a prayer of thanks
that Seth was waiting in the elephant ear line and not next to her. She
accepted the strange looking glob of brown pastry covered in white
powder from the vendor.

"What do you think you're doing?" Her mother's tone was
tense, but she kept her volume low.

"It's called a funnel cake, Mom. Just a pastry. No hard drugs
involved." Maybe it wasn't the best time for a joke, but their reaction was way over the top. Of course she still watched her sugar
intake, but she'd been having a little all summer and hadn't burst
into flames yet.

Seth approached, but seeing her parents, he diverted his path
to a neighboring bench. No doubt he wasn't in the mood for a
scene either. And if they reacted this way over sugar, all bets were
off when it came to him.

"Throw that away." Her father's voice was firm, bordering on
harsh.

Seth's jaw seemed to tighten. She needed to regain control of this conversation before it really went south.

"Dad."

"Grace—"

Seth stood.

"Dad. Relax. I am an adult. You wouldn't want to make a scene over sugar."

That did the trick. Her parents were all about appearances, and the words seemed to bring them back to the fact they were in the town square on the most crowded day of the year. She couldn't help but think about Nate and his daughter. Her dad would have flown off the handle if she'd done what Charis had done in public. It could be a front, but with the way the little girl had curled into his chest moments later, she doubted it. There was a sweetness and love there she never saw in either of her parents.

"Well, if you're going to be ready to return to dancing as Giselle, then you need to be training, not eating junk. And why are you going Sunday and not Saturday like they asked?"

"How do you know all that?"

"That isn't important. What is important is—"

"It's very important. I'm an adult. I have been for years. How would you— Alec?"

"You never took our names off your personnel file. We were the responsible parties when you joined the company. We knew we couldn't count on you for updates, so we've been calling him all summer. Don't think we won't ask about the young man who you showed up with a couple weeks ago."

"You've been spying on me."

Her dad gestured to the funnel cake. "Evidently not well enough."

Seth had come closer now. He seriously might break a molar, by the look of his expression.

"I have to go eat my funnel cake and elephant ear with Seth." As soon as she motioned to him, her parents spun to face him.

"You!" her mom spat out.

"Seth is my friend." Maybe more, but one bridge at a time. "You will be nice to him."

"Do you have any idea—"

"I know everything. And I know that the only reason Gregory got high that night was because he couldn't meet your impossibly high expectations."

She knew she shouldn't have said it the moment her mom's face paled and she took a step back. "You don't know what you're talking about."

"I love you both, but I can't do this right now."

She walked past them toward Seth. Her mother took a step to follow, but her dad seemed to stop her. They had started to make a scene, and several people were trying to eye them discreetly from a distance.

When she got to Seth's side, she leaned in. "Can we just go?"

He nodded, took the funnel cake, and led them to his car. He drove for a little while, but Grace didn't even pay attention as to which direction they turned. The green foliage passed by in a blur as the conversation ran over and over again in her head. She should never have said that to her mother. But why did they have to try to control every move she made?

After a few minutes Seth stopped and shoved the car into park, and Grace looked around. A large sand dune sat in front of the car. "Are we at Little Sable?"

"Yup. Thought it was a good place to watch the fireworks tonight. But first . . ." He reached in the back and lifted both plates. "You earned these. One elephant ear and one funnel cake. Which one first?"

She accepted the funnel cake and tore off a piece and dropped it on her tongue. The pastry practically melted in her mouth. "Wow."

"They're even better when they're still warm." He tore off a bit of elephant ear, then passed her the plate. "Try this one. I honestly can't pick a favorite."

She popped it in her mouth and closed her eyes, savoring the sugary goodness. He was right, amazing.

She opened her eyes and reached for another bite. "Do you ever think about making God happy?"

"With funnel cake?" He popped another bite in his mouth. "Don't think that works but I can't say I haven't said a prayer that these will be in heaven one day."

"Susie said something to me about when she dances, it makes God happy."

He nodded and picked another piece of pastry off her plate. "I guess it's all about why you're dancing. If you're dancing for your parents or fame, then I don't know. But if you let all that go and dance for God, not caring what others think, then yeah, I bet it does."

She started to say she agreed, but the intensity in his gaze stopped her.

Suddenly, she could almost picture this as their date number one thousand rather than date number one. Eating together, laughing together, talking over life together, waiting for the sun to go down to set up their blanket for the fireworks together.

Choosing to be together because there was nowhere on earth they'd rather be. No expectations. Just loving the other for who they were.

Love?

Had she really thought that?

A light knock on the window made her jump. She turned to a smiling Susie waving for all she was worth.

"Are you going to the fireworks too?" the little girl yelled though the glass.

Grace glanced back at Seth for a moment before popping the door open. "We are."

"Great! You can share my blanket." Susie lifted a pink and blue blanket for Grace to see. "And look! My daddy got the night off."

"Susie . . ." Her father, who was carrying a blanket and a small cooler with two camp chairs slung over his shoulder, walked up. She hadn't met him before, but somehow, she'd imagined a bald, overweight grump of a man who was too busy for his daughter. But the man before her, with his military-short haircut and wide shoulders, looked anything but lazy. He dropped the cooler and ran an affectionate hand over his daughter's blonde hair, revealing a tattoo of a trident, eagle, and musket encircled by the words *The only easy day was yesterday.* Maybe there was more of a story to their situation than she'd originally thought. "They probably have other plans."

Grace was just about to agree when Seth leaned forward. "We'd love to."

They would? Maybe she was the only one with love on her mind here. Grace climbed out of the car, and Susie slipped her hand into hers.

Seth walked around and popped the trunk and pulled a blanket out, then nodded at Zane, who'd joined them. They all set off to walk between the dunes toward the lake. A few steps in, Susie let go of her hand and ran up one of the dunes, chasing Zane.

Seth dropped into step beside her. "So, back to Chicago Sunday, huh?"

Her heart sank as she closed her eyes for a moment. She hadn't talked to him about that because she hadn't made up her mind if she was going back. "It's just to talk and maybe dance for them. I haven't fully decided if I'll take it."

"Why wouldn't you?"

"I know it's been the goal all the way along, but suddenly I wonder if . . ." *If what I want is right here.*

225

As if he could read her mind, he shook his head. "This is everything you have worked for. You want this. I'm happy for you."

"You are?" Her gaze jerked toward him over her shoulder.

"I appreciate you standing up for me and the truth you spoke earlier. But I'm only here for a short while—"

She stopped in her tracks and looked at him. "I thought you were opening the ninja gym."

"I'll get it set up, but because of the felony, I found out last night that I can't be cleared to work with kids for another year." He shrugged as if it was not a big deal. It was a big deal. This was his passion. "That's why Nate was there to help today."

"Seth." She reached for his arm, but he didn't stop.

"Don't you get it? They want you back. You have a bright future. The future you always wanted."

It was the future her parents always told her she wanted, but had she ever wanted it for herself? "But what if I don't want that future?"

"I've seen you dance. You do." He turned and walked back toward her a few steps. "Don't let your frustrations with your parents cloud your view. You come alive when you dance."

She tossed up her hands, then dropped them on her hips. "You said the same thing about when I teach."

"True." He shrugged and turned to start walking forward again. "But you can always teach when you're done. Live the dream now."

She hurried to catch up and tugged him until he finally stopped and looked at her. "What about us?"

He shoved his hands in his pockets, only emphasizing the width of his shoulders as his head tilted to one side. "After that little encounter earlier, do you really think that's a good idea? Do you want to always be at odds with your parents? Do you want that for your kids?"

No. Not at all. But that was on her parents, not him. Why did that mean she had to sacrifice him? She'd been forced to sacrifice her whole life. Sugar. Proms. Homecomings. Living at home.

When she did have an answer, he nodded just as Susie ran up, tagged him, then ran off. Seth didn't miss a beat running after her, always staying just a few feet out of reach.

He might think this conversation was over, but he was wrong. She finally found something she wanted to fight for, and she wasn't giving up that easily.

What about us? Seth tried to shove Grace's words from last night from his head. He locked the rec center door and walked back to the desk. They'd had a steady flow of future ninja warriors all day. They could have stayed open longer, but Nate had to be somewhere, and Seth had ink on his record that he'd always be under the shadow of.

He dropped into his chair and dopped his head in his hands. He had hoped that keeping busy today would distract him. It hadn't.

Every time he'd closed his eyes. Every time he wasn't helping someone, all he saw were Grace's eyes begging him to love her. He did. That was no question. But he couldn't tie her to a life in conflict with her parents. He had a life of conflict with his mother, and it was so much harder than she knew.

His phone chimed with an incoming text.

GRACE
I need to pick up my money.

Right. He'd forgotten about that. He flipped open the cash box. It was still there. Between what he'd raked in for the festival and her cash, he had to have close to four thousand dollars in there.

SETH

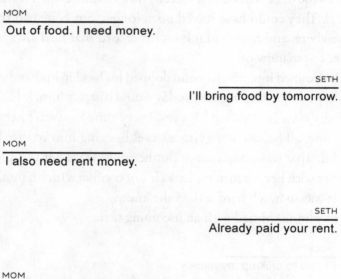

Leaving soon, I'll drop it off.

GRACE

Can you stay and practice the lift again.

Every cell of his body shouted one thing, but his brain didn't agree. His brain won out.

SETH

Pretty busy. But I think we got it.

He slid the phone in his pocket, but it chimed almost immediately. He pulled it out, but it wasn't Grace.

MOM

Out of food. I need money.

SETH

I'll bring food by tomorrow.

MOM

I also need rent money.

SETH

Already paid your rent.

MOM

He said you didn't, and I need it in cash.

Seth leaned back and rubbed his eyes for a moment. Nothing worse than trying to have a conversation with his mom when she was in desperate need of a fix.

I'll be by with food tomorrow, I'll talk to him.

He turned his phone to Do Not Disturb, grabbed his things, and started toward the door. He dropped his keys and when he went to retrieve them his phone nearly slid out of his pocket. He snagged it, flipped off the lights, and headed outside, juggling the phone, a water bottle, the cash box, and keys as he locked up.

There was a missed notification on his phone. He must not have heard the chime with the incoming email. Oh right, it was still on Do Not Disturb. But with the twenty missed incoming texts from his mom, he wasn't turning that off yet.

He tapped on the email and read it over as he walked toward his car.

It was a job offer. A real job offer from JBL, the company in California. The email explained that some of his references had come back slowly but after what people wrote, they had reconsidered. Seth set the cash box and water bottle on top of his car as he reread the email. There was no mistaking it. It was a real, honest job offer doing system analysis starting in two weeks.

He'd told Grace he didn't want to stay in Heritage, but now staring at the opportunity to leave, it didn't feel like he'd expected. Then again, what did he have here? Grace was leaving, and he couldn't open the gym. Jon had dismissed the idea and said Seth would just take over in a year. But who wanted to trust their kids to a guy who had only been legally cleared months before?

He slid his keys into the lock just as movement off to the side caught his attention. Down along the side of the building, Gabe was talking to Zane. They appeared to just be talking, but there was something in the way they stood a couple feet apart that that set Seth's senses on high alert.

He pocketed his phone and stomped that direction. When

Zane saw Seth, his eyes widened. He tossed whatever was in his hand toward Gabe, but it landed on the ground.

Gabe bent over and picked it up. His obvious irritation seemed to melt into amusement as he spotted Seth. "It ain't nothing he ain't done."

"What do you think you're doing?" Seth's words nearly shook.

Zane's gaze darted to him, then back to Gabe, who held the drugs out again to Zane. "Go ahead, take them."

Seth snatched the bag from Gabe's hands and shoved it in his pocket. He'd toss it on the ground, but the last thing he needed was another kid picking it up or a dog eating it.

"I knew you'd come around." Gabe smirked at him. "That's fifty bucks."

"You said it was only ten." Zane's voice spoke from next to them.

Ten? No way that was just ten dollars. Gabe was grooming the kid to be a regular client, and he couldn't even see it. Just like Seth hadn't seen it. And probably like Gabe hadn't seen it with whoever gave him his first.

"Zane, go home." Seth's voice had a steel edge to it that he didn't even recognize. He might be angry now, but he was in the kid's corner whether he knew it or not.

The kid hiked his backpack up a little higher on his shoulder, then hurried past Seth. His footsteps faded but Seth never took his eyes off Gabe.

When he was pretty sure the kid was gone, Seth grabbed the front of Gabe's shirt and slammed him up against the brick side of the building. "If you ever—"

Gabe pushed Seth back, his eyes extra wild. "Who do you think you are? Hammond's new replacement?"

"I'm serious, Gabe. I see you talking to Zane or any other kid in this town again—"

"And how are you going to see me? From what I've heard, you don't plan on staying in town anyway."

"So help me, if you sell one drug—"

"You're going to what? Kill me like you killed my brother?"

"Leave. I'm serious."

"I don't leave. You leave. Over. And over. As soon as someone lets you down—as soon as the cost looks too high, you quit. You quit the *Ninja Warrior* gig, you quit me, and I bet you already have plans to quit this town. The only thing you haven't quit is your mother, and honestly, that's the only thing you should quit."

"Leave my mother out of this."

"But how can I? She's such a valued customer."

Seth heard the crack of his fist connecting with the side of Gabe's face before he even knew his arm was swinging.

He hadn't been in a fight in years, and he hadn't planned on being in one today, but— "You? You're my mom's dealer?" He held up his hand, took a step back before he did something else he'd regret.

Apparently, Gabe had no intention of calling a truce. He threw himself at Seth, wrapping his arms around Seth's middle. Seth shucked Gabe off, but Gabe rounded, and Seth barely dodged a punch aimed at his face. The miss threw Gabe off balance.

Seth sent him reeling with a shot to the ribs. "Gabe, stop! You don't want this!"

But Gabe wasn't stopping. His eyes were full of crazed fury as he came back in.

"Seth! Gabe! Stop." Grace's voice broke through Seth's haze. He searched for her—and Gabe's punch landed under his left eye.

Pain exploded on his face, and he thought he heard bones crack.

Seth pushed Gabe away and stepped back, his vision blurred. He jerked his arms up to ward off the next blow, and his elbow connected with something too soft for this fight.

At the cry from Grace, both guys froze and turned toward her. Grace had stumbled back, landing hard on the pavement.

"Grace!" He could feel a trickle of blood running down his face, but that didn't matter right now.

But Gabe beat him to his sister's side. "Now look what you've done. No one in my family is safe from you."

He wanted to argue, but Gabe was right, it had been his elbow. He hadn't hit her hard, but it was enough to leave a light mark on her cheek that might bruise. Seth reached out for her.

Gabe slapped his hand away. "Don't touch her."

Seth could feel the rage building again, but he didn't move.

Before he could respond, Grace pushed to her feet and put her hands up. "Gabe, go home."

"You're taking his side?"

"You were the one dealing to minors." Seth turned on him.

"Don't believe him." Gabe took a step toward her. "Check his pockets. He's got a bag of—"

"Just leave." She moved closer to Seth.

"Man, has he got you fooled, Grace. Just like he fooled me." Gabe swore a string of curses before he spat blood on the dirt. "When I asked him to a party last week, you know what he said? He said he'd think about it."

"I said no." Seth shook his head resisting the urge to continue the fight.

"After you said you'd think about it. True or not true?"

"It was sarcasm." He glanced at Grace, and she seemed to believe Seth, but there was a seed of doubt in her eyes that hadn't been there before.

"Whatever you say." Gabe held up his hands. "See you later, Seth." He pointed at him as if they might be friends, then took off down through the parking lot.

Jerk. Seth focused back on Grace. "You okay?"

"Let's get you cleaned up." She grabbed his phone from where it had fallen out of his pocket and started back to his car, where she retrieved his water bottle from the roof and the keys that were still dangling from the door. He was feeling woozy enough that he didn't even argue when she got in the driver's seat.

He expected her to take him back to the studio, but instead, she drove to Ms. Bunting's. After helping him inside, she handed him a washcloth and pointed down the hallway toward the bathroom. "Why don't you get cleaned up? I'll make us some tea."

He stepped into the small bathroom and stared into the antique oval mirror. A cold chill ran though him. It wasn't that he didn't recognize his reflection. It was that he did. Only, he hadn't seen that guy in over five years. But there he was staring back as if he'd never really left.

And for the first time, it occurred to him that maybe Grace *would* believe Gabe's words that Seth hadn't changed. And just maybe he deserved it.

fifteen

W HEN GRACE HAD WALKED TOWARD THE REC center, the last thing she'd expected to find was Seth and Gabe in an all-out brawl. She'd never even heard Seth raise his voice except for the one other confrontation with Gabe. But he had a fire in him that she hadn't recognized. A fire she still felt on the corner of her cheek. Grace reached into the freezer and pulled out several ice cubes, dropping them into a baggie. She wrapped the pack in a thin cloth and pressed it gently to her cheek.

She didn't blame Seth. He hadn't even seen her, and she should've never tried to get between them.

The floor creaked with the weight of steps, and Grace turned to find Seth standing in the kitchen by the table. His hands and face were scrubbed clean, leaving the hair around his forehead and temples damp. The tiny cut by his eye had stopped bleeding, but a bruise was already forming along with a fair amount of swelling.

The fire she had seen during the fight was gone, and in its place was an empty, hollow shell. "I should go."

"You need ice." She removed the ice from her face and stepped closer to him, carefully resting it against the bruise on his face.

Seth closed his eyes for a moment as his hand covered hers, revealing his scraped and raw knuckles.

"Grace . . . I'm so sorry." His voice sounded tortured. His good eye flicked to her own bruise. After a moment, he drew a deep breath and took a half step back. "I need to go."

"Not like this." She set the icepack on the table and handed him his phone. "I picked this up. The screen is cracked."

Seth took it and looked at the screen, but facial recognition denied him entrance. He lowered the phone, but he seemed to struggle to see over his swollen eye.

This was too painful to watch. She lifted it from his hands. "What is your passcode?"

He hesitated for only a half second before he rattled it off.

The screen opened on an email. Grace started to close it out when the words "offer of employment," "start date in two weeks," and "California" jumped out at her between the cracks of glass. Was he leaving for California in just two weeks?

She closed it out and sent a quick text to herself. When her phone chimed, she handed it back. "Seems to still work."

"You saw the email, didn't you?" Seth still stood next to her.

"It's none of my business." She started to step back, but his hand landed on her elbow. His touch was feather light, as if he wasn't even completely sure what he was doing.

"I applied for that a long time ago." The words were low but clear as he took a half step closer. "They turned me down at the time, and it never occurred to me they would reach back out to me. I haven't accepted it or turned it down. I just got it."

She blinked several times before lifting her head. As if that could erase all the crazy emotions that were probably on her face. "Are you going to?"

He didn't move. With his hand still on her elbow, his gaze trailed over her face from her eyes, down to her lips, then back. He finally swallowed and blinked. "Are you going back to Chicago?"

When she didn't answer, he brushed the back of his free hand across her cheek with a feather light touch. "Does this hurt?"

"A little." Truth was, it didn't hurt at all. She had completely forgotten about it, but her brain wasn't capable of conveying all that at the moment. All she could think about was Seth. The warmth of his hand was still on her arm. His musky scent surrounded her. The way his gaze pulled her in. Her lungs very well may have forgotten how to breathe, but her heart was pounding hard enough to be heard down the street. If he didn't kiss her soon, she might just combust right in front of him. "What are we doing?"

"I'm sorry." He dropped her elbow, took a step back, then lifted the ice from the table and pressed it to her cheek with a soft touch. "I know I'm sending you mixed messages. I still don't think this will work. But . . ."

"But what?"

He stared at her for a long second then lowered the ice and took another step back. "Maybe I should go—"

"No." She frowned then winced as pain shot through her face. Okay maybe it hurt a little.

His face shifted from longing to concern. As he lifted the ice again, a shiver stole over her. "No ice."

Seth set the bag on the table again. "Do you need pain medication?"

She shook her head and took a step closer, reaching her hand out but not touching him. "But what?"

He closed his eyes a moment as if a war was going on inside of him. "Grace."

"Tell me."

"But . . . I can't stop thinking about you, longing for you, wanting you to be mine. I can't stop loving you." The words came out rough as he gripped the back of one of Ms. Margret's antique chairs. "But it *won't work*. I won't do that to you. I know what it's like to live in conflict with your parents—"

"Do you think we live at peace now?" She closed the distance to him again. "My parents and I have lived in conflict since long before Gregory died."

He rested his hands on her arms. "This would be different."

"I know, but it doesn't mean it isn't worth it." She dropped her head, staring at the floor as she leaned her head into his chest.

When she toyed with the skin at his waist, his grip on her arms relaxed until he almost wasn't touching her. His chest stopped moving for a moment, then his breaths came deeper, more labored. "Grace?"

Her skin hummed everywhere he was touching her, and all she could think about was more. More time. More contact. More Seth.

Drawing a deep breath, she finally looked up. His gaze was uncertain and questioning, but it was also laced with a dark hunger she'd never seen before. It didn't scare her, instead, it seemed to fuel her courage as she rose on her toes and lightly brushed her lips across his. Then again.

When he didn't respond she closed her eyes and started to lean back, but his hand slid to the back of her head, stopping her retreat. He didn't pull her close, just waited until she met his eyes. "Are you sure?"

"You're the only thing I'm sure about."

When he still hesitated, she reached up and ran her thumb the length of his jaw. "Why can't you trust that someone could love you? Trust that I won't abandon you."

Evidently, her confession was all he needed. His lips landed on hers, soft but strong. The last kiss had been hesitant and unsure, but this Seth was no longer questioning. He knew what he wanted, and kissed her like he'd been reliving the last one as often as she had.

His hands trailed down her back, leaving a line of fire and ice behind. It was like every cell in her body wanted him here. Needed him here. Closer. When his lips traveled from her mouth down her jawline and back, her whole mind clouded over. She melted against him as a small whimper escaped her throat.

Her response seemed to add fuel to him, and he deepened the kiss, pulling her closer with no end in sight. Which was fine by her.

A rough, abrupt noise filled the air. Then again. Was someone banging on glass?

Grace leaned back, trying to pull her mind back to reality when the front door rattled with a hard knock for a third time. Grace blinked, regaining her bearings. Right, Ms. Margret wasn't here, and she needed to answer the door. Who could that be? They rarely got visitors and when they did, they didn't usually sound like over-aggressive salesmen.

She pressed her forehead into his, her breath still labored. "I need to get that."

"Yeah." The word agreed but his eyes begged her to ignore it. "But this isn't finished."

"Definitely not finished."

She stepped back, but Seth pulled her close, capturing her lips one more time before he turned toward the sink, drawing a few deep breaths as he went. "I'm going to get some water."

She walked toward the front door, but yelled over her shoulder. "I'll get rid of them."

She yanked the door open, and her euphoria melted away. Her parents' grim faces said it all. They stared at her a moment then walked in without waiting for an invitation.

"We saw Gabe." The venom in her mother's words made her jump.

Her dad opened his mouth to speak, but he froze, his focus on something—or she suspected someone—behind her as all color drained from his face.

Seth's hand brushed her arm. "Everything okay?"

"Don't touch her." Her dad finally found his words as he took a step closer and then spoke to her. "Friends, is it?"

She didn't have to have a mirror to know that her disheveled hair and probably red lips spoke as a testimony against that.

Before she could find her words, her mother jumped in. "Why is he here with you? We saw what he did to Gabe."

Seth stepped up next to her. "Gabe was trying to sell drugs to a kid."

"You want us to believe you?" Her mom narrowed her eyes at Seth then she looked back at Grace. "You're going to trust him over your brother? The only brother you have left."

"It's the truth." Seth took another step, but she blocked his path with her arm. Didn't he realize he wasn't helping? She needed to talk to her parents calmly, but that wasn't going to happen as long as he was here. And she needed to talk to him, but that wasn't going to happen as long as her parents were here.

Grace turned to him. "Maybe you should go."

"Are you serious?" He looked as though she'd slapped him. And could she blame him? She had just said he could trust her to be there for him and now she was kicking him out the first chance she got. But she would be there. She just needed to get her parents out of there first.

"She asked you to leave." Her mother pinned him with a glare.

Seth drew a slow breath and touched her elbow. "Grace—"

"You probably did that to her face too." Her mom reached for her face, but she pulled back.

When Seth didn't answer, her father took a step toward him, hand clenching into a fist at his side. Then as if realizing how much bigger Seth was, he lifted his cell phone. "I'm calling Officer Hammond."

"This"—Grace motioned to her face—"is not his fault."

"You should leave." Her father opened the door and waited.

"I am not leaving Grace." Seth stepped around her, blocking her from her parents. Much like he'd done with Gabe.

The fire was returning, and she knew he was just protecting her, but she couldn't chance him getting in a fight with her dad right now. "Seth, leave. I'll call you later. I promise."

Seth looked ready to say more but finally gave her a curt nod and walked out the door, letting it slam behind him.

A moment ago, she'd been in euphoria and now . . . She wanted to be anywhere but here. Her parents were no doubt ready for a fight. "I love you guys, but I don't care what you think you know. You don't know him."

Her mom opened her mouth, but her dad's hand landed gently on her arm. When her mother looked at him, he subtly shook his head, then turned to Grace. "When are you headed back to Chicago?"

"I . . . I don't know." Her dad always had a way of turning the questions to keep her off balance. "When I make that decision, I'll let you know."

Her dad nodded and then motioned to the door. "We should go."

"I've been teaching a class. Tomorrow is a mini-performance, if you want to come to the gazebo at ten. But I will warn you, I'm doing a lift with Seth."

Her mother's face hardened as she opened her mouth again. But her father stepped in. "We'll see."

When her mother's head jerked toward him, he gave her a look laced with meaning. Then they were gone.

She lifted her phone and dialed Seth's number, but it went straight to voicemail. Probably better to let him calm down first anyway. And maybe by the time he'd calmed down, she'd know what to say about that kiss, because there was no way to pretend *that* one didn't happen.

When Grace said she'd call, Seth expected it would be an hour or two at most. But here he sat at a quarter after eleven and still nothing.

Seth climbed off the couch and walked to the sink for more water. If he'd felt rough earlier, now was ten times worse. His head screamed, and his back and neck muscles were paying the price. He stared at his phone again, willing it to ring. Nothing.

The baggie of drugs next to his phone snagged his attention and held it. He'd pretty much walked in, dumped out his pockets on the table, downed two Advil, and crashed on the recliner. But four hours later, his headache was back worse than ever, Grace hadn't called, and that bag of ecstasy never looked more tempting.

It wasn't the thrill of the high he wanted—he'd gotten over that long ago. This was something different. It was as if his body and mind craved, hungered for the release the little pills could offer. Freedom from pain, freedom from decisions, freedom from thinking.

But that freedom always came with a price. The price of ruined relationships. The price of becoming someone he didn't even recognize. He picked up the baggie and dumped the contents in his hand. This was way more than ten bucks' worth. He'd been right about Gabe grooming Zane. Suddenly, he wished he'd landed a few more punches.

As the frustration rose, so did the hunger and need for what was in his hand. He needed to dump it all and fast, before his last shred of willpower was gone. He carried them to the bathroom and held his hand over the toilet. He hesitated as the too familiar bitter, sweet scent wafted up, resurrecting memories of nights long ago offering promises of escape.

He pressed his lips together as his hands began to shake. Would one be so bad? Yes. It would, but then why couldn't he do this? He was too weak. He refused to be weak. Weak was not who he was anymore. Then why couldn't he turn his hand?

Nate's words and verse from the gym came back. *We're all weak at some time . . . Isaiah 40:29: He gives strength to the weary and increases the power of the weak.*

God, help.

It wasn't his fanciest prayer, but he'd never prayed a more heartfelt one. He closed his eyes and breathed the words out again. "God, help me, please."

There was a series of small splashes and Seth opened his eyes. His hand was palm down, and the ecstasy sat at the bottom of the porcelain bowl.

He leaned forward and flushed the toilet. As soon as the last trace disappeared, Seth gripped the side of the sink as sweat poured over him. He'd done it. So many had believed he'd changed, and now he actually believed it himself. He wasn't the same guy anymore.

He was a new creation.

A new creation with a headache. He pulled the Advil from the cabinet behind the mirror. The swelling in his eye had subsided, but in its place, a nice purple bruise ran from the inside corner of his left eye down his nose and across his cheek. At least Gabe had avoided the mouth.

The memory of the kiss from earlier swept over him again. He'd never let himself believe that he could have the dream. Wife. Kids. House. Two-car garage. But the moment Grace had told him that he was the only thing she was sure about, something changed. And now that he'd passed the ultimate test, the future seemed reachable, tangible. Jon and Grant had been right, the future was his for the taking. His past didn't disqualify him from a future.

He downed two Advil and stepped out of the room just as a heavy knock pounded on his door.

He grabbed a shirt that was tossed across the chair and slipped it on before answering. Jon stood on the other side, clearly upset about something.

He stormed past Seth into the apartment without waiting for

an invitation. "Why aren't you answering your phone? Grace even called me worried about you. Something about Gabe."

"My phone hasn't rung."

Jon scrolled through his own phone then held it up to show he'd called Seth ten times. It was only then that Jon seemed to take notice of the bruise. "What happened?"

"Gabe and I had a disagreement." He walked over to his phone and lifted it and tried to see around the cracks. Shoot, he'd left it on Do Not Disturb.

He checked his history. There were the ten missed calls from Jon alone, three missed calls from Grace, two voicemails, and about thirty texts from his mother.

"You're an adult, Seth. You can't get in a fight with someone just because you don't like him. You have responsibilities now. Like bringing the cash box to Mayor Jameson, who was waiting for it at town hall. Waiting all evening. Like answering Grace's calls so she's not worried sick about you."

"That wasn't—the cash box." Seth lowered the phone as the memory hit him. "I left it on top of the car. But it wasn't there, or Grace would have grabbed it when she gathered my keys and phone after she broke up the fight."

"Are you even hearing yourself?" Jon stormed across the room. "Grown men don't get in fights."

Something on the table seemed to catch his attention. Seth followed his gaze to the baggie lying next to his keys. Jon walked over, picked it up, and sniffed inside. That wasn't good. "Is this a pill bag?" He focused back on Seth, clearly checking his eyes. "I really thought you'd changed."

"You don't understand—"

"No, you don't understand. I went out on a limb when I hired you. I had to fight the board. The town. Even Grant wasn't sure you were ready. But I went to bat for you because I believed you weren't the same kid."

Whoa. That was a lot to take in.

It would have been easier to take another punch from Gabe.

Seth straightened his back, as his chin tightened. "You had your doubts? What happened to there's no one else I want for the job? Everyone's behind you? Was the little furniture handout all an elaborate setup as well?"

Jon flinched at the words. "Not a setup. Not really."

Seth reeled back. He'd meant it as sarcasm, but the truth was written on his cousin's face.

"You had already talked to them. Hadn't you?"

Jon had the decency to look embarrassed. "It had come up."

"And you made it seem all so spontaneous, Seth the local charity case."

Jon grabbed the baggie off the table. "Maybe we should continue this when we've both calmed down. Just give me the cash box, and we can talk about this later."

"I told you. I don't have it. I set it on the car. Gabe was selling to Zane, and I went over to intervene. And everything went south from there . . ."

But Jon's gaze had gone to the floor. A little pink pill resembling a piece of candy rested a few feet away. It must have fallen out of his grip when he'd carried them to the bathroom.

Jon picked it up. Looked at him. A hardness settled into Jon's eyes, and Seth had no doubt Jon wasn't going to believe him this time.

"It's not what you think."

Jon just shook his head, dropped the pill back in the baggie, and marched out the door.

The support? The friendships? People in his corner? Had none of it been real?

No, Grace had been real. Hadn't she? He lifted his broken phone to check the voicemails. One was from his mom. An uneasy feeling settled in his gut, and he pressed play.

"Sethy, I found something to tide me over." Her tone seemed way more relaxed than when she'd texted him earlier. That explained the relaxed state. He was ready to delete when she continued. "I'm close to Heritage. I am coming to see you, baby."

She what? Seth checked the timestamp. It was thirty minutes ago. It could be a lie like before. But there was something in her tone that made him believe it was the real deal. He pulled up the Find My Phone app, praying hers would still show up. It should, considering he paid the bill.

The blue dot appeared, but the map took longer to load. When the words Henderson Road appeared, his heart dropped in his gut. No. The rest of the familiar town streets loaded, just as a commotion came from outside his window.

Her blue dot had stopped . . . in the middle of the square.

He rushed over and peered into the darkness. A car had just driven over the curb and into a booth in the square, its headlights illuminating the white material that had been covering the booth. Luckily it seemed to have missed the schoolhouse.

Seth dropped his phone and sprinted down the stairs and across the street toward the vehicle. The driver's door was open, the engine was still running, and the radio was blaring Chicago's "Hard Habit to Break" into the empty square. Empty of people at least. Could this night get any worse?

Seth leaned forward with his hands on his knees. He swore he hadn't taken even a full minute to get from his apartment to here, but the car was empty and the driver, who he'd bet was his mother, was nowhere in sight. He straightened, still gasping for air as he shielded his eyes from the streetlight and squinted into the night, searching. He came up empty. It wasn't like he could see much in the dark. At least everybody else seemed to be inside already.

Hurrying over to the crushed booth that had been reduced to broken PVC pipe and torn white sheets, he scanned the area. There was no broken inventory, so hopefully that meant the owner had packed up for the night, but that table would never be the same again. He pulled the bent structure from the hood of the car and tossed it aside then climbed into the driver's seat and threw it into reverse. The worn suspension squeaked in protest as each tire dropped off of the curb, but the car didn't seem to have any real damage.

He pulled along the curb across from the studio, then closed his eyes and forced himself to breathe. This would be ok. Hopefully, there wasn't too much damage to the grass, but he'd have to get up early and help them fix the booth before the last day of the festival started. But first he still needed to find his mom. He had just cut the engine when there was a tap on the passenger window.

Seth looked over into the face of Officer Hammond. No doubt someone had called this in. He made a motion for him to roll down the window. Seth hit the button.

Seth blinked as Officer Hammond shone his flashlight in the window, but he kept his hands on the wheel.

"Hello, Seth." The man moved the beam around as if searching the vehicle. The shaft of light stopped on the floor of the passenger seat and Seth nearly threw up. Pills, powders, and various other drug paraphernalia, all laid out for all the world to see. Right next to the open empty cash box.

"It's not mine." That's all he got out before Officer Hammond asked him to step out of the car. He released a sigh. It might be a new record, but it was the same song. He had the right to remain silent. And he had a feeling everything in this car could and would be used against him in a court of law.

Seth tried to resist the overpowering urge to scream as loud as he could. The unfairness of it all was beyond comprehension. He'd faced the ultimate temptation on one of the worst days ever, and he had succeeded, but no one would believe him. His tangible future seemed to crumble right before his eyes.

Seth stepped out of the car and assumed the position. He knew the routine. Miranda Rights. A pat down. Handcuffs. And a phone call. Only who would he call? Jon? Who had caught him with an empty bag in his room? And with his truth bomb back there, Seth now knew that no one else really believed in him either. Even Grant didn't truly trust him. That one hurt most of all.

Their doubts, combined with the missing money and about four grand of drugs in the car all added up to one thing.

Seth was guilty until proven innocent.

sixteen

*S*ETH HAD BEEN MAD, BUT GRACE HAD NEVER
expected him to ghost her last night. She tied her left pointe
shoe, then stood and walked over to the speaker and connected
her phone. At the very least she expected he'd show up for today's
performance. But everyone was set to meet at the gazebo in an hour
and still nothing. She opened the Spotify app, then closed it and tried
his phone one more time. As it rang, the familiar "Dancing Queen"
ringtone could be heard faintly from above her.

He was here. He was just up those stairs and still not answering.
Grace lowered her phone, not even bothering to leave a voicemail
this time. Maybe he was punishing her. She had pretty much kicked
him out to talk to her parents, but he had to understand that they
couldn't be reasoned with while he was there. She'd thought he'd
been different from her parents, but maybe there wasn't different.
Love came with high expectations—always.

The front door rattled, and she turned to it with a forced smile.
But it wasn't one of her students. Her parents stood on the steps,
all smiles. Had they come to watch?

Grace only hesitated a second before she walked over and unlocked the deadbolt.

As soon as it was unlocked, her mother turned the knob and walked in. "You need to reconsider going to Chicago today. If you want your chance, you need to do all you can."

"I can't." Grace glanced at her phone which was still in her hand. "I have a show at ten."

"This isn't a show. It's barely a recital. Your students will understand. This is your shot to return as Giselle, not to mention to prove you're ready for the summer show. But we have to leave right now." Her mother picked up her bag and handed it to her. "I have food for you in the car along with a pair of backup pointe shoes."

"You have a pair of my pointe shoes?" It was high school all over again. No wonder she'd agreed to go to Europe. All her dance decisions filtered through her parents.

"I stopped by Margret Bunting's house, and she helped us find what you need."

Her parents were right, her students would understand. But it was all happening too fast. She couldn't leave. Not like this. Her gaze flicked to the ceiling. Maybe she should just go up and knock on the door.

"Don't bother, he's in jail." Her dad's harsh words jerked her back to the moment. "Where he belongs."

"What are you talking about?"

He pulled up his phone and then turned it toward her. "I thought you would have heard about last night."

The video was dark, grainy, and a little shaky. But she'd recognize those shoulders anywhere. But it didn't make sense. With the way his arms were spread on the car and the lights of the cruiser, it seemed as if they were arresting him. She'd never seen the car he was standing over in her life.

"If rumors can be believed, he was arrested for car theft, reckless driving, drug possession, and open containers, but I wouldn't be surprised if they can file more once they get his drug test back."

None of this made sense. "But yesterday—"

"It only takes one hit to pull a drug addict back down the rabbit hole. You know that from your brother. And from what we heard, he had access to a large amount of cash recently."

Yeah, her cash.

"We tried to warn you about him."

She'd known he was upset when he left, but she just didn't see how that would turn into a stolen car, a drug bust, and driving recklessly into the square. But if Gabe had taught her anything, it was that the obvious connection often wasn't anything more than just falling off the wagon.

Everything was crumbling down around her. It couldn't be. This was supposed to be different. *Seth* was supposed to be different.

Another knock rattled the front door just before Jon Kensington walked in. With a dark scowl on his normally warm face, and the fact that Leah wasn't with him, she guessed he wasn't here for the performance either.

Jon stopped next to her and her parents. He greeted each of them before focusing on Grace. "Can I have a moment?"

"We need to go." Her mother stepped forward, but Grace held her hand up.

If this was about Seth, she had to hear it. She nodded at Jon and walked to the far side of the room with him. She lowered her voice then showed the video to Jon. "Is it about this?"

He narrowed his eyes on the poor quality video. "I hadn't seen this yet."

Jon closed his eyes, and bile rose in her mouth at the defeat on his face. He drew a slow breath and opened his eyes. "Seth said that after you broke up the fight between him and Gabe you grabbed the stuff Seth had with him. What was there?"

"His keys were hanging in the door of his car and his phone was on the ground. And a water bottle on his car."

"You didn't see a cash box?"

"That old blue one he has? No, it wasn't there. I would have noticed that."

"Did you see anyone else around?"

"No, and I looked because I wanted help breaking them apart." Grace eyed him for a moment. "Did he say I could verify the cash box had been there? There has to be an explanation."

"I want to think so too, but the cash is gone and then . . ." He motioned to the video, then ran his hand roughly through his hair. "The empty cash box was found in the car with everything else."

"Do you know what he was charged with?"

"Car theft and possession. I'm still trying to figure out the timing of it all. But before I go to talk to Hammond, I wanted to ask you about the cash box."

"I wish I could say I saw it, but I just didn't. Do you think he used it to buy the drugs?"

"He had about four grand of a variety of drugs on him. But he'd only claimed to get about two from the festival event. So I am not sure—"

"It was mine."

"What?"

"He was holding two thousand dollars for me. He was going to bring it to me when the fight happened."

Her vision began to tunnel. How could she not have seen it? She'd been pulled into his lies just like she'd been pulled into Gabe's lies in the past.

"I don't want to believe it either, but I found this in his apartment last night." He pulled a baggie from his pocket. "It's an ecstasy bag. I found this and a pill in his apartment last night."

"Check his pockets. He's got a bag of—"

Of ecstasy. He had it on him at the fight. Grace's stomach turned over again. Then she'd sent him home. Had he taken a hit to relieve the pain? She knew it wasn't a far jump from an addict's "one hit" back to where they had once been.

Jon's phone rang, and he pulled it from his pocket. "This is Jon."

The guy's jaw tightened as his gaze flicked to Grace.

"Is it him?" She mouthed the words more than spoke them.

Jon nodded and Grace reached for the phone. "May I?"

He passed it over and she drew a slow breath. "Why did you say I would know where the cash box was?"

There was a long pause before Seth's voice—stretched thin—came over the line. "I didn't. I said you might have seen it. The last I saw it, it was on the car before the fight. Please tell me you saw it."

The desperation in his voice nearly broke her.

"Is the baggie that Jon has the bag Gabe was talking about in the parking lot when he suggested you had drugs in your pocket?"

"Yes, but—"

"What about the drugs in the car? Were they yours? Did you use my money to buy drugs?" She didn't know what she was looking for. Denial or just honesty? Because how could it not be? When he still didn't answer, she pushed. "Are you going to answer me?"

"If you're really asking those questions, then my answer doesn't matter . . . and there's nothing more to talk about." With that, the line went dead along with everything inside of her.

Had she been wrong? Or was he so deep in his lies he couldn't see out? She thought she'd known him better than that, but once she'd thought she'd known Gabe better than that, and he'd snowed her.

She handed Jon back his phone. "Thank you. I need to go."

Her parents must have heard her because they had the door open before she even got over there.

"No. I will go to Chicago. But I will go by myself and on my own schedule. Sunday is soon enough. I have a few things I need to do here first."

Nothing made sense anymore. Her only hope was redemption in Chicago. But first she'd follow through with her girls' show.

This wasn't the first time Seth had slept in this jail cell, but it was the first time he'd done so while innocent of any crime. Not that it mattered. Once a criminal, always a criminal, at least in Heritage. He couldn't believe he'd thought things would be different this time. That Jon believed in him. That Grace believed in him.

"Trust that I won't abandon you." She wouldn't abandon him until it was uncomfortable, that was.

Seth stood and paced the ten feet of cell. His muscles, still sore from the fight, protested the movement, but it was better to keep moving. There were two cells in the precinct, and he'd been the only resident last night. At least he could be thankful for that.

The outside door opened, and Hammond walked in with a tray of food, then passed it through the bars. "You sure there's no one else you want to call?"

Seth shook his head as he took the food. Who would he call? Twenty-four hours ago, he had a whole list of people he'd call in a bind. Jon had thinned that list to one last night, and today's phone call had dropped it to zero.

Hammond offered him a sad smile, then disappeared out the door again.

"I had to fight the board. The town. Even Grant wasn't sure you were ready. But I went to bat for you." Those words were on a nasty little repeat in his head. Maybe he wouldn't feel as stupid had he known. But the fact that the whole diner event with the furniture had all been nothing more than a theatrical production for his benefit, he couldn't swallow that. He was the town's little charity project. A charity project no one believed would succeed.

He plopped down on the bench and eyed the bologna on white

bread with a side of applesauce. Could be worse. He downed the food and set the tray aside as the outer doors opened again.

Gabe, with his hands cuffed behind his back, was led to the neighboring cell. He glared at Seth from his non-swollen eye then turned away as they uncuffed him. In addition to the swollen eye, Gabe sported a bruise on his chin, testifying to their fight yesterday.

Hammond took Seth's tray before walking out, letting the metal door slam behind him. The room remained silent for a moment before Gabe leaned back against the far wall. "You rat me out?"

"Rat you out? No one has even asked about the fight. Not everything is about you, Gabe."

He dropped into a sitting position on the bed and rested his head against the brick wall. "Really, because all my problems seem to begin and end with you."

"How do you figure that?" Seth took a step toward the shared bars but not so close that it would seem threatening to the cameras. The last thing he needed was an assault charge added to this. "It was you who gave me my first hit. Not the other way around. You were there the night Gregory died, but you walked away. Whatever they pulled you in for, I'm pretty sure you'll manage to get off this time as well. Life's always on your side, Gabe."

"My side? Are you kidding me?" Gabe pushed off the bed and took an aggressive step toward the bars. "My parents are impossible to please, my brother is dead, and now any relationship I had with my sister is gone because of you."

"Me? I never said anything to her that wasn't true."

"Right, because Seth is perfect now. Seth's not a screwup like me anymore. Let the whole town rejoice because the prodigal son of Heritage has returned, reformed." Gabe's fist clenched but he seemed to spot the camera mounted in the corner and stepped back. "If I have to hear another person in town tell me how amazing you've turned out, I might throw up."

"This town hates me."

"Hates you? Is that why people just hand you jobs? Hand you furniture?"

"The furniture was staged. They don't care about me."

"Let's see, half the town hatched a plan to help a guy who has his pride wrapped so tight around him there was no other way to get him to accept the help. Sounds terrible."

For a second, the words tripped him up, but he found his footing. "Please. They were just waiting for me to mess up. Car theft, reckless driving, and drug possession. I showed them."

"Like any of it will stick. The car was lifted from the gas station twenty minutes away, but your car was still at your apartment. What did you do? Run to the gas station only to drive back home? Not to mention the drugs were all used, but just guessing you were sober when they brought you in. You'll test clean."

"How do you know all that?"

"What can I say? I'm in the know."

"In the know or you were in the car?"

He shrugged with a smirk, then glanced at the camera again. "I wasn't in the car."

"But you were there. You know, I don't have a hard time believing that you'd put the cash box in the car to frame me. But I can't believe you let my mom drive when she was high. She could have killed someone."

Gabe leaned against the wall and then finally looked up at him under hooded lids. "Like mother, like son."

"I am nothing like her." Seth gripped the bars between them, his knuckles whitening. "Do you hate me so much that you want to take down anyone I care about? Because that's what it feels like."

When Gabe didn't answer, Seth knew he'd landed close to the truth.

"Why?" Seth walked back to the bed and sank onto the bunk

and leaned forward, dropping his elbows on his knees. "You were there. You know I didn't kill him."

A beat. Then Gabe looked away, his voice raw. "It should have been one of us who died, not him. Never him."

Seth drew in a breath, his voice dropping. "Don't you think I believe that too? Don't you think if I could have traded places with him I would've? I have no memory of buying that third bag, and I didn't give it to him on purpose. You said as much while we were waiting for the ambulance right before you abandoned me."

"I abandoned you? I was grieving my brother and trying to deal with my parents." Gabe launched himself off the wall and stopped in the middle of the cell. "After the trial *you* abandoned *me*."

"You let me take the fall. Do you know what that has done to my life?" Seth dropped his gaze to the floor. This was so messed up. Because as much as that had been the worst time of his life, that conviction was what saved him. Or at least had driven him to the only One who could save him.

"Then again if you hadn't . . ." Seth leaned forward propping his elbows on his knees. "I'd probably still be right here in jail, only I'd be guilty. Because I would've never gotten out of that life."

He sat up again and met Gabe's gaze. "I did abandon you. I found a way out of that dumpster fire of a life and didn't look back. I had to start fresh. Cut unhealthy ties. I had to."

He never would have dumped those pills if he hadn't. Even if no one believed him, it confirmed he wasn't the same guy.

And just maybe the guy best suited to save people from drowning was the guy who almost drowned himself. His mind flashed back to the scrawny seventeen-year-old he'd been. He'd been half high on pot when Grant had stepped into his life on the street in Heritage and told him he could help him quit. It was another year before that kid's desperation would drive him to get help. But that day was the first time he'd felt seen. Felt hope. Considered he could have a future.

He stood and eyed Gabe through the bars. "It doesn't have to be this way."

"What doesn't?"

"You feel trapped, alone on an island with no way off. But people are willing to build a bridge to help you. You just have to stop burning those bridges to the ground. Grace cares what happens to you. I care what happens to you. You need to start caring about what happens to you."

Gabe didn't answer, but a bit of the hardness of his glare fell away. He opened his mouth to speak when the metal door opened and Hammond walked in and started unlocking Seth's cell. "Looks like you're free to go. Your mom showed up demanding we release her car and her *possessions* from impound."

"So she confessed?"

"Not sure she was in her right mind. Once she's through processing we'll let her sober up here before we try to get the full story out of her. But that, combined with no traces of drugs or alcohol in your results, and the fact someone showed up giving you an alibi at the time of the car theft." God bless him, Hammond sounded genuinely happy about it. "No reason to hold you, son."

He didn't know when the car was stolen, but he couldn't help but hope it was yesterday around five because then that person might just be Grace.

Hammond opened the heavy metal door that led out of the holding cells.

Not Grace.

Jon stood by the far wall with Nate and Grant.

"Zane confessed to taking the money this morning." Nate took a step forward. "Told me about what happened."

"He told us the baggie of drugs was Gabe's." Jon shook his head. "It was a setup. To get the money. Gabe had some dirt on Zane and threatened to tell us if he didn't take the cash for him."

"You got the money back?"

"Oh, we're pretty sure it was used to buy those drugs." Grant flipped his keys over in his hand then again.

Then the last of the pieces fell into place. The money. The dealer holding out on his mom to try and draw her to town. "Gabe set it all up for me to take the fall."

"Looks that way." Officer Hammond handed him an envelope with the few possessions he had on him when he'd been arrested. "We're holding him on some overdue parking tickets, but we're hoping your mom's confession can connect everything to put him away."

The news should come as a relief. And in some way, it did. But he'd been honest with Gabe when he said he cared what happened to him. Gabe had been the only one there for him when he'd been cold and hungry as a kid. He couldn't forget that. But he also couldn't help someone who wouldn't help himself, and Gabe might just have chosen to burn his last bridge.

seventeen

"I F YOU'RE REALLY ASKING THOSE QUESTIONS, *then my answer doesn't matter…and there's nothing more to talk about.*"

Grace landed her final pirouette of the piece and struck her pose. She closed her eyes against the blinding spotlight as the music faded. She'd done it. Her jumps were high, her turns solid, everything had been perfect. The movement hadn't even put a strain on her knee. Stepping back into the part of Giselle for tonight's performance would be seamless.

"Thank you." Alec's voice echoed through the vacant auditorium, his face hidden among the dark rows of chairs. She assumed Madame Laurent was out there as well, but she really couldn't see beyond the fifth row. "Send Mallory out to do her solo."

She walked off stage and dropped on a bench to unlace her shoes. She'd stuck to her guns and come down Sunday, much to the protests of her parents. But she had wanted to see her girls dance even if the lift didn't happen. Waiting had also allowed her to think, clear her thoughts, and piece things together.

"Just perfect." Her mother approached her from down the hallway, her father a few feet behind. "If that doesn't land you the leading role, then you need to consider moving to another company."

"What are you doing here?" She couldn't remember the last time they'd shown up for a practice or an audition. And then as if she'd said nothing, her mother leaned forward and hugged her. After that, her father stepped up and put his arm around her. What was going on?

"You don't think we'd miss our daughter's return to the stage, do you?" Her father pulled his phone from his pocket and started tapping at the screen.

"We even got tickets for the show," her mother said.

"Fourth row, on the left?"

"Of course." Her mother reached out and squeezed her hand. "But we were thinking about slipping out to get some food. Do you want anything?"

What? She shook her head.

"Okay. We can't wait to watch you return to the stage tonight. We're very proud of you, darling, and all your hard work." Even her father smiled at her as they left.

Strange. She slipped her shoes into her bag then pulled the convertible tights over her toes before sliding on her Crocs. Her phone vibrated with a text.

MARGRET

Seth has been released and cleared of all charges.

Thought you'd want to know.

Grace sank against the wall as tears burned her eyes. A weight that had been pressing against her since she'd first seen the video lifted, and she wasn't sure if she wanted to laugh, or cry, or do a little dance.

She tapped his name on her phone and let it ring several times before going to voicemail. She tried again. Nothing.

"Madame Laurent wants to see you in her office," Alec said, emerging from a door.

Grace eyed her phone again, then slipped it into her bag and hurried down the hall. She stopped in front of the large ornate door and knocked.

"Enter." The thick French accent was a welcome sound.

Grace pushed the door open and took in the grandeur of the room. The dark paneling combined with the sconces that mimicked candlelight transported her back to when this nineteenth century theatre had opened. But it also made it hard to see. Grace blinked several times, letting her eyes adjust before they landed on Madame Laurent.

It wasn't her office since they were at the Auditorium Theatre rather than their studio, but she sat behind the stately dark oak desk with a straight back and tight bun like she owned the place. Without even a hint of a smile, she pointed to a chair opposite the desk. "Sit."

Grace offered a polite smile as she circled the antique Empire chair and sat on the deep red velvet, taking care not to sink back no matter how much her body was sagging with relief right now after the news of Seth.

"What was that?" Madame Laurent's French accent was thicker than usual and laced with an icy tone that was punctuated by the woman slapping her desk.

Grace sat up a bit straighter. "I hit every turn, every mark, every—"

"Your knee is healed. Anyone can see that." She dismissed the idea with a flick of her hand. "But that was not a performance. That was rote memorization. You may have healed your knee, but in that process you have lost your heart."

Lost her heart? Madame Laurent no doubt meant her heart for dance, but Grace's mind went to Seth.

"No one will take a role on my stage who doesn't love the piece. It shows."

"I can do better."

Madam Laurent leaned forward on her elbows, her eyes narrowing as she seemed to be trying to look into Grace's very soul. "I don't think you can. I have seen you dance for five years and *that* was the worst performance you have ever given. Maybe not technically, but where it counts. I'm putting you in the chorus."

The woman sat up, slipped on a pair of dark-rimmed glasses, and began making notes on the paper in front of her.

"The chorus?" She didn't disguise the horror in her tone. It wasn't even a secondary role. She hadn't been in the chorus since her first year with the company.

Madame Laurent paused her writing and sent Grace an icy stare above her glasses. "Would you rather have nothing?"

When Grace didn't immediately answer, Madame Laurent leaned forward again, this time her arms crossing on the desk in front of her. "I will give one hour to decide. That's when the chorus will take the stage to review their dances. I assume you know the part."

Grace nodded. She'd never danced the chorus, but Madame Laurent had always been adamant about every dancer knowing every part just in case she needed to move someone around at the last minute.

"You may go."

She stood—numb—and turned toward the door.

Where is your heart?

She had no doubt where her heart was.

In Heritage. Maybe this was a message that it was time to wrap up her time on the stage.

She walked out to the hall and dropped back on the bench. She pulled out her phone and checked it again. She had to talk to him. She tapped Seth's name and waited to leave a voicemail, but on the third ring, he answered. "What do you need, Grace?"

The detached tone gutted her. "I heard you're out."

"Yup."

"I'm sorry I didn't immediately believe you. But as soon as—"

"I get it. You've been burned before. Don't worry about it." His voice softened. "Did you get the part?"

The part? Oh, Giselle. Madame Laurent's words rang in her mind. *"You have lost your heart."* No kidding. "I got *a* part."

"I knew you would. I'm sure you'll do great. Best of luck to you, Grace." Then his voice dropped lower. "You were made to dance."

Why was he saying goodbye? Why wouldn't he listen to her?

"Seth." The desperation in that one word was way more telling than she intended, but this couldn't be it. "Will you . . ." *Forgive me? Give me another chance? Ever trust me again?* ". . . come to see me dance?"

He hesitated a long moment before his voice came through rough. "I'll try. Goodbye, Grace."

The line went dead. He wouldn't come. That had been a final goodbye. She imagined the despair if she were in a cell, wrongly imprisoned, and the people she trusted most assumed she was lying. She hadn't immediately believed him and had left him standing alone. And it seemed he'd never forgive her for that.

She slipped the phone in her bag and walked back down the hall. When it rang a moment later, she yanked it out, but it was just her parents. She sank onto a nearby bench and accepted the call. "Hey."

"Darling." Her mother's voice was lighter than it had been in a long time. "About the show tonight—"

"I'm in the chorus." Her voice didn't crack. It didn't betray any emotion. The whole thing felt like an out-of-body experience. When there was no response, she tried again. "Did you hear me? I won't be Giselle tonight, I'm in the chorus."

A pause and then her father's voice came over the line. "Absolutely not. This is unacceptable. I won't let you take it." Of course, she was on speakerphone.

She sank forward on her knees. "That's my decision, not yours."

"What reason did she give?" Her mother again, but the lightness in her tone was gone.

"That I lost my heart."

"It was that boy." Her mother nearly spat the words.

"He's not a boy." She stood and paced to the opposite wall and back. "He's a man. An innocent man at that."

Her father's voice broke in again. "I looked up a few other dance companies that—"

"I'm staying. I'm dancing in the chorus." She'd planned on thinking about it more, but what was there to think about? She wasn't going back to Heritage. Not if Seth was there, because he didn't want her. Besides, what choice did she have?

Would you rather have nothing?

That was exactly what she'd have. Because without ballet she had nothing. And she was no one.

You are more than a ballerina. Seth's words rolled over her.

Maybe he'd believed that at one time, but this brief conversation put that idea to rest. She had failed him, and he was done with her.

She would dance the chorus, forget the past month had ever happened, and just maybe convince Madame Laurent she was ready for center stage by the fall show. "I'm not going back to Heritage, or anywhere else."

"Don't expect us to go to that show tonight."

"I don't. Believe me, I don't." And for some reason the words just sort of released a knot inside of her. "I actually don't need you to go to any of my shows. It's your choice. I need to go. I need to let Madame Laurent know I'm taking the part."

She ended the call and looked back at Madame Laurent's office door. She still didn't know how long she'd dance but . . . she'd dance today. She was no longer dancing for her parents. And in the chorus, she wasn't dancing for fame. Maybe it was time to dance for God and for the love of dance He'd given her.

Seth sat for a long time in the grass with the open envelope in one hand and a blue-and-red ribbon in the other. He didn't move. He could barely breathe. He might as well be one of the gravestones he sat among.

His eyes lingered on the photo clipped to the top of the document bearing the same name as the marble grave marker in front of him.

William Roger Warner.

His dad's face in the official photo held a serious expression, but still carried his characteristic kindness in the eyes. The close-cropped brown hair brought back memories of joyous homecomings from a deployment, and sad farewells for the next.

He lifted the photo again. The top of the paper read: Official Military Personnel File. He'd had no idea what to think when he found a large envelope from the Department of Defense in his mailbox this morning. He'd peeked inside, been unable to breathe for a minute, then decided to bring it with him to look through it here. Seemed fitting. That he had found it on his way to the cemetery was too much to be a coincidence. This was a gift from God.

After what seemed like forever, he began leafing his way through his father's military life with his one free hand, the other still trailing over the ornate ribbon. Most of it was mundane administrative stuff, but it was a treasure to him. Farther on, the tears began again as a new picture of his dad formed.

. . . posthumously awarded the Army Distinguished Service Cross . . .

. . . for extraordinary acts of heroism . . .

. . . despite having received wounds of his own, Cpl Warner refused evacuation, returning to the line of fire twice to rescue wounded comrades . . .

. . . pronounced dead on arrival at base medical facility . . .

His dad was a hero.

The last page was in reference to a one-time replacement of service medal. No doubt his mom had hocked the first one.

Seth opened his other hand and studied the intricate details of the golden cross. He ran his thumb over the golden eagle that was superimposed on it then drew a deep breath as he focused back on the grave.

William Roger Warner. Husband, father, and hero of our country.
Now that felt like an understatement.

He placed the medal on the photo and dropped it all back in the envelope to keep it clean. Leaning forward, he brushed away a few leaves that stuck to the surface of the gravestone. His life could've shaped up so differently had his father lived. Not just his life, but his mom's. She hadn't cooperated with the police once she'd sobered up, and they couldn't hold her on anything more than a drunk and disorderly charge.

Movement to the left caught his eye and he froze. Gabe stood over Gregory's grave. His head low. Had it been just four days since the two had been in jail together? Seth stood, and the two men locked eyes.

"So the rumors are true." Seth took a few steps toward his old friend. He didn't know the details, but it didn't matter.

Gabe's parents had gotten him off because of a lack of evidence connecting him to the theft or the drugs. Gabe had been careful not to leave prints in the car, that was for certain. All they had was Zane's testimony, but even if there was some way to corroborate that to make the charges stick, all Hammond could slap Gabe with for that was contributing to the delinquency of a minor. Max punishment was five hundred dollars or ninety days in jail. Or a deal with the DA.

Gabe always came out on top. What burned Seth most was for a second there, he thought he might have actually gotten through to him in the cell. "Must have been some deal."

"I gave them some names. I do make friends in low places." Gabe shifted his gaze back to his brother's headstone then back to Seth. "I also told them more about a crime from a few years back. It didn't affect my deal, but they did seem pleased to set the record straight."

"Well, I hope you do something good with your freedom."

Seth turned away, but Gabe's voice came again, stopping him. "Turns out a guy convicted of possession with the intent to distribute, didn't actually distribute."

A cool chill ran through Seth as he spun to lock eyes with Gabe. "What are you talking about?"

Gabe shoved his hands in his pockets and stared off for a moment as if he couldn't handle meeting Seth's gaze. "Gregory brought his own stuff that night."

"What are you saying?"

"When he called to ask where we were"—Gabe met Seth's eyes—"he told me he'd bought them off a kid at college."

So many emotions hit Seth at once, the world seemed to spin around him. He leaned forward, bracing his hands on his knees and took a calming breath. Then another.

He hadn't killed Gregory. It hadn't been his fault. He'd been dumb, but the blood wasn't on his hands. As the relief passed over him, it was replaced by the same unwelcome rage he'd felt the day of the fight. It welled in his stomach. He stood and took a step toward Gabe. "Why didn't you say anything before now?"

"Because I was mad." He turned his head to the sky a moment before locking gazes with Seth again. "I was mad at myself for not stopping him. I was mad at the unfairness of it all. You and

I spent half our senior year high, and Gregory has one bad night and he's dead."

What could he say to that? It was true, and the same thoughts had crossed Seth's mind a hundred times.

"After you were arrested, my parents sent me to a facility in Detroit for six weeks."

"How did I not know that?"

Gabe shrugged and kicked at the ground with his toe. "You know my parents. Keep it all quiet. When I came home, I planned on coming clean, but you were gone."

Serving his sentence, but also gone from Gabe's life. He'd thought a lot about that since their conversation in the jail. And doing it all over, he wasn't sure he'd choose a different path. He'd needed a fresh start. "So why come forward now?"

"Maybe because it was the right thing to do. Maybe hearing that you actually cared about what happened to me made me think. Maybe the idea that my sister still cares about me—" He cleared his throat and gazed off into the distance again. "I honestly thought there was no one left who cared about me anymore."

"A lot of people care."

"Yeah well, if Grace can get past your history, then—"

Seth flinched and looked away.

"So you messed that up?"

He pinned Gabe with a stare. "Don't fool yourself. She's not past my history."

"What are you talking about?"

"She doesn't trust me. Turns out no one trusts me."

When Seth didn't elaborate Gabe pushed further. "So, you still going to take a job out of state with the first company that offers no matter what this town has done for you?"

"What have they done for me?"

"The whole town has been looking out for you your whole life.

Where do you think the groceries came from that showed up on your steps?"

Seth's head jerked toward Gabe. "I thought it was you."

"Where would a kid get the money for groceries?" He shook his head. "Nah, it wasn't me. It was neighbors and the churches and people who saw your mom and cared. But she was too proud to accept any help. And you're just like her. You're going to lose the best thing that ever happened to you—my sister—because you're wrapped in that stupid cocoon of pride."

"That's not true." But maybe yeah, it felt a little true.

"You push everyone away." Gabe's hands began to shake as he lifted them in the air in frustration.

Seth shook his head. "You need to get clean."

"How?"

"You have parents."

"My parents are complicated. That and the fact I've burned them so many times. I'm pretty sure they're done with me."

"Others will help you."

"Who? You?"

"Yes."

Gabe's look said it all.

Yeah, he wasn't sure where that came from either.

"You hate me." Gabe shoved his shaking hands back into his pockets. "With good reason."

"I may not want to help the Gabe that got me thrown in jail—not once but twice. But I want to help the Gabe who snuck me food, blankets, and even into your place a few times when the night was too cold. I have to believe that Gabe is still in there."

Gabe pulled his shaking hands out of his pockets as he shifted his weight—no doubt the guy was in desperate need of a hit. "I think I'm too far gone."

"No one is too far gone. I have to believe that."

"Why?" Gabe's blue eyes, so much like his sister's, pierced into him.

"I once believed I was too far gone. Grant helped me find the answers I needed."

"You mean religion?" Gabe scoffed and shook his head.

"Faith. And belief that God has saved me for a reason."

"A reason? Is that reason walling yourself off from the world?" Gabe walked away a few feet, then back.

When Seth didn't respond, Gabe held out a brochure to him. "Don't let the person who believes in you more than anyone else pass you by."

Seth took the brochure. It was for the production of *Giselle*. He shoved it in his pocket. If that person did believe in him, it would have been easy. But that person didn't. How could he be with someone if he had to constantly prove he wasn't guilty before she'd believe him?

Gabe turned to go, and the words from his dad's file flashed in his mind.

. . . despite having received wounds of his own, Cpl Warner refused evacuation, returning to the line of fire twice to rescue wounded comrades . . .

"Gabe." Seth took a step to follow him. "We both know if you go anywhere by yourself right now, you won't be sober within the hour."

Gabe stopped walking, but he didn't turn.

"Come with me."

"Where?"

"Nate's." He didn't know where that idea had come from, but it made the most sense.

Gabe finally faced him again. "The pastor?"

"He's been through it, and I'm sure he has resources. You can trust him."

Gabe took a step. "Why are you doing this?"

Seth tapped the file in his hand, then glanced back at his dad's headstone. "No man left behind."

Even if people had failed to stand with him, he'd be a son his dad would be proud of.

eighteen

I T HADN'T BEEN A FULL WEEK OF PERFORMANCES, but who knew that being in the chorus could be so much fun? Maybe it was that she no longer had the pressure of the lead. But more likely it had to do with her decision to dance for God rather than trying to please her parents. But there was no doubt that for the first time in a long time, she was enjoying dancing again. She wouldn't quite say loved, but enjoyed definitely fit.

Grace sat at her dressing table and carefully undid the bright red clip in her hair. She dabbed a cotton ball on the makeup remover and then began the tedious process of scrubbing her face. She squinted against the bright mirror lights and sent up a word of thanks that they had given her back her private dressing room, which didn't really make sense as a chorus member. But whether it was a clerical error or a subtle hint from Madame Laurent to step up her game, she'd take it.

Not that she didn't love the energy of the group dressing room, but lately the quiet was her best friend.

It was when she was quiet that she thought about the little girls in her class and what they might be up to. She thought about Ms.

Margret and how much she missed her daily Yoda-isms. And she thought about Seth. Or more like she tried not to think about Seth. Wondering if he took the new job. If he didn't.

And occasionally, when it was really quiet, she would think about God. Ms. Margret had been texting her verses from the Bible every day. She didn't understand them all, but she found herself looking forward to them. Whenever she read them, Seth's words would come back. *"I could really understand who I was, I had to understand how God saw me."*

So every time she read a verse, she tried to picture how God saw her.

An usher appeared in the reflection of the mirror. "There's a gentleman to see you, Miss Howell."

A gentleman? Her father made it clear he had no intention of coming. What other gentleman was there in her life?

Seth.

Her pulse picked up. She focused back on her reflection, only now it was half covered in stage makeup and half a swirl of black and brown smudges. "Did he give his name?"

"No. But he said he was from your hometown."

She swallowed and scrubbed faster as she did her best to keep her breath even. As soon as she was smudge free, she stood and turned back to the usher. "Thank you, could you please show him in?"

Why was she standing? Did that look weird? She sat at the table again. But she didn't want to stare up at him. She stood once more, closed her eyes, and drew a slow breath.

Who knew why he was here? Maybe he had just been in the area. But he had come. It had to mean something.

The door clicked, and she opened her eyes as Gabe stepped around the doorframe. Her shoulders deflated, and she gripped the chair to steady herself.

"Am I not the face from Heritage you were hoping for?" Gabe

stepped forward and presented her with a rose and a fat manila envelope. Dark circles weighed under his eyes, his face pale and clammy. Was he ill? He pointed to the envelope. "Those are from your students."

Her students. She couldn't keep the smile from her face as she peeled back the tab. Crammed inside were a dozen homemade cards made mostly out of construction paper and yarn.

She set the envelope on her dressing table and turned back to her brother. His hands were shaking slightly. He leaned against the door, his gaze hesitant.

"Why didn't you just tell him you were my brother?"

"I wasn't sure you'd let me back here." He wiped his hand across his forehead and then on his pants.

"Because you set up Seth or because you're obviously in desperate need of a fix." She stepped back toward her chair and set to removing more of her makeup. "Are you here to ask for money?"

"I'm not . . ." He blew out a long breath. "I'm trying to quit. Three days clean—wow me."

She met his gaze in the mirror. Was he really trying to get sober? She hated to assume he was lying, but she'd heard this song and dance before. "Then what do you want?"

He stared at the floor a moment then back at her. "He said you might actually care what happened to me, so I thought I'd tell you—"

"Who said that?" She paused her scrubbing and met his gaze in the mirror again.

"Seth."

She spun back toward her brother. "You talked to him? How is he?"

"Stubborn." He offered a half shrug. "But good. He's helping me get clean."

"How?"

"That's another reason I came." He glanced back at the door and then at her. "I'm going away for a while."

"To Quinn Ranch?"

"I might land there eventually, but I need to go through basic rehab. A detox." He held up his shaking hand as evidence. "Nate and Seth helped me find a program here in Chicago. Nate's out there waiting. He's taking me there after this. Guess they didn't trust me to not give in before I got to the door."

Her gaze trailed to the open door. They?

"Seth isn't with me." Her brother obviously read her like a book. "He helped me get connected with Nate, but he had to work today."

Had to work or had to stay away from her?

Her brother nudged her shoulder. "He's an idiot, you know."

"It doesn't matter. Seems like I was made for this." Grace stood, spread out her arms, and motioned to the space around her as she made a little turn.

"That's nonsense, and you know it."

She halted halfway through her turn and glared at him. "What?"

"You're an amazing dancer, sure. And dancing was your passion for a while. But your heart wasn't in that." He pointed roughly in the direction of the stage.

"Would people stop saying that?" She dropped on her stool and started pulling the pins from her hair.

"What? The truth? You looked happier about those ridiculous cards I brought you than any one of your dances out there."

Had she? She worked the hair screw out of her bun and then dropped it on the table.

"If you want to dance, then dance." He appeared over her shoulder in the mirror. "But if you would rather be in Heritage teaching those kids, then there's nothing wrong with that."

"Can you imagine what Mom and Dad would say?"

"Couldn't be any worse than what they said when they found out Seth was helping me. Does that mean I shouldn't get help?"

She spun on the stool to face him. "Who are you and what have you done with my brother?"

"Crazy, right?" He stepped back and leaned against the wall. "Turns out when you stop beating yourself up constantly, you don't hate everyone else as much either."

She stood and took a step toward him. "So, is this goodbye?"

"For a while." He offered her a quick, shaky hug and then stepped toward the door. "I'll look you up when I get out. And I will support you whether you're still here on stage or back there in Heritage. Just make sure you follow what's in there."

He pointed to her heart, then was gone.

Grace collapsed into her chair. She reached over to the envelope of cards and pulled the stack out. The top one was a crayon drawing of what she thought was her standing by the mirror teaching. The rough image had her wearing a large smile and a pink tutu. Awkward, misshapen letters spelled out *Thank you for making me love dance*. At least that's what she thought it said.

Her heart filled at the words. She had shared her love of dance with someone else, and that knowledge brought her more joy than any she'd gotten while taking the stage.

One of the cards slipped to the floor, and she bent to get it. It was fancier stationery with flowers and script that looked more like an elaborate font than handwriting. It was from Ms. Margret.

1 John 3:1

See what great love the Father has lavished on us,
that we should be called children of God.

Grace read it and read it again.

Was that how God saw her? As his child?

Was that a good thing or bad thing? Her mind flicked to her

own father, who expected perfection. The image faded in her mind, replaced by others. Nate holding Charis tenderly even after she'd thrown a temper tantrum. Susie's dad who worked two jobs just so she could dance. Seth's dad had been kind, loving, giving.

She dug through more of the notes, each one gripping something inside of her. Maybe she had left her heart in Heritage, but it wasn't only with Seth. She'd left her heart in that studio and with those kids.

Because she was more than a ballerina.

She was a teacher.

She was a friend.

But most of all her identity was God's child. Even if she was only just beginning to understand what that meant.

And for the first time, she began to believe that God loved her whether she had the starring role of the biggest production in Chicago or no role, no job, unknown to anyone. She was known to Him.

She wasn't sure she was ready to give up the identity of a dancer yet, but she did know that just as God gave her the gift of dance, He also gave her the gift of teaching. He gave her the gift of friendship. And God loved her no matter what she chose.

Grace stood and rushed out to find Alec. "I will finish this show, but tell Madame Laurent that I will not be auditioning for the fall show."

He hesitated for a moment, then flipped through the clipboard. "Probably for the best."

She marched back to her dressing room. She wouldn't let robotic Alec kill her mood. According to Ms. Margret's text that morning, *the Lord is good, and His love endures forever.* For the first time she had a clear view of who she was, and her future looked bright.

There had never been a stress or a regret he couldn't outlift. Then again, he'd never known heartbreak could feel like this. Seth did another ten reps on the bar, but that didn't help either. He set it in the stand then ducked under it as he sat up.

"Switch?" Nate came around from where he'd been spotting and waited for Seth to move.

Seth grabbed the towel, dried off the bench, then assumed the spotting position.

Nate lifted the bar and did one press, then a second. "What has got you so wound up on a Saturday night? Is this about your conversation with Jon?"

"No." But that wasn't helping either.

Nate came up short on the third rep and Seth helped him get the bar back on the stand with a clang.

Nate sat forward and reached for the towel. "I have to say I side with Jon. Taking that desk job in California when you could set up the gym here is dumb. Your record is expunged. Or it will be soon. This is what you have wanted, why run now?"

"I'm not running." Now that he knew how Jon really felt about him, he just couldn't go there. "A new start will be good for me."

"The gym is a new start. When do you leave, anyway?" Nate sighed.

"Next week."

Next week would be a new start where he didn't still feel slightly betrayed by his friends. A new start where he didn't have memories of Grace everywhere he looked. Nate stood up and Seth pointed to the weight rack. "Let's add ten to each side."

Nate just raised his brows then stepped over to help change the weights. "How long are you going to punish yourself—punish us?"

"I'm not punishing anyone. I just want more weight." Seth disconnected the lock and waited for Nate so they could add the weight at the same time.

"Of course." Nate nodded and they each added ten pounds to

the bar. "Look, we're sorry we failed you, but news flash. People *will* fail you. You can't toss relationships aside just because people aren't perfect."

His own words to Grace hit him square in the face as a memory flooded back. *"Real love isn't based on your performance, it's based on who you are. We all have wins and losses. People who love you are with you for both."*

Nate secured the lock at the end, then took a step closer to Seth. "Don't kick us out of your corner because we weren't perfect. Jon, Grant, myself . . . Grace."

"I don't want to talk about Grace." Maybe he was being unfair to the guys, but Grace should have known. Her question still burned inside of him. He couldn't spend the rest of his life with someone who always wondered if he was one step from falling off the wagon. Seth returned to his position on the bench. "I'm glad she's happy back in Chicago. Haven't even thought about her."

Liar.

"Great." Nate positioned his hands to spot the next round of reps. "Then you don't care that Gabe and I saw her perform before I dropped Gabe off at the center."

Seth lifted the bar. The added weight definitely took more focus. "Great."

He did one rep and held.

"And you probably also don't care that she was dancing in the chorus."

"What?" Seth was mid press when that bit of knowledge dropped along with the bar on his chest. "*Uff.*"

Nate grabbed the bar and lifted it back to the stand. "Maybe we should take a break."

Seth sat up again and reached for his towel. "What do you mean she had a role in the chorus? Isn't she Giselle?"

"Nope."

"Why?"

"Shockingly, they didn't put that in the program."

Seth stood, walked over to his desk, and pulled the pamphlet Gabe had given him from the drawer where he'd shoved it. He hadn't even really looked at it. All of it had been too painful. He studied it over and then again. Sure enough, Grace's small name was listed in the chorus.

Why hadn't she said anything on their phone call?

The door to the rec center opened, and after a long pause, a hesitant Zane walked in. His hands were shoved in the front pocked of an oversized hoodie, and he shuffled toward them, gaze down.

"What's going on?" Seth finally asked. The kid was clearly not dressed for a workout.

"I wanted to say I was sorry." The words came out mumbled and rushed together.

Seth walked around the desk and stood in front of the kid and waited for him to look up. When he did, there was fear in his eyes.

Seth nodded. "It's time to put childish ways aside, Zane. Stand up and say it like you really mean it. Unless you don't."

The kid lifted his chin and drew a slow breath. This time keeping his gaze fixed on Seth. "I am really sorry."

Seth patted his shoulder. "I forgive you. I'm just glad you listened to your conscience and came forward in the end."

Seth walked to the other side of the desk.

"But I didn't." Zane's boyish tone was back.

Seth crossed his arms over his chest and studied the boy. "What do you mean? You did come forward."

"No, I mean I didn't listen to my conscience. I listened to Grace."

Grace?

The one word had the power to knock the wind out of him. He dropped into the chair and leaned forward on his knees. "What are you talking about?"

Zane's eyes darted between Nate and Seth. "I . . . I thought she told you."

Nate settled into a chair then nudged one closer to Zane. "Why don't you tell us."

"I went to Susie's show that morning they were dancing in the gazebo. As soon as it was over, Grace cornered me and asked me all these questions about Gabe, about the cash box, about the ..." The kid looked at his feet a moment then back up. "...about the drugs."

"And?" Seth's ears were pounding so loud he could barely focus on the kid.

"She had me in circles, and I couldn't keep my own lie straight. Once I told her the truth, she told me if I didn't come forward, that she would." He stood and walked closer to Seth. "I was really mad at the time but now ... I really *am* sorry."

Seth nodded but his mind was completely on Grace. She'd unraveled the truth out of Zane? He looked at Nate, who had an eyebrow raised, and Seth just wanted to bang his head against the cement wall. He'd been wrong. Grace was the best thing that ever happened to him, and he had tossed her away because she'd failed him. Or at least he'd thought she had.

"Call her." Nate stood next to the desk.

"And say what?"

"Honestly, I don't know. Maybe you'll know when you hear her voice, but I have a feeling things aren't done with you two, and at the very least you need to talk."

Seth nodded and tapped her name. It rang a few times before she picked up.

"Hello?" Her soft voice was full of uncertainty.

"Hi." The silence stretched. He looked to Nate for help, but the space where he'd stood was empty. He noted that Zane was missing too, just as the main door clicked shut in the distance.

"Seth, I have to get ready, so if—"

"You're the one who convinced Zane to come forward."

There was a long pause and some shuffling on the other end.

He almost had given up on her speaking when there was a sigh. "Yeah, I was."

"You *did* believe me."

"Honestly, I didn't know what to believe at first, but it didn't take long to put the pieces together."

"I should have given you a chance to explain."

"Yes, you should've."

"Grace, do you think—"

"I need to get ready. The curtain lifts in less than thirty minutes."

"You're dancing in the chorus?"

"Yup."

"How do you feel about that?"

"I've enjoyed it, actually. I've learned that the role I dance is just that, a role, it isn't my identity. A role may be how others see me, but it isn't how God sees me."

"How does He see you?"

"Beautiful, lovable, perfect—with a fair amount of room for growth." A small chuckle from Grace traveled through the line and settled deep in Seth's chest.

"Yeah, I can identify with that." Seth ran his hand over his sternum, but the pressure only increased. "I was thinking—"

"Seth, don't."

The words hit him like a punch, and he sat back. He closed his eyes and drew a slow breath, waiting for her to continue. Because honestly, he couldn't form words right now.

"I know you have regrets, so do I, but before I broke up that fight between you and Gabe, he said something . . . and I think he's right."

Seth leaned forward and rubbed his eyes with his free hand. Even after the guy turned his life around, his actions were haunting Seth. "And that was?"

"'As soon as someone lets you down—as soon as the cost looks too high, you quit.'" She took a slow breath then continued. "Hon-

estly, at the time I didn't see it. But I asked you one question—
one—and you tossed me aside as if I was barely more than an
inconvenience."

"That's not—"

"True? When you were helping me on those tilting discs you
told me the only way to succeed is to go all in. Don't hesitate. That
I had to focus on where I was headed, not worry about where I'd
been. Don't you see? You're so fixated on your past mistakes, on
others' past mistakes, you miss what's in front of you."

He clenched his jaw. He wanted to tell her she was wrong, but
his mind became a slideshow of examples. His resistance to start
the ninja gym with Jon. His refusal to return to *Ninja Warrior*. His
refusal to really trust the guys again. Even what she'd said about
how he'd treated her. He'd been so fixated on the past he couldn't
even see the future.

"I really do need to go, Seth."

"Can we talk again?"

"I don't know. Bye, Seth."

The line went dead, and Seth dropped his phone on his desk
and pressed his palms into his eyes.

What was he going to do now? He seemed to have pushed
everyone and every good thing out of his life. All he was left with
was a pathetic apartment and a job he had no doubt he'd hate,
come next week.

His head jerked up as the door opened and Nate walked back
in. "Sorry, forgot my bag."

Nate lifted his duffel from the floor, then paused next to Seth's
desk. "Phone call not go well?"

"You could say that."

"Sorry, man. Maybe it was the closure you need. But the rest of
what I said was true." Nate tapped on yet another invitation the
Ninja Warrior production had sent him. "People care about you."

Seth sent his friend a skeptical look. "The TV show cares about me?"

"Absolutely not! They want to make money off you. But your fans care and they keep talking online about how they hope you'll return to regionals. You inspire them—"

"But if they knew—"

"If they knew everything, then you would inspire them more. You inspire the rest of us. Why do you think people were willing to go along with Jon's charade with the furniture? That took no small amount of planning."

"Jon's well liked."

"No, because you're well liked. People here have been rooting for you your whole life. And your success inspires them. Let go of your past."

"Even with my record expunged I just don't know if I can be that open with the public."

"Why? Don't you think that God could use it? Your past doesn't exempt you from a good future." Nate settled into a chair and stretched his legs out. "For so long I let my own past be an anchor around my neck. I pushed Olivia away because I thought she deserved better. But what I came to realize is that by doing so I was slapping God's hand away when He was trying to give me a gift."

"You think Grace is a gift to me? I'm pretty sure that phone call says that gift is gone."

"Maybe. But God is giving you other things." He waved to the space around them indicating the gym in progress and then tapped the invitation again. "Don't slap God's hand away."

Could he really believe that? He'd told Grace over and over that real love wasn't based on performance, and yet that was exactly how he lived. With her. With the guys. With God.

Somehow, he'd convinced himself that God loved him less because of what he'd done, and he was earning his way back into favor. But that wasn't what the Bible told him. And it wasn't what he'd been preaching to Grace. What could he do about that now?

Tomorrow's a new day with no mistakes. Great. First Grace, now his dad. Why were all these memories plaguing him every time he turned around today? Because just maybe it wasn't the memories. Just maybe God was trying to get his attention.

Because God refused to give up on him. Because God's love didn't change. Because God wouldn't fail him.

Seth lifted his phone and punched in Allen Mets's number.

"Seth, tell me something good. We have a week until shooting, and we just lost one of the top-rated guys. Did a header off the Diamond Dash in practice. Separated shoulder. Please tell me you're coming."

"You got your wish. The Storm's coming back."

"And the interview?"

"Whatever you want." It was time to embrace what God was giving him. Win or lose he needed to go all in, full tilt—no hesitation.

Nate clapped his hands, stood, and grabbed his phone. "I'm calling the guys." Then he hesitated, lowering his phone. "Unless you don't want anyone to know."

"I want you all in my corner, if you'll come."

"We wouldn't miss it."

nineteen

THIS WASN'T HOW IT WAS SUPPOSED TO GO. For all his resistance to competing, Seth had never actually thought about the possibility of losing. He took an extra second under the water, letting it cool his face before standing and staring at the blue Chicago sky as he wiped the water away from his face. The sun was low, but the network had plenty of flood lights trained on his face, so everyone at home would have a good view of his humiliating fall.

Awesome.

He stared up at the red spinning cylinders above his head that had beaten him, then made his way to the edge of the splash pool. He offered the crowd a wave before making the awkward climb out over the side. As if falling hadn't been humiliating enough.

A guy in a black T-shirt and headset handed him a towel then pointed him to where his friends stood next to a woman in a red dress holding a microphone. He ran the towel over his head a few times but before he could even exchange one word with Grant, Nate, or Jon, the microphone was shoved in his face.

"Up until the fall, your pace was a full ten seconds ahead of the top finisher tonight. We were heartbroken to see you fall." The blonde was all smiles. Yeah, she looked real heartbroken. "Can you tell us what happened?"

He fell, that was what happened. But it wasn't like he could say that. Instead, he forced a smile and leaned toward the mic. "I just missed my footing."

"You faced the Log Runner in city qualifiers and had no difficulties. Can you tell us what was different today?"

Thanks for the reminder. He ran the towel over his head again to stall for time as he searched his mind for a response. Because what happened was that a certain blue-eyed ballerina had distracted him.

She wasn't there, but she might as well have been. All he'd thought of was Grace on the tilting discs. Of her comments about him not being all in. Her saying that he'd tossed her aside. With all that filling his head, he'd hesitated just long enough to send him spinning. Just like she said he did in life. Always looking back. Always losing focus.

But things were supposed to be different. He'd signed the contract for the gym with Jon. He'd even agreed to put The Home of The Storm on front of the building in neon letters.

She must have given up waiting for his answer because she pulled the microphone back. Her smile was more strained by the second. He had to pull himself together. "I know this wasn't the outcome you hoped for, but I know many of your fans were so glad to see you back."

"Thank you, it was good to be back." And that was the truth. It felt good to be out there. And maybe next time he wouldn't hesitate, but for the first time in a long time he was looking to the future.

"One last question. This year, fans can vote in three of their favorites who didn't make it to the finals to get another shot. What would you like to say to your fans out there?"

No doubt she wanted him to look into that camera and remind

everyone to go online and vote for him. But that just wasn't his style. Instead, he smiled and nodded. "I am sure whoever they bring back, it will be an amazing show."

The woman's smile dimmed as she focused back on the camera. "Thank you, Storm. Allen, back to you."

The crowd was already going crazy for the guy behind him who had progressed on obstacle three. The Spider Wall. *Good luck. Next one is a doozy.*

He walked to his friends as they made their way beyond the barrier. They walked toward the makeshift locker room. Although with the security flanking the door, he supposed his friends would have to wait outside.

They had almost reached it when Nate spoke up. "Sorry, man."

"It's all good. I'm glad I did it."

"No regrets if they run the editorial on you?"

"Nope. This is a gift." He motioned to all the production around him. "Nothing I could have ever planned. Might as well see what God wants to do with it."

Seth hurried into the locker room and emerged fifteen minutes later with dry clothes and wet but combed hair. He walked to where Grant, Nate, and Jon all waited against a fence.

He crossed over yet another barrier only to suddenly be surrounded by a sea of young faces, several with a large gray cloud painted on them.

"Storm! Will you sign this?" One boy rushed forward, shoving a paper in his face. That seemed to open the floodgates as several pushed forward.

He dropped his bag and accommodated them one at a time, even posing for a few photos before the small crowd dispersed. He lifted his bag again, catching a glimpse of the guys leaning against a fence a few feet away.

Nate stepped forward. "Can we get your autograph, Mr. Storm?"

"Funny." He motioned down the street in the direction of the parking garage. "Let's get out of here."

They were part way down the street when a poster advertising *Giselle* caught his eye. He stopped and looked around. How had he not realized they were right in front of the Auditorium Theatre? He walked over to the sign and, sure enough, *Giselle* was playing tonight, and it was marked as the final show.

"You going to go?" Nate stopped next to the sign. "I'm not one for ballet, but it was a good show."

"I'm not sure she would want to see me." And yet he couldn't seem to move on, his feet cemented to the sidewalk. "Can't say I blame her."

"Show her that you've changed. If her fear is that you'll abandon her again—" Grant stepped forward and dropped a hand on his shoulder. "Then show up. Again and again until she knows what we know."

Seth looked at him over his shoulder. "And what's that?"

Grant shoved his hands in his pockets, seeming in no hurry to move on. "There are few more loyal than you."

"But I—"

Nate moved to stand shoulder to shoulder with Grant. "You thanklessly care for your mother."

"You helped Gabe when many in your position would not have." Jon joined the wall as if they were all physically blocking him from walking away. From giving up.

Nate spoke up again. "You still stop by Margret's to check on her even though Grace has no idea."

"Tell her you love her and let her decide." Grant crossed his arms over his chest as if to emphasize the wall.

When he still hesitated, Jon gave his shoulder a shove. "Where's the brave Seth who didn't hesitate to help his mom when she drove into the square or The Storm who just owned the spider wall?"

Seth shook his head as his gaze traveled toward the lights in the distance of the competition. "You do realize one of those led to jail and the other led to the dunk tank of failure thirty seconds later."

"Yup." There was amusement in Jon's tone.

Seth looked back at the sign. "So you think this will end in disaster too?"

"Honestly, I have no idea." Jon landed a hand on Seth's shoulder. "But I do know what will happen if you don't go."

"What?"

"Nothing." His hands flew up in frustration. Then he motioned to the two guys next to him. "We're always in your corner no matter what. Give her a choice to be in your corner too, don't say no for her."

Seth looked at them, then the box office, then back at them. Finally, he sighed and walked over to the window. "Do you have any seats under the name Scooby-Doo."

The woman on the other side of the window sat up a bit straighter as a smile filled her face. "We do."

She pulled an envelope from a box and slipped it under the glass. "Enjoy the show."

"You could have told me you have season tickets," Nate shouted after him as he headed inside.

This too could end in disaster, but it was time to go all in and trust she just might want to catch him.

She had expected that her final show would feel different than this. Bigger. More daunting. But in the end, it just felt like another show. Grace checked her hair one more time, then lifted her shoes from the bag.

There was a swift knock on the door before it swung inward, and Mallory stepped in. "Stephanie from tickets sent this to you."

Stephanie? Why would she? Unless her parents . . . She tore open the note and sure enough.

Scooby-Doo seats claimed but it wasn't your parents.

Not her parents. Why would Stephanie think she cared about some of her parents' fancy friends claiming the tickets? She lifted the note again.

It was The Storm. You have been holding out on me! We need to talk.

She looked up at Mallory and the girl gripped her shoulder. "Seth is here."

"You read it?"

"Of course. I was not delivering it until after the show if it was about your parents. You don't need that." Mallory tugged her to the door. "Let's go see."

"How?"

"There's a great little spot where you can see the audience, but they can't see you. You aren't supposed to, but I use it all the time."

Mallory led Grace to the little opening. They were in darkness, but the theatre was still in full lights. Grace's gaze travelled the room. Fourth row left. Her eyes landed on the seats, and she nearly froze.

She would have wondered if her eyes were playing tricks on her if Mallory hadn't released a little squeal. "It's really him. He loves you."

"You don't know that." Their last phone call was running though her mind. She had been so harsh with him.

"I guarantee that he's here for one and only one reason. He loves you. So the question is, do you love him back?"

"I . . . I don't know." Grace walked a few steps away then back, her fingers twisting in front of her. "I told him it wouldn't work. I basically told him I didn't trust him."

"Ouch. He's brave to come back." Mallory peeked through the gap again. "Why can't you trust him?"

"Because he got so mad when I asked him if the drugs were his. Because he's so hung up on his past that he won't move forward, commit to anything, or trust anyone. Why would it be different with me?" She paced as she spoke but then gripped Mallory's arms. "He was so hung up on his past that he even refused to return as The Storm."

"But he did." Mallory's brows rose like Grace was missing something big. Maybe she was.

"What are you talking about?"

"It hasn't aired yet, but it's all over social media, people posting photos of him tonight. He must have come right here." She tapped her phone and then turned it around.

Grace lifted it from her hand. Sure enough, that was definitely Seth. The image had caught him on the Hanging Bridges just as he jumped from one obstacle to the next. She lowered it and looked at Mal. "How did he do?"

"They won't release that until the show airs, but here are some selfies some kids took with him."

"He returned as The Storm." She picked up her pacing again. "Why would he do that? He said he'd never do that. And now he's here. What does it all mean?"

"Back to my first guess. He loves you. So, let me ask you again. Do you love him?"

Her pacing stopped. "Yes."

"No hesitation this time." Mallory gave a little clap with her hands. "Progress. Now you just have to tell him."

"Tell him?" She peered through the curtain gap again.

"After the show." Mallory pulled her back.

Right.

Grace's hand flew to her face. "Wait!"

"What now?"

"He knows I'm in the chorus, but I doubt he knows that means

I'm only in a few dances." She motioned to her less-than-remarkable costume. "I'm just a nameless character."

"I could be wrong"—her friend lifted one brow in her direction—"but I am guessing he isn't here for the ballet."

"But he's expecting—"

"You." Mallory pointed to the stage. "Now go out there and dance for him. And if he really loves you, it will be enough. By the way he looked at you last time, I'm guessing you could go out there and fall off the stage and it would still be enough."

"Love isn't based on your performance." Seth's words came back. He had failed her, but she had also failed him. Love wasn't about perfection. It was about forgiveness and choosing the other person every day. *"A new day with no mistakes."*

He was here, and this was her last performance. All in, no holding back.

She couldn't see his face well while she was dancing. The problem with her role was that she was always stationed toward the back of the stage rather than up front where she could see the audience. But her spot on the stage didn't matter. She danced like she hadn't danced in a long time, and it felt good. Free.

By the time the final curtain call came she was ready to leap off the stage and run to him. Madame Laurent would love that. Instead, she rushed to her dressing room and started pulling off the elastic arm decorations. Hopefully he wouldn't leave.

"That, my darling, was the Grace I have been looking for." Madame Laurent strode in with Alec two steps behind. "You are finally back, and the lead in the fall show is yours if you want it."

The lead. Everything she had worked for was at her fingertips. But suddenly, she didn't want it. Because all she could think about at this moment was seeing Seth.

"Take it. You have earned it."

She stilled, then turned. Seth stood in the doorway, his gaze fixed on her. Oh, he looked good. And it hit her just like it had when he showed up in her studio dressed in workout clothes. This man had presence, power, and a place in her life. At least she hoped so.

He stepped into the room, his eyes on hers. "You should take it. And I'll be at every show."

"Every one?" She took a step toward him. "That's a long drive."

"What can I say?" He shrugged. "I am committed . . . to the ballet."

Grace bit back a smile and then turned to Madame Laurent. "Before, you said I'd lost my heart, and you were right. Ballet used to be everything. But now . . . I think I'm ready to let go. Move to the next stage of life. See who I was created to be."

"Don't do anything rash." She placed a gentle hand on Grace's arm. "Today I saw that heart again. *You're back.*"

"Maybe." Grace laid her hand on Seth's chest. "But I left my heart in Heritage, and I think it's time to go home."

"I will let you think on it." Madame Laurent narrowed her eyes, then disappeared out the door with Alec on her heels.

"How did you get back here?" She took a step forward.

"Mallory."

Right. Deep breath. She could do this. "I'm sorry for the phone call it was—"

He closed the distance, his expression solemn as his hands landed gently on her arms. "Honest. Hard truth I needed to hear. I was scared. I've never been in love with someone before, and—"

"You love me?" She gripped the front of his shirt.

"I do." His face softened into a smile. He ran a finger over her cheek. "Very much. But if you don't want—"

Grace pulled him forward, pressing her lips into his. She drew a deep breath, savoring everything about the moment. How he tasted of mint and smelled a musky scent that was uniquely Seth. Against all odds, they had made it work. She was his, and he was hers. And every day she would choose him.

His fingers laced though her hair as he eased her back, a teasing grin on his face. "Does that mean you do want something?"

"I do. I love you so much. I want . . . forever." That's all she got out before his lips covered hers again. Grace sank into the kiss. For the first time after a performance, she felt loved and seen, and it had nothing to do with the dance. He'd come for her. And he'd come again. Because he knew her, saw her, and still loved her.

He eased her back ever so slightly. "I'm serious though. You were amazing out there. You have your joy back, and if you want to stay for another season, we'll make it work."

"I'll admit that was my best show I've had. But it wasn't because I remembered why I love dance."

"Then what was it?"

"Don't you know?" When he just stared at her blinking, she reached up and ran her fingers along his jaw. "You're the reason. You're the reason I loved dancing tonight. You're the reason I found a way to dream again. You're the reason I can't wait to return to Heritage."

Seth's lips pressed against her again as he dug his fingers into her hair, catching them on her pins. Without breaking the kiss, he began removing them one at a time until her hair hung free at her shoulders. He ran his fingers through one more time as he pressed his forehead to hers. "And you're the reason I ran the Ninja Warrior course."

"So the rumors are true. How did it go?"

"Poorly." He released a small chuckle as he ran his thumb over her chin. "But I was done being held back by my past. It was time to go all in."

"All in."

He leaned back and ran his fingers again though her hair sticking out at all odd angles. "I love it like this."

"Like this?" She leaned back and shook it out. "It's a mess."

"We all are. And I'll be there for your messes every step of the way."

"And I'll be there for yours. We will be beautifully messy to-gether."

He pressed his lips to hers once more, and she let herself be lost as her senses exploded with all things Seth. This was better than dancing.

After a few more moments, Grace leaned back. "Did you ever get anything in the mail about your dad?"

"That was you?" He pressed his forehead into hers as if he couldn't get close enough. "How did you—"

"Ms. Margret connected me with Grant, who helped. He was in the Army. I did it the day after we got back from Chicago."

He closed his eyes as if the words pained him. "I am so sorry I didn't listen to you. That I thought I couldn't—"

She covered his mouth with hers again, drawing out the kiss before pulling back. "All is forgiven. Every day's a new day."

He pulled her close, wrapping her in a hug. "Can tomorrow have more of that?"

"Of course." She pressed one more quick kiss on his lips. "Now let me change so we can go."

"Go?"

"I believe it's time to go home. Home to Heritage."

Epilogue

T HE LAST THING SETH EXPECTED WAS TO BE voted by the fans into the final round, but here he was in Las Vegas, staring down the bright lights and big cameras as he waited for the green light to give him permission to run across the Floating Steps one more time. He bounced on his toes a few times and waved to the crowd as they cheered. But they weren't the reason he was doing this.

He glanced to the side where his crew waited. Half of the group wore fluorescent green T-shirts with the words Thunder Arena: Home of The Storm. The other half wore pink T-shirts that advertised Grace's dance studio, Dance with Grace. They had unveiled the sign a week ago with a party that even Otis had shown up for, and already her roster for fall was almost full. No doubt the word was spreading to neighboring areas that a prima ballerina would be teaching.

He glanced down at his own shirt.

Leah had fashioned him a half-fluorescent-green, half-pink T-shirt like he was the kaleidoscope of Heritage businesses. But he didn't mind—after all, these were his people.

He didn't even care if he finished in record time or finished at all. This journey had been about so much more than this run. His future was full of endless possibilities. His future was good. And the future started right beyond those steps.

The green light lit as the buzzer sounded, echoing through the arena.

Seth gave Grace one last look then jumped . . . all in.

READ ON FOR MORE FROM THE

Home to Heritage

SERIES

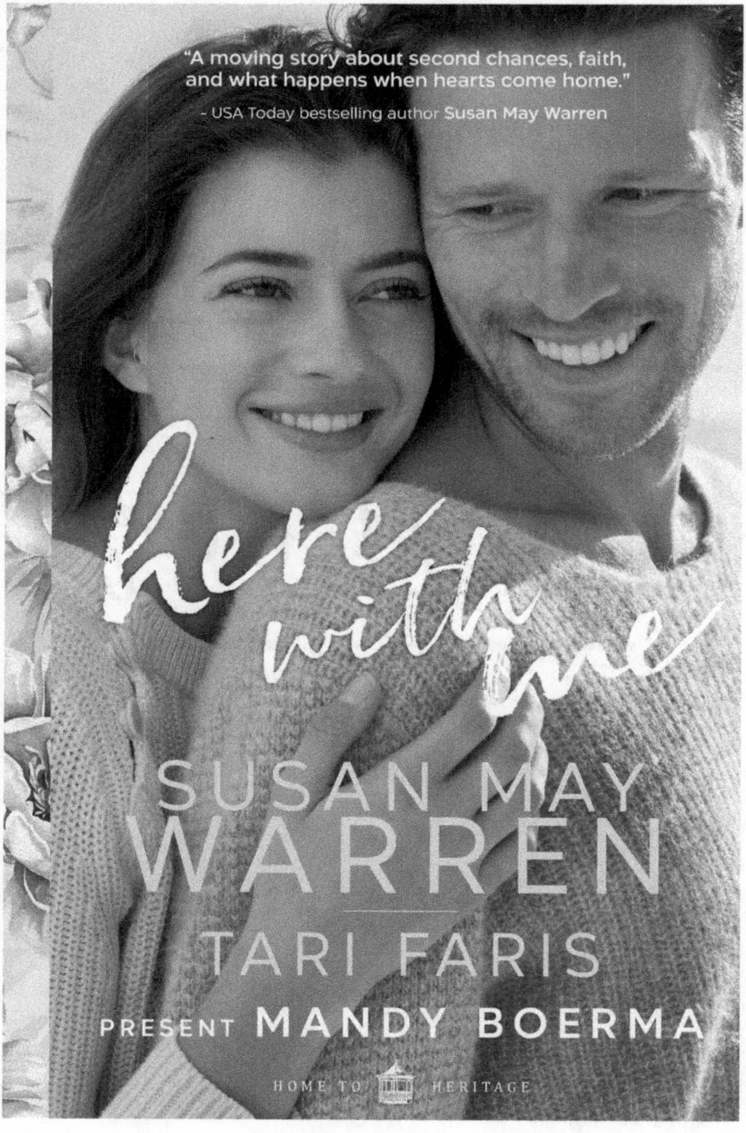
"A moving story about second chances, faith, and what happens when hearts come home."
- USA Today bestselling author Susan May Warren
here with me
SUSAN MAY WARREN
TARI FARIS
PRESENT MANDY BOERMA
HOME TO HERITAGE

Inheriting her best friend's daughter and a store on the brink of collapse, Sadie Hoover is determined to provide Lottie a stable life and keep the family business afloat. But her resolve is tested when the past walks in, wearing a tool belt and a smile that still weakens her knees.

Is he back to break her heart?

David Williams, once the love of Sadie's life, returns to Heritage not as the missionary he was, but as a man in search of healing and purpose. Tasked with community service, he's thrown into the daily grind of nuts and bolts, unaware that the hardware store's troubles—and Sadie's struggles—are more than just loose hinges and unpaid bills.

What will it cost her to fall for him again?

As they grapple with financial peril and the echoes of a love once lost, David and Sadie are forced to confront what they truly want. The store's impending foreclosure looms over them, a testament to their joint past and the future they must shape.

If the store fails, they lose not just a legacy, but the second chance life has offered them. Can they rekindle their love while saving the heart of Heritage, or will their dreams rust away like forgotten tools?

Can love be rebuilt from the ruins of their shared history, or will the fight for survival drive the final wedge between them?

one

I T WAS TIME, BEYOND TIME, TO LEAVE HERITAGE, Michigan, and return to Costa Rica—if only David Williams could convince his directors at Christ in the World Mission that he was ready.

To be needed.

To help people.

To go.

Instead, David was stuck in a tiny town, practically trapped in his late grandparents' old farmhouse. His only use? Fulfilling his sisters' designs to turn this place into an Airbnb.

The cool August breeze whispered over his skin as David worked at a makeshift table, a couple of sawhorses for his miter saw, in the driveway of the old farmhouse.

Gravel crunched under tire wheels, but he didn't need a distraction now.

"Still working I see." Nate Williams, his cousin, walked across the gravel driveway.

David set the board aside. "These are the last shelves I need to cut to finish up the built-in."

Picking up one of the freshly cut boards, Nate nodded to the front door. David grabbed the remaining two pieces on the saw, checked to make sure the power was off, and followed Nate toward the front door.

"Heard anything from Lance?" Nate pushed through the door of the old, two-story farmhouse and tossed his keys on the table.

David set the boards against the new built-in he'd constructed in his grandparents' living room. "Do you know what they decided?"

"I sent off my recommendation yesterday via email, but I'm not part of the meeting today."

David tried to hold back a wince. He had hoped Nate was part of it. After all, it could only help to have his cousin and pastor of the local church on his side. But maybe the letter from Nate would be enough to convince the board he was well enough to return to his job as a teacher for the children of missionaries in Costa Rica.

Nate ran his hand along the last set of shelves David had installed. "This looks good."

David grunted a thanks. The shelves did look good. Especially as a backdrop to the two couches and coffee table that his sisters had ordered. They called it "farmhouse chic"—whatever that was. All he knew was that it was the last project his sisters wanted before they listed the place as an Airbnb. Of course, they couldn't do that until *after* he returned to Costa Rica. Who knew how many people would want to come vacation in Heritage?

The clock chimed the bottom of the hour. The day was ticking past him at a snail's pace. With the offices closed for Labor Day, surely the director wouldn't make him wait until Tuesday for an answer, or would he?

David picked up his cordless drill on the coffee table then pulled a couple of wood screws out of his carpenter's belt—he was almost out of them. Hopefully he had enough to finish installing the shelves.

David measured and marked where the shelf would go, and Nate stepped closer, taking the shelf and pressing it against the wall. Then he picked up the level and set it on top. "Are you sure you're ready to leave all this behind and return to Costa Rica? Your sisters have enjoyed having you here these past six months."

David adjusted the shelf and checked the level. "School is starting next week. I really wanted to be back before this new year began. Besides, I haven't seen them much. They're busy with their own lives." Leah with her new baby, and Caroline had her hands full with two girls and another baby on the way.

David lined up the screw in the predrilled hole then lifted the drill. When his hand started to shake, he lowered it as his gaze shot to Nate. The guy's stare fixed on the wall—at least he hadn't seen. He drew a slow breath and stretched his fingers then tried again. This time he connected with the screw. David slipped his hand into his belt for more screws and pulled out the last three. Just his luck. Short three screws for the final shelf. "I'm gonna need to run and pick up more screws to finish these last few shelves."

"You should have messaged. I could have stopped at Hoover's on my way over."

Hoover's. The local hardware store—the one he'd turned his back on all those years ago. No way could he shop there now. It would be easier to drive to Ludington.

"I'll run to Lowe's." David looked at the time. Three forty-five. "But I'd like to be here when that call from Lance comes in. I hate talking and driving."

"You don't have to continue to hide out here." Nate walked into the kitchen and filled a glass of water at the sink.

Hiding hadn't crossed his mind. But he liked to keep the past in the past.

David followed, pulling out a root beer from the fridge. He opened the top, and the pop fizzed before he took a long drink, taking his time to respond to Nate. They'd had this conversation a few times now. "I get out. Talk to people when I do."

"You've been home six months, and you've hardly left the house."

"I've counted every day I've been here. That's why I need to get back." David picked up his wallet and keys to his grandpa's Subaru Brat and walked to the front door.

Nate, close behind, grabbed his own keys off the table by the door as he followed David outside. "If you're eager to get back to work, you could do that here. You could be out in the community. There are people here that need encouragement. For example, would it be hard to run to Hoover's Hardware? It would certainly take less time. How hard could it be to say hi to Gary?"

Gary wasn't the problem. It was Sadie. But if she was in town, Caroline or Leah would have mentioned it. They'd certainly told him when Sadie had moved away. He hadn't believed them, because for as long as they'd dated, her dream had been to take over the family business. It had become their dream. Proof that dreams changed.

Still, David had managed to go all summer without going to Hoover's. Why change that today? Heading there might dig up memories best forgotten. Memories he worked hard to keep buried.

Once they were on the porch, Nate's phone pinged.

His cousin pulled it out then shook his head as he typed out a quick message. "I've gotta go. Church duty calls."

Nate hurried to his motorcycle and buckled his helmet in place before heading back toward town.

The sun beat down on David, the temperatures hinting of the changing leaves and the cooler weather sure to come. He checked his watch. Three fifty-one. Gary Hoover had always closed the hardware store at five back in the day. If that was still the case, David could be there and back in under thirty minutes. Maybe Nate had a point. He could easily pop in and say hi, get what he needed, and be home. Bonus, it wouldn't take as much time as traveling to Ludington.

Almost ten years had passed since David had spoken to Gary in person. When David and Sadie had broken up, he assumed Gary would disappear from his life. But Gary hadn't. Just like a true father, he'd stayed in contact, even sending monthly support.

David drove into the city center of Heritage. Otis, the bronze hippo that moved around the town square, sat in front of the new ballet studio, almost like he enjoyed the fresh entertainment. Never able to figure out how Otis moved, David accepted the lovable town oddity.

David stopped at the intersection of Second and Teft. No matter how many times he pulled into town, the updated square surprised him. Long gone was the Manor and the row of condemned houses. An old schoolhouse had been renovated and turned into the library. It sat on one corner with a gazebo in the middle. A playground filled the southern part of the square. Maybe his sisters weren't too far off base with the Airbnb idea. The town did hold a certain small-town charm.

Up on his right, the diner's front window sparkled in the afternoon sun, and directly in front of him a huge banner hung over the street advertising their 150th town anniversary in October.

David continued through the intersection down Second Street until he found a parking spot along the square and cut the engine. The shop sat on the corner of Richard and Second just across the street from the southeast corner of the square. It was right next to the bank, but the entrance had been moved around the corner to Richard Street on the southern side of the building. That would have been Sadie's and his first change to the store. He shook away the memory as he got out of the truck and hurried across the street.

As soon as he turned the corner, the rusted Hoover's Hardware sign greeted him. The letters had faded even more, so that one of the *o*'s was completely gone.

The friendly jingle of an overhead bell announced his entrance into the shop. Gary had always kept the store in immaculate condition, but today, dust laced the air and the endcaps of the aisles held anything from paint brushes to hammers—seemingly with no rhyme or reason. Charlotte's web had nothing on the huge cobweb spun along the wood paneled wall behind the register. Gary had never allowed spiders free rein of his store.

"Be right with ya!" The distant voice came from somewhere among the shelves, but there was no mistaking Gary's deep timbre.

The man's gait faltered for a second as he stepped out of the aisle, his eyes widening. He set down a five-gallon paint bucket. And there was just enough of a pause that David's heart sank. Maybe this hadn't been a great idea. But before he could think of what to do next, Gary rushed forward and grabbed David's shoulder and looked him over. "Ten years looks good on you, son. The final bits of boy have disappeared."

Son. David's throat tightened. Gary probably used the term with every male under the age of forty, but it still triggered a sense of what had been. What could have been. The guy almost looked proud of him.

Before David could consider what to say, his gaze landed on Gary's arm that was wrapped in a blue sling and seemed to be strapped down to his chest. "What happened to your arm?"

The older man offered a slight shrug, lifting his uninjured shoulder. "I fell working on the upstairs guest bath a month ago. Landed on my shoulder wrong. Emergency surgery on my rotator cuff, and my arm is useless until it heals. Just a few more weeks in the sling."

One month ago? How had he missed this tidbit of gossip? David had been working away in his grandparents' home a month ago. Maybe this was what Nate meant when he said that David should get out more and see the needs of people around him. Guilt clung to him like day-old sawdust.

Gary walked back to the bucket and bent to pick it up.

"Let me." David didn't know much about rotator cuff surgery, but lifting heavy objects probably wasn't part of the recovery.

Gary slapped David's back. "I appreciate that. I'm getting too old for this. Definitely time for the next generation to take over. But kids are busy these days. One of my daughters only pops in and out maybe once a month now."

Gary had three daughters, but he must mean Sadie, otherwise he'd just name his daughter. With their complicated past, he couldn't blame Gary for being vague. He couldn't ask. Wouldn't ask about Sadie. So, he nodded, and Gary kept talking.

"The high schoolers looking for volunteer hours just don't work for us, with all the heavy machinery and specialized merchandise."

David followed Gary to the register at the front of the store, and set the bucket where Gary directed.

Gary patted him on the back, squeezing his shoulder. "Now tell me, what brings you in today?"

Business. Good. David could handle that. "Need a box of two-and-a-half-inch wood screws."

"Ah. Screws. Those are on the back wall, just like always. It's a bit disorganized—things have just gotten away from me—but I'm pretty sure they're back there somewhere."

David's phone chimed in his pocket, and he pulled it out. *Finally*. He held up his phone. "I need to respond to this. I'll be right back."

"Take your time, son. I'll be here." Gary continued toward the back of the store, and David turned and stepped outside, looking for shade so he could read his phone screen. The afternoon sun slipped behind a cloud as he walked to the back of the building, away from the square.

Lance
_____
Let's chat next week. Tuesday morning. 10 EST

No. No. No. No. No. This couldn't be right. If they'd approved him to go back, they'd simply say the words. The only reason Lance would want to talk was because they weren't going to send him back yet.

David

School starts next week.

I'd love to work through things ASAP.

Chat now?

Lance

Marco can't right now.

Tuesday morning. 10.

Marco wanted to talk, too? David clenched his fist and then stretched his hand. If they wanted to bring in the executive director, it meant he'd officially miss the first day of school in Costa Rica. This couldn't be God's will. But then again, what did he know? No matter how much he prayed lately, God still seemed to be silent.

Anytime, God. I'm ready.

Still no response.

Nothing more could be done today. Tucking his phone away, David walked back to his grandfather's gold truck and opened the door and plopped down in the driver's seat. Ugh. He still needed those screws. Not that he had a pressing deadline to finish the built-ins anymore. No. He wasn't giving up that easy. He'd fight for what he wanted.

He left the truck and hurried back up the few steps toward the hardware store. The bell welcomed him a second time.

"Coming." A feminine voice rang out, and David could hardly process the familiarity before Sadie stepped out of the back aisle.

She froze. Her long, light brown hair was braided, hanging over her shoulder. Her hazel eyes took him in, a touch of vulnerability in her gaze. "You." The word came out breathy and tense.

"Sadie." His voice wasn't any better. But it had been ten years. Ten years since she'd talked to him. Ten years since he'd held her. Ten years since she'd broken his heart right before their college graduation. He opened his mouth again, but nothing came out. His brain had stopped working.

The softness in her gaze vanished, and the welcoming smile disappeared as she held out a box. "I take it you're the wood screw guy."

She was mad at him? She was the one who'd stomped on his heart, not the other way around. She'd been the one to walk away and never look back. He opened his mouth but snapped it shut. He'd moved on and so had she. They didn't need to have this discussion again. His throat tightened, and he worked to swallow the moisture before it evaporated from his mouth. "Two-and-a-half-inch wood screws—that's me."

Her left ring finger was bare. He'd heard she'd gotten married, but maybe he'd heard wrong. He tried not to dwell on news of Sadie, so on the rare occasion one of his sisters brought her up, he quickly ended the call. But hearing she'd gotten married would have been hard to forget. Even so, there had been no one since Sadie, because no one had measured up.

She briefly nodded and walked to the register without a backward glance.

"It's been a while." Almost ten years. And not a day went by that he didn't think about her.

"We don't have to do this, David." She rang him up, not looking at him.

Do what? Catch up? Find out how she'd been? How long she'd be in town? David gulped and looked at his shoes as he pulled out his wallet.

Sadie said the total, and he handed over the cash, his hands oddly still. He wanted her to look up again. To see her eyes, catch a glimpse of her smile. But it was better if he didn't. He couldn't consider those things anymore. Not since her wedding.

She handed him his change and the screws. Her fingers barely touched his skin, yet little sparks shot all the way up his arm. She looked up, holding eye contact now.

"You been here long?" He should go. He had his change and his screws. But seeing Sadie again...well, he wasn't ready to walk away just yet. Not if it was going to be another ten years.

"Just got into town." She tucked her hands in her back pockets and rocked back on her heels. "Have a good one, David." She nodded to the door.

He could take a hint. He stepped closer to the door without looking away from Sadie. "You too."

David pushed the door open, and the jingling of the overhead bell broke the moment. He hurried out of the store. And that was why he should have gone to Ludington. Because seeing Sadie Hoover? It only reminded him of everything he'd lost. Everything he'd never have.

One thing was certain, he wouldn't be back. Ten years hadn't been long enough to swallow the disappointment of today. He'd lay low and continue to do the one thing he'd done the last ten years.

Avoid Sadie Hoover at all costs.

She'd waited ten years to move back to Heritage, ten years to chase her dream of owning the family hardware store, and ten years of visits to her parents, praying she wouldn't run into the man who'd torpedoed her life.

Too bad it couldn't have been eleven or twenty. Or never.

Instead, she'd had to reset the count—four days had passed since she'd seen David Williams. Hopefully, that number would continue to go up. Sadie Hoover pulled the ham and provolone from the fridge and set them on the counter of her kitchen in her new-to-her apartment.

The alarm on her phone sounded, halting her movements. Great. Where had she left her phone? The vintage kitchen was barely big enough for two people, so how could she lose her phone?

She paused and followed the muffled notes of the alarm to one of the half dozen cupboards. She opened it. Of course, next to the bread. She grabbed both. This was David's fault. It was the wrong season for a visit from the spirit of Boyfriend Past. "Lottie! That's the fifteen-minute alarm."

"I heard it, Mom." Lottie's voice carried a thick layer of nine-year-old sass.

The front door burst open, and Romee, Sadie's youngest sister by four years, burst into the apartment. Romee's long brown hair tumbled around her face in wild curls, her glasses slipping to the end of her nose. She closed the door with a flourish and pushed her glasses up with one fluid movement.

"Look at this place. It's really coming together." Romee toed off her black flats by the door.

"Really?" Sadie scanned the area. It was definitely cleaner than a few days ago when everyone had helped her move in the furniture, but all she could see were boxes. On the vintage oak coffee table she'd found thrifting last month. On the dining room table that had once been Jeremy's grandmother's. She even piled them at the end of her queen-sized bed. At least she'd gotten Lottie's room ready. First day jitters at a new school were enough without being lost in a sea of boxes.

"So, Dad said David is back." Romee squeezed by Sadie in the kitchen and selected a mug.

Leave it to a sister to make herself at home, even before Sadie had. Turning back to the sandwiches, Sadie layered ham and cheese on two slices of bread. "He was in the store, *not* back. I think he still lives in Costa Rica, which means it was a one-time thing. By the look on his face when he saw me, he'll make sure of that. I just wish he'd gotten fat. Or gone bald."

"What you're saying is that he's still hot." Romee eyed her over the rim of Sadie's favorite Cedar Point mug.

Hot didn't really cover it. David always had been good looking with his coffee-colored eyes and auburn hair. Clean shaven, incredible bone structure, and full, kissable lips. And boy, had he known how to use them. So okay—yes, he was still hot. "He's older. Broader. And not in my life."

Romee wiggled her eyebrows. "But he could be." Her sister gave a questioning look at the sandwich. "When did Lottie start eating like a linebacker?"

Sadie blinked at the sandwich then started pulling off the layers. If David had her this discombobulated after one encounter, she prayed he'd be leaving the country soon, very soon. Maybe she'd offer to buy his ticket.

Sadie packed up the now normal-sized sandwich and put it in Lottie's new tie-dyed lunch box. Romee picked it up, zipped it closed, and put it in Lottie's matching backpack by the front door.

"No more talk of David." Sadie shook her head. Her chest ached, and her heart squeezed. Hadn't she gotten over the pain of his departure years ago? "He chose to leave me behind. He didn't want me then, and he definitely doesn't want me now. Besides, I have Lottie."

Swallowing another big gulp, Romee looked over the top of the cup. "Jeremy would want you to move on. And he liked David. Well, except for the whole dumping you and taking off thing, but it's been ten years. Maybe—"

"No. I have a new life." Sadie turned from Romee and walked out of the kitchen into the main room, past the dining room table.

She squeezed between the sectional sofa and a row of boxes to the small hallway that led to two bedrooms. "Almost ready, Lottie?"

Lottie's heavy footsteps came running out of her room, her purple hairbrush in her hand. She now had a huge bump on top of her head that hadn't been there when Sadie braided her hair after breakfast. Her freckled nose wrinkled as she waved the brush around. "Mom, I hate my hair. Fix it."

Sadie took the offered brush. "Fix it, *please*."

Lottie acquiesced to the proper request, and Sadie quickly brushed out the braid and re-did her daughter's thick red hair. She might hate her hair now, but give it a few more years, and the girl would love it. Thick, wavy. The color would cost women hundreds in a salon. She had her father's hair and her mother's beauty. "Five minutes, kiddo. Have you made your bed and brushed your teeth?"

"Going now. Hi, Aunt Romee!" Lottie gave a quick wave and rushed back to her room, straightening her lilac T-shirt as she left.

"*Mom*. It's still surreal to hear her call you that." Romee leaned against the wall outside the kitchen and sipped her coffee.

"We still talk about Bonnie and Jeremy often. But when she asked if she could call me *Mom*..." Sadie's throat tightened.

Romee pushed her glasses up. "When is the adoption finalized?"

"October twenty-second. And it should be pretty easy. I do wish Jeremy could be here to see it, even if his sister, Doris, is unhappy with me for moving away from Grand Rapids."

"Let Doris be unhappy. Jeremy was clear in his will that he wanted you to take custody of Lottie, not his sister. Lottie is going to love it here. We both know Heritage was an amazing place to grow up. Even if it moved you farther from me."

"We're going to miss your daily drop-ins, but you could always move home."

"Because Heritage is full of promising violinists looking for an instructor. Grand Rapids is my home now. My music school is there. Besides, you are going to keep plenty busy with the store." Romee picked up the store key on the counter and placed the ring around her finger, spinning it.

"It's a little crazy to think I'm taking over." Sadie had always pictured taking over the store as a child. When David had started talking marriage, she pictured taking it over with him. Then he'd left, and she'd let the dream die because she couldn't fathom taking over the store without him. "Do you think it's a mistake? I mean, I thought I had two years to get ready for this."

"Dad needs you now, and you need a job. It makes sense for everyone."

"I just feel like I should know more about the state of the store before I take over. Did you know Dad's accounting isn't even on the computer?"

"So, you'll learn on the job. And you'll get to set it up the way you like. Which is perfect for your control-freak personality."

"I'm not a control freak." She crossed her arms across her chest. "You're just a slob."

One eyebrow shot up, and Romee stepped to the closest box. Without breaking eye contact, she opened the flaps and pulled out what must have been the first thing she touched. Then without even looking at the purple cut glass vase, walked over and set it on one of the empty shelves in the corner. That was Sadie's favorite vase, and she always kept it on a wood trivet in the center of the dining table.

For one heartbeat Sadie stared at it then turned away. She'd fix it later. After she unpacked the trivet. It would be in the box with the vase.

Maybe she did like to have a certain order to life. But with David leaving her, then Bonnie, and eventually Jeremy, she'd learned that everything went smoother when she only depended on herself. She even stopped asking God for His input. Let someone else take the wheel? No thanks.

Just to prove to Romee that this hadn't bothered her, Sadie walked back into the kitchen and opened the cupboard above the coffeepot and pulled out a mint green tumbler. The final alarm sounded as she poured the coffee. "Lottie! Time to go."

Lottie dashed back into the living room and slung her new backpack on her shoulder. "I'm ready. Bye, Mom."

"Not so fast there. Don't I get to take you today? It's the first day of school." Sadie picked up her computer bag off the small dining table, pulled the strap onto her shoulder, and held out her hand for the store keys Romee still held.

"Please, Mom. I'm almost ten. I can walk to the bus stop. Alone. Oma said Annabelle will be there. We're going to be best friends." Of course they would. Because Lottie made friends wherever she went, just like Bonnie had.

Sadie bit back the chuckle wanting to escape. Lottie—little Miss Independent. "Very well. Find out if Annabelle is in ballet. Maybe you could take lessons too?"

Lottie bounced her backpack on her shoulder. "Sure thing."

"Let me snap your picture real quick." Sadie pulled out her phone, and Lottie posed in front of the door. "Can I at least walk downstairs with you since I'm heading to the store?"

Lottie threw open the door. "Okay. But no farther. And don't stand at the door and cry when I walk away."

Together, the trio walked out of the apartment and down the wooden stairs to the alley that ran behind the hardware store. The cool morning air hinted at the start of fall.

"The leaves will change soon." Lottie pointed at the fall tree full of green leaves behind the shop. "Dad would've loved that tree."

Sadie slid her arm over the little girl's shoulder and hugged her to her side. Grief, the unwanted companion that it was, showed up at unusual times. "He sure would've."

Lottie shrugged off Sadie's arm and twirled when they made it to the bottom of the stairs—the moment of grief passed. "Okay, Mom. I'll see you after school. Bye, Aunt Romee."

Lottie skipped ahead of Sadie, stopping at the corner and running back. "Mom, Otis is sitting in front of the hardware store. Almost like he's trying to peek in on you."

The cool morning breeze rushed down the side of the building as Sadie walked up to the corner. Romee kept pace with her. The sun peeked over a grove of pine trees behind them, casting their long shadows down the sidewalk toward the square. Sure enough, Otis sat on the sidewalk at the corner of Richard and Second, right under the window that faced the square, as if trying to draw attention to the big, dirty window of Hoover's Hardware.

"Otis always knows what's happening around town. He's in on all the big events." Sadie pulled in a breath. Maybe Otis's watchful eye meant her new endeavor would be a success. Otherwise, Otis would have a front seat to her making a mess of things.

Lottie jumped up to kiss Sadie on the cheek and then dashed off again.

Sadie waited while Lottie made her way all the way to the bus stop at the corner of Richard and Henderson and gave her a final wave then fell into step with another little girl. Maybe it was Annabelle.

Romee stood beside her, sipping her coffee. "I'd hoped I could walk a little farther with her."

"Nope. Lottie's determined to meet Annabelle. And don't go stealing my mug. I love that one."

Romee inspected the old mug. The words Cedar Point could barely be seen on the side. "You're attached to this mug? Looks ancient."

If thirteen years was old for a coffee mug. She got it just after her freshman year of college. Maybe it was ancient. She and David had met at college, both involved in the same outreach program on campus. One weekend, the group had gone to Cedar Point in

Sandusky, Ohio, where she'd found the mug in the amusement park's gift shop, and David bought it for her. Maybe it was time to let the memories rest, a final release to prove seeing David again after ten years hadn't wrecked her mental state. "No attachment. Maybe you should keep it. Or better yet, trash it."

Romee waited for more, but she'd be waiting a long time, because Sadie had talked about David about as much as she was willing.

Her sister finally shrugged and turned toward their parents' place. "Well, I'll run home before anyone notices I'm missing. And I'll be back to bug you at the store in a bit. Maybe I can bring you lunch before I head for home?"

Sadie waved as Romee walked off before climbing up the few steps to the front door of Hoover's. She pushed her store key into the lock, but there was no resistance when she turned it.

The store was unlocked? She ran through her memories from yesterday. Maybe she had been a little distracted after seeing David, but there was no doubt that she had closed and locked the door last night.

Wrapping her fingers around her keys like they were brass knuckles, Sadie wondered if the crime rate in her small hometown had skyrocketed. Unlikely, but still, maybe she should invest in something other than her keys for protection.

Five aisles stretched inside the store with the front counter running along the side wall, but nothing looked different from last night. The register was still closed. And everything smelled the same—a mix of sawdust, paint, and sweat.

"Hello?" Sadie's voice wobbled through the empty store only to hear a familiar and gruff response from the office.

Shoulders relaxed, Sadie shoved her keys into her jeans pockets. Dad.

Sadie walked down the third aisle. A paintbrush had fallen on the floor, and she picked it up to hang it back up, except the paint brush sat between a hammer and a flathead screwdriver. Why wasn't it with the paint supplies? Below the hammer sat a different brand of paintbrush, a garden shovel, and a Phillips head screwdriver. Looked like she'd be reorganizing soon.

She hung the brush up and headed to the back of the store. "Dad, I thought you were taking some time off. Not coming in to open the store on my first official morning." Sadie bent over and brushed a kiss on her dad's cheek as he flipped through the ledger on his desk. Goal one: get the books online. "That's an awful deep V between your brows."

"It's all good, kiddo. Just making sure the books are in order for you. It might be a little harder to let go of the reins than I imagined."

"You thought you had more time. Me too. But it's okay. We'll figure this out."

"You're so good at organizing. But I remembered a few invoices I hadn't recorded yet. I wish I was handing it to you in better shape." Her dad stood up, stretching to his full height. His shoulders were a little rounder, his back not as straight as it had been before the fall. His dark hair held some gray, and the wrinkles in his forehead were deeper. These last few months had been hard on him. It might have changed her plans, but it was time to take over. Her dad needed the break.

"I'm sure it will be fine, Dad. I'll get everything online and fix whatever chaos is in those books."

"I don't think entering numbers into QuickBooks or whatever you're using will change the numbers." Her dad stepped behind the chair, his good hand running slowly over the back. "I guess this is yours now."

So, it was. After all these years, even without David. This was hers. Her dad pulled the chair back and gestured for Sadie to have a seat. She placed her bag on the desk and sat down.

Her dad walked to the door. "About those books..."

"It's fine, Dad. I've got this. And I'd like to hire a few people to help around the store." Sadie pulled out her computer and opened it up in front of her.

Her dad's feet shuffled on the ground. "I can help out at the store some."

"I know, Dad. But you still need to heal from your surgery and make it through rehab, too. That's part of the reason I'm here. Plus, I need time to settle in as the new proprietor. Make the store mine, you know? Oh, did you bring the keys to the back room?"

Her dad's face turned into what she could only describe as a grimace. "About the back room—it's sorta a mess."

His phone rang out and he pulled it from his back pocket, a sheepish grin on his face. "Your mother is calling. I'd better get home. I'll be back later."

"Please bring the key next time. And tell Mom I said good morning." Sadie settled behind the desk as her father exited the office and answered his phone.

When the bell jingled to signal he'd exited the store, Sadie opened her purse and pulled out a framed picture of her and Lottie for the desk. They'd been at Jeremy's favorite cabin on Lake Michigan, north of Chicago, and they were both windblown, sun-kissed, and all smiles. The reminder of her why—why she was back in town, why she wanted the store to be successful, and why she had pulled it all together after another heartbreaking turn in life. To make sure Lottie had a comfortable home, surrounded by people who loved her.

Four hours later, Sadie wished for those smiles. Her eye twitched, and she rubbed at new wrinkles on her forehead. When her dad mentioned the books weren't in great order, Sadie had wrongly assumed he meant they were disorganized. Not that the store operated in the red.

In. The. Red.

For months.

Sadie pulled open the top drawer of her dad's desk—hers now—and dug around inside. And since it was her desk now, she could raid his secret chocolate stash without guilt.

Instead of pulling out candy, her hand found a stack of envelopes. From the bank. She opened the top one and scanned the letter inside. Her stomach tightened and turned over.

There's no way this letter was right. But there was no mistake—payment due September 30th. When had her parents taken out a mortgage on the business?

Why had they taken a mortgage out on the business?

Hoover's had been in the family for years. And they'd missed a few payments, so the bank was recalling the loan. The full amount due.

Sadie closed the computer and placed the note on top. If they couldn't make the payment by September 30th, Sadie wouldn't have a store to run. She had twenty-seven days to fix this.

This was why she'd wanted two years to get ready to take over. Diving into any decision without all the details never ended well. She'd jumped blindly, making this move, changing her life, to chase a dream she'd given up on.

All for what? To discover the store was underwater. How could this happen?

Her hand trembled. But the red letters stamped across the page couldn't be ignored.

She looked down at the statement again. When she trusted people to handle the details, bad things happened. Two words stared up at her, cementing that thought.

Past Due.

More Heritage Novels

Home to Heritage
You're the Reason
Here With Me
Christmas With You

Restoring Heritage
P.S. Goodbye (prequel novella)
You Belong With Me
Until I Met You
While It Was Snowing (novella)
Since You've Been Gone
Upon a Midnight Snow (Christmas novella)

P.S. Goodbye

What if a woman who's all about the goals and plans falls in love with man who no longer believes his life has a purpose?

A novice life coach needs to cement her reputation with one great success story. When a wounded ex-Army officer walks in looking for a job, she decides to work with him—a win-win for them both.

If Caroline Williams had her way, she'd help everyone in town find their purpose in life—unfortunately, no one seems to want her help. But she refuses to give up, and her new status as a certified life coach should provide her with some badly needed credibility. All she needs is her first client. When Grant Quinn walks in looking for a job, Caroline knows he needs more than that—he needs a new plan for his life. But when Grant refuses to be honest about his dreams and his struggles, Caroline's business might come crashing down before it starts.

Wounded former Special Forces operator Grant Quinn understood the cost when he enlisted and served his country with pride. The scars on his face are reminders of what he lost, but he is moving on—now if he could just convince his family that he's fine. When Caroline steps back into his life and offers to help find him a job in exchange for being her Guinea pig in her new life coaching business, he agrees. After all, what better way to show his family he's okay than with a new, stable job? But when the anxiety he's been running from ruins his one interview, his plans come crashing down. Can he trust Caroline enough to be honest about everything?

Get your free copy today!

Want more Heritage now?

Come see what has one Goodreads reviewer saying "I love this small town of Heritage, MI . . . where gossip blooms like wildflowers but also where love, acceptance, and mercy flow like a wild river." (MJSH, Goodreads)

Six books, nine couples, and one mysterious hippo!

Start where it all began with Tari Faris' FREE prequel novella *P.S. Goodbye.*

Scan for a free download or go to: www.tarifaris.com/my-free-novella

More Sweet Sunrise Romance

Faith. Forgiveness. A future they never imagined.
It's time for a fresh start for the Fox Family.

Return to Susan May Warren's beloved town of Deep Haven now!
Find out more at sunrisepublishing.com.

Connect With Sunrise

Thank you again for reading *You're the Reason*. We hope you enjoyed the story. If you did, would you be willing to do us a favor and leave a review? It doesn't have to be long—just a few words to help other readers know what they're getting. (But no spoilers! We don't want to wreck the fun!) Thank you again for reading!

We'd love to hear from you—not only about this story, but about any characters or stories you'd like to read in the future. Contact us at www.sunrisepublishing.com/contact.

We also have a monthly update that contains sneak peeks, reviews, upcoming releases, and fun stuff for our reader friends. Sign up at www.sunrisepublishing.com or scan our QR code.

Acknowledgments

Every book is a lot of work and I am so thankful for the help and support I get along the way.

Scott Faris – my husband, my champion, and my ultimate hero. Not only do I see a bit of you in every one of my heroes, but you also make it possible by holding the fort down while I am in deadline mode.

My children who support me with each and every book.

Susan May Warren – Thank you for believing in this book and for your amazing editing skills that really made it shine.

Barbara Curtis – who is so kind to answer all my little questions even after her amazing editing is done.

My daughter Danielle who answered a plethora of ballet questions, all mistakes are mine not hers.

And all my writer friends who talked me through scenes when I'd get stuck – I love my writing community!

About the Author

TARI FARIS lives in the Southwest with her amazing husband the three coolest kids on the planet. She loves writing in Heritage, because although she lives in the suburban desert now, a part of her heart will always be in the small Michigan town where she grew up. In her free time, she love coffee dates, traveling adventures, and time with family. She loves to hear from readers.

Connect with her at tarifaris.com.